'What a pleasure to read this smart, original, wholly satisfying portrait of the good people who, through adoption, became one big, not-always compatible family. The plot thickens: who should adopt the yet-again-pregnant birth mother's next baby? Eleanor Brown's beautiful writing, brilliant concept, and deliciously wry point of view spins that question into a big-hearted page-turner.'

**Elinor Lipman, author of *Good Riddance*
and *Rachel to the Rescue***

'Brown brings compassion and insight to exploring the hopes and vulnerability that make us first human, then family. Highly compelling.'

Isabel Costello, author of *Scent*

'Funny, wise, heartbreaking, and heart-mending, *Any Other Family* explores what it means to be a family, in all its messy complication. Emotionally complex, immensely readable, and deeply affecting.'

**Christina Baker Kline, #1 New York Times bestselling
author of *Orphan Train* and *The Exiles***

'*Any Other Family* offers deeply necessary insight into adoption, non-traditional families, and too-little discussed topics like postpartum depression in adoptive parents and grief associated with infertility, but beyond that, it is a beautifully written, elegantly assembled exploration of the joys and complications of family, any family, no matter what it looks like.'

**Laurie Frankel, New York Times bestselling author of
*This Is How It Always Is***

ANY OTHER FAMILY

ELEANOR BROWN

Legend Press Ltd, 51 Gower Street, London, WC1E 6HJ
info@legendpress.co.uk | www.legendpress.co.uk

Print ISBN 9781915054470
Ebook ISBN 9781915054487

First published in the US in 2022 by G. P. Putnam's Sons, an imprint of
Penguin Random House LLC | www.penguinrandomhouse.com

Cover Design by Grace Han
Cover art © Rachel Campbell / Bridgeman Images

Printed and bound by CPI Group (UK) Ltd, Croydon CR0 4YY

Eleanor Brown is the New York Times bestselling author of *The Weird Sisters* and *The Light of Paris*, and the editor of the anthology, *A Paris All Your Own*. She holds an MA in Literature and teaches writing workshops at writing conferences and centers nationwide. Born and raised in the Washington, D.C. area, Eleanor lives with her family in Highlands Ranch, Colorado.

For Liz, who knows.

There was once a woman who wished very much to have a little child, but she could not obtain her wish. At last she went to a fairy, and said, "I should so very much like to have a little child; can you tell me where I can find one?"

"Oh, that can be easily managed," said the fairy. "Here is a barleycorn of a different kind to those which grow in the farmer's fields, and which the chickens eat; put it into a flower-pot, and see what will happen."

—"THUMBELINA," BY HANS CHRISTIAN ANDERSEN

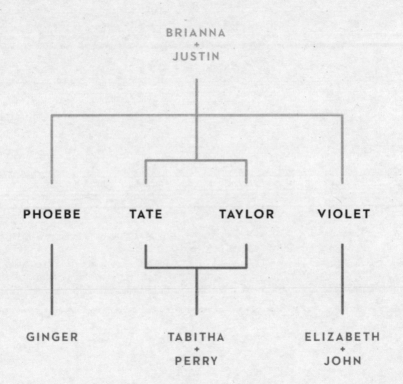

PROLOGUE

THEY LOOK LIKE any other family. A real one: cousins, siblings, aunts and uncles, brothers and sisters. They look like any other family with a past, with shared stories and traditions and jokes, memories of childhood summers and hundreds of holidays, carrying old wounds and the echoes of kept and broken promises.

But they are not like any other family, not exactly.

Does that mean they are not a family at all? Each of them stumbles over the word occasionally, searching for the right label to explain their relationships to outsiders, never feeling quite understood, not quite certain themselves of what the right term for this is.

Still, that name, *family*, is as close as they have found. They are a family, formed by three sets of parents who adopted from the same group of biological siblings.

Once upon a time, there were three children: Phoebe, the eldest at five, and the twins, not-quite-toddlers. When their grandmother, who had been raising them, died, there was no one else to turn to. Their mother, Brianna, had been so young when she had them, was more like a sibling to them than a parent, and was no more prepared to care for them than she had been when they were born.

As the social workers began casting about for options – fostering? adoption? – little Phoebe took her own destiny in hand and asked to live with Ginger. This was a surprise to everyone, most of all Ginger herself, whose only connection to Phoebe was her volunteer work in Phoebe's kindergarten class as a reading tutor. But she had fallen for Phoebe in the same way the child had fallen for her, and she was happy to open her home.

Tabitha and Perry, who had married later in life and were hoping to build their family through adoption, were asked if they would care for the twins, busy and curious and energetic, an exhausting joy. They had just completed their home study and were surprised but delighted to have Tate and Taylor come home with them so quickly.

Splitting up siblings who got along so very well and had already lost so very much was generally seen as a less-than-ideal arrangement, but when Tabitha suggested a new way of thinking of it – the children living in different houses but still raised as siblings – the social worker and the judge and, most important, Brianna embraced the plan, and so they became one family and many families at the same time.

Tabitha has always loved the idea of this magical new thing they were making. It was what she had been dreaming of her entire lonely childhood and beyond: being part of a big, happy family. They all come together to celebrate birthdays with piñatas and cake in the backyard, to share gratitude at Thanksgiving, and to have dinner every Sunday night, including Brianna, when she can make it.

Ginger, who came from a complicated family and escaped it as soon as humanly possible, likes this familial closeness rather less, even though she believes firmly, agrees entirely, that keeping the siblings as close as possible is the right thing for the children. She had never thought she would be a mother at all, and it couldn't have happened any other way. Sometimes Ginger considers the millions of decisions that led her to exactly that place so she could catch Phoebe as she fell from the sky, and marvels at the happenstance that brought her this child.

It is only that after spending her entire adulthood building a life of happy solitude, in addition to motherhood, she has inherited a complete set of quasi-relatives. Sometimes Ginger feels as if she spends all her time going back and forth to Tabitha and Perry's house (everything happens there, of course). When the parents were first working out the boundaries and rules of this tiny nation they were forging, they had committed to weekly family dinners and holidays together as their baseline. Now it seems to have grown far beyond that, especially since Violet arrived.

Ah, yes, Violet.

They had been a semi-family for four years when Brianna called Tabitha to say she was pregnant again. The children's biological father had come back into Brianna's life, and she hoped this time, now that they were older, they might stay together, raise this child.

He had managed to stay until Brianna was seven months along and then disappeared, as everyone else had known he would. The parents keep their mouths shut on the topic of Justin. He is, after all, the father of their children, but he is also nobody's favorite person because he has broken Brianna's and the children's hearts too many times.

So there was Brianna, alone, twenty-four and pregnant again. She cried and told Tabitha she couldn't do it, couldn't parent this child, she absolutely couldn't do it; what was she going to do?

And so came Elizabeth and John. They were young, or relatively so, having met in college, married immediately after, and then spent several painful years trying to have a child. When they adopted Violet, they went from the fog of fertility treatments straight into the fog of parenting a newborn. The adoption happened so quickly, and Violet was a colicky baby, angry and red-faced, for months that felt like years, an endless, stumbling routine of nighttime feedings. The colic has passed, but Elizabeth is still so tired, so overwhelmed, she hardly knows what happened.

All of which is to say that if anyone asks Elizabeth what she feels about their Very Special Family, she might look blank for a moment, as if trying to remember a distant acquaintance, then shrug.

Theirs is a strange way to become a family, each of the mothers has thought at some point, though how is it any stranger than any other way people create families, based on things no more scientific than the accidents of genetics or a common interest in bowling or opera, or simply rather liking the look of someone on a particular Tuesday night? At least they have a purpose, a reason to stick together, a common cause: the children they love as much as any parent, maybe even more.

Because they are all committed to the children, to letting them be a family as much as they can be. After all, who gets to say what it means to be a family? There are no names for the relationships they have to each other. There is only this broad word they are shaping around themselves: *family*, even though they aren't exactly a family; that word isn't exactly true, isn't exactly right.

At least not yet.

1

TABITHA

TABITHA SAID SHE would get the flowers herself, and then she had forgotten.

Well, of course she hadn't forgotten. Tabitha does not forget things. She keeps lists and she checks things off those lists and she follows up on things from the lists and at no point does she ever forget anything. But Perry has been on work calls all day, so she has been tending to the children, and now there are no flowers in the guest rooms, which is a small detail, she knows, but all perfect moments are composed of small details, are they not?

And she so wants this vacation to be perfect. She wants this to be the moment when their big, busy family truly becomes real, when she and Ginger and Elizabeth bond like sisters, when they create the moments where years from now they can ask, *Remember when?* and all laugh the way they had the first time it happened, or ask, *Remember when?* and look at how the children have grown and yearn happily for these days.

They do have some of these memories already, but they are never quite how Tabitha wants them to be, and even so, shouldn't there be more? There just never seems to be enough time. Ginger is always leaving early because they have so far to drive and she always has some reason the moms can't do a day out together, and poor Elizabeth always looks so overwhelmed and tired. Once, during Sunday dinner, she fell asleep at the dinner table and got risotto in her hair. But here, Ginger cannot leave, and Violet is getting older and sleeping through the night, so Elizabeth will get some rest, and Tabitha just loves playing with Violet anyway. It will be different this time.

There is a fizzy excitement in Tabitha's chest when she thinks about the next two weeks: the plans she has made, the adventures they will have on this summer vacation, the first of many wonderful trips together, a chance to make memories and become the happy family she has always known they can be. She and the twins have been up here in Aspen for a week already, and Perry flew up from Denver a few days ago, but finally it's Friday and the others are coming, and now the vacation can really start. Tabitha has planned bike tours and a hike to a waterfall and a horseback ride with a stop to go fishing and pancakes for breakfast and a moms' day at the spa – she can hardly remember everything on the schedule. It breaks her heart that Brianna can't take the time off from work to join them. Still, having the rest of them here will be wonderful. It is all going to be perfect.

If she could only figure out the flowers.

The twins, who have been swimming basically since they woke up, burst out of the pool like fireworks, sparks of water flying over the deck and onto the table where Tabitha is sitting. "Can we have popsicles?" they ask, crowding close to her. They have always been so physical, for which she is grateful. Sometimes it feels like they want to climb inside her, their desire to be close to her, to touch her, to sit in her lap and stroke her arms is so intense. They were already just over a year old when they came to her and Perry, and she had been so worried about attachment. But through a lucky combination of their sweetly clingy dispositions and her fierce devotion to motherhood, their connection is solid and loving, which gives her such a swelling of pride in her own mothering capabilities she would almost be ashamed for anyone else to find out. She gives them each a little squeeze, dropping a kiss on Taylor's forehead before he squirms away, enjoying the miracle of their existence.

The children smell of chlorine and leaves, and they are dripping wet, their hands pressing against her skin. Taylor's hair stands up in wild spikes; Tate's is pulled forward over her shoulder, where it drips steadily onto Tabitha's white capri pants.

"Popsicles? It's not even noon!" Not that she would be likely to acquiesce even later in the day. They are scheduled to have s'mores tonight after everyone else arrives, but she can hardly tell them now or they'll be unbearable, begging for them all day. Even the promise of sugar turns them into monsters.

"It's summer!" Taylor argues. He still looks like a baby to her sometimes, his belly slightly convex, while Tate has fully leaned out, an inhale of girlhood before the exhale of adolescence, already so close Tabitha can feel it on her skin sometimes, looking at them and seeing the people they are going to become.

"As though good nutrition doesn't apply in summer. Besides, we don't have any popsicles," Tabitha says, which is true.

Then, as though the three of them have orchestrated the entire thing to make a fool of her, Perry steps through the sliding glass door, carelessly leaving it open behind him. "Who wants a popsicle?" he asks, waving a box of Bomb Pops, the top torn raggedly open. They must have been buried in the deep freezer in the garage, because if Tabitha had noticed them, she would have thrown them out immediately with all the other junk food.

Tabitha pushes air out between her teeth as the twins abandon her, running to their father. He takes one for himself and gives one to each of the kids, who quickly abandon the empty box on the steps and vault back into the pool, bounty in hand.

"There were only three left," he says, sitting down at the table beside her. "Want to share mine?" He peels back the wrapper, but the popsicle has freezer burn, and tiny shreds of white paper stick to the red portion at the top.

Tabitha glances over at the twins, but they are already eating theirs as they swim clumsily, one-armed. Probably eating the bleached paper along with whatever chemical horrors are in the popsicles themselves.

"Really, Perry," she says. She tries so hard to take care of the children, to give them every chance, and he just offers them sugar willy-nilly.

Perry, unconcerned, sticks his popsicle in his mouth and leans back. "It's vacation," he says, gripping the ice with his teeth as he talks.

He clasps his hands behind his head the way Taylor does when he finishes eating, stretching in pleasure. It delights her to see herself and Perry reflected in the twins. So much of them is like their grandmother, and so much of them is like Brianna. But they are also clearly her children, and Perry's, tiny mimics of their voices and movements and phrases she does not even realize she says so frequently until she hears them echoed.

"If it's vacation, are you done working?" she asks.

Perry nods and slurps at his popsicle, pulling it out of his mouth. His lips are already stained lurid red. "I've got another call in an hour, but that's it."

"But Ginger and Phoebe will be here in an hour!"

Perry shrugs and turns back to the twins and his popsicle, as though it doesn't matter when everyone else arrives, as though he isn't hosting, too. "It shouldn't take too long. Are you going somewhere? They can let themselves in."

Tabitha whistles air out between her teeth again, because obviously she is not just going to have her guests "let themselves in" like they are running a motel. "I just need to finish getting things ready. I want everything to be perfect." Anxiety pulls taut in her chest.

Perry reaches over and pats her leg in a way that manages to be both sweet and condescending. "I know you do. It will be. It always is. Everything you do is always perfect."

She gives him a tight smile because that isn't true. She leaves things undone or underdone all the time, but she doesn't want to argue, and he is watching Tate and Taylor play in the pool anyway, not even looking at her. When he pulls his hand away, she can see a pale blue spot where his thumb touched her white pants, a damp drop from the melting bottom of his popsicle. The children are probably dripping theirs in the pool, too.

"I'm going to go check the guest rooms," she says, trying to sound light again. She doesn't want to ruin things.

Perry turns to look at her. It is unfair how handsome he is, even with a silly rocket-shaped popsicle sticking out of his mouth, a drop of red dye on his chin. His dark hair is curly and uncombed, and he replaced his glasses frames recently with round tortoiseshell ones that she never would have picked but she has to admit give him a sexy professor look. He is wearing a linen shirt and cargo shorts (they are so awful that she had disposed of the previous pair, but Perry only assumed he'd misplaced them and bought new ones) and he looks deliciously like summer. She is so grateful for him, for the twins, for this family they have found themselves in.

Looking over at the pool in order to admire the children, she finds they have abandoned their stained popsicle sticks on the edge and now appear to be attempting to drown each other. As Taylor pounces on Tate, she dives down, her hair rising up and spreading out, splaying across the top like seaweed.

Perry turns and opens his mouth to stick out his tongue, which is a truly alarming shade of purple.

"Charming," she says. "Are you okay watching them?"

"Watching my own children? Yes, I can handle this assignment," Perry says.

In the laundry room, she finds a stain wipe and dabs cautiously at the blue mark Perry's thumb left. Now there is a wet spot, but it will dry. She doesn't have time to change. Hurrying upstairs, she checks the children's room, picking up the nightclothes they abandoned when they changed into their swimsuits that morning and placing them in the hamper, bringing bottles of water from the upstairs pantry into the guest rooms where Ginger and Elizabeth and John will sleep, and checking the closets for extra blankets.

The dryer buzzes, and she pulls out Tate's sheets and makes her bed. She feels, as she always does, a little twist of anxiety as she tucks the sheets in. Despite the fact that the twins are seven, Tate still wets the bed every night, and even has accidents during the day sometimes. It quite literally makes Tabitha's heart ache – she wants so much for their lives to be happy, easy, for the obstacles to be smoothed out of their way, but this particular problem seems impossible to solve, no matter what Tabitha does.

The doctors say it's no one's fault, but who else but their mother could possibly be at fault? In Tabitha's worst moments, she wonders if Tate would have these problems if her grandmother were still raising her, or if Brianna had chosen to parent. Because otherwise it must be something Tabitha has done, or not done. So every morning Tabitha strips Tate's bed and washes the sheets, and every few months she buys entirely new sheets, and every day she wonders, what is she doing so wrong?

The flowers! Hurrying downstairs, she pulls a couple of lowball glasses out of the cabinet in the butler's pantry. On the kitchen table is a gorgeous arrangement, a welcome compliments of the house's owners, that she put in a lovely Baxter & Motts vase she found in the butler's pantry. That will have to do. She picks out stems until she has two passable bouquets. They all match, as if she bought them at the grocery store, but she can't do anything about that now. Running back upstairs, she puts the glasses on the bedside tables in Ginger's and John and Elizabeth's rooms, brushing her hands on her pants and then looking down to make sure she hasn't smudged any pollen on them.

It is not perfect. But it is so very close.

2

GINGER

"WHAT ARE WE doing the day after that?" Phoebe is asking from the back seat.

Ginger, who only drives in the mountains under great duress and is gripping the steering wheel with a level of force that she is aware is potentially exacerbating her tension, glances back in the rearview mirror. She has made a wrong turn somewhere, and instead of the relative comfort of a broad and anonymous highway, they are climbing over the mountains on narrow roads, frequently trailing behind groups of cyclists, white-haired men in lurid spandex bike gear moving slowly and determinedly up the hills even her car is straining to summit.

Phoebe has earbuds in and there is a book lying open on her knees, but she has spent most of the drive looking out the window, watching where the road falls away into steep slopes of rock and evergreen trees as they twist their way, up, up, up toward the house Tabitha has procured for this, the First Official Basnight-Kowalski-Evans Family Vacation.

Tabitha is in love with that phrase, while Ginger has

slightly more trepidation, as *First* implies there will be more, and Ginger would like proof of life after the nine of them have been in one house for two weeks before she even considers a second.

One of Phoebe's earbuds is dangling from its cord against her shoulder, tangled in the corn silk of her hair. When the family is all together, she is often mistaken for Elizabeth's or Tabitha's daughter, both of them blond and fair like Phoebe, whereas Ginger is redheaded and freckled. But the biggest difference between Ginger and Phoebe is how beautiful her daughter is.

Ginger has never been beautiful, and has, in fact, always been actively uninterested in her appearance, though which of those is the chicken and which the egg could be up for debate. Her hair was once the brilliant carrot orange people are kind enough to call red, though now that she's firmly into her fifties, it has faded into a white-streaked rust that she keeps pulled back and clipped into a knot but refuses to cut. She wears a uniform of her own making: boxy, square shirts and loose pants and comfortable sandals. Her greatest delight in growing older has been that her age finally matches her preferred wardrobe.

"Honey, I don't remember off the top of my head what we're doing every day," Ginger says. The itinerary – because of course Tabitha made an itinerary – is printed out and in her bag, but she can't bear to think about the endless stream of activities. It's not so much the organization she minds; she quite likes that, in fact, but she prefers a little less "together time" with the entire family than is on the schedule.

"Can you check? Pleeeeease?" Phoebe whines.

Ginger has to resist rolling her eyes.

"I can't look now; I'm driving," Ginger says, hoping Phoebe will let it drop.

Phoebe does, for now, but she won't let it stay dropped for long. She likes to know what is going on ahead of time as much as is humanly possible. Her preference for preparedness is completely understandable; she was the only one old enough to be knowingly affected by the loss of her grandmother. Phoebe still goes to counseling, though often only once a month, but Ginger holds firm on the advice she was given at the beginning, which is to ensure Phoebe feels as secure as possible. Which is just fine by her. Who likes change? Who likes unpredictability? No one sensible. And Ginger is, if nothing else, quite sensible.

"We're going to go horseback riding, though, right? And on a boat at the lake?"

"It's a reservoir, not a lake, but yes, that's the plan," Ginger says. She remembers those things from the itinerary, but she does hope there won't be a quiz on when they are happening. With Tabitha, one never knows.

"I'm so excited, Marmee," Phoebe says happily.

Ginger glances back at her daughter, who is smiling out the window at nothing in particular, and cannot help but smile herself. She loves hearing Phoebe call her Marmee. When she began volunteering at Phoebe's school, the children called her Miss K., but that had seemed awkward and unwieldy when Phoebe came to live with her. Still, it had persisted for a while, even after the adoption was finalized. She already had a Meemaw, and she called Brianna "Mama Brianna." Ultimately, Phoebe had solved the issue when they were reading *Little Women* together by looking up at her one night and announcing, without preamble, "I'm going to call you Marmee," a choice that had pleased them both.

"I'm so glad," Ginger says. And she is. Since she had not expected motherhood, she had not expected the joys that come from it, most notably the way Phoebe has of lifting her mood, of making Ginger feel happier simply because Phoebe is happy.

Phoebe is unusually thoughtful for a child, always aware of other people's feelings, and Ginger appreciates the way Phoebe sits with questions and thoughts before she expresses them. From the moment they met, there was something in

Phoebe's peaceful nature that reminded Ginger of herself, and she understood for the first time why people like seeing themselves in their children: not out of vanity but a sense of connection and the comforting notion that you might not be so peculiar after all.

She delights in all the children, in fact, not just Phoebe, but the twins as well, and even Violet, though she is not what one might call a "baby person." It is the parents she finds a little more difficult. She knows she is a disappointment to Tabitha, that Tabitha would have preferred a mother for Phoebe more like herself, sunny and efficient and overinvolved. Yet here is Ginger, introverted and cautious and allowing Phoebe to roam about underscheduled and with absolutely no green juices in her diet. But Phoebe is the one who asked for Ginger, and therefore Ginger is what Phoebe, and therefore by extension Tabitha, got.

They have managed to get along fine thus far, mostly because Tabitha makes the plans and Ginger generally acquiesces to them. It isn't worth fighting over. She can maintain her boundaries and keep them both safe from the general familial pandemonium by living far away and departing Sunday dinners and birthday celebrations at promptly 7:45 p.m.

It is just that, over time, Tabitha's determination to make them a Real Family has grown into an obsession. In addition to the Sunday dinners and the sleepovers and birthdays, Tabitha has doubled down on ensuring the family celebrates Every Single Holiday together (Arbor Day, with tree crafts! Kentucky Derby Day, with horse crafts for the children and real mint juleps for the grown-ups!). And then, almost as soon as Violet arrived and Elizabeth and John officially joined the family, she introduced the idea of a vacation together: "All of us! For two weeks! Just like a real family!"

Being an only child, Tabitha doesn't understand family at all. Ginger, on the other hand, understands family all too well. When she read fairy tales about changelings as a child, she felt certain that's what had happened to her. She is deeply introverted by nature and was sure she had been destined for a nice, quiet life among the fairies, and had instead been swapped into her loud, social family.

Her father was in sales – that's how he said it, "I'm in sales" – the old-school kind, handshakes and back slaps and cigars and, worst of all, constant travel and moving. Whenever he changed jobs or territories, the family would pack up and follow him. Ginger had attended five different elementary schools alone and lost count of the number of houses they lived in before high school.

Every day when she woke, she kept her eyes closed, trying to remember where she was so she wouldn't be blindsided by the shock of staring at an unfamiliar room. When she objected to this peripatetic lifestyle, pointing out that wherever they lived, Mr. Kowalski would be traveling from Monday to Friday anyway, her mother responded that their father took care of them, and it was the least, the very least they could do to return the favor. This was difficult to argue with, though one might quibble with a definition of *taking care of* that involved putting one's children through such constant change, but Mrs. Kowalski was also friendly and extroverted, and being the new stay-at-home mother in one town after another never seemed to wear on her. She unpacked the boxes, baked some banana bread, and went around introducing herself to the neighbors until she was the epicenter of the social circle.

Ginger's brothers – one older, one younger, Ginger in the miserable middle – took after their parents, thriving in the constant resettlement. It was like a challenge to them, she thought as she observed them swaggering easily ahead of her into yet another new school. How quickly could they make friends, swing a spot on a team, start dating, win an election for homecoming king? Meanwhile Ginger slunk along the edges, never sure of how to find her way in or if she even wanted to, mocked by her brothers for being an outcast, pushed by her parents to go to dances and games and participate in the school musicals, as if any of these were things she would be interested in.

So when Tabitha talked about how *fun* these two weeks were going to be, how they would all be one big happy *family*, Ginger remained unconvinced, because *family* means something very different to her. *Family* means instability and discomfort and being forced to be someone you don't want to be.

"Did you tell everyone about TGA?" Phoebe asks suddenly.

"I haven't told anyone yet," Ginger says. "Did you want me to?" TGA is The Global Academy, where Phoebe has been moved off the wait list and offered a spot for sixth grade in the fall.

Getting that email from TGA had been one of the few moments in Ginger's life when she wished she were closer to... well, anyone. Someone she could call and crow to. *My daughter got into one of the top schools in the city!* she would say. *Phoebe is going to do amazing things, and it is all going to start right here*, she would say.

But she isn't close to anyone, rather intentionally, so she told Phoebe how proud she was of her, how amazed she was by how Phoebe had wanted this thing and pursued it, and now it was happening.

Initially Ginger had assumed Phoebe would go to the neighborhood middle school with her eternally sworn best friends, Esperanza and Charlotte, and was surprised when Phoebe insisted on applying to TGA, a charter school, as well. Phoebe had been wait-listed, which had disappointed her, but Ginger knew it would all be fine. The local school was quite well regarded, and Phoebe would be with her friends. There would be nothing to worry about.

But after she had gotten off the wait list and the excitement had settled, it turned out there was a great deal to worry about. How would Phoebe manage without the girls she had been best friends with since first grade? How would she find her way around an unfamiliar building at least three times the size of her elementary school? How would they get her to and from TGA, all the way in the city, near Tabitha and Perry? What if she started there and she didn't like it – it was too much change, or there were bullies, what if someone pulled the fire alarm and she was scared (Phoebe could be so sensitive to sudden loud noises), or the college preparatory curriculum didn't suit Phoebe, who far preferred to be able to direct her own time?

There were so very many things to worry about.

"I want to tell everyone," Phoebe says confidently.

"We haven't had a chance to talk about it yet, have we? Whether you're going to go."

"Marmee," Phoebe says flatly. Lately she has taken to addressing Ginger like she is a complete idiot, as if she were already a teenager. "Why would I not go."

Ginger notes the lack of a question mark at the end of what is indeed a very good question. She wants Phoebe to be able to go, to have this wonderful experience, to take advantage of everything her hard work has earned her. It's just complicated, isn't it?

"For starters, we'll have to plan how you'd get there and back. It's easily an hour each way in rush-hour traffic, and I'm not sure how I'd be able to get to work on time. Or pick you up in the afternoon." Ginger's job, as a technical writer for a software company, is fairly flexible, but the company has offices in multiple time zones, and she constantly feels like she is running behind from the moment she wakes up in the morning.

"I can take the bus," Phoebe says.

"I have thought of that," Ginger says. "But I'm not sure it's an ideal solution for such a long trip." She smiles at Phoebe in the mirror, appreciating her attempt at a creative solution to the issue. But transportation is only the beginning. There are all those other things to be afraid of, all the other question marks that come with considering such a dramatic change.

Underneath that is the fact that Phoebe is growing up faster than Ginger would like, the years since they met slipping through their fingers, and there is something about her going to this school that feels so much more like a passage into a world that leads to a thousand things beyond. No one warned her parenthood would feel so much like you were losing something every day.

After passing through the valley that leads them to the center of town, they begin to climb again, the houses set back from the road, protected by stands of aspen trees and bristlecone pines, insulated by their steep driveways and distance from the mundanities of civilization.

They pull into the driveway, and the house comes into view, a house so large it cannot possibly be a vacation home, but Ginger doublechecks the address and laughs aloud. She has known Tabitha and Perry for a fair amount of time now, but she remains unfailingly amused by how very Tabitha-and-Perry Tabitha and Perry are. Heaven forbid they just rent a cabin for a family vacation when they could get the Aspen equivalent of a château.

"Let's discuss this more later, honey, okay?" Ginger says as they park, reaching back blindly to pat Phoebe on the knee.

"Okay," Phoebe says.

"We'll keep it between us for now," Ginger says, but Phoebe has spotted Tate and Taylor running out of the house and she leaps out of the car to greet them, and Ginger isn't sure if she's heard.

3

ELIZABETH

ONE DAY, AS she wrestled Violet's bucket seat into the car after baby gym (which, who came up with *that* bullshit?), Elizabeth saw a couple emerge from the building, put their child in the car seat in the back, and then get into the front seats and drive away. Both of them! In the front! Like real people! Elizabeth was stunned. Was that a thing people did? Put the kid in the back while one parent drives and the other – well, what do you even do in the passenger seat of a car? She can't remember. Listen to the radio? Read? Stare out the window? *Nap?* At some point she must have done those things, but it feels like a thousand years ago. Now all of those choices feel like an impossible luxury.

Either she or John (spoiler alert: it's always her) sits in the back with Violet, who hates the car seat and protests mightily unless she is plied with snacks and toys and games of peek-a-boo and endless, endless repetitions of "The Wheels on the Bus." That fucking bus. Jesus. If Elizabeth ever meets the asshole who wrote that song, she will punch him in the neck.

Because for sure it was a man. No woman would betray the sisterhood that way.

On the drive to Aspen, Violet screams until she miraculously falls asleep. John misses all the fun, having put in his earbuds to listen to the endless fountain of podcasts he loves but Elizabeth finds infuriating.

His checking out, especially during a four-hour drive, fills her with rage, but she is generally filled with rage these days, latching on to whatever has the misfortune to float across the transom of her mind. Specifically, lately, that has been this vacation, and everything related to it, all of it feeling like yet another demand on her flagging energy. She likes Tabitha and Perry and Ginger, and she adores Phoebe and the twins. Some days she even likes her husband. She is just so tired. So, so tired. Tabitha and Ginger are never this tired. What is wrong with her?

As they exit the highway by Glenwood Springs and slow for the drive into the valley, their aging flatlander car almost exhaling in relief, Violet wakes up. Elizabeth closes her eyes to pray for strength, then opens them and forces a smile onto her face.

"Hello, sweet girl," she says, pretending to be the cheerful mother she knows she ought to be, and not the withered thirty-something husk of a woman who hasn't had a good night's sleep in far too long.

Violet begins to wail. You can't bullshit a bullshitter.

John takes out his earbuds. "Is she okay?"

"She's hungry. Probably ready to get out of the car, too," she says, trying to sound as though she doesn't want to scream herself. She suspects Violet needs a diaper change in addition to a snack, and she cannot wait until her daughter can express these things in words instead of crying. She is so, so sick of the crying, all the goddamned crying, the endless wail of Violet's disappointment in her. She loves Violet so much, and it makes her feel like such a tremendous failure that she can't make her happy.

At the bottom of the diaper bag, she finds a pouch of a fruit-andvegetable slurry that sounds horrific – something like broccoli-applepassionfruit-quinoa-kale – but allows her to at least pretend she is the kind of mother who feeds her child kale. She offers it to Violet, who grabs and begins to suck, stopping periodically to reiterate her displeasure with a half-hearted wail in case anyone has forgotten she is not one thousand percent delighted to be there.

"We'll be there in a few minutes. I can't wait. It's been so hot I'm ready to jump into the pool with all my clothes on. Aren't you excited?"

Elizabeth would like to throw him into the pool with all his clothes on for that question alone. "This is going to be a long two weeks," she says instead.

"Hon, if you come into it like that, of course you're not going to have a good time," he says. "It will be fun."

She doesn't doubt it will be fun for John. He loves Perry, idolizes him, in fact, and this is like fraternity bonding for the two of them. She would bet good money that Perry will have brought cigars for the two of them to smoke in the evenings, a smell that nauseates her when John comes to bed with it lingering in his hair, and that the two of them will take off more than once to golf, abandoning her with Violet.

Her feelings for Perry are the same as her feelings for Tabitha: irritation mixed with admiration and gratitude. The two of them always look so confident, always have everything under control. Her resentment of and eye-rolling over Tabitha's itinerary is tinged with something else, jealousy, maybe, or gratitude – thank heavens there is a grown-up taking care of things because she certainly can't do it.

She has the same feelings about Tabitha's relationship with Violet. Tabitha loves spending time with Violet, practically sweeps her out of Elizabeth's arms when they come for Sunday dinner. Elizabeth is, on the one hand, grateful when Tabitha claims the baby so she can have a break and, on the other, utterly confused by why Violet seems to like Tabitha more than she likes her own mother.

When they first started trying to have a baby, Elizabeth knew exactly the kind of mother she would be. As a teacher, she has taken years of classes and seminars on child development, and even though she prefers teaching middle school, where the kids can be royally shitty to each other but also creative and hilarious, and, perhaps most important, are capable of taking themselves to the bathroom, she knows more than the average bear about child-rearing. She would breastfeed, practice baby-led weaning, and then make baby food from scratch. Her child would only play with open-ended toys made from sustainably harvested wood. There would be no plastics, no melamine, no bottles, cloth diapers. She would wear her baby in a sling or a wrap, as though it were an extension of her body, which everyone swore babies loved.

Almost six years later, after multiple rounds of IUIs and then IVF, after miscarriages and then the sudden, unexpected adoption of Violet, Elizabeth figures the kid should consider herself lucky she doesn't have to sleep in a dresser drawer and eat Twinkies three meals a day. Elizabeth had enough of hormone-addling drugs and didn't want to take any more to induce lactation so she could breastfeed, making baby food was a pain in the ass, they couldn't afford handcrafted toys, cloth diapers were a joke, and Violet hated being worn the same way she hates swaddles and the car seat. She hates being contained in any way, but the wraps and slings and baby carriers were the worst, Violet squirming and kicking until Elizabeth finally surrendered to carpal tunnel and started lugging Violet's dumb bucket seat around, which the baby was no happier about but at least didn't involve Elizabeth getting kicked in the spleen like a metronome.

John doesn't understand, has the privilege of not having to understand the way mothers are judged, the way Elizabeth knows she is judged in particular. She sees the way other mothers look at her when Violet is crying, the way Tabitha always jumps in with some gift that feels like a veiled stab ("I found the most darling little socks, don't want her feet getting cold!"), the way the moms at music class and baby gym give her a tight smile when Violet cries and she pulls out a bottle instead of breastfeeding. She literally sweats when Tabitha is around and she has to do something with Violet like feed her or change her diaper, because she will undoubtedly do something wrong and Violet will scream and Tabitha, perfect Tabitha, will know Elizabeth cannot handle this.

It is not that she doesn't love Violet. She loves Violet beyond all understanding. She is not a crier by nature, but sometimes when she is rocking Violet at night, singing to her or reading a book, Violet warm and sleepy in her arms, Elizabeth is so overwhelmed with love for her daughter she weeps. (She does not tell anyone this.) She tries not to fall into the trap of maternal exaggeration, but Violet is genuinely smart and curious, and when she is not crying, she is a total and complete delight.

Pulling the car into a driveway with a swish of confidence as though he belongs here, among these insane mansions that are actually people's second homes, John accelerates up the steep drive to the house, which looks even more enormous and understatedly elegant than it had in the photos Tabitha sent.

Violet is still screaming as John parks the car and jumps out. Tabitha comes out the front door, looking perfectly crisp in white capris and a shirt that probably costs more than everything in Elizabeth's closet put together. John bounces over to Tabitha, who gives him a hug. Elizabeth, on the other hand, tries to stand, but her legs have locked up from sitting for too long, so she ends up staggering out of the car as though she has been drinking. This is, sadly, not the case, but she wonders if she should start carrying those tiny airplane bottles of vodka in Violet's diaper bag. They would make excellent portable Molotov cocktails.

"Oh, my goodness," Tabitha says, and while Elizabeth is still reeling around on the other side of the car, trying to shake the pins and needles out of her feet, Tabitha pulls Violet out of the car seat. Violet immediately stops screaming when she is free. "You are making quite a ruckus! Your poor mama!"

Lifting the baby high in the air, Tabitha pretends to nip at her toes, and Violet squeals in delight. Two tiny red spots on her cheeks are the only remaining evidence of her recent fury, and they only make her look more cherubic.

"How was the drive? Ginger came over Independence Pass somehow and is just worn out. Such a pretty drive, but so dangerous! You came on the highway, didn't you?" Tabitha asks John, but before he can answer, she lowers Violet and sniffs her bottom. "My goodness, someone has a very wet diaper! Let's go inside and Aunt Tabitha will get you changed." She puts Violet on her hip – Elizabeth cringes at the thought of the very wet diaper staining Tabitha's very perfect clothes, but no diaper would have the nerve to soil that expensive outfit. That is the kind of thing that would happen to Elizabeth, not Tabitha.

As Tabitha plucks the vodka-free diaper bag from the car and heads into the house, talking to Violet the whole time, Elizabeth gives John a look.

"What? She's helping. You're always saying how tired you are – let someone help without making it into a whole big thing."

He is irritated with her, which makes her irritated right back. He doesn't understand because it's not the same for men. He doesn't understand because his exhaustion is nowhere near hers. When Violet wakes up and shrieks to announce her presence, John continues to sleep, but Elizabeth's eyes pop open, her body immediately surging with adrenaline. How he can sleep through his child's crying is a mystery for the fucking ages. *Your baby is crying, and you are sleeping*, she wants to scream. But she doesn't. She goes and gets Violet, changes her, kisses and hugs her, brings her back into their bedroom, and wakes John up by dropping Violet onto his chest while she goes to pee. This abrupt wake-up is intended to piss him off, but it never does. He loves waking up to Violet's patting his face, which she does, rather adorably, while Elizabeth tries to find a pair of clean pants in the pile of laundry on the floor.

For this they lost five years of their lives. For this they are carrying a hundred thousand dollars in debt. For this they underwent endless tests and injected her with appallingly expensive and ultimately useless drugs. For this she wept and prayed and endured.

The problem with motherhood, Elizabeth thinks, is that it is like shaving your head. You never know how it will turn out until you do it, and by then it is too fucking late.

The problem with motherhood, Elizabeth thinks, is that she hates it.

John practically skips up the front stairs into the house, carrying a suitcase – his, of course; hers and Violet's are still in the car. By the time Elizabeth gets inside, Tabitha has already changed Violet and the baby is happily sitting on a towel Tabitha has laid over the fashionable slate of the kitchen floor, playing with measuring cups.

Elizabeth looks at the clock on the stove. Perry, who is a wine expert, likes to start drinking before dinner. She hopes he brings out a bottle soon.

Maybe Violet will sense they are on vacation. Maybe she will sleep in, or maybe she won't but John will wake up early for once and Elizabeth can sleep in. Ha. Haha.

"Oh, goodness, I didn't even say hello, I was in such a hurry to get my hands on the baby," Tabitha says. She is over by the sink, assembling a snack that is more like an hors d'oeuvre you might find at a fancy restaurant – Tabitha is an incredible cook, another thing she does with effortless ease – but she stops, brushing her hands off on her pants, which remain inexplicably, pristinely white, and comes over to give Elizabeth a hug. "I'm so glad you're here. Isn't this going to be wonderful? Ginger's with the children out by the pool, and Perry will be down in a moment. I'll take this outside and get

Violet, and he'll pour you a glass of wine and you can put your feet up."

In many ways, being around Tabitha is an assault. She never stops moving, doing, fixing, preparing, and she does it all so perfectly Elizabeth finds it unbearable to watch sometimes. But as Tabitha hugs her, smelling like fresh air and her signature perfume, Elizabeth finds herself relaxing, almost collapsing into the other woman's arms. To sit by a pool in a house she and John could never even begin to afford with her feet up while someone else brings her expensive wine and takes care of her child, this sounds like the most indulgent of pleasures, like a gift she is so unworthy of she nearly wants to cry.

• • • • •

A SINGLE MAN

• • • • •

When I was younger, everyone said to get a good job and I would find someone. I did get a good job (lucky I was analytical by nature right when everyone was looking for software developers) but I was still alone. They said to save for the future and I would find someone. I saved, first to have a nest egg in case anything went wrong, then for a down payment on the house, then for retirement. When all of those accounts were full, I was still alone. So I started a savings account for the child I didn't yet have.

Then they told me to buy the house and the family would come to fill it. So I bought the house, me, alone, on this suburban block where I can hear children playing all day from my home office, see them walking home from the pool on summer afternoons. On spring evenings, they are lined up in someone's driveway, awkward in tuxedos and long dresses, posing for photos, tilting on the edge of adulthood, and I have to go back inside because I cannot stand to watch their parents' joy. They come to the door selling things to support their schools, their parents hanging back on the sidewalk and letting them do the work, and I buy everything. I buy cookies and popcorn I will not eat; I buy wrapping paper for gifts I will not give; I buy discount cards to local family-friendly establishments when I have no family.

They told me to "work on myself" and I would find someone. So I took salsa dancing lessons where I was the youngest person by twenty years, and watercolor classes where all the older women told me they'd love to set me up with their daughters, or they would if only their daughters weren't already married. I joined a church that is full of families, and I sit alone during the service and smile at babies who smile at me while their parents scrabble under the pews for dropped pacifiers and Cheerios.

I went to my friends' weddings, and then their second weddings, and I danced with women who always seemed to be looking over my shoulder for something better. I met friends for drinks, always the first person there, and I looked hopefully at the groups of women laughing together. Surely one of them must be single. One of them must be as lonely as I am.

None of them ever were.

My sisters had children and I was their favorite uncle, and we made play dough and played dress-up and swam in the pool and I rocked them to sleep, but it wasn't the same. And then, on my fortieth birthday, I realized that if I wasn't meant to fall in love, I could still have a child. That could be my family. We could be a family of two, or three. I knew parenting would be hard on my own, but I could afford help, and my sisters and their husbands would help, too.

But whenever expectant mothers and social workers looked at my file, they all said the same thing: it's too strange that a single man wants to be a dad.

It has been two years since that birthday, and I still don't have the family I have longed for, still don't have the child I have waited for my whole life. They say why have children when there are so many children out there waiting for a home? But what if none of the people looking for homes for those children pick you?

It will cost $150,000 for me to have a child now. I will pay a fertility clinic, and an egg donor, and a gestational surrogate, women who are willing to give pieces of themselves to me so I can be a father. One hundred and fifty thousand dollars. Maybe more if it takes a few tries.

This is money I have. This is money I will gladly spend because I have wanted to be a father my entire life. Yet I can't help wondering, what about the men who are like me but don't have this money, this crazy amount of money to create something that other people get for free? What about the men who have been dreaming of a child since they were rocking a baby doll to sleep? What about the children who would be so happy and loved and cared for in their homes? Where are their families?

4

TABITHA

THAT EVENING, AFTER everyone has arrived, Tabitha is finishing up the preparations for dinner, watching the kids play in the backyard. Ginger and Elizabeth are both upstairs, John and Perry outside, talking and kicking the soccer ball back to the kids when they overshoot, which is frequently.

She loves every part of this – well, perhaps not the part where Ginger and Elizabeth have disappeared – but seeing the kids playing, Violet crawling along the sidelines by John's feet and then pulling herself up on a chair and surfing around it, even John and Perry together. There is something easy and special to their relationship that she wishes she had with Ginger and Elizabeth. Some of that is caretaking: John is sweet, but has a bit of lost puppy about him, and he sees Perry as the older brother he never had. Though Ginger is technically the eldest, Tabitha feels like an older sister to both her and Elizabeth, who is a good fifteen years younger. She has tried to copy the men's dynamic with the two of them, but Ginger and Elizabeth are both inexplicably prickly, even when she is only trying to help. Well. This is why they are on this vacation, isn't it? To bond. By this time next week, the three of them will be like sisters – she just knows it. She always wanted sisters, always hated being alone, and this family has given them to her, even if they don't feel like sisters just yet.

She hears Ginger's steps on the stairs, solid and slow, at the same time as her phone rings on the countertop. Her hands are slick from chopping the red onion for the cauliflower couscous, but she leans over and looks anyway.

It is Brianna calling, which is wonderful. The only real disappointment about this vacation, other than her mistake with the flowers, is that Brianna had to work and couldn't come with them. Unless she is calling to say that her schedule has changed and she can come after all? Preemptively overjoyed, she answers, onion-stained fingers and all, pressing the speaker button so she doesn't have to lift it to her ear.

"Brianna! How are you?"

"Hi, Tabitha," Brianna says, and starts to ask something, but Tabitha cuts her off, because Ginger is just stepping into the kitchen, and Tabitha waves her over.

"Ginger's here, too! I've got you on speaker!"

"Hey, Ginger," Brianna says cheerfully. She always has so much energy. Tabitha tosses the red onion into the bowl with the rest of the salad. Just the olives and the dressing and it will be done. Ginger leans over to look at what she is making, and Tabitha bats her away. She's as bad as the children. Next thing she'll be sticking her finger in the bowl for a taste.

"Please tell us you're calling to say you can come up after all! There's plenty of room!" There is: there are three extra bedrooms Brianna could choose from, but Tabitha is sure she'd be more comfortable in the corner room, the one with that lovely Serena & Lily bedding.

"I wish I could! You are so sweet, but I have to work. And my car's in the shop again anyway."

Tabitha frowns. This is one of those times she wishes Perry would let them help Brianna a little more financially. They funded Brianna's cosmetology school, but even then

Perry insisted it come under the guise of a "scholarship." That training helped Brianna land a good job at a dermatology office that also does cosmetic procedures: Botox and lip fillers and skin resurfacing and tattooed eyebrows. Brianna is like the kids, energetic and enthusiastic, impossible not to love, and Tabitha suspects she herself might be talked into having botulism injected into her face if Brianna were on the other end of the line. She wishes she could save Brianna, not just because she is the woman who gave her the unimaginable gift of her children but because she was motherless and fatherless too young, and it makes Tabitha feel so good to help.

"Oh no! What's wrong with it? Can you get to work?"

"Yeah, there's another girl at the office who lives near me who's giving me rides. Anyway, how are the mountains? How are the kids?"

"It's gorgeous up here. The kids are having a wonderful time, but everyone just got here, so there's lots more fun to come! When your car is fixed, maybe you could come up for the weekend?" Tabitha asks hopefully.

"Maybe," Brianna says, but she has the same tone to her voice Perry takes when *maybe* means *no*. Tabitha is glad she didn't even mention Brianna's joining them to the children; while they are used to the intermittent schedule of her visits, they are nonetheless always disappointed when she doesn't show. At some point she should talk to Brianna about this, but until then, Tabitha has learned not to advertise Brianna's presence at any event until she has actually arrived.

Elizabeth marches in. "Where's Perry? I need wine," she announces loudly.

"We're on the phone with Brianna," Ginger says.

"Oh, hey, Brianna! Are you coming up?" Elizabeth asks, unapologetic. She looks into the bowl, too, picking out an olive as soon as Tabitha puts them in.

"Elizabeth," Tabitha says, pulling the bowl away, but Elizabeth only pops the olive in her mouth and shrugs and smiles, as though it is all out of her control.

"I can't make it," Brianna says again. "Work. Maybe I'll see you when you all get back."

"Do you want me to go get the children so you can say hello?" Ginger asks, stepping toward the door.

"No, no, actually I wanted to talk to you guys," Brianna says, and then pauses.

Tabitha hears something in her voice, and in the silence, some shift from her normal cheer. "We're here," she says, before Elizabeth can say something insensitive like, *What's up?*

"It's complicated." Brianna laughs uncomfortably. "So the thing is, Justin was back in town for a while a couple of months ago."

Now it is the mothers' turn to be silent. Their eyes meet over the phone, but none of them says anything.

Elizabeth mouths, *Fuck.*

"How is he?" Tabitha asks finally. She has a sinking feeling about where this conversation is going.

"He's gone now. He got a line on some job in Alaska. Said it was too hot here." She laughs a little, but it is a tinny sound, not like the normal bell of her laughter. She says it like she doesn't care, but Tabitha is sure she does.

"That's a shame," Tabitha says.

"You know how it is, easy come, easy go." Brianna gives that awkward laugh again, and then, with no warning, says, "The thing is… I'm pregnant."

There is a silence.

Fuck, Elizabeth mouths again.

"Wow!" Tabitha says. *Congratulations* doesn't seem quite right, the way the story is coming together. "How are you feeling?"

There is another pause, and then Tabitha can hear a little sniffle from the other end of the phone. "Oh, honey," Tabitha says. "It's going to be okay."

Ginger and Elizabeth, other than Elizabeth's silent profanity, say nothing. Tabitha's mind is spinning. Brianna can't be that pregnant, can she? If Justin was only around a few months ago? *How many months?* she wants to ask. *How long was he in town?*

"I know," Brianna says around her tears. She still manages to sound upbeat even when she is crying. "I know it's going to be okay. I have you guys. I don't know what I would do without you."

Tabitha holds out a hand, as if she can reach through the phone to calm her. "I'm so sorry, honey. This sounds so stressful. Can I ask... how far along are you?"

With a sigh so long it sounds like a crackle across the phone line in an old movie, Brianna says, "Like three months? I'm due in December."

They are all silent again. Not too far along to terminate, but Brianna has never talked about that. With Phoebe and then the twins, she says, she was too scared to tell her mother she was pregnant until it was too late for an abortion, but Tabitha doubts she would have made that choice anyway. And the year before, with Violet, Brianna and Justin had planned to parent together, but he hadn't held up his end of that bargain, and Brianna was too scared to raise a child on her own. No one faults her for that.

"Have you thought about what might happen now? What does Justin think?" Tabitha asks.

"He says it's my decision," Brianna says, sniffling again. Ginger reaches up and rubs her fingers along her forehead when she hears that, and Tabitha knows how she feels. Justin's answer is both the right response and completely the wrong response. "This is why I wanted to talk to you. Because you know, I was sitting here feeling all alone and then I was like, I'm not all alone. Because I have you guys."

"We are always here for you," Tabitha says, and she feels herself tearing up a little bit.

"Totally," Elizabeth agrees, and Ginger nods, though Brianna can't see it.

"It's just, I was thinking about you guys, and the kids. You all took me on when I didn't really have a family anymore, and I am so, so grateful to you. So I was thinking, like, maybe Elizabeth and John… like, when I met you, you said you'd always wanted a big family, and I was thinking maybe you might like to adopt again?" She ends this in a rush.

Well. Tabitha was not expecting that. She looks over at Elizabeth, who clearly was also not expecting that. Her eyes are wide, and she looks up at Tabitha and this time mouths, *What the fuck?*

"My goodness, Brianna," Tabitha says, because someone has to say something. "We love you so much."

"I love you all, too," Brianna says, and there's another sniffle there.

"Are you sure that's what you want to do?" Ginger asks.

Elizabeth hasn't said anything yet.

"Are you kidding? Sure I do. I love you guys. And I love our kids, and I know you are the best family for them."

"Okay," Ginger says, because what else can they say?

"What do you think, Elizabeth?" Brianna asks.

"Oh, wow," Elizabeth says. "I… wow. I am so honored. So touched. I just don't know – Violet is so young, and I have to talk to John…" She trails off.

"Oh, sure," Brianna says, and she sounds relieved, like Elizabeth and John will just talk it out and it will be fine, but looking at Elizabeth's face, Tabitha wonders if it might not be that easy.

But it will all work out. It has to. A new baby! The whole family together at the house! Elizabeth and John will adopt this baby, and Brianna will be around more during the pregnancy, like she was with Violet. Tabitha cannot wait for the children to go to bed so they can start planning.

5

GINGER

"WHEW, " PERRY SAYS, collapsing into one of the chairs by the fire pit, a fresh bottle of wine in his hand. "I thought they'd never go to bed."

"I imagine they won't fall asleep for another hour," Ginger says.

Phoebe and the twins are always so happy to be together, and to have a two-week-long sleepover is their dream come true. And as if by some miracle, there is a room just for them in this house, a specially designed children's room, with three sets of bunk beds. The children will be up until all hours giggling and probably leaping off the bunk beds as if they were abandoning ship. One of them will end up in the emergency room before the trip is over, she is certain of it.

"We'll go up and check on them in a bit," Tabitha says. "We need to make sure Tate uses the bathroom before lights-out anyway."

Ginger watches Tabitha set an alarm on her phone, as though she might forget.

"So." Perry grimaces theatrically as he pulls the cork on the wine. Ginger demurs, but Elizabeth reaches out easily, even though Ginger is fairly sure she is already quite blurry around the edges. "It seems you all had an interesting call with Brianna earlier."

They hadn't wanted to discuss Brianna's announcement in front of the children. Their family policy has always been to let the children in on the conversations that affect them early, but the parents also try to discuss things together before presenting them to the children, in an effort to convey a united front and avoid confusion. Ginger finds it all very sensible.

Still, it was hard not to think of it, not to speak of it, as they made s'mores, Elizabeth's marshmallow catching on fire, the children dancing around in glee as Tabitha grabbed the stick and blew out the flame. They'd wanted to eat the charred remnants, but Tabitha had thrown it away, complaining about carcinogens, which was very Tabitha, denying a child the pleasure of a burned marshmallow over a vacation campfire.

But Ginger had seen Tabitha and Perry conversing quietly in the kitchen when she passed through to use the facilities, and Elizabeth and John, heads bent together for a moment on the side patio before he took Violet up to bed, so everyone must be slightly caught up.

"Have you two had a chance to chat about her request?" Tabitha asks, nodding at Elizabeth and John. John, who always seems to be smiling gamely at nothing in particular, is doing so now, but Elizabeth is leaning back, her wineglass held loosely between two fingers like a cigarette, her eyes closed as if she is going to drift off to sleep right there. Ginger, of course, never had an infant, and whenever she sees how tired Elizabeth is, she is grateful to have missed out on that experience.

"You have literally been with us the entire time," Elizabeth says without opening her eyes. "There has been no chatting."

"But Elizabeth told you?" Tabitha asks John.

"She did," John says. "It's really something, isn't it?"

Ginger isn't sure what he means – Brianna's pregnancy, or her asking Elizabeth and John to adopt again, or maybe the fact that they have barely been here for twenty-four hours and everything has been upended. As though things hadn't already been in upheaval since Brianna announced she was pregnant the last time.

"How did she sound?" Perry asks. "She was so upset when she called us about Violet, remember?"

"That was different. She had thought Justin would stay and they were going to raise the baby together. I think she was mostly upset about being abandoned, and then the pregnancy just made it worse," Tabitha says.

"I genuinely do not understand her luck," Elizabeth says, opening her eyes this time.

"Babies aren't made through luck," Perry says lightly, but Ginger sees Elizabeth's expression through her glass, and her face is sour.

"Didn't she go on birth control after Violet?" Tabitha asks.

"She couldn't. She had that blood clot in her pregnancy with Violet, remember? Can't do anything hormonal," Elizabeth, who had gone to OB-GYN appointments with Brianna when she was pregnant with Violet, says.

"Still, though…" John says, but he stops talking when Elizabeth looks at him with some unreadable expression.

"It's just amazing to me that she doesn't want to parent this kid, either," Elizabeth says. "I don't know how she can just get pregnant and then…" She trails off.

Across the circle, in the dancing light of the fire, Ginger sees John's hand reach out for Elizabeth's, but she doesn't respond. Her fist is clenched tight on the arm of the chair.

"You had an extra-hard time of things, though," Tabitha says. "Perhaps it's different for Brianna."

"Maybe," Elizabeth says, though she doesn't sound particularly convinced.

"I think she'll always be that scared child, the one who

was still practically a baby herself when she found out she was going to have Phoebe," Tabitha says.

"Is she... she's not that far along. Do you think she's thought about an abortion?" Perry asks.

"I'm sure she has, but I didn't ask. She's never really considered it as an option before, so I don't think that would change now," Tabitha says.

"And Justin is..." He makes a gesture with the unfinished sentence.

"Adiosed to Alaska," Elizabeth says.

"That guy," Perry says, shaking his head. "Why can't she just tell him to get lost?"

They do genuinely love and enjoy Brianna, all of them, but Ginger knows they all also have opinions and concerns about her choices, especially about Justin and her relationship with him. Their conflicted feelings about their children's first family is a dichotomy Ginger has tried more than once, and failed as many times, to resolve.

The children – the twins and Phoebe, for now, and Violet will receive the same explanation when she is older – know why they were adopted. They understand that Brianna loves them but feels she cannot take care of them in the same way their parents do. And in a way that awes her, the children love them all equally, if differently – Brianna, and Justin, and their parents, and each other.

"Why do you think she wants us to adopt?" John asks.

"She said she remembered us saying we wanted a big family," Elizabeth says.

"And you're wonderful parents to Violet," Tabitha says kindly, but Elizabeth looks startled, as though this were an undeserved compliment. "Why shouldn't she want you to adopt this baby?"

"I don't know. Because this is her fourth pregnancy, and she's not parenting any of them? Because she could have an abortion and not have to have another pregnancy, which, given the blood clot with Violet, is riskier this time? Because she's gotten stuck in this pattern where she keeps having kids with this guy and he doesn't care?"

"Elizabeth," Tabitha says, correcting her. "Let's look at it another way. Let's say that she knows how hard you tried to have a child. Let's say she knows that she has had a hard life but that this is a way she can give something to the world, make it a better place. Isn't that a kinder way to think of it?"

"I guess," Elizabeth says, but she sounds like Phoebe when she doesn't want to admit she has lost a fight.

"If that's the case, perhaps it would be better to view it as the miracle it is. Imagine, a full sibling for Violet! She won't be an only child. And a new baby for you two!"

Elizabeth mutters something Ginger can't quite catch, and then looks at Tabitha and Perry. "What if we don't want to adopt this baby?"

"Bethy," John starts to say, but Elizabeth holds up her hand without looking at him.

"What if we don't? Do you two want to adopt again?" she asks Perry and Tabitha.

There is a brief pause as Tabitha looks back at Elizabeth in surprise, and then turns to Perry. Their eyes meet and she smiles wistfully. "Oh, wouldn't that be wonderful?"

"It would be wonderful, but we're too old," Perry says.

"Oh, come on," Elizabeth says. "You run circles around all of us. I get tired just watching you."

"We'd be fine now. But we want to make sure we're around for our children as long as possible. If we adopted a baby now, I'd be almost seventy by the time the kid graduates from college, which is older than I'd like," Perry says.

Tabitha nods in agreement.

"Ginger?" Elizabeth asks, and now she sounds a little frantic.

"No, thank you," Ginger says, trying to sound polite, as though someone has offered her a meal for which she doesn't care. "But Elizabeth, Brianna asked *you*. Not us."

"She'd be fine with it. She's always just cared about the

53

kids being able to be together somehow." Elizabeth lifts her wineglass and drains it, then sets it down on the edge of the fire pit, where Tabitha scoops it up and puts it gently on a tray off to the side.

"That's not quite true," Tabitha says. "Ginger is right. Brianna asked you, not us."

A feeling of alarm sounds in Ginger's mind at being used as a shield. It never occurred to her that Elizabeth and John would not adopt another baby. Elizabeth is such a wonderful mother. The kids took to her and John within minutes of meeting them, and the way she is with Violet, giving and giving even though it clearly costs her so much.

And the thought strikes her, deep and bone-shaking as the tolling of a bell, that if Elizabeth and John don't adopt this child, who will?

The way this family looks is still finding its form, constantly changing. Their numbers increased by fifty percent with Violet's arrival, and now it will increase again, even if it is only the baby. More instability, more change, more disorder. Ginger presses her fingers against her forehead as though she can push the thought away. It is all so complicated, and it was all supposed to be so simple.

"Well, I think it's wonderful," Tabitha says when no one else has spoken. "Another baby! Just in time for Christmas! We'll have to reserve the photographer now, maybe someone who can do pictures in the hospital like we did when Violet was born."

"We're not doing it," Elizabeth says, cutting Tabitha off. Everyone, including John, looks at her, startled.

"Not adopting? Oh, don't be silly. You'll want to take some time to talk about it, of course," Tabitha says.

"No," Elizabeth says. "We won't."

"That's ridiculous!" Tabitha says. "Honestly, Elizabeth. This just doesn't *happen*."

"Yet it has happened twice. Funny, that," Elizabeth says.

"Wait," Ginger says, an uncomfortable realization dawning

on her. A loose feeling of panic begins to rattle around in her chest. This family is already so much, everyone's needs and noise around her a constant drain on her energy. She leaves Sunday dinners with headaches half the time. And Phoebe – how is she going to handle this much disruption? A new school, a new sibling, and a new set of parents, too? That is too much change.

"What if you don't adopt? Does that mean there will be another adoptive family? That would make... what, twelve people?" Ginger asks, speaking her worries aloud.

No one answers her.

"Should we tell the kids?" Perry muses. He and Elizabeth have drunk a great deal of wine tonight, and he is getting a little sloppy, swallowed by drunken bonhomie. Tabitha takes his empty glass and sets it on the tray with Elizabeth's.

"We don't know anything yet," Elizabeth says. "Like, what would we even say?"

That question adds another layer of anxiety. Phoebe had been distressed when Brianna first told them she was pregnant with Violet, and that she and Justin would be raising the baby, and then confused when the plan had changed, and Ginger doesn't want to put her through that uncertainty again. But the parents must agree to a plan before she can approach Phoebe. That is the rule.

Elizabeth's questions have left Ginger feeling slightly off-kilter, as though she is moving on an unsteady sea. "Elizabeth is right. Let's wait. Just a day or two. Until everything is all settled."

6

ELIZABETH

WHEN BRIANNA SAID she was pregnant, Elizabeth wanted to scream. *Again? AGAIN?*

How in the world is it fair that Elizabeth tried for years – years! – to have a baby and could not manage to have a single pregnancy stick, and Brianna is pregnant *again*?

It makes her doubt the existence of any rational god.

And then to have Brianna ask her if she and John would adopt again. The only answer is no, obviously the only answer is no, but how can she say no? Brianna made her a mother, and despite whatever flaws she has, she is a very sweet person, and she is offering to give Elizabeth the thing she claimed she wanted only a year ago, which is another child. She is asking if it's okay if she just gives Elizabeth a human being.

To which Elizabeth's response is a big fucking *NO*.

The worst part is that she can't say that. She can't say why. She can't say anything because it is fucking omertà to say anything negative about being a mom that isn't like, *Wine o'clock!* or *Toddlers be like…* She can't say that she is so fucking tired, and weirdly sad, and that she loves Violet with an intensity that surpasses even the degree to which people told her she would love her child while at the same time hating being a mother. It is inexplicable, and because she can't say anything, or not anything honest, no one can explain it to her.

Because here she is, with a mind-bogglingly large credit card debt from those goddamned endless treatments that only ended up with their very expensive and ultimately very useless reproductive endocrinologist shrugging her shoulders like an emoji, her period still insane from the hormones (her gynecologist swears that isn't possible, but fat lot she knows because she isn't the one waking up in a pool of blood every three weeks), her twenties wasted on the futile effort of trying to have a baby, exhausted all the time, and it turns out – *Haha, joke's on you, Elizabeth* – that being a mother sucks.

The day she met Tabitha was supposed to be the end of things. That morning she went for a blood test to see if the last embryo transfer had worked (which she knew it hadn't, but god forbid they not go through the whole delightful fucking charade), and they usually called before lunch, but they hadn't, and one of the eighth-grade boys broke his arms when someone else dared him to jump over the stairwell railing and then there was an interminable faculty meeting and finally, when she called the nurse herself to ask for the results, even though you'd think a nurse at a fertility clinic would be trained to have a little fucking empathy, she just said, "Didn't anyone call you? It was negative."

Elizabeth hung up without saying goodbye.

She isn't a crier by nature. One time when she found out a pregnancy wasn't going to stick, that she was having what they called a "chemical pregnancy," which, fuck that term and the horse it rode in on, she punched a hole in the drywall near the pantry. (It is still there, and she feels a weird pride every time she looks at it.) But that day there was no drywall to punch, so she got her things and went to her car to go home. Stuck at a traffic light, she was staring at nothing when she saw the cars next to her beginning to move. Stepping on the gas without looking, she drove straight into the back of the very large, very expensive SUV in front of her, which was very much not moving.

The SUV was fine, but the hood of Elizabeth's car, which was small and old and had been cheap to begin with, crumpled, one headlight popping out like a loose eyeball in a cheesy horror movie, and Elizabeth sat there until the woman in front of her, who she did not know at the time was Tabitha, climbed out of her car and Elizabeth realized she should do the same. Tabitha didn't even stop to look at her own car, simply hurried back to Elizabeth, asking if she was okay, and instead of answering, Elizabeth hurled herself into this stranger's arms and began to weep inconsolably.

They stood there, traffic diverting around them like the parting of the Red Sea, only with more horns and middle fingers, and Elizabeth cried and cried and cried. Finally Tabitha took Elizabeth to her SUV and installed her in the front passenger seat, Tate and Taylor in the back looking wide-eyed and confused, and then Tabitha, as she does, took care of everything. She had the car towed to a body shop, found Elizabeth's phone and called John to tell him what had happened and where to meet them, and then she drove them all back to her house and sent Tate and Taylor to the playroom while she gave Elizabeth a cup of tea and listened to her whole story.

And then Tabitha said the words that had changed Elizabeth's whole life. "You're not going to believe this," she said, leaning forward over the island, a sleek poured concrete that should have looked industrial and unwelcoming but somehow looked comfortingly cool, "but I think we can make you a mom."

It had been easier to say yes then, before she knew how miserable this is, how somehow her love for and ease with children doesn't translate to her own child. Now she knows better, and there is no way she is doing it again. It isn't fair to anyone – not John, not herself, not Violet, and not whatever child would have the misfortune to end up with her as a mother.

She has said no to adopting this baby, but she has the feeling no one has heard her, no one cares what she wants, that they are going to force her into it. John tried to talk to her after the conversation around the fire pit the night before, but she had let herself get far too drunk, angry drunk, and had just said no, no, no, we are not adopting again, don't make me do this again, and then she had collapsed into her pillow and slept until Violet's crying woke her up far too early, her mouth dry and woolly and sour.

After breakfast, while everyone is running around trying to get ready to leave for Tabitha's Fun Family Activity Du Jour, John's phone rings, and he steps outside to take the call. Elizabeth has no idea who is calling him at nine o'clock in the morning on a Saturday, and she doesn't particularly care. Mostly what she cares about is that he has wandered off to the backyard where there is a putting green – an actual putting green at a house, don't even get her started – and is yammering on the phone while she goes upstairs to wrestle Violet into a romper and sunscreen and then back out of the romper when she sees a poop face and then into a new diaper and then into the romper again and sets her on the floor while she tries to pack the diaper bag.

But when she comes back downstairs and sees John walking in, his face looks ashen.

"I need to talk to you," he says.

One of the reasons she first fell in love with John was his easygoing nature. It is a trait that, now that they are responsible for keeping a tiny human alive, she frequently finds less charming, but it also means that when she looks at him now, the serious expression on his face and the way his throat pulses hard when he swallows, she can tell that something is very, very wrong.

She looks at Violet. "What do I do with her?"

Perry is passing through and he reaches out his arms. "I'll take her," he says, lifting Violet and tossing her in the air with an ease Elizabeth has never mastered. "General Tabitha would like us to report to the driveway in ten minutes," he says.

John and Elizabeth go out to the side patio, walking to the chairs by the fire pit. It is shady and cool by the stream, and she shivers, slipping her arms into her sleeves. "What's wrong?" she asks.

John sits down on the edge of one of the chairs, elbows resting on his knees, hand still gripping the phone, but loosely, as though he might let it fall and shatter. A thousand things run through her mind – he is sick, his mother is sick, he is leaving her.

"It's happening. The layoffs," he says. He doesn't look at her.

"Oh no. Oh no," she says. He mentioned the possibility of layoffs a couple of times, but there had always been something to interrupt the conversation (usually Violet), and to be honest, she'd put it out of her mind. But here it is, and suddenly that thing that hadn't seemed so urgent is as urgent as it gets. Elizabeth gropes around for the edge of the fire pit behind her before she sits, the stone pushing into her thighs. This isn't possible. This isn't possible! "Tell me they're not laying you off."

John still doesn't look up. "I told you it might happen. Things haven't been great for a while, and I haven't been making my numbers."

John does – well, *did*, she thinks – something dull and inscrutable in sales for a company that does something dull and inscrutable in telecommunications. He has a mind for technology but a heart for people, and though this has never been his dream job, it was steady and reliable, and when he took it, even though more of his salary would be dependent on commission than felt safe, the company's health insurance included a round of IVF. Back when they assumed one would be enough, a thought that makes her laugh bitterly when she thinks about it now.

She isn't laughing. She feels sick, sicker than the few times she had been so briefly pregnant, when the waves of nausea rocked her constantly, and then remembering those times makes her feel even sicker.

She has the feeling this is a moment when she should be A Wife, when she should hold his hand and tell him things like they are stronger together, or they have made it through worse, but mostly she wants to throw herself into the fire pit. Which isn't even currently on fire and would therefore only end with her covered in ash and the charred remains of the marshmallow carcasses the twins lost off their skewers.

"This is not good," she says, which is the understatement of the year.

He doesn't say anything.

"Fuck. We need that money. We need your salary."

"I know," he says. He sounds miserable, which only makes her angry.

"What have you even been doing? Why didn't you tell me how low your numbers were? Why didn't you tell me they were actually going to do these layoffs?"

"I've been trying! I've tried to talk to you about this a dozen times!" His voice is high and loud, and then he suddenly seems to deflate. "I figured it might be okay. A big contract could always come through at any time, and we had some stuff in the pipeline. I knew it wouldn't happen overnight, but I thought…"

He doesn't even finish his sentence.

"You can get unemployment, right? While you look for a new job? Wait, it's Saturday, right? Why are they doing this on the weekend?"

"They did everyone else yesterday. I think they forgot about me because I was already out of the office," he says, that thought making Elizabeth ill as well, all these other people driving home from work last night with the same sick feeling in their stomachs.

"Okay, fine. So you can call for unemployment on Monday. Or go online tonight." Her brain is spinning wildly, a thousand what-ifs and maybes all going at once.

"Yeah, but unemployment is only a percentage of my base salary."

Elizabeth's belly clutches. A percentage of what might as well be nothing is nothing. "Okay, calm down," she says, more to herself than to John. "Let's think about this."

Like she wasn't thinking about it already. All she does is think about money. The money they don't have, the money they owe. How much things cost, how much money other people have, the various miracles that could make their problems go away. It is a dull worry, unromantic, but a terrifying one, a cartoon anvil that hangs above her head, swaying precariously whenever she breathes.

Her parents could afford to help them. Could, if they wanted, make all their problems – the financial ones, at least – disappear. But she can't ask them. They know nothing about Elizabeth and John's financial issues and hardly anything about their fertility treatments. She has thought about going to them for a loan a thousand times, but the emotional price would be too great. She'd have to tell them where the debt came from, and then her mother would raise an eyebrow and point out that *she* never had any problems getting pregnant, and her brothers and sister would agree, saying they only had to look at their spouses to get pregnant, hahaha, a joke Elizabeth had never found funny even before she knew it would take a lot more people than just her husband to get her pregnant. They would ask whose fault it was, as if one of them had planned it. Her sister, Rebecca, would certainly know one or more dental hygienists whose cousin had a miracle pregnancy and wonder aloud why Elizabeth hadn't been able to arrange something similar. Someone would ask if she had tried yoga and one of her brothers would suggest they start eating paleo and someone else would say they should relax more, and all of that together added up to a big fat NO when Elizabeth thought about asking them for help.

"We could always…" John trails off without finishing the sentence, but she already knows what he is going to say.

"No. No, no, no. No way."

He stands up, like he is taking control now, like he has a plan. "Come on. We have to at least consider it. It's the only thing that makes sense. If we stay here, even if I get another job, it's going to take us at least ten years to pay off the debt. It's like being on a hamster wheel. We're never going to get anywhere. What if something happens? What if one of us gets sick? What if Violet gets sick?"

"Stop, stop." Elizabeth puts her hands over her ears, unwilling to hear any more.

What she is not letting him say is that they should move to Russell, the small town on the plains in eastern Colorado where his family lives, where he grew up. They have talked about it before – his family, closeknit and happy in each other's company in a way Elizabeth has never understood, would be over the proverbial moon – but she has always said no. It would make so many things easier, she knows. Free childcare, courtesy of John's family. A cost of living half of what it is in the metro area. A dependable job for John working for his uncle, a dependable job for her working in the local school – the town being so small, there is only the one.

The price there is also too high, in other ways. John left Russell because he felt suffocated by its smallness, and she knows he romanticizes it now from a distance, but there's no question he would feel the same if they returned. As for her… well, John's sisters do genuinely seem to get pregnant on a whim, and she can't stand being around them, listening to their endless joking litanies about the difficulties of pregnancy as though they were not things she would have given anything to endure. His mother would indeed provide childcare, but it wouldn't be free; they would pay in opinions and intrusive questions, and the salary working for his uncle would include perks like health insurance and lots of vacation days and his family knowing exactly where they were every second of the day.

John's family is similar to hers in their intrusiveness, but there is a kindness to their meddling, a genuine concern rather than a desire to extract the best opportunities for one-upmanship and criticism. The closeness, which he delights in and was happy to find a replica of in this family, does make it hard for her to breathe sometimes, but she could suffer it for the ease and comfort it would bring them, couldn't she? If it would mean the end of their financial anxiety?

It would also mean leaving this family behind, the end of Sunday dinners and the children gathered together like this, and that is hard to imagine. Let alone the issue of telling Tabitha because, hoo-boy, if Tabitha is ignoring what Elizabeth is saying about the adoption now, just imagine the level of denial that would kick in if they tried to move.

"Is that really what you want? For us? For Violet? To be stuck in the middle of nowhere? To have your family hovering over our lives all the time?"

"You're making it out like they're evil. They're not. They love us. They want to help us."

"What about the family?"

"Which family?" John asks. That term has become confusing for them. There is John's family and his siblings' extended families and Elizabeth's family and her siblings' extended families and Violet's birth family and their own family of three, and then this crazy-quilt family with the kids at the center, and they often have to correct each other. "No, the sibling family," or "No, my family in Russell," or "No, Violet's birth father." She is already dreading Violet's having to do a family tree assignment at school. She'll need a whole forest.

"You mean them?" he asks, gesturing vaguely at the house. She can hear Violet squealing happily and the kids shouting, and General Tabitha is probably in the car already, tapping her watch. "We'd still see them. We wouldn't be moving to Mars."

"It's not the same. They're Violet's family. There's going to be another sibling. It's not fair to her. To the kids."

"Don't use the kids as an excuse," John says.

"I'm not!" Elizabeth says, but she has the sick feeling that she is. Isn't she always complaining about how tired she is, how often they have to go over to Tabitha and Perry's, wishing she could have one weekend, just one, without something to do for this family so she could get some rest, for crying out loud?

Knowing she is in the wrong, she stands up, as though that gives her moral righteousness. She is an inch taller than John, which isn't usually noticeable, but he hasn't put on his shoes yet, so the difference is visible. She puts her hands on her hips. "I'm just saying it's not only us now. We can't make decisions just about us."

"If we moved to Russell, we could afford to adopt again," John says, and the silence falls hard between them.

She has never felt so far away from him. They just talked about this and she said no. Jesus, does he not see? Does he not understand how exhausted she is, how awful this is, how she would give anything for Violet to age five years overnight so she wouldn't be caught in this Sisyphean trap of diapers and feeding and crying, all the crying, so much crying? Does he really not know?

Elizabeth knows she picks fights. She gets angry sometimes, that's all, can't stand having to suffer whatever is being thrown at her, needs to stand up for herself. But for once she doesn't feel like fighting at all. She is too tired to argue, too tired to explain to John what he should already know. Instead she simply says, "Yeah, no," and for the first time in their relationship, she turns and walks away from her husband in the middle of an argument.

·····

THE RUN

·····

People say we're strange. Maybe we are. Though I don't see how we're any stranger than anyone else.

We started running together. He was on the cross-country team in high school, but I had never been a runner before. It was good to have him with me. At first, I thought it was boring. So we'd run and talk, and that kept my mind busy. We ran pretty slow when we started. I didn't know it at the time, but he was holding himself back for me.

He's built like a runner. Or rather like a marathon runner, which is quite different from a sprinter. I've always thought that was interesting. Like when you watch the Olympics and they're all athletes, but their body types are all different depending on which sport they do. Anyway, he's like a greyhound. I'm more like a pit bull.

Then we started racing. I call it racing even though neither of us cares whether we win. Not even him. We are just doing it to know we did it. We did a 5K. Then a 10K. Then a half-marathon. Then a marathon.

One thing I like about running with him is that he never leaves me behind. I know he could go faster. Could go longer. Instead he stays with me. He tells me jokes to make me laugh when I'm getting tired. He always knows when I'm getting tired.

I was the one who heard about ultrarunning first. Initially he was a little bit cautious about it. More cautious than I was. Maybe because he knew he was going to have to entertain me for that whole time. Our first marathon took us over five hours. Or it took me over five hours, and he stayed with me.

I wanted to do a 100, but he told me to slow down. Ironic. We did a 50K first because that's only a little longer than a marathon. I have to say, I'm fairly sure I liked it more than he did. We kept working up, and now we do 100 miles.

We like the challenge. We like the focus it takes. We like having a purpose. Something that gets us up in the morning. Neither of us ever wanted fancy careers. We wanted a family and an interesting life. We have the interesting life part; now we're just looking for the family. We travel a lot for races. And because we're running, we get to actually see the place we're visiting. Not just the tourist attractions.

I've been looking at jogging strollers. I see people running with them. I don't think you can run a marathon that way, but maybe. Sometimes the races have 1K family routes, so one of us could do that with the kids while the other one ran something longer. Now that I know I can do it alone, it doesn't worry me so much.

I see families running with their older children and I think, We could be like that. It could be something we all do together. My family never did anything together. My parents got divorced when I was eight and my sister was six, and mostly what I remember is being tossed between their cars every couple of days. Which was pointless because they always had to work anyway, so we never even saw whoever we were with.

Maybe that's why I don't care about having a big career. I do like having something to work toward. We're registered for a lot of races this season, but if we do adopt a kid, we'll figure something out. The kid will fit into our lives; we won't change everything to fit theirs.

Like I said, people think we're strange doing what we do, but sometimes I think they're strange, too. People love all kinds of stuff. Knitting and cat shows and stamp collecting. Why not running? It makes me happy. It's made us better as a couple. Soon it will make us better as a family.

7

TABITHA

IT WOULD HAVE been a perfect morning if John and Elizabeth hadn't been in such bad moods. They made everyone late having an argument in the yard, and have been quiet and sulky ever since.

Other than that, the day has been wonderful. They all took the gondola up to the top of the mountain and played disc golf, which the kids adored, and then found a spot in the sun for a picnic. Tabitha has prepared snacks for them, nothing fancy – kalamata olives because Taylor likes spitting out the pits; refrigerator-pickled carrots for Perry, who prefers things with so much vinegar you can literally see his lips pucker; *melón con jamón* on sustainable bamboo toothpicks; and the most adorable little spinach-and-goat-cheese quiche bites. Oh, and butter bean dip and fresh pita crisps. Tabitha doesn't believe in feeding children differently from adults, and while she is certain Ginger and Elizabeth give Phoebe and Violet things with nuclear colors and chemical-laden ingredient lists when she isn't around, she tries to show them when they are all together that children will eat adventurously if it is modeled for them. It's really quite simple.

When the older kids are finished eating, they go off to try to fly a kite. John is sitting at the edge of the blanket looking at the ground, Violet using him to climb around, her bottom sticking out adorably. Elizabeth is at the far end of another blanket, lying on her stomach, eyes closed.

"How are you two doing?" Tabitha asks.

Perry, leaning back with his arms crossed under his head, looks over at her and then at John and Elizabeth. Elizabeth opens one eye and then closes it again.

They don't say anything.

"I texted with Brianna a little bit this morning. Just to let her know we support her and we are here for her," Tabitha says.

"How is she?" Ginger asks.

"She's not in an easy situation, but she seems optimistic," Tabitha says. Privately, Tabitha wonders if there is something behind Brianna's apparent altruism, the way she leapt so quickly to the idea of Elizabeth and John adopting this child. Is it a way of whitewashing the fact that she has let Justin abandon her again, that even though she promised she wouldn't see him anymore, she obviously has? A way to make it look as though she meant to do this all along? A way of seizing power and attention in a life that has so little of both?

But she can't think any of those things. Brianna is part of their family, and she is reaching out and they will reach back.

There is a strange trick of adoptive motherhood, she has found, a necessary blindness to the bifurcation of your child's life. If you spend all your time thinking about the life your child might have lived, how things might have been different if they stayed with their birth family, you will rob them of the life they are living, and drive yourself crazy to boot.

On the other hand, she cannot help but think of that life, cannot help but see Brianna in the graceful way Phoebe moves, hear her laughter in Taylor's. To deny that first family, that part of their lives, would be to deny who they are.

So Tabitha tries to walk the tightrope between shutting her eyes to that shadow life and never forgetting the miracle of what they have, of these children and Brianna, who had needed them just when they needed her. If she thinks about it too much, it makes her teary, her heart swelling with gratitude.

"I think Brianna is eager to hear you say you two will agree to adopt this child."

"We are not doing that," Elizabeth says testily.

Tabitha would like to say a thousand things, but she forces herself to take a deep breath. She doesn't understand why Elizabeth is being so stubborn. When the universe offers you a gift, you say yes! "I know you've just had the one night to think about it. It must seem to be going so fast. Is there something you'd like to talk about? Some reason you're feeling reluctant?"

Elizabeth and John look at each other, and then Elizabeth looks away again, back toward the kids, who have managed to launch the kite and are running back and forth in a panicked attempt to keep it aloft. Violet has found a pita crisp and is gnawing it into sogginess.

"We're not sure we are ready," John says.

"You weren't ready for Violet, were you?" Tabitha intends to sound lighthearted, because who is ever prepared for parenthood, but she hears something hard-edged in her own laughter, and Perry glances over at her again and shakes his head.

"Why do you even care? What's it to you?" Elizabeth asks sharply, so sharply Tabitha literally draws back.

"You're my family. I want you to be happy. And Brianna is our family, too. It's like what she said, when we met, you and John talked about having a big family, and it just doesn't make sense…" Perry reaches over and brushes his hand down her arm, and she stops herself, calms the rising pitch of her voice. "It just seems like fate."

"It's complicated," John says.

"Is it just because Violet is so young? Because she'll be

nearly two when this baby is born. It is so different when they can do more for themselves," Tabitha says. This is a slight exaggeration of the timeline, as Violet won't be even eighteen months, but she will be so much more independent by then.

"That is true," Ginger agrees. Surprised by the support, Tabitha gives her a small appreciative nod.

"Two kids under two is still a lot," Elizabeth says.

"I've been there," Tabitha says, and Elizabeth at least has the dignity to look sheepish.

"The thing is," John says, swallowing audibly, "I've been laid off."

Elizabeth turns her head quickly to look at her husband, but her expression is unreadable.

"Oh no," Tabitha says. "Oh, dear." But she takes a little comfort in this knowledge, that at least there is a reason for their reluctance, and such a minor one at that. Money, after all, is only money.

"That's so rough. Is the company going under?" Perry asks, and Tabitha appreciates how calm he sounds.

"They're struggling a little bit. The sales numbers were always impossible to hit, but the product's gotten a little behind the industry. They've been talking about layoffs, but they hadn't told us for sure. Really, I just wasn't making my numbers," John says.

Tabitha sees he is avoiding looking at Elizabeth. Violet has crawled over to Ginger, who is humoring her by beeping the tip of the child's nose so Violet laughs. It is the one trick she has with young children, but it works.

Elizabeth closes her eyes for a moment. "I don't think we need to talk about this right now," she says.

"I'm just telling them why we're feeling a little hesitant about adopting," John says, and now it is his turn to sound sharp. Tabitha raises an eyebrow. She has never quite understood John – Elizabeth has a forceful personality, and John just… exists. Perfectly nice, quite helpful, but not terribly interesting. It's rare to see him express any opinion forcefully.

"I don't think this is any of their business," Elizabeth says, exhibiting an uncharacteristic amount of control by not swearing.

"Don't be silly. We're family," Tabitha says. "We are here for each other."

"You will find another job, though, won't you?" Ginger asks.

"I hope so," John says. He offers a weak smile.

"Sure you will," Perry says heartily. "The market's good; you're a smart kid."

"Absolutely," Tabitha agrees, her voice calm, almost a coo.

"So we don't know what that means about adoption," John says. A silence falls as they consider this. "You know, adopting another. Because we were thinking…"

"John," Elizabeth says again, and this time her voice is tighter, warning.

He looks back at her, and his jaw tightens.

Violet makes her way back over to Elizabeth, who reaches for her. "It's fine. It'll be fine," she says, offering a tight smile, but Tabitha is not fooled.

When they were adopting the twins, Perry had to remind her again and again that they were not also adopting Brianna, that Brianna was technically an adult and in charge of herself, and that Tabitha could not fix her or her problems. He had been on board for helping with her cosmetology school tuition, but he draws the line at more direct interference. Tabitha knows he is right, but it is so hard to keep quiet sometimes. It is the same with Elizabeth. Tabitha can so clearly see the right path – Elizabeth and John should adopt this child because they said they wanted a big family and if they do, it will keep the children together without introducing even more disruption into the family – yet she has to sit here and watch Elizabeth make precisely the wrong choice. "She is not yours to rescue," Perry always says, about both Elizabeth and Brianna. But it is very, very hard not to try.

"So what will we tell Brianna?" Ginger asks.

"We'll call her together," Tabitha says. After all, she has

known Brianna for longer than Elizabeth, and will be able to manage the conversation better. Manage it toward what, though, she wonders, and feels a little shiver of something that might be fear. Because what will Brianna say when Elizabeth says no? What will happen to this child, this child whose life has been turned upside down before it is even born? What will happen to all of them?

She and Perry could, they could, adopt again. But Perry is absolutely opposed, and if she is honest, she loves their family as it is.

No, Elizabeth and John must adopt this baby. They must. It is the only answer.

"We'll call her together," Tabitha repeats. "But later. And we can mention that we're not firm on the timeline. So you and John can have a little more time to think about things." These words are like an incantation, a prayer for Elizabeth and John to change their minds. Because the alternative is… well, Tabitha doesn't know what it is, and that is a problem. Knowing what to do is her job in this family.

Before Elizabeth can respond, the kids come running back up. The air is cool, but the sun is intense, and she can feel the heat coming from them as they hurl themselves against her, bounding off almost immediately and turning toward the refreshments. Tate grabs her water bottle and starts gulping at it as if she were a freshman at a frat party. "Tate, are you sure you want to drink that much?" she asks her daughter, and then, "Taylor, don't spit the olive pits in the grass."

Perry turns to say something to Ginger, and Violet starts to cry, and Tabitha watches them all, her family, wondering how to keep them moving in the right direction.

8

GINGER

"DO YOU HAVE Phoebe's school calendar yet?" Tabitha asks later that afternoon when they are back at the house, out by the pool while the children swim.

Ginger, who has leaned back in one of the pool lounges, hoping for a cat nap in the afternoon sun, opens one eye and looks over at the table. She doesn't think of herself as a napper, but being with this many people all day exhausts her: the constant flow of conversation, the sheer number of Organized Activities, the perpetual motion machines that are the children (and, if she is being honest, the other adults – doesn't anyone else like to just sit down and *read*?).

Tabitha is sitting at the table by the pool with her day planner in front of her, alert and perky, while Ginger feels slightly less so. Their outing that morning had been pleasant, but the weight of the conversation about the new baby, how things might change, has made the task of being around so many people all the time even more exhausting. She only wants a little silence.

"Tabitha, it is summer. Why are we talking about school calendars?"

"I need to start planning the holidays for the fall."

"I appreciate that, but does it need to be done right this moment?"

"Why not? You're here, I'm here, I have Tate and Taylor's calendar. Have you ever heard the expression *Strike while the iron is hot*?"

"Have you ever heard the expression *Let me take a nap*?"

"Hahaha," Tabitha says. Taylor chooses this moment to cannonball into the swimming pool, sending up a splash completely disproportionate to his size, and giving Ginger a generous sprinkle as he does.

"Taylor," Ginger says when he emerges. He tosses his head, shaking off more water, and grins at her.

"Sorry, Aunt Ginger," he says, but clearly he is not the slightest bit sorry.

"What's the name of her middle school? I'll look it up," Tabitha says, sitting with her pen like an eager student, ready to take notes. She has a strict rule about not being on her phone or computer when the children are around (a rule Perry is somehow exempt from, she has noticed), which Ginger respects but also thinks is rather extreme. Which, come to think of it, is how she feels about Tabitha a lot of the time. Tabitha is so devoted to perfection and all things good and right you would think she was the eldest of the mothers, and not Ginger.

By now, their conversation has gotten Phoebe's attention, and she pops out of the water like a dolphin at SeaWorld. "I'm going to The Global Academy," she announces, with a significant amount of ceremony and self-importance. "They call it TGA."

"TGA? The one in the city? Really?" Tabitha asks.

Ginger clenches her teeth. "We're not sure, actually. We just heard about the wait list a couple of days ago." She says this quickly and apologetically. She could have told Tabitha when they found out, she realizes now. Tabitha would have loved sharing in Phoebe's triumph. But Tabitha would have done then what she does now: take over.

"Oh, Ginger, why didn't you call us? Phoebe, that's wonderful, sweetheart! Congratulations! We'll have to celebrate tonight. Oh, I wish I'd known, I would have made a special dinner." She appears genuinely upset, which is rather silly. Tabitha cooks as if every meal is a special meal. If she knew how often Ginger and Phoebe eat nothing more complicated than frozen macaroni and cheese for dinner, she would probably have an aneurysm.

"Thanks!" Phoebe says, and jumps out of the pool. "Can we have a snack?"

"Here," Tabitha says, reaching over and lifting a lid off what Ginger had thought was a decorative box but turns out to be a pleasingly arranged platter of crudités and fruit. This is on top of the gourmet snacks she provided for their outing, and lunch. Phoebe wraps a towel around herself and sits down at the table, and Tate and Taylor, sensing the presence of food, climb out of the pool and join her.

"I'm so happy for you, Phoebe," Tabitha says again. She reaches over to give Phoebe a side hug, managing not to get her shirt wet even though Phoebe is positively dripping. "You're going to love it there."

"It's not for sure yet," Ginger sings, hoping the light tone will keep the sharpness from her voice. Phoebe turns and looks at her with disappointment. Ginger makes a face back that is supposed to mean, *We spoke about this*, but she thinks probably looks more like, *I have a golf ball in my mouth that I would like to spit out.*

At the other end of the table, Perry has been reading something on his phone, but now the conversation has registered with him, too, and he looks up. "I thought you were going to school with your little friends," he says. Perry has a funny way of sounding like he is a father from a 1950s sitcom, which could be an act, but she thinks is genuinely the way he is.

"I *waaaaas*," Phoebe says, stretching the word out to clarify. "But then I got off the wait list for TGA. So now I'm going there."

"You *might* be going there," Ginger corrects in as gentle a way as she can. She understands Phoebe's excitement, shares it even, but Phoebe does not, cannot, understand how much there is to think about before they make any rash decisions.

"What do you mean? Why wouldn't she go? TGA is great. It was on NPR last year," Tabitha says. "Honey, get your hand out of your glass," she says to Taylor, who has indeed, somewhat inexplicably, thrust his hand down into his glass of lemonade. He pulls it out, the liquid slipping down his fist, and then giggles and sucks the liquid off his fingers.

"Weird, buddy," Perry says indulgently, and goes back to reading.

"It's not that she won't go. It's complicated and we haven't talked it through yet. We weren't going to bring it up until we had a chance to do so," Ginger reiterates, looking again at Phoebe with an expression that she hopes this time is closer to *Be quiet* and further from imminent golf ball swallowing.

"Isn't that the school by our house?" Tate asks. She is kneeling, and Tabitha reaches over and gently nudges her to sit down.

"It certainly is," Tabitha says. "It's just around the corner."

"Yes!" Phoebe says. "You can come to all my debates!"

"Let's see," Tabitha says. She has broken her own rule and is consulting her phone and then looking at a printout of what must be the twins' calendar. "Your first day of school will be the same as Tate and Taylor's. That's perfect!"

Ginger's heart is racing. Wasn't she just settling in for a nap? What is happening?

"How come Aunt Ginger doesn't want you to go?" Tate asks, as though Ginger isn't sitting right there within earshot.

"She thinks it's too far away," Phoebe says, in a tone that

indicates precisely what she thinks of that argument. She sits up and rifles through the tray and then leans back with a handful of grapes, popping one sullenly into her mouth.

"I didn't say that," Ginger objects. She wonders if she can steer this conversation better if she moves over to the table, so she does, standing awkwardly by Phoebe, concerned that if she sits down she will be agreeing to participate, accepting the turn things have taken, allowing everyone else to change their entire world without her having a say in it.

It's too late because Tabitha has spotted an entrée into one of her favorite subjects: Why Ginger and Phoebe Should Move to the City. "Oh, when we get back to the city, we should go look at some houses near us for you and Phoebe!"

Tabitha has been pressuring Ginger to move closer to them from the beginning. While normally the social worker, Sunny, would have tried to keep the siblings together, both Sunny and their family therapist had encouraged the idea of the children living in separate homes. That arrangement permitted Phoebe to gain some independence and release the feeling of responsibility she had developed for taking care of the twins, and offered Tate and Taylor the attention they needed to overcome some gross motor delays. No one had raised any concerns about how far apart they lived at the time, and Ginger takes umbrage at Tabitha's continuing to harp on the subject. She would like, someday, to counter with the idea that Tabitha should move closer to *them*, but she has not yet had the courage. Besides, now Elizabeth and John live near Tabitha and Perry, and it's two against one. But why does she always have to be the one to move?

"That's quite premature, isn't it? We're not ready to move. Perhaps we should discuss this later," Ginger says, referring to both the idea of moving and of Phoebe's going to TGA. She feels a creeping sense of self-righteousness. The family rule is to discuss issues among the adults before the children are involved. Tabitha knows this. She shouldn't be rushing ahead.

"What time does TGA's day end?" Tabitha asks, as though

she has not even heard Ginger, which she probably has not. Tabitha's hearing is highly selective.

"3:38," Phoebe answers promptly. "But then there are after-school activities. I'll have dance, and cross-country, and Chinese club, and Model UN."

Ginger hadn't realized Phoebe had already invested so much time in researching and imagining her life at TGA. Is this her fault for not paying attention, for not listening? Or has Phoebe already come to the age where her life outside of Ginger is expanding, where the two of them will no longer be a nation of two? They have been so happy in their safe, cautious little bubble. The thought of it popping breaks her heart.

Ginger had never considered herself particularly maternal, but when Phoebe came to live with her, she had no other option but to discover that part of herself. They were perfect together: Phoebe looking for shelter from the proverbial storm, Ginger having spent her adult life perfecting the art of calm shelter. Phoebe twined herself around Ginger like a vine, so close she sometimes found it hard to breathe, but she learned to gasp for air and then dive back down because that was what Phoebe needed her to do. Now it feels as though the time has gone so quickly, Phoebe's adolescence looming in front of them, change and separation coming too soon. Do all parents feel like this, she wonders, or is it only because she didn't have Phoebe for the first years of her life that she feels such a strong impending sense of loss?

"Can you pick her up that early?" Tabitha asks Ginger.

This is exactly why Ginger needs time to think this through. She can't be in the city to pick Phoebe up at 3:38, which is a ridiculous time for anything to happen anyway. Still, she doesn't want to move. It is their home! And what if Phoebe isn't happy at TGA, or changes her mind, and then they will be just as far away from everything safe and familiar. This is impossible. All this on top of the baby – how is she supposed to manage it?

"Oh! You can come to our house!" Tate says, hopping up

on her knees and slapping the table with an open palm. "Our mom can pick you up when she gets us."

"Yessss," Phoebe says, and slaps her hand down on the table, too.

Ginger sees the situation spinning out of her control and is unsure how to reclaim it without upsetting anyone. On the one hand, it makes perfect sense. TGA is a wonderful opportunity for Phoebe, and Ginger really does want her to be able to take advantage of it, if they can do it in a way that feels safe. And the school is quite close to Perry and Tabitha's house. Tabitha wouldn't even have to pick her up; Phoebe could walk to their house. Tabitha is home anyway, and the children do love to spend time together.

On the other hand, and this hand is quite large, she has only survived thus far with her sanity intact because of the physical distance between them, a bright line that keeps her from getting too drawn into anyone else's business or them into hers, which holds everything on a level without conflicts or problems. She and Phoebe have created a comfortable, predictable routine Ginger does not want to upend, for everyone's sake. It is her job to protect Phoebe and make her feel safe. She must balance every opportunity, no matter how wonderful, with this charge.

"We'll think about it," Ginger says. A pause to think is always best anyway. Abrupt change is not helpful for anyone.

Perry puts down his phone abruptly, rescuing her, though it is probably coincidental. "Who wants to play badminton?" he asks.

"Me! Me! Me!" the children, none of whom have ever, to Ginger's knowledge, played badminton, shriek in delight.

"Tate, go to the potty before you play," Tabitha says, brushing Tate's hair back from her face as she slips out of the chair. Tate rolls her eyes but runs off to the house while the other kids follow Perry.

"I'll help you set up," Ginger, who also has not, to her knowledge, ever played badminton, says, hurrying to follow the others before Tabitha can take advantage of their absence and say anything else.

She has been lucky so far in this relationship, skating along the edges of Tabitha's vision, agreeing to whatever Tabitha wants. The trap has been that, at least until now, whatever Tabitha wants has been either easy to give or, frankly, a great idea in the first place. Things have been that way for so long that Ginger never stopped to consider what would happen if Tabitha pushed for something she couldn't give. It is a delicate thing they have built here, a house with no foundation of blood or memory, only a promise. Her promise to keep Phoebe safe. Whatever may come, she must keep this promise.

9

ELIZABETH

"HEY, BRIANNA, IT'S Elizabeth," she says when Brianna answers. "Tabitha and Ginger are here, too." She looks up at the other mothers as though they might have wandered off while the phone was ringing.

"Hi, mamas!" Brianna says, so upbeat Elizabeth cringes, hating the news she is about to deliver. "Where are the kids?"

"We sent them off on a little hike with Perry and John so they can work up an appetite before dinner," Tabitha says. "They'll be back in a bit if you want to say hi."

"Did you tell them about the baby?" Brianna asks, still excited. Both Brianna and Elizabeth had been present when they told the kids about Violet's impending arrival, and Elizabeth feels surprised that Brianna thought this time they would tell the kids without her there. You would think they'd have figured things out by now, they'd have some protocol for managing family situations, but everything about this family seems to be permanently under construction.

"Not yet," Elizabeth says. "We thought we would work

some things out before we told them." She stops, catches her breath, though she has no reason to have lost it.

"Oh, guess what?" Brianna blurts out as though Elizabeth hasn't spoken. "I got that blood test done, and it'll tell us whether it's a boy or a girl!"

"Wow, so soon?" Tabitha asks. "That's amazing."

"I know! I'll text you guys as soon as I find out. Elizabeth, do you and John know whether you want a boy or another girl?"

She says this so easily, sounds so happy, Elizabeth presses the heel of her hand to the bridge of her nose, the pressure of expectations too much.

"Brianna, I can't tell you – I mean, you will never know how grateful we are that you would think of us to adopt again. It's just… the thing is, John and I don't feel like we can adopt this baby."

She pauses to catch her breath. There is silence on the other end of the line.

"Oh, wow," Brianna says. "That's so sad! Are you sure?" She definitely doesn't sound angry. She doesn't even sound sad, exactly, and Elizabeth can't tell whether that is Brianna's natural good humor or whether – maybe she doesn't care whether Elizabeth and John adopt after all? That thought unsettles Elizabeth, makes her wonder if Brianna knows how much she has been struggling, and that stab of guilt comes at her hard.

She feels like she needs to explain their refusal but doesn't want to say too much. The family knows nothing about their fertility debt. Nothing. Sunny, the family's social worker, knows from their application process, but Sunny is silent as the grave. She is sure that Ginger, who is always talking about incredibly dull things like retirement planning and probably hasn't bought a new piece of clothing in the last decade, and Tabitha and Perry, who have never worried about money a day in their lives, would not understand. She hardly understands it herself, is so embarrassed by it she has to steel herself to open the credit card statements every month. She finally signed up for paperless billing so she could make it less painful, could avoid holding her failure in her hands. A touch on a keyboard and it is gone, at least until the next time. She was sick to her stomach at how quickly, how easily, John told them all about his being laid off, and she practically had to smack him to get him to stop talking.

And they know nothing about how she truly feels about motherhood, how she has to drag herself out of bed every day to face the work of raising this child, this child she loves beyond belief.

From her own family, Elizabeth learned to hold anything she cared about close to her. The youngest of four children, two brothers and a sister, and parents who were highly competitive and, now that she thinks about it, narcissistic, everything she did was mocked or derided. Being the youngest, Elizabeth had nothing new to offer, so when she cried, she was an annoyance, when she walked too slowly, a hindrance, and when she needed help, an inconvenience. She is who she is, she believes, because she is so determined to stand up to bullies the way she could never stand up to her family. Everything she did was fair game to tear apart. Her sister would pry her open with flattery and promises that they were best friends, and then take anything Elizabeth confessed and share it with the rest of the family so they could all have a hearty laugh at her expense. The feeling she most associates with her family is one of powerless fury.

Elizabeth only remembers fighting physically once with Rebecca. She can't even recall what the fight was about, only that they were standing in their parents' room at the foot of the bed shouting, and Elizabeth reached out and grabbed her sister's hair, pulling it and throwing frantic, furious arms. They fell onto the bed, struggling, slapping, and pinching, Elizabeth's breath short and gasping. Rebecca was on top of her, and though her sister was long and thin, a stripling of a dancer, she was also so much stronger, and Elizabeth felt as if she were pushing up, up, straining as though she were being buried alive.

But the worst part, and the thing she most remembers, is that while she was struggling so violently, fighting so hard, Rebecca was laughing. It couldn't have been easy for Rebecca to keep her pinned there; it couldn't have been. Elizabeth was solid and square where Rebecca was light and birch-bodied. Yet despite their sizes, despite Elizabeth's fighting as hard as she could, drawing on nine years of wrath, Rebecca was able to laugh. "Go on," she said, and the smile on her face as it hovered above Elizabeth's was so cruel in its ease. "You can do it. Come on."

There are a thousand things she could say to these women, the three most important women in her life for now and maybe for always, so many things she could tell them that might help them understand, but all of them would open her up in a way that feels unsafe.

So she decides to stick to what is already public knowledge.

Forcing an apologetic smile onto her face because they say you can hear a smile in someone's voice, Elizabeth says, "We're sure. John's been laid off, and the timing is just hard."

"Oh, my gosh! That's awful! And poor John! No wonder you're worried. I'm sure he'll get another job, though! There's a long time until the baby is due. You could change your minds!" Brianna says, a rush of optimism at the end.

"We could…" Elizabeth says, struggling with what to say. She can't very well scream *NO!*, even though that is very much what she would like to do. Everything else seems like a lie, like false hope. She is amazed by Brianna's generosity, that she would carry another child for them. In their darkest moments when they were struggling through fertility treatments, Elizabeth used to fantasize about being able to afford a surrogate. She never could have dreamed that someone like Brianna would come along and offer her even more, and ask nothing in return except that she care for this child as her own. How can she say no to that? But how can she say yes?

Tabitha coughs politely, announcing her entry into the conversation. "We all hope they will change their minds. It makes so much sense, doesn't it? I know how much you want to keep the family together." She smiles at Elizabeth here, as though she didn't just totally throw her under the bus.

Elizabeth has to resist the urge to punch Tabitha in the throat.

"I do! And you guys have only had like twenty-four hours to think about it."

Elizabeth doesn't say anything.

"Tabitha, I don't guess you and Perry... or Ginger...?" Brianna sounds hopeful, but also can't finish the sentence.

"I'm afraid not," Tabitha says. "We both know our families are complete."

Elizabeth almost wants to laugh. Tabitha gets to decide when her own family is complete, but god fucking forbid she extend Elizabeth the same courtesy.

"So this baby is going to have different parents?" Brianna asks.

"I guess?" Elizabeth says when no one else says anything.

Brianna gives a long sigh. "It's just that I just hate going through the parent books from the adoption agency. They make me so sad. I wish I could pick all of them."

"Did you have to look at them last time?" Ginger asks.

"Sunny made me. I mean, my mind was totally made up after I met Elizabeth and John, but she said I should look at some other options, just to be sure. It just kills me. There are all these perfectly nice people, and then you have to, like, close the book on some of them. Literally. It sucks. I don't want to be that person."

Everyone is silent for a moment, even Tabitha, who has never been without an opinion in her life.

"Except maybe..." Brianna starts, and then trails off.

"What's that?" Tabitha asks.

"I'm just thinking, like, what if you guys chose the parents? You're going to be seeing them more than I am, right?" She gives an uncomfortable laugh, and the three mothers look at each other over the phone, each of them wondering if the others might have the answer. Does this suggestion make sense? Or is this just another way for Brianna to duck out of responsibility? It is incredible to Elizabeth how this thing that was impossible for her comes so easily to Brianna. *Sure, no problem, just grow yet another human in my body by accident.* And for fuck's sake, how is this happening again? Hasn't anyone ever talked to her about condoms? Why is it that she won't have an abortion? Does she have to be the saint of all fertility? Jesus Fucking Christ.

"What do you think?" Brianna asks, hesitant since none of the women have spoken.

"We could help," Tabitha says. "But it would have to be your decision. The way it was with Elizabeth and John. And with us, for that matter."

"Oh, totally, sure," Brianna says in a rush, "Seriously, I would love it. I would love your help. I mean, Sunny will send you the parent profiles, and you'll see. It just kills me. I don't even know how someone is supposed to decide. Thank goodness you ran into Tabitha's car, Elizabeth, or I would still be looking at those agency profiles. Honestly, it makes sense for you to do it instead of me, you know? You're going to be their family, too, right?"

"Right," Ginger says, as though she has suddenly seen the wisdom of this plan.

"And if Elizabeth and John change their minds, then we're still fine, right?" Brianna adds.

"Exactly!" Tabitha says, and she sounds almost as enthusiastic as Brianna, which shouldn't be a surprise because there is nothing Tabitha loves more than a project. "I think this is a wonderful idea. We'll talk to Sunny and help narrow things down a little, and then you can make the decision when it's time."

"Right, and if Elizabeth and John change their minds, then no problem," Brianna says again, and Elizabeth has to clench her teeth.

She had been right – this is turning out to be the least relaxing vacation in the history of ever. They have been here for what? Like, a day? And already everything has fallen apart.

And then, as though they have not just had a conversation about setting the course of a child's life and however many hopeful adoptive parents they will have to look at and abandon, Tabitha starts updating Brianna on the schedule for the rest of the vacation.

In some ways, it's a blessing John lost his job, right? Because it gives them an out. A way to say no to Brianna, to Tabitha and Ginger and Perry. A way to say no to Violet. To say no to Phoebe and Tate and Taylor.

It is that thought that hits her hard, that she is saying no to all of them, making a decision that affects everyone. The adults will be okay. But this will change things for the kids, too. Because as much as their lives now are about managing the other adults, it is the kids who are their real family, a thought that finally struck Elizabeth when Tabitha and Perry said they were too old to adopt an infant. She knows she and John are the youngest, but other than occasional joking comments about their ages, it doesn't really matter. They're all parents. Equals.

But she sees it in the future, how at some point, odds are it will be just Brianna and her and John and the kids, that Tate and Taylor and Phoebe – and god, this new baby; even if they don't adopt this baby, it will still be theirs – will become theirs as well, more than they already are. She has loved that, loved being part of Phoebe's and Tate's and Taylor's lives, having them as nieces and a nephew. And Phoebe has cousins, though Tate and Taylor do not, and they will always have Brianna, but Elizabeth feels the gravity of her responsibility to all of them now in a way she has not before, not even with Violet. It is like marriage, the way that by taking on one person, you take on their whole world. They thought they were adopting Violet, but they have adopted a whole family, and now it is too late to change any of it. 'Til death do they part.

AN EMPTY QUIVER

·····

"When you are a mother," they said in Sunday school when I was little, when I was not so little, when I was a teenager, when I was a young woman preparing for marriage. "When you are a mother." I took it as a promise. There was no *if*. There is no *if*. It is my purpose, as it is the purpose of every woman, of every marriage. Large families are a blessing from God. *As arrows are in the hand of a mighty man; so are children of the youth. Happy is the man that has his quiver full of them: they shall not be ashamed, but they shall speak with the enemies in the gate.*

If I cannot have children, then what is my purpose?

We have prayed. Our pastor says God opens wombs all the time. Isn't this the promise in Samuel? *For this child I have prayed, and the Lord has granted what I asked.* We must not have prayed hard enough because my womb is still closed.

Or is it that we are not worthy? That we carry some sin or betrayal or weakness in our hearts that we have not confessed to, have not repented for? Children are a reward from God, yet we still have nothing. Neither of us knows what our sin is. We have been faithful. We have been honest and loving and trustworthy. I will admit that sometimes I have been angry, envious of women for whom children come easily. I pray for forgiveness and try so hard to remind myself God has a purpose for this I don't yet understand.

When the bishop first suggested we consider adoption, my husband and I reached out, without even looking at each other, and clasped hands. We have always been able to communicate without speaking. In that moment, our hands said a million words, words of despair and hope and grief and anger and loss and joy.

I don't know if I can explain to you what it's like to know that it is your greatest purpose to be a mother while watching the women around you bloom and grow and produce child after child while you have none, watching yourself fail and fail again to do the one thing a woman was born to do.

Some people are called to adoption. Is this us? Should we grow our family in our hearts and not in my body? Scripture tells us that God believes in natural families, in keeping families together. But scripture also teaches us to defend the orphans and the fatherless, and what are we to make of the story of Hannah?

Here is what we have. We have a strong and loving marriage. We have a comfortable home with space for children. We have friends and family and neighbors to surround our children and our family with love and friendship. We have a strong community and a strong faith. My husband is a teacher who loves to work with children, and I want to stay home with our family. Our home is ready. Our hearts are ready. We are ready for God to grant us the family we have prayed for.

10

TABITHA

HOW DOES ONE even go about choosing a parent for a child?

Early the next morning, Tabitha is lying in the darkness of the silent house, meditating on this question. She has slept, she thinks, but not for long. Tate came in because she'd had an accident – Tabitha knew she should have stopped her from drinking so much milk at dinner – and she had to change her sheets. She has been awake ever since. She is humming like a plucked string and cannot keep her mind still.

Ginger was chosen for Phoebe – or, rather, Phoebe chose Ginger – because they already knew each other.

Tabitha and Perry were chosen for the twins in part because they were available and waiting, in part because they had said in their application they would be willing to take siblings, including twins, and older children. Sunny had told them this is unusual: people are fascinated by the idea of twins, but when it comes to actually parenting them, they flee in fear. As they probably should, Tabitha thinks. No hand-me-downs, no second chances, no breaks. Get one to sleep and the other wakes up. Get one off the potty and it's time for the next one to get on. It takes patience to manage that uninterrupted cycle, let alone enjoy it.

As for Elizabeth – well, Tabitha thinks about that sometimes. If she and the twins had left a minute later for piano, if Elizabeth had gotten a call from the nurse earlier in the day and hadn't been so distracted, if, if, if. Tabitha had thought the way they met was meant to be. It was so perfect; it could have meant nothing else. For all of them, the more they told the story, the more natural and inevitable it became, their families as seamlessly joined as if they had conceived the children themselves.

Now Tabitha is forced to truly consider the mechanics of things, to look at events as chance rather than luck, as coincidence rather than fate. Because there are so many families who would love to adopt this child, who have ached or prayed or wondered. Out of all of those people, how do you choose? What if you choose the wrong family for a child? How would you even know?

Ultimately, it is not their decision. It is Brianna's decision. She also knows Brianna trusts them, even relies on them. When Justin left (the last time) and Brianna decided to make a plan for adoption, Sunny promptly set about finding candidates for adoptive families through the agency. If Tabitha is honest, she suspects Brianna only ever truly considered Elizabeth and John because they came recommended by the family. It is easy to say that choosing who parents this child is not their decision, but she knows in some way it is.

Last night, she emailed Sunny, who had already talked to Brianna, and requested that she send them some books from suitable hopeful adoptive parents, and she has already drafted a post to share online in local adoption groups, but even that action makes her feel sad, like she has lost, like she is betraying this child by aiding Elizabeth and John's inexplicable refusal to adopt. They said they had always wanted a big family, and Elizabeth is just so wonderful with children. It's the right thing for Brianna, and the right thing for the family, but it's really the right thing for Elizabeth and John. No one who loves children that much could be happy with just one child.

"Perry," she says.

Perry, sleeping blissfully beside her, does not move. She reaches out and pokes him with a sharp elbow. "Perry," she says again, a little louder.

His eyes blink open, and he looks at the ceiling in confusion, as if wondering where he is, before turning his head to look at her. "Are you okay?" he asks, his voice throaty and sleep-laden. "What's wrong?"

"I need to talk to you."

He sits up slightly so he can check the time on his watch and then collapses back onto the bed, rubbing his hand over his face. "It's not even five a.m. What are you doing? Have you been up all night?"

"No," she says, though this is a lie and they both know it. "Listen, Elizabeth and John need to adopt this baby," she says, rolling over on her side. She keeps her voice low, urgent, their faces close together as if they are sharing a secret.

He slaps a hand on his face, covering his eyes. "Honey, come on."

"No, listen to me for a minute, okay?"

Perry squeezes his eyes shut and then rolls over onto his side, as she had known he would. "Okay," he says. "But you're insane."

"I know. Now listen. When we met Elizabeth and John, they said they wanted a bunch of children, right? So we have to make sure they adopt this baby. What if Brianna never has another child, or she decides to parent the next one?"

"Then they'll adopt a different child when they're ready?" Perry asks, as though the answer is obvious.

"What if they don't? What if Violet grows up an only child?" Tabitha asks.

"Ah, I see," Perry says. He rolls back over onto his back, nodding as though he has it all figured out. "Okay, so first of all, Violet is not an only child. I don't know if you've noticed, but she is actually our children's sister. As is Phoebe. That's the point of this whole arrangement, isn't it?"

"You know what I mean. Of course they're siblings. But it's one thing to have siblings who are like your cousins, especially with how much older Phoebe and the twins are, and it's another to have one who lives in your house, who's raised by your parents, who grows up right beside you."

"Being an only child isn't the worst fate in the world. You're a terrible example, but most other only children turn out okay. By your definition, Phoebe's an only child, right?" He says this jokingly, lovingly, and she pokes him playfully, but immediately turns serious. She knows when he is trying to get her to lighten up, and sometimes it is soothing and encouraging, but right then she needs him to listen. And he doesn't understand. He and his brothers are so close. He doesn't understand what it feels like to grow up alone, how she still craves the family she never had like a wild hunger, how she chases friendships with the other mothers in Tate and Taylor's classes, desperately trying to find the connection that will fill that void. She wonders sometimes, now that she is distant from it, if she got into event planning because it was a way of surrounding herself with people, of staving off the loneliness even if it was just for one night.

"That's different. Phoebe wasn't an only child until Lorna died, right? Tate and Taylor were there. She understands the connection, what it's like to have a brother and a sister. If Violet grows up alone, she won't. That's what worries me."

"Okay, so Violet cannot suffer the tragic fate of growing up an only child, and Elizabeth and John told us at one point in the distant past they were interested in having multiple children, even though they have not mentioned that recently. Have you forgotten John lost his job? That they already said no to Brianna?"

"He'll get another job. And Brianna was so eager to have them change their minds. You should have heard her."

Perry shifts again. The windows behind him are letting

in the fading glow of the moon, so clear and white up here, and it outlines the edge of his shoulder in a way that looks like a painting. "I think you are forgetting what it's like to be young. We can say jobs come and go, but we've got savings to fall back on and retirement money and investments. If the worst were to happen, we would be okay. But they're not us, honey. They are still young, and I'm betting they spent every penny they had, if they had any, trying to get pregnant and then adopting Violet. Do you remember Nancy and Elliott? They did a cycle of IVF that cost almost fifty thousand dollars, and that was ten years ago."

"That was Manhattan, though," Tabitha points out, but she does wonder, now that he has brought it up. Is there more to their financial concerns than just John's losing his job?

Perry puffs out a breath, and she looks up to see him rub his eyes with the heel of his hand and then push his fingers through his hair, leaving it standing straight up, charmingly, like a mad scientist. "I am so glad we didn't do that," he says. "The money is one thing, gambling like that, but the emotional fallout is another thing entirely."

As Tabitha had been almost forty when they married, and Perry five years older, they had briefly discussed fertility treatments, but neither of them had a strong attachment to having biological children. Perry was an advocate for adopting from foster care, which was how his muchadored youngest brother had joined his family. Tabitha had only cared about growing their family quickly, so adopting from foster care was the choice they had made. And as soon as they met Tate and Taylor, not long after their home study was approved, it had felt like there wasn't even a question. This was their family.

The irony is Perry and Tabitha could have afforded the cost of fertility treatments, even surrogacy, at least in terms of money, though not time. Whereas Elizabeth and John, who had plenty of time, had likely struggled for the money. It was all dreadfully unfair.

"Anyway," Tabitha says, interrupting her own thoughts,

determined to get the conversation back on track, "we should ask them why they said no. Because if it's just the money, if they can't afford it, we could offer them a loan. To cover the adoption, so they don't have to worry about that while John looks for a new job."

Perry's mouth pulls down in disappointment. "I don't think that's a good idea," he says.

She pops up onto her elbows so she can look at him, excited by her own idea. "Why not? It would make a huge difference to them, and it would make no difference to us. Isn't that what money is for?"

"That's really generous, but money does weird things in families. You know that. Look at Brendan."

Perry's oldest brother, charming and charismatic and always sure his next big break was around the bend, had convinced the family time and again to invest in his ventures, always blowing through the money and then returning with a bigger and better idea. Finally everyone had agreed together to stop financing Brendan's new business ideas. But it would be different with Elizabeth and John.

"Family and money don't mix," Perry says firmly. He pulls her close and hugs her. "One of the things I love most about you is the way you want to take care of everyone you meet. You have the most beautiful heart. But you can't rescue everyone, okay?"

"I'm only trying to help."

"I know. And that's wonderful. But it doesn't work that way. People have pride and all kinds of other feelings, and especially when it comes to money people are weird anyway."

Tabitha is not surprised by his rejection of this idea. In fact, she has just come up with another plan. "Okay. Here's the other thing – what about hiring John?"

"At PBD?" Perry asks, surprised. "Isn't he in telecom?"

"I believe so, yes, but he's smart and nice, and I'm sure he's hardworking. I'm not saying make him a designer. But there has to be something he can do there, right?" She is a silent partner in their business, and usually has no interest in stepping out of that role. But these are not usual circumstances.

"Tabitha," Perry groans, rubbing his face again so her name half disappears into his hand. "That's the same thing as giving them money."

"No, it's not."

"It's that same entanglement where everyone has two priorities. What if he is terrible and I have to fire him? What would Sunday dinner look like then?"

"He won't be terrible," Tabitha says.

Perry doesn't reply.

"Come on. Think about it, okay?" She moves up and kisses his ear the way he loves, and he sighs happily. "Please?"

"I'll think about it. What a telecom sales guy would do at the agency I have no idea," Perry says.

"You're a smart guy. You'll figure it out," Tabitha says, and slides back down and snuggles in, pleased with herself for finding a way out of no way, as she always does.

There is silence for a moment, and she assumes Perry has fallen back to sleep. She is about to get up – might as well get a head start on the day since she is awake – when he says something else. "What if it's not the money? I mean, not only the money? What if it's something else?"

"Like what? What else could it be?" Tabitha says. She sits up again, leaning on her arm. The palest hint of daylight is coming up, the white sheets glowing pink.

"I don't know. Just having a baby is a lot. Don't you remember it?"

"Remember what?"

"When the twins came home. We were so tired all the time."

It comes back to her in a rush, those days. She understands now why people decide to have more babies, because babyhood comes at you when you are too worn out to enjoy it, let alone remember anything after it passes. The twins were just over a year old when they came home, and Tabitha and

Perry doubled down on the time they had missed, both to cement attachment and for the pure pleasure babies bring.

Tabitha loved the moments of stillness in the night when she rocked in the darkness, one or both of the twins sleeping on her chest, the tiny, peaceful rise and fall of their breathing underneath her palms.

"But we were so happy," Tabitha says, the memories of that soft-scented time making her tender.

Perry looks at her as if she's grown another head, and then barks out a laugh. "Yeah, and you had a complete crying breakdown about twice a week because you were so overwhelmed."

With a start, those memories come back to her, too. The twins were lovely, the kind of babies you dream of, but even perfect babies are babies. There had also been the endless laundry and the confusion, the feeling of never knowing, never doing things exactly right, of finally mastering something just in time for them to move on to a new stage where your skills were no longer useful. Tabitha, who prides herself on being prepared for every situation, had never felt so outclassed. She remembers in particular one time about two weeks after they came home, sitting in bed, appallingly unshowered, holding one of the twins out to Perry, sobbing so loudly she could hardly speak, telling him she couldn't do it, they needed to find someone else to take care of the children because she was failing so terribly at it.

She can't recall what happened afterward; probably Perry took the babies and sent her to take a shower and eat something, and probably, because that was unfairly the way it always happened, the twins had settled down immediately when they were with him, but she remembers that helpless feeling. It was like being a child in the ocean, knocked over by an unexpected wave, the gasping shock and indignity of being caught so unprepared. He had argued again and again for night nurses or nannies, and she had refused, a decision about which she has no regrets, but the intensity of the memories startles her now.

"I'd forgotten," she says, surprised by how surprised she is. Sometimes the twins ask to see photos of themselves when they were babies, and she shows them the photo books she made, the selfies she took when they slept on her chest, the pictures of them at baby gym and music class, fat rolls of dough. She hadn't taken pictures of her tears, or when she stumbled out of bed to the cries of one bare minutes after she'd gotten the other back to sleep.

"I'm pretty sure forgetting what having an infant is like is designed to protect the continuation of the species," Perry says. "And the twins weren't even colicky like Violet. Poor Elizabeth and John. They both look like they are about to keel over from exhaustion. Those kids have been through the wringer, for sure." He reaches up, folding his arm backward and palming the back of his head, rubbing the hair there.

"They have had a hard time, haven't they," she says, not even a question as she thinks through John's and Elizabeth's lives. The losses, and then the adoption on the heels of the last fertility treatment, the newborn sleeplessness and Violet's colic and generally finicky nature, and now John's job. They have been through so much. Which makes it even more important that she and Perry help them through it. What else is family for?

11

GINGER

GINGER HAD ASSUMED only the children would participate in that day's activity, a trail ride on horseback followed by fly-fishing. What business does a grown woman have on a horse? What interest did she have in catching fish? So when she had seen *jeans* on the packing list, she had only packed a pair for Phoebe.

Before Ginger can finish explaining why she can't go on the ride, Tabitha, ever prepared, produces a pair of jeans in Ginger's size. They must have been expressly purchased for this occasion because Tabitha is the size of a hummingbird and one could fit about thirty of her into a single pair of Ginger's pants.

"I have just the thing!" Tabitha says. "I washed them a few times, so they'll be nice and soft already."

Ginger looks at the jeans. So much for that. "Thank you," she says. When she comes back down wearing them, Phoebe laughs. Ginger never wears jeans or skirts, only loose, comfortable pants without buttons, and Phoebe has never seen her in anything else. To be fair, she knows she looks ridiculous, as if a child has put the wrong legs on her body in a matching game. When the hilarity is over, with the usual kerfuffle of transport required in going somewhere with eight people – Violet is staying home with a babysitter Tabitha magicked from somewhere – they are at the stables, hay and dust drifting in the bright sunlight. The children run from stall to stall, offering each horse baby carrots, laughing as the animals' mouths kiss their palms.

Phoebe, who in contrast is overflowing with delight, runs over to Ginger and gives her a hug, laughing and chattering about the horses. Watching her joy eases Ginger's apprehension slightly, though she still wouldn't say she is looking forward to it.

Despite the fact that she has chosen to live in this state that considers itself aggressively outdoorsy, she is not even mildly so, and feels no guilt about it. Look at the traffic down from the mountains on the weekends during ski season. Someone has to stay inside with a book for the sake of the environment.

Long walks are one thing – she quite enjoys those – but once, Tabitha wrangled her into a hike to a waterfall that involved more scaling of uneven rocks than Ginger would have liked. From this she learned that Tabitha, like most Coloradoans, uses the term *hike* to cover all manner of sins from a stroll along a paved sidewalk to scaling the side of a mountain, and *easy* includes anything that doesn't involve crampons and carabiners. Therefore she has been suspicious of the label *horseback ride*, as it could encompass anything from riding a pony around a paddock to running the Triple Crown.

Thankfully, today's ride is somewhere in the middle, the guides offering instructions and a jaded teenager helping her aboard – is that what one says? – the horse with a disinterested hand on her rear. The horse is terribly large, which Ginger finds disconcerting, though perhaps its size will keep it from running with any great speed. There's something deeply unsettling about a mode of conveyance with a mind of its own. Fortunately, the horse seems familiar with unqualified riders, because as the others move ahead, the lead guide and the children, followed by Tabitha and Perry and John and then Elizabeth, it lumbers into gear with no coaxing from her and follows the pack.

The horse's intentions appear to be in line with her own, which are to move slowly and cautiously until it is all over. They pick their comfortably unhurried way along a path through the trees, the children shouting eagerly ahead somewhere she cannot see them, and Ginger grows rather fond of her horse, finding in it (him? her?) a kindred spirit, lazy and careful and happy to follow along without any showboating.

Emerging into an open space, she sees Tabitha and Elizabeth have stopped, and her horse ambles to a stop, too. She pats its neck with silent gratitude for not killing either of them thus far.

"Isn't this view amazing?" Tabitha stands up in the stirrups and drops down easily from her horse, swapping out a lens on her professional-style camera and lifting it to photograph the vista in front of them. One of the things Ginger has never understood about people's desire to go to the mountains is that once you are *in* the mountains, you can no longer see the mountains, which is, as far as she is concerned, the whole point of mountains. But Aspen is different, low in a valley where the mountains rise all around, and here they are in a meadow, wide and flat, the mountains preening before them.

"Gorgeous," Elizabeth says.

Ginger makes a noise of agreement, but she has ceased to be truly awed by Colorado. The only possible response to its boundless beauty is fatigue, like going to Europe and becoming numb to all the cathedrals and churches. Everything in Colorado is awesome – in the truest sense of the word – even the flat brown of the prairie in the summer, and you can't stop to admire it all or you'll never get anywhere. Yes, this vista is beautiful, but it is no more beautiful than the view of the mountains she has when she drives to work, albeit with fewer cell phone towers.

"Maybe we should come up here for Christmas." Tabitha climbs back onto her horse easily, with neither the box nor the supportive shove from the guide Ginger had needed. "Or we could go to Steamboat? Or Telluride?"

"Why?" Ginger asks. Tabitha does something to make her horse move, and Elizabeth's and Ginger's follow.

"It's just so nice to be away, don't you think? And the mountains are so lovely at Christmas. Phoebe hasn't learned to ski yet, has she? It would be great to give her a sustained period of lessons – it'll go much more easily if she skis every day for two weeks."

"Two weeks?" Ginger says aloud, unable to stop herself. Leaving aside the issue of the exorbitant cost of two weeks of skiing, and the fact that Phoebe has expressed zero interest in learning to ski at all, another two-week trip would make it a full month of the year they would all spend together, not counting the dinners and birthday parties and playdates.

"We can't do Christmas," Elizabeth says. "We have to go see John's family."

"They're only two hours away! You can see them any time!" Tabitha says. They have crossed the open land and are dipping into another patch of aspens, lodgepole pines rising up behind them. It is sunny but cool and breezy, and Ginger feels grateful now for the jeans, though she would never admit it.

"Oh, we do," Elizabeth says sarcastically. "But the break wouldn't be worth the price afterward. They'd punish us all next year with techniques banned by the Geneva Convention, like passive-aggressive family texts and weepy phone calls any time we didn't come for the weekend."

John's family is big, four sisters or so and then John, but also a pile of cousins and aunts and uncles. They are a sprawling family that not only includes relatives like second cousins once removed but understands what the terms mean. Ginger met them all once when they came to town when

Violet's adoption was finalized, and it was overwhelming: a tsunami of hugs.

Then she remembers the new baby, and the new family that will come with it, and the way she is already so, so tired by all these people, how every Sunday night she comes home from dinner and has to sit in silence with her eyes closed just to recover. How does everyone else manage? Already this trip has descended into madness – Brianna's pregnancy and the enormous task of finding a child's parents, Elizabeth's inexplicable moodiness, and now the resurgence of Tabitha's interest in forcing them to move, throwing poor Phoebe's future further into question.

"Let's talk to Perry and John about it. We'll have to start planning. I'm sure most places are already booked," Tabitha says over her shoulder as the path narrows and they fall into a line.

"Won't the baby be here by then?" Ginger asks. "We can't go running off on a vacation right after the baby is born."

"Oh, that's right!" Tabitha says. "What am I thinking? Okay, maybe next Christmas. That will be better anyway, won't it? We'll be able to find a place for sure, then."

Win some, lose some, Ginger supposes.

What seems like an interminable amount of time later, they come to a stop by a pond, a beaver dam holding in the water, the standing trees spreading shade over one side. The women who have been riding with them tend to the horses while the children, holding fishing poles Ginger is fairly sure are going to end up poking someone's eye out, jump around at the edge of the water. Perry and the fishing guides are trying to wrangle them, but John is getting into light saber battles with Tate and Taylor, judging by the sound effects, and she suspects if they are relying on today's catch for lunch, they will be going hungry.

"Oh, I meant to tell you," Tabitha says, pulling her horse alongside Ginger's. "I talked to my real estate agent, and she's going to start pulling some properties near us – well, near TGA – for you to look at."

Ginger supposes she must look like a fish, the way her mouth is opening and closing in surprise with no words coming out. Hadn't she told Tabitha she wasn't ready to move? She hasn't even had time to think about it! She and Phoebe haven't even decided whether Phoebe will be attending TGA.

"I know, I know, but it's just looking," Tabitha says, holding up her hand.

Ginger feels an unfamiliar shaking in her body.

One of the guides is coming toward them to help them down, but Tabitha swings down easily on her own. "You can see what's available. I asked her to look for properties to buy and rentals as well. I told her you insist on renting even though you know better, and heaven knows in this market it's probably too late to buy anything reasonable, but it's worth looking, right? I told her to search by TGA, which would also put you by us. Then you and Phoebe can come over all the time!"

Tabitha starts to walk away, as if the conversation is over. And here is where everything changes.

"Except, Tabitha," Ginger begins, though she doesn't quite know what she is going to say.

That turns out to be the least of her issues because while she is looking at Tabitha and trying to imagine how she can stop this insane runaway train, the guide is trying to help her down from her horse. What happens next is neither the horse's fault nor the guide's fault; it is Ginger's fault for not paying attention to the instructions the guide is trying to give her.

She has one foot still in a stirrup, leaning forward inelegantly as she tries to drag the other over the horse, feeling very much like a manatee trying to do gymnastics. When she gets that other leg free, she reaches blindly backward to step onto the stool the guide has set up for her. Then she cannot quite get her other foot out of the stirrup, and she lets go of the horse to lean down and pull it loose.

As it turns out, this is a terrible idea. As she shifts her weight, the stool tips, and she falls backward, one foot still firmly lodged in the stirrup.

Ginger can feel, actually feel, something tearing in her ankle, and as she puts out her hands to catch herself, she lands hard and feels something twist sharp and painful there, too.

"Marmee!" she hears Phoebe call in a panic, but her vision has tunneled and all she can feel is her ankle and her leg throbbing and all she can smell is the dirt by her face and her leg is still half in the air, but she is afraid to move because it is going to hurt, it is going to hurt, it is going to hurt so much.

"Hold on, hold on." Elizabeth rushes over, and she and the guide move Ginger gently, pulling her foot free and laying her back on the ground. Elizabeth kneels down beside her on one side, and the guide on the other. "You're going to be okay. Don't move yet, okay? Does anything hurt?"

"Marmee!" Phoebe says again, with an anguish to her voice that makes Ginger try to sit up and reach for her, an instinct that sends her head into dizziness and her leg and wrist into a scream of pain.

Both the guide and Elizabeth lay their hands on her, gently pushing her back down. "Shh, shh, hang on, sweetie," she hears Tabitha say, and then Phoebe kneels beside her, bending so close Ginger can feel her warm breath on her cheek.

"Are you okay?" Phoebe asks, looking panicked.

"I'm okay," Ginger says, making her smile as wide as she can, though it probably looks more like a rictus. She isn't a big smiler at the best of times, and her arm and her ankle throb insistently.

Phoebe touches Ginger, moving her hands from her hair to her shoulder to her arm, as if making sure she is really there. The guide and Elizabeth are talking to each other in low voices.

"I'm okay," Ginger says again, moving her good hand up to Phoebe's and giving it a squeeze.

"Come here, honey, let Aunt Elizabeth and Miss Cheyenne take care of your mom," Tabitha says, pulling Phoebe gently back.

For once she is grateful for Tabitha's bossiness because

Phoebe does move away far enough so Ginger can whisper to Elizabeth, "Is it broken?"

"I don't know. I'm going to be honest, it doesn't look great. You're going to have to go to the ER." In college, Elizabeth worked as an EMT, though they've never had much cause to use her first aid skills for much more than bandages until that moment.

"Is she okay?" Phoebe asks from under Tabitha's arm.

"She's going to be fine," Elizabeth says. "I think we'll have a doctor just double-check. Hey, did I ever tell you about how one time I fainted when I was teaching? Passed out in front of the whole class. When I woke up, they were all running around like Muppets." She raises her arms above her head and waves them around, making a silly face. "But I was fine."

Phoebe gives only a tiny smile, but Ginger can see her shoulders relax.

Cheyenne has called the stables, and they send an ATV with a trailer to take Ginger back. She has a bumpy ride back with ice packs on her wrist and ankle. Tabitha kneels beside her in the trailer, trying to hold her leg still to avoid the worst of the bumps, and Elizabeth follows on her horse. They drive her to the hospital, Tabitha staying and checking her in while Elizabeth drives back to get everyone else.

It isn't that Ginger has never wondered what would happen if there were an accident. The older she gets, the more she is conscious of how many things can go wrong at any moment, and having Phoebe has deepened that awareness. She considers herself a sensible person, part of which includes planning for potential problems. So she has wondered, has played out a series of scenarios, that if she were to suffer a medical crisis, she would call Esperanza's mother and they would take Phoebe, who would be happy to stay with them. Though Mrs. Lopez does travel a great deal and Ginger isn't sure what would happen if Mrs. Lopez happened to be out of town, and what if it were Phoebe something happened to, who would feed the cat while Ginger took Phoebe to the hospital, or what if it were both of them, heaven forbid, and Tabitha and Elizabeth do live quite far away, and she isn't sure she'd want to call either of them anyway...

As she lies there in the ER, Tabitha out cracking the whip over the staff to get her released with her crutches, the analgesic kicking in, forcing the pain to recede to a dull throb, she considers whether she is wrong about moving to the city. If they were all there, if they were all nearby, if something were to happen, it would be wiser to be close, wouldn't it?

That is silly. She and Phoebe have been a pair for five years, and this is the first time this has happened. Is it worth giving up all her – their – hard-won stability to be surrounded by a family whirlwind for a scenario that is likely to happen only once a decade?

"Finally," Tabitha says, marching in, a cowed staff member following behind her with a wheelchair. Tabitha is wielding a pair of crutches like a majorette. "They're bringing in the paperwork for you to sign on the way out."

Ginger has been on her own, essentially, since she came to Colorado for college and settled in to stay, relieved to be able to build her life without being yanked around by her family's ever-changing whims. But she notices, as Tabitha busies herself with making sure they have all their belongings and that Ginger is treated with the amount of care she deserves, tucking her into the back seat of the car, that instead of feeling suffocated, she feels pleased. Comforted. Cared for. Part of something in a way that feels safe, despite the unknown questions looming ahead.

12

ELIZABETH

THE NEXT MORNING, when John's mother calls, Elizabeth knows she should not answer. But motherhood has changed her, made catastrophe feel so close. When they brought Violet home from the hospital, Elizabeth hardly slept, waking every few minutes with a gasp, resting her hand on the tiny body beside her to feel the light, steady movement of breath.

Every day since then has felt similarly threatening, as though she could fall at any moment and take Violet down with her. She feels as though she is falling already, failing her daughter all the time. It feels so heavy, the responsibility she has been given, not only the trust of this child in her but everyone attached to her – the family, yes, the twins and Phoebe, yes, but also Brianna and Justin and Sunny and Lorna and everyone beyond them, the infinite spiderweb of family. She should have thought of these things ahead of time, but she had focused for so long on getting pregnant, sustaining a pregnancy, that she never had the time to think beyond that, to imagine a future that wasn't one of loss and failure, let alone the leisurely nine months many women have to contemplate parenthood before someone plops a baby in their arms. Letting one of them down means everything collapses. In this way, adoption is so different, or at least she thinks it is. Adoption demands seeing two lives and constantly ensuring Violet is living the better one.

Now things seem even more fragile. John's job (or lack thereof, really), Brianna's pregnancy, the way Tabitha and Brianna and even John seem so certain she will change her mind, and now Ginger has sprained both her ankle and her wrist. That diagnosis was actually somewhat of a relief because when Elizabeth saw the way Ginger's ankle was swelling after the fall, she had been sure it was a break. But even a minor injury is an injury, and this vacation has already been, as she had feared, not relaxing in the slightest. Everything feels like it is tilting off-kilter.

So when the phone rings, she cycles quickly through the list of potential horrors – death, illness, collapse – in her mind and answers. Besides, this is the second call from Bonnie today, and if Elizabeth doesn't answer this one, either, Bonnie will panic and go straight to calamity and calling the police for welfare checks.

"Hi, Bonnie," she says, trying not to sound resigned. She does like Bonnie – truly she does. She is high-strung and overly involved, but also well-meaning and enthusiastically kind. She is like Tabitha in that way, Elizabeth thinks, a connection she had not made until then but which might be why Tabitha pushes her buttons so easily.

"Oh, Elizabeth," Bonnie says, and she sounds half unhinged. "I always knew this was going to happen! I told John that company was no good from the start!"

"Oh, yes. That Fortune 1000 company. Totally fly-by-night," Elizabeth says sarcastically.

"Exactly!" Bonnie says, launching into an extended monologue on the company's shadiness. Elizabeth half tunes her out as she walks up the stairs to get her shoes.

She and John have hardly had a moment alone to sit down

and seriously think about what their next steps will be, let alone talk about what he is telling his family, but John is not cautious about sharing information with them the way she is with hers. *Well, too late now*, she thinks wryly.

"...so then I talked to Mrs. Pierce, you met her at Kathryn's baby shower, you remember, she's the school principal, has been since Abigail was in kindergarten, and she says she thinks Peter Williams is ready to retire, and you don't know him, I don't think, but he teaches elementary school, and I know you work with older kids, but just think, a job right here would make it so much easier. I told them you'd call this week – tomorrow is Thursday, so you'll be fine."

"I'm sorry, what?" Elizabeth asks, tuning back in and scrabbling to catch up. "You're looking for a job for me? In *Russell*?"

Her mother-in-law sounds surprised that Elizabeth is surprised. "Yes, in Russell! You can't stay in the city without John having a job, and how is Violet supposed to grow up without her family around anyway? I don't know why you would live there in the first place when everyone who matters is here. All Violet's cousins and aunts and uncles would love to have her around, and we'd just love to see you all more than just a day or two a year."

Elizabeth is going to have to ignore that particular exaggeration. "Bonnie," she interrupts, "we have family here, too. We can't abandon them."

"What family?" Bonnie asks. She could be genuinely confused, or she could just be acting dramatic. Odds are fifty-fifty with her most of the time.

"You know, Violet's brother and sisters. And I don't know if John told you, but their birth mother is pregnant again, so there will be another sibling. That's Violet's family, too. That's our family, too."

She feels a twinge of guilt as she speaks, for using the family she has been pushing away as a shield now that it is convenient.

"Wait, another baby? Oh, honey, you'll have to move here,

then. You can't handle two littles all by yourself!" Bonnie says, triumphant. Elizabeth cannot figure out which issue to argue with first, so Bonnie generously adds another. "Besides, we don't live on the moon! You easily can go down for a day or two in the summer!"

Elizabeth finds a blank space on the wall and silently beats her forehead against it. Bonnie demands Elizabeth and John come to Russell for at minimum one entire weekend a month, and in the reverse situation she offers a day. Or two.

"Yeah, that's not equitable," Elizabeth sidesteps the issue of the assumed adoption. "It doesn't matter. We can't move there, so it's a moot point. I already have a job. And John has a better chance of getting one here than there."

"Honey, he's going to work with his uncle. It's all set up." Her mother-in-law sounds genuinely perplexed.

A rock falls in Elizabeth's stomach. Has John actually agreed to this? It's impossible. She wants to hang up without saying anything but pushes herself to be polite enough to interrupt whatever Bonnie is saying with a hasty, "So sorry, but everyone's ready to leave. Talk soon!" and hangs up.

It is a white lie – no one is going anywhere right now. Ginger and Tabitha came home late from the ER the night before, and while Tabitha had been up at the crack of dawn when Elizabeth woke up with Violet, Ginger is still sleeping, as far as she knows. But she has to talk to John. She finds him on the putting green behind the house with Perry.

"Perry and I are going golfing," he says, and he sounds like a five-year-old who's been invited to Chuck E. Cheese.

"That's great. Where is our child?" Elizabeth snaps. If he has sold them out to Russell, Colorado, he deserves the pointiest ends of her collection of emotional knives.

John steps back as Perry swings, sending a ball soaring toward the far edge of the property. She hears it thwack into a tree. "She's with Tabitha and the kids. What's wrong?"

"I need to talk to you. Privately," Elizabeth says.

"I'll go," Perry says. He heads off, whistling, and Elizabeth thinks of Tabitha taking care of Violet with one hand while cooking some Michelin-starred meal with the other. She bets Tabitha never wants to strangle Perry the way she does John.

"I just got a friendly call from your mom," Elizabeth says when Perry is out of earshot.

John is swinging the golf club idly. She wants to yank it away from him, annoyed by the motion.

"My mom called you? Why?"

"So, funny story, she somehow has the impression that we're basically packing up and moving there tomorrow and that you're working with your uncle and they're going to force some teacher to retire so I can work at the school. Oh, and I told her about Brianna and the baby, so now she's decided we're adopting it, too."

"Yikes," John says.

"Is that what you told them?"

"No. I told them about losing my job, and they did ask about moving to Russell, so I said it was an option, which it is."

"Oof," Elizabeth says, sitting down on one of the chairs under the eaves of the house. "That is super not what she heard."

"Yes, well, we've all met my mom. My guess is she's trying to make it sound like a done deal so we don't argue. But—" He bites off the sentence and swings the golf club again. Elizabeth stands up and grabs it from him, trying not to use it as a weapon.

"What?" she asks. She suspects he is right about his mother's manipulation, but seriously. Does Bonnie think they don't talk to each other? Like Elizabeth would hear her plan and say, *Oh, well, guess it's all done, better start packing*?

John rubs the bridge of his nose and then looks at her for a long moment before he speaks. "It's our best option. You know it is." He reaches out his hand for the club and, when she gives it to him, puts it back in the bag with the others and then sits down in the chair she vacated.

"It is not our best option. It is *an* option, but it is a *shitty* option. For everyone involved, especially Violet."

He holds up his hands, a stop or maybe a signal of surrender. "Every option has drawbacks. Look, I am sorry I told them without talking to you first, but I figured we were probably going to have to ask them for a loan, and I didn't want it to come out of left field. But we have to talk about it. What's not fair to Violet is not considering all our options, and we can't do that if you fly off the handle every time it comes up. I need you to be rational."

"So now I'm irrational?"

"Don't pick a fight. I'm not going to fight with you. I know this is hard. I feel awful. But we've been through harder, haven't we?" Standing up, he walks over to her and takes her hands.

He is right; she is trying to pick a fight because she is angry and confused and overwhelmed, and she has nowhere else to put it. It's an amazing thing, she thinks, that we marry a person because we claim to love them so much, and then punish them by making them tolerate all our worst qualities. She tries to let it go as he pulls her in tight and closes his arms around her.

"It's not your fault," she says. "Stuff happens."

"Yeah, well." He shrugs.

"You're right. We have been through so much worse. We are going to figure this out." She doesn't know how, but they will. Haven't they always? Struggling to have a child drives a lot of couples apart, but at the time it had brought them closer. In their worst moments, they stood like this a lot, arms wrapped tightly around each other, faces turned together and away from the storm. She has mourned this, the connection they sacrificed for Violet. Now they pass in the night, often literally; their mornings are rushed, their conversations transactional. It had been easier when Violet was a newborn, when she slept so much, but now Elizabeth is startled to realize how long it has been since she felt like she was talking to him instead of instructing or directing him.

They're silent for a moment, and then John pulls back. The air around them is bright with the ceaseless sunshine, warm and cool at the same time, and she can hear the rustle of breeze through the trees and the distant chirping of birds. In the front yard, the kids are playing badminton – they have been delighted by the game since Perry introduced them to it.

"Are you sure about the adoption?" he asks.

"You mean not adopting the new baby?" Elizabeth asks. The question drains her. It brings back so many memories of the people they used to be. They were different, both of them. Lighter. Warmer. Funnier. Those people had thought they might have three kids, four, more. Who cared? They were young. They were magic. And now she knows what life is really like, and she both hates and misses the person who thought everything she wanted would come true, just like that.

"Right, the new baby," John says, because what else would he be talking about? There are no other babies on offer.

Elizabeth hesitates. Before, they had no secrets. Before, she would have told him how she really felt. Then again, before, they never fought, and now she feels like they fight all the time, mostly over things she really shouldn't have to tell him, like that the diaper pail bag needs changing or that Violet's laundry is not finished until it has been folded and put away, not when it is just sitting in the dryer. And she shouldn't have to tell him that she made a mistake, either, that she clearly wasn't meant to be a mother, that she should have stuck with teaching, where she is happy and the kids love her as much as she loves them, instead of this constant tussle she has with Violet's moods. She shouldn't have to tell him because he should know; he should see it. Once upon a time, she thought he knew her better than anyone in the world.

Telling him would be admitting she has failed him yet again, that first she could not have the children they wanted, and now that they have one, she cannot be the mother she is supposed to be.

"No. We just can't afford it right now," she says. "And Violet is so young still. If she were a year older maybe…" She lets the thought trail off, a half promise that will never be kept.

····

LOVE MAKES A FAMILY

····

Sometimes my wife gets mad because it's so unfair – you can have an accidental pregnancy in a straight relationship, but not if you're gay. I tell her this is not something worth getting upset about, in the grand scheme of things. We are lucky to live in a time when there are lots of ways to have a family. She tells me I'm right, but then she gets upset about it again later. Which is okay. It's one of the things I love about her, how concerned she is about justice and fairness. This is why she became a lawyer; this is why she teaches law – employment law, because she knows all the ways people can be discriminated against and how losing your job can change your whole life, and she wants to be sure new attorneys know about those things and care about them. She's a fantastic teacher, and a lot of her students do go on to do social justice work, even if it's not specifically employment, which makes her insanely proud.

We're a funny pair in a lot of ways. She is serious and driven and always wants everyone to do the right thing, and I'm happy just to go along to get along. I never went to college, and she has so many letters after her name it's like a whole new alphabet.

My wife was adopted from China when she was two.

Growing up in a white family wasn't always easy for her, so she is frank about the things her parents did wrong in raising her, both because of her background and in general. She is also insanely close with them, and they love each other like no other family I've ever known, including mine, where we all like each other but there's a lot going on and sometimes we forget about each other completely.

I love my job. I love flowers, and I love spending my day making people happy, and when I go home, I can relax and be with my wife and our dogs and not have to spend all night answering emails. When we first met, she would always ask me if I wanted to open my own shop, and it took her a long time to understand that I am happy doing what I do. That I don't want more or bigger or better, and I don't want the stress of all the things the owners of the shop I work at have to deal with, like lease terms and unemployment insurance and accounts receivable. I just want to design and make arrangements and then go home and cook dinner while she goes over her lecture notes for class the next day.

We got married the October right after it was legal, which is another thing you shouldn't get her started on. Our wedding was in the Botanic Gardens, and I did the flowers myself, which everyone said I was crazy to do, but it made me so happy. We'd been together for five years then, so it was way past time anyway, and it was a huge party, which we had on a Wednesday night because it was the only way we could do it quickly, but even though it was short notice, people came in from literally everywhere and it was the biggest celebration you've ever seen, and when there was a big sale on canvas prints, I got a bunch of the pictures printed and they hang all over our house and they remind me of that day and how happy we all were and how much we love each other and how lucky we are that we found each other.

So anyway, we always wanted kids, and since she feels strongly that adoption is such an important way to make a family, we decided that we were going to adopt. We have two golden retrievers and a house, and we both have flexible jobs, and we live near some amazing parks, and we're ready for that part of our lives where we go to Home Depot on Friday nights and tour Montessori schools in our free time, so we have the perfect family setup already and now we just need the kids.

We've talked about international adoption because she'd like to adopt a kid from China, but international adoption has been getting weirder and weirder, for good reasons and bad, and it is going to take a long time and we're ready to start our family now, so we're looking at domestic adoption for our first child while we start working on the rest of our family. It's all expensive, which makes her start on her thing about unfairness and accidental pregnancies, so I calm her down and agree that it is expensive, even though she makes a good living, though not as good a living as when she was working for the corporate soul-suckers she worked for after she graduated from law school, just long enough to make some killer bonuses to fund her retirement and buy this house and put some money away, which thank goodness she did because now we have that to help.

I don't know how you choose who gets a child. I think we'd be great parents. I know we'd be great parents. How do you even decide a thing like that? How do you look at a family and know that it's the right family for this child? How would someone know it's us?

13

TABITHA

"WHAT'S THIS?" ELIZABETH asks, pulling an envelope off the stack of mail Perry's assistant overnighted them from home. Tabitha is trying to prepare a frittata for breakfast tomorrow, but Elizabeth is hanging around like a listless teenager, yawning and getting in the way. Tabitha had tried to take Violet that morning when she woke up early, let Elizabeth get some sleep, but Elizabeth had turned her down, for yet another unknown reason. Now it isn't even dinnertime and she is wandering around the house like a zombie.

Honestly, sometimes Ginger and Elizabeth make it so difficult to help them. Ginger was fussy before she fell off the horse, and she's been even worse since then, grumping around and refusing reasonable suggestions like making up a bed for her in the office so she doesn't have to go up and down the stairs.

Forget getting anyone together to do anything important, like actually find parents for this child. Tabitha hasn't pressed it so far, because she is waiting for Elizabeth to say they have changed their minds, but she did share the note she'd written with the online adoption groups, and Sunny has been emailing links to profiles of families the agency is working with. Better to be prepared, and she has the suspicion that seeing other families will set Elizabeth's head straight if it doesn't happen on its own.

Glancing away from the vegetables she is dicing, Tabitha sees Elizabeth is holding a purple envelope. "It's addressed to Tate. Looks like an invitation."

Something catches in Tabitha's chest, and she reaches over for the envelope. "Let me see," she says, plucking it out of Elizabeth's hands and looking at the return address.

She is right. This is it. The invitation that will change Tate's life.

Her hands shaking, Tabitha tears the lavender envelope open without using a letter opener, and the air erupts in glitter.

"Damn," Tabitha says, watching the sparkles spill, catching the light as they wreak their shiny havoc on the way down to the floor, reaching out for her pants, her skin, a nearby chair, finally settling in cruel satisfaction into the mortar lining the slate tiles of the kitchen floor.

"Language," Elizabeth says, pretending offense. Which is a joke. Elizabeth's language is quite blue, and if she doesn't watch out, Violet's first words are going to have four letters.

Tabitha moves over to the sink to finish opening the envelope even though she knows by moving she is spreading the glitter all over the floor. Who does this to another mother? She hopes it won't become a trend simply because Pamela Preston did it. Spending all of the next year opening envelopes as if they might contain the craft equivalent of ricin would be a miserable existence.

It is worth all the pain of the glitter when she sees what is inside: a hand-lettered invitation written in graceful swooping arcs and bends bearing Tate's name and then Serafina's. A curious seltzer bubbles in her chest. It is going to be okay. It is all going to be okay.

Serafina is one of the girls in Tate and Taylor's class. She is a charmless girl with thin hair and an enthusiastic overbite, but the latter two will be cured with cosmetic intervention and the former will become irrelevant, her lack of charisma smoothed over by the patina of money and the casual confidence that comes from it. In any case, Tabitha can see the social role Serafina will continue to inhabit in school going forward, and Tate will need someone's wing to shelter her, not only because of her sweetly immature and aggressive nature but also because of the accidents, if they happen to continue. Which she is certain they won't, but just in case.

Pamela Preston is the mother around whom Country Day's social world turns. She is tall and willowy and beautiful, always perfectly dressed, equally stunning in leggings for barre class or a gown for the Gala, so effortless it makes Tabitha ache with jealousy. Pamela's husband was once a professional football player and is now a motivational speaker, and she hears rumors Pamela herself was a model, maybe even a *Playboy* centerfold back when there were such things, depending on which circle of parking lot gossip she finds herself in.

"What is it?" Elizabeth asks.

"It's an invitation to a birthday party," Tabitha says, because she cannot think to explain how important this particular invitation is, what a gift it is that Tate has been invited.

Ginger comes clumping into the kitchen. The silver lining to her sprains is that she sprained her right ankle and her right wrist, so she is able to navigate around on one crutch until she regains the use of her hand, even if she does sound like a herd of elephants banging around when she moves.

"Whose birthday party?" she asks, collapsing into a chair. She winces as she lifts her leg up to elevate it, Tabitha stepping over to move a chair into position for her.

"A girl in Tate's class. It's really quite wonderful."

Elizabeth comes over, carrying the invitation, leaving a trail of glitter along the floor. Tabitha winces. If only she could have a word with Pamela.

"A little young for a slumber party, aren't they?" Elizabeth asks.

"It's not a slumber party," Tabitha says, going back to the counter to wipe up the glitter Elizabeth has spread there. For goodness' sake, they are going to be tracking this mess around for the rest of the vacation.

"Uh, it's a slumber party," Elizabeth says. "Look."

Quelling an annoyed huff at Elizabeth's inability to read a simple party invitation, Tabitha dries her hands on a towel and takes the invitation, scanning down past the girls' names to the date and time.

"Seven to nine p.m.," she says, pointing to the time.

"Yeah, no," Elizabeth says, a phrase she uses all the time that drives Tabitha batty. She leans over, pointing at the hours. "Look. Seven p.m. to nine a.m. It's a slumber party. Look." She moves her finger down to the bottom, where in tiny, pale script it reads: *Party design by Sweetest Dreams Slumber Parties.*

"Oh," Tabitha says. Then, "Oh," again.

It is a slumber party. A slumber party! They are seven! Well, she supposes Serafina will be turning eight, but that is hardly any better. Who sends seven-year-olds to a slumber party? Tate cannot go to a slumber party! She is still a baby. They are all babies. What is Pamela even thinking?

And Tate cannot go to a slumber party, because at a slumber party there is no way Tabitha can shield Tate from the fallout if she has an accident, and if she has one before they are in bed or even if they are in bed and she wakes up and cannot get out without their seeing her wet nightgown, the girls will tease her, and girls can be so cruel and they never forget.

Yet Tate has to go. She has to.

This is a nightmare. Tabitha shouldn't have had to deal with this for years. She never went to a slumber party herself, but she remembers the first time one of her classmates had one. In sixth grade, where Phoebe is heading and the twins will be any moment, one of her few friends, a bland girl named Kara who was mostly friends with Tabitha because she was new and didn't know anyone else yet, was invited to a slumber party by one of the girls in their class. Kara was worried because she didn't have a sleeping bag, only a comforter her mother had sewed ribbons on to close the sides. Tabitha assured Kara this would be fine, and then went home to cry into a pillow. She had a sleeping bag, but she had not been invited. She rued the unfairness long after Kara had ridden that invitation to a higher social stratum, leaving Tabitha alone again.

So, sixth grade. Eleven or twelve. A safe four years away, at least. They will have resolved Tate's issues by then; she is sure of it. So why would Pamela do this now?

"Pamela Preston. She hired a company to design her daughter's slumber party. Tate has been invited to a slumber party." Tabitha looks at Elizabeth as if she might have an answer, which is ridiculous. Elizabeth never has answers. Tabitha is the one with the answers.

"Like I said, kinda nuts for a bunch of seven-year-olds," Elizabeth said.

"I know!" Tabitha says, sounding hysterical even to herself. She lifts her hands in the air, stupidly, because it sends another shower of glitter down onto the floor. *Screw Pamela Preston*, she thinks uncharacteristically. *Screw her.*

"Whoa," Elizabeth says, grabbing Tabitha's arm, then taking the invitation from her hand and putting it on the edge of the terribly low and inconvenient farmhouse sink – those are all the rage right now, and they do have a look, but why would you put something so awkward in such a wonderful kitchen? Putting the invitation in the sink doesn't help – both her and Elizabeth's hands are already covered in glitter, and she can see some on Elizabeth's arm and, yes, on her feet, the contagion spreading unchecked.

"Let's sit down," she says.

"Wow," Ginger says, blowing out a low whistle, "if those parents want to manage a dozen seven-year-olds, good luck to them."

"No lie," Elizabeth agrees.

"Tate can't go," Tabitha lowers her voice and leans forward, whispering fiercely.

"Why not?" Ginger asks.

Elizabeth and Tabitha both look at her silently.

"Oh," Ginger says, realizing belatedly. "Yes. I see."

"What if she, like, wears a pull-up or something? Under her nightgown?"

"She swore those off ages ago. She refuses to wear them." Tabitha has mostly learned to tolerate this. She understands Tate's objection to them, and sympathizes, but also perhaps they should be forcing them on her. Maybe that would help? Oh, she doesn't know.

The doctors and therapists can offer her nothing, or nothing that works. Tabitha is helpless, which is a painfully unfamiliar situation for her. It is so rare that she encounters a problem that she cannot solve through either diplomacy or force of will, and it is, if she is being honest, if she is being absolutely honest, infuriating. It makes her both want to scream and cry.

"Not even for this?" Elizabeth asks.

"Not even," Tabitha says. "She's in denial about it. Every night, she thinks it won't happen, and every night, it does. I am at my wit's end!" She has raised her voice, which she tries not to do, and forces herself to calm down. "In any case, the other girls would know. She insists on those horrible, thin nightgowns, and you can see everything through them."

Her eyes flick over to Ginger as she says this, but Ginger doesn't seem to notice. Tate's obsessions with these awful plasticky nylon nightgowns with Disney princesses on them is Ginger's fault. The first one had been Phoebe's, left behind after a sleepover. Tate claimed it as her own and wore it to tatters, the cheap netting on the shoulders tearing, Princess Jasmine's face distorted and fading from washing and threads pulling, and then asked for another.

She still won't wear anything else, not the adorable Mini Boden nightgown with the unicorns and the ruffled sleeves, not the Petite Plume in the sweetest pale pink gingham that looked so lovely against her skin, not the Tea Collection pajamas with wide flowers that made her eyes shine. Finally, Tabitha stopped fighting it, because the child has to wear something, and ordered the least odious polyester princess nightgowns she could find, still awful and made of nylon, but at least she could choose the princesses who are less simpering and more diverse – Moana and Mulan and Tiana and Merida, who is white but has the temerity to have red hair and a fierce independence. Tate was delighted and wore those all to shreds, too, at which point Tabitha tried to replace them with something less horrible and was, again, refused.

In any case, the nightgowns are thin and scratchy and would show the outline of a pull-up if Tate were willing to wear one, which she would not be. The risk is too great anyway. What if it leaks? What if she has an accident before they even change into their nightclothes? This is one reason she appreciates Country Day's uniforms. Every day she sends Tate to school with two duplicate sets of clothes so if she needs to swap during the day there will be no sartorial interruption.

"What if she doesn't go to the party?" Ginger asks.

Tabitha scoffs. "She can't not go. All the other girls will be there. Serafina is the most popular girl in school, and all the other mothers love Pamela."

"The most popular girl in… first grade?" Elizabeth asks doubtfully.

"Yes," Tabitha says. Of all people, Elizabeth should understand that popularity and social mechanics begin quite young. "If Tate doesn't go to this party, it's entirely possible Serafina won't want to be her friend. Then where will that leave her in middle school?"

"Middle school?" Ginger asks in confusion. "That's years away."

"Exactly," Tabitha says, looking at each of them in turn, but they still appear confused. Of course she can't expect them to understand. Ginger doesn't have any friends and probably doesn't care if Phoebe has any, either, and Elizabeth was undoubtedly queen of her school the whole way through.

"You don't think you're maybe… overreacting a little bit?" Elizabeth asks.

"I know you think I am crazy, but I am not. She will be in school with these people for the next decade, and they will remember. What if she goes and has an accident? Her classmates are not going to forget that. It could brand her for life. They could make fun of her forever. Seriously. Is that what you want?" Tabitha tries to be patient, tries to explain, but ends up snapping at them.

Elizabeth holds up her hands and leans back. "Whoa, whoa, of course I don't want that for her. I get what you're saying about kids having long memories, but trust me, there will be plenty of things that happen later in their lives that will supersede a potential bed-wetting incident now. It is unlikely her entire life is going to be ruined because of one party. Most of my students have been going to school together since pre-K, and they are way more concerned with who barfed in the lunch line yesterday than who wet their pants in elementary school, probably because they all did that at one point or another."

"It could happen! Things can happen like that, and I refuse to let her go through her whole life alone and miserable!" She can hear her voice is sharp, maybe even shrill. Her hands are shaking, and she takes a break to bring herself back under control.

"Okay, okay," Elizabeth says. She lifts her hands in a gesture of surrender. "We are here to support Tate, and you. You just let us know what we can do to help."

Tabitha opens her mouth but finds she has nothing to say. Tate is going to the party. That is the beginning and the end of it. She just has to figure out how to make it work, which she will do herself. She is not the one who asks for help. She is the one who gives it. She wouldn't even know how to ask. She'll figure it out. She always does. Just like finding parents for this new baby, like getting Brianna into cosmetology school, like finding Ginger a place to live that isn't in the back of beyond, like planning this whole vacation and keeping this family together when it is absolutely fraying at the seams no matter how hard she tries. She will make it happen.

Tabitha had always thought she would be the mother of boys. Taylor is so much easier in so many ways. The things that loom ahead of Tate make Tabitha shudder: the weight of party invitations, the cruel social Darwinism of middle school, the permanent castes in high school. Taylor, athletic and cheerful and simple in his needs, will be fine. But Tate, who is louder and more energetic than most girls, who is sweet, so sweet, but ever-so-slightly immature, and then there are the accidents – she is a different story.

Tabitha's own parents had been older, and she had come as quite a surprise to them. Everyone else she knew had siblings coming out of their ears, houses the same size as hers but where children had to share rooms, stacked in bunk beds where they could whisper and play far past lights-out, station wagons and minivans like clown cars where the children spilled out in an endless stream on their way to some adventure, matching pajamas on Christmas morning, and wild backyard adventures on summer afternoons.

To Tabitha, whose house was quiet, always, her parents delicate and bookish, set in their ways, those lives had seemed preferable to her own. Her summer afternoons consisted of desultorily jumping through a sprinkler alone while she listened to shrieks and laughter from other backyards. She and her parents didn't have adventures, only long car trips to see her grandparents in nursing homes. Her father drove, humming tunelessly along to old folk music that gave Tabitha a headache, and her mother read. Tabitha sat in the back and imagined she might meet a secret sister in the family room at the nursing home and they could play together and be best friends forever. But there never was a secret sister, and the drives home were even sadder without that daydream to lift her spirits.

Maybe because she didn't have any siblings, or maybe because her parents were so antisocial, or simply because of her personality, Tabitha was lost at school. She had been a small child, pale and petite, forgettable as paper, and was never able to make anyone notice her for more than a moment, and never anywhere near long enough to cure her aching loneliness.

She'd always liked to draw, and there was a brief moment of celebrity because of that in seventh grade, when she absentmindedly sketched a popular girl who sat next to her in math class. The girl had been flattered, and instantly it had become all the rage among the girls to have Tabitha draw them. She had done it gladly, with the forgiving eye of a royal portraitist, cleaning up their blemishes and flyaways and making them look happier than anyone could ever possibly be in seventh grade, and they were each delighted, clamoring to be next, begging her to sit at their lunch tables, posing in hopes that she might see their beauty and decide to capture it next.

Then the weekend came, and she begged her mother to take her to buy new art supplies, but when she came back on Monday, the trend was something else, lip gloss, maybe, and she stood in the hallway clutching her pristine sketchbook and pencils to her chest, wondering where her moment had gone.

This will not happen to Tate and Taylor. They will not be left out or left behind. She has signed them up for everything from the beginning. She is the one who suggests to the moms in music class that they have picnics in the park after class or come over for playdates on rainy afternoons. She is the class mom and always has a craft and a snack for the kids and a glass of wine for the moms when anyone comes by. She will do whatever it takes to make sure that Tate and Taylor never stand in a hallway looking lost as everyone else passes them by.

14

GINGER

IF ONLY SHE hadn't sprained both her ankle *and* her wrist. Either would have been enough. With both, she's practically a prisoner. She can hardly use the crutches to get around. Mostly she puts one under her good arm and hops around.

Her sudden dependence feels like suffocation, reminds her why she never wanted to be married. She delights in being able to keep her own company, in the silence and the ability to do something, anything – nap, read, cook – without being interrupted a thousand times to respond to someone else's capricious desires. Over the years she has realized her lack of interest in a partner was a desire for total independence, the ability to make her own decisions, to manage her environment when her childhood had been all about a wild lack of control of even the simplest things. Unlike Tabitha, she has no interest in controlling everyone around her. She simply wants to keep her world safe and calm, and the best way to do that is to minimize the noise around her, both literal and figurative.

Now Tabitha keeps finding her trying to ambulate and forcing her back to a couch or a chair, calling on Perry to bring more pillows to prop up Ginger's leg, or hurrying back into the kitchen for one of the endless ice packs she has and swapping it for a heating pad on Ginger's wrist or ankle. She ought to have been a field nurse, Ginger thinks, observing as Tabitha efficiently rewraps a bandage that has come loose.

Despite her instinct to ward off Tabitha's endless tending, she admits it is comforting, and it's relaxing to have Perry help her over to a chaise that still has some sun on it, the cushion warm from the day's light. She is surprised by the feeling of reprieve that she does not have to do it herself, that she does not have to keep track of when she should alternate heat or ice on her joints, that she does not have to figure out how to navigate the stairs from the house to the pool with her crutch and her bad ankle and wrist, that someone is there to help her. It is as invasive as it is pleasurable, and she is unsure of where to file the experience.

Without this family, she wouldn't have been on that fool's errand of a horseback ride in the first place, but suppose she had injured herself in some other way at home when Phoebe was at school or at her friend Esperanza's? What would she have done then? And how would she maneuver around her apartment alone? Elizabeth helped her in and out of the shower this morning, handing Ginger a towel to cover herself and then cracking jokes, rendering her too busy laughing to feel ashamed or embarrassed about either her body or her sudden uncomfortable dependence.

What about when the vacation is over? She'll go back home with Phoebe, and then what?

She told herself she wouldn't worry about that, but now that the thought has crept into her mind, she cannot *stop* worrying about it. What if she isn't okay by then? It has been two days already, and she is still in a great deal of pain. She does know people – she's not a complete recluse

131

– but they are acquaintances from book club or church, or the parents of Phoebe's friends. She doesn't seem to have any help-you-out-of-the-tub-and-make-you-laugh or remember-to-change-your-ice-pack people in her life. Except for Tabitha and Perry and Elizabeth and John. And do they even count, really?

"Marmee!" Phoebe and the twins, followed by Elizabeth, come around the corner, looking for all the world like cartoon characters, windmilling their arms and practically skidding to a halt on their heels. Phoebe hurls herself down beside Ginger, who tries not to flinch at the way the impact makes her leg shift, setting a spark of pain through her still-tender ankle. Tabitha badgered the doctors in the ER until they relented and gave Ginger a prescription for the pain, but she has avoided taking it thus far in case it makes her woozy, which also means, unfortunately at that moment, she is surviving on ibuprofen and sheer grit.

"Are you okay?" Phoebe asks.

"I'm doing fine," Ginger says, carefully shifting so Phoebe can curl up beside her. The children are in their swimsuits, the twins bouncing on the chaise next to her. "Are you all here to take a swim?"

"Yes! Aunt Tabitha said you were probably sleeping, so Aunt Elizabeth said she would watch us, but you're not sleeping at all!" Phoebe says.

Ginger would like very much indeed to be sleeping, but she will not be now. "Here I am," she says. "You don't have to stay. I can watch them," she says to Elizabeth, who hovers on the edge of a chair beside her.

"Oh, but what if someone needs a heroic rescue and I miss my chance?" Elizabeth says dryly. "Besides, can you do this?" She stands up and hoists first Taylor and then Tate into the air, hurling them into the pool one after the other, like so many empty barrels off the side of a ship. She is heading for Phoebe, Ginger marveling at her strength, when

Phoebe squeals, jumps up from the chair, jostling Ginger unpleasantly as she does, and dives into the pool.

"I'm pooped. How's the patient?" Elizabeth sits down in the chaise beside Ginger and puts her feet up.

"I'm fine," Ginger says, which is not true. Her wrist is improving, but her leg and her ankle continue to swell and throb painfully. She tries not to look because she doesn't want to have to deal with it. Internally, she vacillates between gratitude at being taken care of and fury at Tabitha's nagging, which is how she ended up in this situation in the first place. If Tabitha only listened, only left well enough alone, Ginger wouldn't have fallen off that damn horse.

She forces herself to take a breath, and they are silent for a few moments, watching the children swim.

"I'm sorry about John's job," Ginger says finally.

"Me, too," Elizabeth says. She is still looking at the children, but Ginger can see something tighten in her jaw. What she really would like to know is why Elizabeth and John seem so set against the idea of adopting again, but that seems inappropriate to ask directly.

She settles on, "I don't mean to pry, but is everything okay? Between the two of you?"

"Other than the fact that John has lost his job and we're going to be living in a cardboard box in a month? We're swell," Elizabeth says.

"Surely it won't be that bad," Ginger says with relief. If Elizabeth is being her normal sarcastic self, things can't be too terrible.

"Yeah. Well," Elizabeth says.

"I guess I'm just wondering… if you don't adopt this child, who will?" Another baby is one thing. It comes with its own adjustments. But yet another family? Another couple, or another parent at least? The aftershocks of John and Elizabeth's joining their family still feel like they are happening. And now they will have to do it again?

She wants to tell Elizabeth that it will be fine, John will

get another job, but surely they will not have another chance to adopt a full sibling for Violet. It would just be so much easier for everyone. And Phoebe, who was so unsettled before Violet's arrival, has enough on her plate already, doesn't she?

But their conversation is interrupted by the children.

"Taylor, stop!" Phoebe shouts. Ginger turns to look and see Taylor swimming away from the girls, a smirk on his face, and Phoebe marching up the steps from the pool, pushing her hair away from her face.

Her daughter grabs a towel and comes over and sits sulkily down beside Ginger, and she sees Elizabeth relax, perhaps grateful for the distraction.

"What's wrong?" Ginger asks Phoebe.

"Taylor keeps trying to drown me," Phoebe says.

"Yet here you are, still alive to see another day," Elizabeth says, and Phoebe tries not to smile. Ginger is a little envious sometimes of Elizabeth's ease with the children, with Phoebe especially. She and Phoebe have been close for so long, but Elizabeth can make her daughter shake off the growing moodiness of tweenhood in a way Ginger cannot. She has always tried so hard to take Phoebe's concerns seriously, and now she wonders if that is the wrong approach, if she should be more like Elizabeth. But that doesn't seem right, either, both because Elizabeth can be so dismissive – when Violet bumps her head and cries, Elizabeth picks her up and kisses her, but also says, "Shake it off, slugger!" – and while it seems to work, Ginger is afraid of dismissing an actual problem.

"Hey, congratulations on getting into TGA," Elizabeth says to Phoebe, reaching out a fist. "That's a big deal!"

Phoebe removes her hand from the cape she has created from her towel and bumps her fist against Elizabeth's, a gesture Ginger has never seen her daughter perform. She is noticeably brighter at the mention of TGA, but Ginger cannot help but blink her eyes closed for a moment and wish

Elizabeth hadn't brought it up. Tabitha must have told her. She wishes Phoebe had listened when Ginger had asked her not to talk about it.

"Thanks!" Phoebe says. "I am really excited. Except I don't know if I can go."

"Wait, what?" Elizabeth asks. "Why not?"

Phoebe looks guiltily at Ginger, who presses her lips together. She shifts her leg, and her ankle shouts in pain.

"Marmee says we have things we have to talk about first."

"Oh, yeah, Marmee? Like what?" Elizabeth asks. She bends her knees, sets her elbow on the chair's arm, and rests her chin on her hand, looking at Ginger, who is feeling terribly put upon.

"Don't ask it like that," Ginger says.

"Like what?" Elizabeth asks, looking surprised.

"Like I'm just being difficult. We need to discuss the feasibility of it. Practical matters. How Phoebe will get to and from school given my work hours. Whether she – you," she says, interrupting herself to address Phoebe, reminding herself that it is her future they are discussing, and Elizabeth is not technically part of it, "whether you are okay going to a school where you don't know anyone. A different school from Esperanza and Charlotte."

She worries about her daughter's friendships more than Phoebe does herself. When Phoebe came to her after their grandmother's death, she had been in an understandable state – grieving and confused and traumatized. The first few months especially had been filled with urgent and frequent consultations with her teacher and social workers and therapist and pediatrician, an exhausting series of conversations even for someone far more extroverted than Ginger is. Though they made it through the worst of Phoebe's grief and transitions relatively unscathed, Ginger does not want to let down her guard. This new school is a clear example of disruption and loss, whether Phoebe believes she wants to make the change or not.

"I hadn't thought about it exactly like that," Phoebe says, and she looks anxious. "If they're going to school together, won't they forget about me?"

Ginger is about to respond, but Elizabeth does instead. "I doubt they will forget about you. Best friends don't forget about each other. But not being in school with them would be different, yes."

"And if we have to move to the city, you will definitely see them less outside of school, too," Ginger adds.

The moment Ginger says that, she regrets it, thinks less of herself for it. She is not wrong, but it feels manipulative.

Phoebe doesn't say anything.

It is Elizabeth who rescues her. She looks at Phoebe thoughtfully, with a level of empathy Ginger doesn't associate with Elizabeth, sharp and loud and brisk. "Saying goodbye is a tough thing to do. But when you say goodbye to something, you also get to say hello to all the things that are going to take its place. Like if you go to TGA, for instance, what do you want to do?"

Phoebe brightens again. "Like debate and cross-country. And Chinese club."

"That sounds fabulous," Elizabeth says enthusiastically. "So those things are all the gifts you would get to say hello to. And middle school can be really fun. You get more independence, you get more variety because you're moving from classroom to classroom, the schools are bigger, so there's more activities, there are more kids, so you get to make more friends and meet different kinds of people. All that is intimidating, but it's also really, really cool."

"It is a fantastic opportunity. It's a big change, though," Ginger says, and Phoebe nods. She doesn't think Phoebe genuinely understands what she is talking about doing. A different house, a different school, different friends. A different restaurant for Friday night Chinese food, a different grocery store. A different morning and after-school routine,

136

a different bedroom when her room has hardly changed from the day she moved in.

"It's going to be a year of a lot of changes, that's for sure," Elizabeth says. She meets Ginger's eyes quickly, the secret of Brianna's pregnancy weighing on both their minds. "Look. Things change. This is a fact of life. But you have survived one hundred percent of the changes in your life so far, which means the odds are high you're going to survive whatever comes next, even if you don't know what it is right now. Right?" She reaches out and squeezes Phoebe's hand, and Phoebe squeezes it back.

"So can we talk about it, Marmee? Like talk about it for real, not like when you say we'll talk about it later but we never do."

Ginger feels Elizabeth's eyes on her and avoids them. "Yes, we'll talk about it. We're talking about it right now, aren't we?"

"Yes, but when Tate and Taylor and I were talking about it the other day, you got all weird." She waves her hands in the air vaguely.

A feeling of guilt settles on Ginger, a fear that she is standing in the way of what is right.

"Yes, let's talk about it later, just us two," Ginger says. It will give her time to think, time to determine how to address the issues of change and instability in a thoughtful way without obviating how impressive Phoebe's achievement is and how excited they both are about the opportunity.

"Tonight," Phoebe says. "Not later, tonight."

"Tonight," Ginger promises.

Phoebe nods, as though this has all been dispensed with, and stands, letting the cape fall off her shoulders. She is starting, Ginger sees, to develop, the long, slim lines of her body shifting ever so slightly, and it makes her want to brace for impact, thinking about five-year-old Phoebe weeping in her arms, wondering where her grandmother had gone. That had only been yesterday, hadn't it? Can she be faulted for not wanting to set this poor child's world askew any more than it will be naturally?

She and Elizabeth watch Phoebe cannonball into the pool, and instantly join Tate and Taylor's game of Marco Polo.

"You need to let her go," Elizabeth says bluntly, looking at Ginger.

For a moment, Ginger isn't sure what she means, and she has an image of herself grasping for Phoebe as she steps off a balcony, a wisp of fabric in the air, and then gone, and she reaches out as though it is real, pulling back abruptly because of course that's not what Elizabeth means. She just means let Phoebe go to TGA. Which is ridiculous. She's not *stopping* her. She just wants everyone to be aware of all the aspects of this decision.

"It's not that I don't want her to go. It's complicated. It would require a lot of details she's not aware of."

"Like where you live," Elizabeth says. The sun has moved, and Ginger is now largely in shade, the last of the sun falling onto Elizabeth's legs, stretched out on the chair. Leaning her head back against the cushion, she looks over at Ginger. Shadows so deep they are nearly purple hang under her eyes, and she yawns, scratching her head.

"Yes, that's part of it. And whatever Tabitha may have said to you, it's not inconsequential. I have lived there for ten years, and Phoebe has lived there since she came to me. Disrupting that firm foundation is not something to rush into. And they're going to be dealing with a lot of change already with the new baby, and new parents, if it comes to that already."

Something flickers across Elizabeth's face, but she just says, "I know. You don't have to defend yourself to me, okay?"

"Sorry," Ginger says, realizing she is becoming prickly. "But it is our decision, and I don't like being pressured into it by anyone."

Elizabeth runs her hand through her hair, making one of the curls stick straight up until she pats it down again. "I'm not pressuring you into anything. I'm telling you that your child really, really wants to go to this school, and in my professional – hahaha – opinion, she will thrive there. So if the only thing that is keeping you from enrolling her is that it makes you nervous to be close to the rest of us, I'd recommend thinking hard about who you are protecting."

"Don't be ridiculous," Ginger says, but there is a queasy feeling in her gut, as though Elizabeth has seen something in her she has not.

"I get it. I totally get it. Lord knows Tabitha has zero boundaries. But maybe it would also be good. And just FYI, it's not like we see them any more than you do because we live closer. In reality, we probably see them less, because of all the sleepovers Phoebe and the twins do."

"Oh, but we *would* see them more. Tabitha seems to have decided she's opening an after-school care program for Phoebe. The children made this whole schedule for the time they'd spend together after school. I would literally be there every day."

Elizabeth looks at the sky, squinting into the last of the sun for a moment. "Okay, fair. I'm having a hard time feeling bad for you for getting free childcare, but I understand. But also, it's not like every night would be Sunday dinner, right? You'd snag Phoebe and go home. All evidence to the contrary, Tabitha does have a life outside us. She doesn't seriously want to spend every waking second with you. No offense, you're scintillating company—"

"You're being optimistic. If it were Violet, you would feel quite differently."

"Maybe," Elizabeth says. She turns back to the children. "No drowning each other on my watch, please!" she calls out to Taylor, who is attempting to dunk Phoebe under the water again. He stops, but more because Tate beans him in the head with a wet tennis ball than because of Elizabeth's warning.

"It's not only about being too close. It's about all the change Phoebe has been through, and how much more she can handle at once. We simply need to make this decision in our own time. I don't believe it makes me a bad mother because I'm not instantly doing whatever my child prefers."

"No," Elizabeth says, stretching the word out like taffy, as though she is thinking about something else. "Really, though, Ginge. Is it worth torpedoing something that might be really great for Phoebe because you're scared of change?"

15

ELIZABETH

AFTER DINNER, THE children scatter to play a new game of their own invention called Screaming Mimi, which does indeed involve a fair amount of screaming. Elizabeth wonders idly what the neighbors, who all have spent equally ridiculous amounts of money on their houses, think of the noise. She looked online and saw there is a house at the top of this very road that is for sale to the tune of forty-nine *million* dollars. For a second home! For that price, she imagines, someone would expect fewer screaming mimis in their yard.

As usual, Tabitha prepared a complicated and elaborate meal when everyone – Elizabeth included, or maybe Elizabeth especially – would have been happy with baby carrots and chicken nuggets. Now Perry is feeding himself grapes at the other end of the table as though he is at a Roman feast, leaning his head back and dropping them in one by one. The pleasant weight of a good meal and her afternoon in the sun on top of a truly excellent wine is making her feel pleasantly sleepy until Tabitha turns to them all and says, "It's time to make some choices about adding to our family."

Elizabeth, who had been letting her lead loll back, falling halfway asleep, sits upright quickly.

"Unless Elizabeth and John have changed their minds?" Tabitha asks, her voice tilting up at the end, buoyed by hope.

"Tabitha," Perry says gently, a warning. Tabitha looks at him with a raised eyebrow, and he shakes his head so gently it is almost imperceptible.

"Nope," Elizabeth says. She leans over and takes a bunch of grapes from Perry's plate. John looks up at her, as if he is going to say something, and then thinks better of it.

She doesn't bother looking at Tabitha's expression. She has said no.

How many times will she have to say it?

Tabitha looks disappointed. "I was afraid of that, so I've taken the opportunity to get the ball rolling, as it were." She reaches over to her planner and pulls out a stack of papers. She hands one to each of them, Ginger passing one to Elizabeth, and she sees it is a packet, stapled neatly in the corner.

"What the hell is this?" Elizabeth asks, flipping through the pages. Each one has names at the top, photos of strangers, bullet-pointed lists, and what look like screenshots of messages.

"This is a sampling of the prospective parents Sunny shared with us, and a few who responded to my posting."

"What posting?" Elizabeth asks. She flips through again, now that she knows what she is looking at.

"The posting I put on some of the online adoption groups to help find families," Tabitha says. She sounds irritated, as though she has explained all this (she has not) and is having to repeat it like they are refusing to understand.

"When did we talking about doing that?" Elizabeth asks. She is flipping the packet one-handed, shaking the pages until they move forward, her other hand still full of grapes.

"We're talking about it now," Tabitha says. She has put on her reading glasses. She doesn't wear them often, and

Elizabeth guesses they are an affectation, so she can peer over the top of the lenses in a way that feels annoyingly performative. Tabitha was an only child (which Elizabeth knows because she has harped endlessly about how terrible it was, like she'd grown up in a workhouse in a Dickens novel), but she obviously desperately wants to be an older sister.

"No, before. Did we talk about this? Where is the posting? Who wrote it?" Ginger says.

"I did," Tabitha says, and she sounds sharp, unusually so. "Someone had to do something. This baby is coming, and Brianna has asked us to help her find the child's parents. And we're only all going to be together like this for another week. We can't sit around and wait. Brianna needs us. The baby needs us."

"Yeah, but we're supposed to be doing it together," Elizabeth points out.

John is still spinning his fork and has not looked up. There is a cold war between them at the moment; she is actually rather proud of herself for keeping their child alive while managing to basically not talk to him since their conversation about his mother's call. But now she could use his support and he is silent.

"I didn't see you stepping up to do anything," Tabitha says.

Elizabeth stares back at her. "It's not like the baby is coming tomorrow. We have months to figure this out."

Tabitha sighs impatiently. "You would be surprised how quickly months go by."

Elizabeth would like to object, but Tabitha isn't wrong. It's not like she wants to have extra family dinners to hash this out when they get back home. If they even survive until then.

"Can we see this posting?" Ginger asks.

"It's on the first page," Tabitha says, looking over the tops of her glasses again. Elizabeth flips back to the first page one-handed, even though she has finished the grapes, and there it is.

We're looking for the perfect parents to join our very special adoptive family. We are three families who became one when we adopted biological siblings. Their birth mother is pregnant again and has honored us by asking us to help her find this child's parents.

Our pledge is that our children will grow up as siblings, even though they live in different homes. We have family dinners once a week, celebrate birthdays together, visit over school breaks, and even go on family vacations! Our children's birth parents are part of our family and welcome in our homes as well.

You must be committed to our unique and wonderful open-adoption family, as we will be to you. Because of our arrangement, we are only looking for families without children. You must live in and be committed to staying in the Denver area.

If you think you are the perfect match for our family, please tell us about yourselves!

It is infuriatingly perfect.

"This is great," Perry says, and Ginger nods, but so gently it could have been a twitch. This is the problem with Tabitha. She is often right, even when it is unfair for her to be.

"What's this part about families without children?" John asks.

"That was something we realized with you two," Tabitha says. "Because of the siblings. It would be confusing that some of them have siblings that the others don't. It would dilute their relationship with each other."

"They all have relatives the others don't have," Elizabeth points out. "Violet's and Phoebe's cousins and grandparents. Tate and Taylor's uncles and aunts."

"Yes, but not siblings. I do remember talking about it in regard to you two. Extended family is different," Ginger says.

"What if we want to adopt again, though? Later?" John

asks, looking up for the first time. He is sitting hunched over in his chair, elbows resting on his knees, his back curved like he is carrying something heavy, dragging it behind him.

Elizabeth looks over at him, a sharp caution.

"If you're planning to adopt again, why aren't you just adopting this child?" Tabitha asks, lifting her hands up in exasperation. Elizabeth has seen Tabitha rattled more frequently on this trip than she has in their entire relationship. She has never seen Tabitha this way, snappy and irritated. As though she is worried, as though she has lost control, as if that would ever happen. The evidence of Tabitha's complete control over everything is in her hands, in the form of this tidy packet of dossiers on people whose lives they are controlling, if only for a moment.

"We're not adopting this baby. We told you this," Elizabeth says firmly. She says this as much to John as she does to Tabitha. Her chin juts out defiantly, and she forces herself to lower it. It's a habit from childhood, trying to stand up, be tall enough to argue back. Her sister and brothers always mocked her for it.

"Why don't we talk about imaginary babies later and focus on the real one now?" Perry says gently. He holds his hands out wide, palms down, as though he is pushing the tension back.

Tabitha shakes her head, as if trying to clear out her annoyance. "Now, Sunny did send over some files from the agency, but none of them are quite right for our family, so the ones here are—"

"Wait, Sunny said they weren't right?" John asks.

"No, I said that," Tabitha says.

"So you're picking the parents now? Then why are we even here?" Elizabeth asks, making a show of tossing her packet onto the table. Tabitha's mouth closes in a thin line.

"I am not picking. I am a central point of contact. But trust me, they would not be appropriate."

"Why not?"

"Well" – Tabitha pushes back her shoulders and sits up straight – "for various reasons. We have a schedule we follow as a family, and traditions, and it would be difficult to fit some of them in. One couple, for instance, are competitive runners. Ultrarunners. They train every day and travel for races almost every weekend. I can't imagine how they think they have time for a child, let alone our extended family. Another is lay leadership in their church – they practically run everything, so their weekends are spoken for, too. There's one where the wife travels for work every week Monday through Friday and she'll hardly see the baby, let alone us. That sort of thing."

"This family does take up a lot of time," Elizabeth says aloud, though she hadn't meant to phrase it exactly that way. Tabitha looks at her sharply.

"That's hardly true," Tabitha says, and she sounds hurt. "In any case, there was one family – a single man, actually – who sounded quite wonderful, but I—"

"No single people," Elizabeth says abruptly.

Ginger looks at her, surprised. "Why not?" she asks.

"I don't mean you, Ginge," Elizabeth says. "I don't even mean single parents in general, and I'm sure this guy is swell. But come on – a newborn? As a single parent? That is a lot to ask of someone. There are two of us and we have nearly lost our minds."

"People do it all the time," Tabitha points out.

"I know, but I'm just saying it would be hard. So maybe we should look for a couple? Just since it's a baby?"

No one answers because right then Tabitha's phone, which is facedown on the table, buzzes loudly. She picks it up, and Elizabeth sees her face change to delight.

"It's a boy!" Tabitha says, turning her phone so they can see the text from Brianna.

Elizabeth feels sick.

She goes upstairs, using checking on Violet as an excuse to escape, and then steps out into the hallway, intending to go back and join the others outside, but halfway down the stairs

146

she is overcome with a strange, heavy feeling. She isn't sure what is happening at first as she struggles to breathe, choking and gasping, until she begins to cry, so heavily she doesn't hear the door downstairs slide open, and starts when John comes bounding up the stairs.

"God, Bethy, what's wrong?" he asks, pulling her to him. "What happened?"

Elizabeth cannot speak, and she wouldn't know how to answer anyway. What the hell is wrong? What the hell is wrong with her, besides everything?

Once upon a time, she had been fun. She had been funny! She had been the person she pretends to be every day at school when she gets up in front of twenty-five eighth graders and tries to make them care about velocity and chemical reactions (letting them throw things and blow them up – in a controlled way, obviously – is the secret). She had laughed all the time.

She can hardly remember who she was before this – before Violet, before the thousand years of fertility treatments and all the failures. The closest she's gotten to who she once had been was when she and John went to their college reunion just before their last transfer. For just a few days, they'd been the people they once were. They hung out with their old friends and their old teammates; she drank all the alcohol she hadn't been drinking because the expensive, useless doctors had told her not to, not that, she could point out, it had made any difference. They had sex whenever they wanted to, unencumbered by their reproductive endocrinologist's schedule; they danced and sang with their friends until the haze of dawn crept over the sky and they stumbled back to the hotel room to sleep late, and when they woke up, they feasted on a forbidden breakfast containing a metric fuckton of gluten and sugar.

One afternoon that weekend, she walked down a hallway in the old sciences building with Terra, her roommate from junior and senior year. Terra made a joke, and Elizabeth cracked up and was startled to hear the sound of her laughter echoing along the empty walls. She'd always had a great laugh, people told her, rough-edged like her voice, like she'd been up too late singing in a bar. It had been her laugh that caught John's attention, at some sticky-floored party in a dorm basement sophomore year. The music had fallen just as someone said something funny. Elizabeth had laughed, and John heard it all the way across the room and worked his way over to her just to hear her laugh again.

Who had that person been, even? Where had she gone?

It doesn't seem worth holding a grudge against John right at that moment, and she relaxes into his arms. She allows his touch to soothe her, lets her breathing relax, and the sudden and alien tears abate. "I'm fine," she says, pulling away, embarrassed. "I seriously don't know what's wrong with me." Wiping her eyes with the back of her hand, she gives a long, unladylike sniff and tosses her hair back, blinking like she is trying to adjust her contacts. She gives him a fake, wide smile that probably looks like she is going to eat him, but he does not pull away.

"Is it Brianna?" he asks. He strokes her hair tenderly, and she finds herself unwittingly leaning into it, like a cat asking to be scratched behind the ears.

"What? No," Elizabeth says. "Why would I be crying about Brianna?"

He hesitates, as though he doesn't want to name it. "Because she's pregnant," he says.

"What? God, no," Elizabeth says, but there is a lump in her throat that wasn't there before, and that sour twist in her stomach has returned. She has a child. She doesn't need to get pregnant. Doesn't want to get pregnant anymore anyway, because pregnancy would only lead to another miscarriage, and even if it didn't, it would lead to another child, which she also emphatically does not want.

"I don't know," John says. "Her being pregnant is hard for me. It's so easy for them. It just happens for them and they don't even want to be parents. It's not fair."

That's exactly it, Elizabeth thinks. It's not fair. It's not fair it's not fair it's not fair. None of it is fair.

When she sees a pregnant woman, she rushes to avert her eyes, and a strange anger crawls from her belly into her chest. She remembers the women in the mothers' group she was dumb enough to go to after Violet was born, all of them smugly breastfeeding while they watched her give Violet a bottle with a critical eye, telling stories about their pregnancies and labors while she sat silently, wanting to scream. The women cooed when she told them Violet was adopted, told her how amazing she was, what a gift that was, but she always felt something underneath those words, a sense of relief and superiority that they hadn't had to adopt, because what a wonderful thing for *other* people to do, just not them, thank goodness they didn't need to resort to that.

She knows it is not Brianna's fault, not the fault of any of the women she takes an instant dislike to, not the fault of the women in that fucking group, all of whom she would happily kick in the ear if she saw them again. But knowing and feeling are two different things, and even as she sits there, one of John's arms around her shoulders and the other resting, steady and warm, on her thigh, her fists begin to clench as if they are looking for some nearby drywall to punch through.

DIAGNOSIS

Some people with my wife's condition manage to get pregnant and carry the baby to term. Most of them don't. Mostly they don't get pregnant in the first place. Then, if they do, either they die, or the baby does. I told her I wasn't willing to take that risk. I could live without having a child. I couldn't live without her.

But from the moment she told me she was sick, I have spent every day knowing that someday I will have to live without her.

We have it under control. Medication, a careful diet, exercise. Still, somewhere out there, looming, is the day she will die. She can live a long time, or she might not. Odds are she will be gone in twenty years.

Then again, isn't that true of all of us? Any one of us could die tomorrow. Any one of us could live a long time or be gone today. So why shouldn't we live our lives the way we want to? Why shouldn't we have a family and dream about our future? Why should her illness rob us of the simple happiness of life while we have the chance to live it?

The social workers tell us birth parents won't choose us because of the diagnosis, but also that we can't keep it a secret.

So I tell them everything else about us first. I tell them that my family fostered children when I was growing up, so I know what it means to create a family that doesn't look like everyone else's but is still filled with love.

I tell them how we met, that we were at a concert by a lake and she turned around and looked at me and I was so struck by her eyes, a soft amber like a jewel, that I couldn't speak.

I tell them I have the best job in the world, that I work at a zoo because I want to share everything animals have to teach us, and I promise them our children will feed the giraffes and pet the reptiles and watch the hippos get a bath more than any other children in the world.

I tell them my wife is calm and patient, that everything she does is precise and full of care. She is a pediatrician who works in the ER at Children's Hospital, and she makes everyone feel better, even the parents.

I tell them I make the best blueberry pancakes every Saturday morning and I can even make them into shapes and animals.

I tell them my wife has the biggest collection of records you've ever seen, and our home is never without music when she's around.

I tell them her father was the first Black professor at his university and he is smarter than anyone I know but also he knows how to make sailboats out of sandwiches and whittle sticks into tiny birds and he lives with us so he can help take care of the kids when we are working.

I tell them everything that matters. I tell them all the reasons to choose us.

Then I tell them that my wife has a medical condition that has made her sick sometimes, but that most of the time she is fine, and we take good care of ourselves, we eat healthy food and go for long walks and swim in the reservoir and go to the doctor for checkups, and that our children will do the same.

Because isn't that what matters? That we will be a family, with all the question marks and unknowns of any other family?

That we will do our best and be our best and we will teach our children to do the same because the only thing that matters is the moment we are in and the future is unknown for all of us?

She asks me again and again if I will be okay with the idea that someday I will have to do this alone. She asks me if I understand that the odds are high she will not be there to see our children get married and she will never be a grandmother and maybe she won't even be there to see our children graduate high school.

I tell her of course I am not okay with that, but we all have to be okay with it. All of us. Because there are no guarantees. Nothing is known, and so much is unknown. The only thing we can do is hold hands and walk into the future together with hope.

16

TABITHA

THE NEXT DAY, Perry volunteers to take the older children to one of those bounce house places so the rest of them can continue discussing the prospective parents. Tabitha is relieved that he is taking them, honestly. She finds children's places of that ilk cavernous and depressing, the lights too high and not bright enough to illuminate everything, the walls painted black or gray, so something that should be cheerful feels prison-like. She imagines the experience is similar to living in a castle, a real one in the Middle Ages, heavy dark stone and smoky torches and candles, damp and cold and winter-dark even in the brightest days of summer. Not to mention the objection she holds in principle to the idea of "family-friendly" activities, as if children are a unique species who must be caged in special areas, far from normal humans.

But Perry, bless him, will take off his shoes and jump on the inflatable pads with the children, scattering them like jacks every time he lands. She packs some extra clothes for Tate, because all that bouncing around is an absolute recipe for accidents, and insists on including some snacks, though she imagines Perry will give them money for the vending machines instead and they will return with their teeth stained orange from cheese dust, their bodies rattled with sugar.

"Shall we go outside so Violet can play in the grass while we talk some more about these hopeful adoptive parents?" she asks the others. Tabitha feels bruised and is trying to be overly careful, given how fussy everyone was about the work she is doing to find parents. Which is ridiculous, because someone has to do it, and Ginger has been out of commission, and Elizabeth is either snapping at someone or sleeping.

"I guess," Elizabeth says now, as if it's a burden. Well. Tabitha will just let that go. For the sake of the baby.

She already has a blanket and toys ready for Violet, and she grabs them along with her planner, leading John, who is carrying Violet, and Elizabeth, who is helping Ginger, out to the yard. She flips the blanket out, letting it fall to the ground and tossing the toys across it. John places Violet in the center of the blanket, where she immediately reaches for a little wooden car. The sight of Violet playing with it cheers her, because it reminds her of what lies at the end of this: a new baby; more time with Brianna, at least for a while; a reminder of how happy they can be when everyone isn't being difficult, and how special the family they are building is.

When they are finally settled, after Tabitha sends John back to the kitchen twice to ferry out the drinks and snacks, because even though they have only just finished breakfast someone might be peckish, she opens her planner and pulls out fresh packets. They had only held them for thirty minutes or so the night before, but some people had already ruined theirs. It was fine; she had to reprint them anyway to take out the single parents and those with other children and also to include some new prospective parents she has heard from: a married couple, one of whom was adopted from China herself as a child; a husband and wife who live quite close and do an impressive amount of volunteer work, and another couple who live on an intentional community farm. Tabitha feels a little sense of pride at the number of responses she has received in such a short amount of time.

"This is so odd, isn't it?" Ginger asks, fingering the tabs Tabitha put on the edges of the pages.

"What is?" Tabitha asks. She feels a pang of anxious shame and flips through the packets to see what she has done wrong.

"This whole thing. Choosing who will parent this child. It feels like we are playing God, doesn't it?"

"It's like we're in charge of someone's happiness. For the rest of their lives," Elizabeth says.

"We're not choosing. Brianna is," Tabitha points out.

"Obvi," Elizabeth says. "But we are recommending someone, right? Or someones? So we're going to be saying no to other someones. And you just, like, say that? Say 'No, sorry, you can't have a kid'?"

"I don't even know what we're looking for," John says. "How do you even know what kind of parent a kid needs if you don't know the kid?"

Elizabeth turns to him. "That's always how it is, though, right? Like if we were talking about a biological family, we assume the parents are right for the child because they are genetically related, when it's entirely possible they are the wrong parents for that kid, or shouldn't be parents, period. I can tell you from sad experience there are a lot of kids in this world who would be better off matched with someone randomly than with their own biological parents. And a lot of parents who shouldn't be parents at all."

"That's true. I was absolutely raised in the wrong family by the wrong parents," Ginger says.

"Why do you say that?" Tabitha asks. It feels like a strange thing to say, disloyal, even. She loved her own parents fiercely, firmly, though she harbors so much misbegotten nostalgia for the childhood they never gave her, hadn't known how to give her. Then again, she never asked for it.

"They just had a tolerance – perhaps even an appreciation – for chaos that I do not. But my brothers seemed fine with it.

My parents were not bad people, per se; we were just ill-suited to each other temperamentally."

Tabitha is surprised by how self-aware Ginger is. She is so resistant to the smallest things – moving, for instance, even when it is clearly the correct choice and Tabitha has even volunteered to help her find a place. Does Ginger realize this about herself? And if she does, why doesn't she change it?

"So you're saying we might as well throw a dart at a board while we're blindfolded," John says.

"Thank you," he says to Violet, who has drooled all over one of the wooden cars and handed it to him. He makes a face and wipes his hand on his pants while Violet gabbles at him, hands on his thigh as she rocks back and forth.

"I wouldn't say that. It's not scientific, but it's not pure luck. We will make decisions based on what's best for our family and what we think would be best for a child – any child. Financial stability, for instance," Tabitha says, casting about for something no one can argue with.

"What does that mean, though?" Ginger asks. "There are widely varying levels of financial stability."

"Perhaps a couple who is on solid enough financial footing for someone to stay home with the baby for the first few years. A stay-at-home parent would be ideal, but—"

"Wait, why would that be ideal?" Elizabeth asks, looking affronted.

"Well, wouldn't you have liked to stay home with Violet longer?" Tabitha asks.

"Ah – no," Elizabeth says.

Tabitha laughs lightly, and then realizes Elizabeth is not joking. "Oh, well, I didn't mean – I'm not criticizing you. It would just be nice to have another stay-at-home parent in our family. I could help with the baby, too, which would be great."

"So you want us to pick someone to what, be friends with you?" Elizabeth asks, as if this is the worst thing in the world that could happen, that someone would be nice to Tabitha for a change.

"I didn't say that," Tabitha says.

"Honey, don't," John says.

Tabitha cannot tell whether he is talking to Elizabeth or his daughter. Violet is handing him a pile of unfinished wood cups and then promptly taking them back, stacking them out of order and howling in rage when they refuse to nest that way.

"This lady's a yoga instructor," Elizabeth says, randomly flipping to a page in the packet. "Do you want us to pick her so you have someone to do yoga with?"

Tabitha cannot think what Elizabeth, of all people, has to be upset about. "At least I'm doing something," she says, and her voice is sharp and high-pitched, unnatural and unexpected. "I don't see you doing anything to help find this baby's parents."

"How can we? You won't let anyone else do anything," Elizabeth says, throwing her hands up in the air, rather overdramatically, Tabitha thinks.

"I am literally here trying to discuss the people who have responded to the message. If you have an opinion, now would be an excellent time to voice it," Tabitha says primly. She is thinking about Elizabeth's crying when they first met. Tabitha preferred that Elizabeth, of whom she has seen neither hide nor hair since that day, to this shouty one, who makes regular appearances and is never welcome.

Tabitha feels vindicated when Elizabeth does not attempt to argue her spurious point and instead begins flipping loudly through the packet. For goodness' sake, what is she supposed to do? No one else ever does anything, so is she just going to let this child be born and have no parents at all? Elizabeth may think they have ages, but really, time will go quite quickly, especially if everyone continues to be so resistant.

She lets the silence go for a few minutes and then, having made her point, suggests they look at the families who have replied.

"I'm no on number five," Ginger says.

John flips to the page and scans the profile. "What's wrong

with them? They're only forty-five minutes away; they don't have any other kids; she wants to quit her job and stay home with the baby, so Tabitha's in. What's wrong?"

"They're part of one of those churches that thinks women are useless unless they have a thousand babies," Elizabeth says, looking at the page. "Ix-nay on them, for sure, though may I add, that poor woman. Being in one of those churches and not being able to have kids has to be a nightmare on a whole different level." She says this flippantly, but Tabitha senses something more behind it.

From the day she met them, Elizabeth and John were swallowed in a tsunami of adoption and parenting-related tasks. And while Tabitha has always assumed Elizabeth's tears the day they met had been a moment, an aberration, she wonders now if it was only that the grief had been buried by all that action, all those things to do.

"No single parents? Is that where we landed?" John asks, flipping through. "I liked that one guy."

Elizabeth and Ginger exchange a glance that Tabitha cannot read.

"Elizabeth has a point about single parenting an infant. Though he sounds like an excellent candidate otherwise," Ginger says.

"So that's just it? He's out because he's single? Didn't his whole thing say he wasn't being picked because he was single? It seems like such a little thing," John says.

"They aren't small things. They feel superficial, but if we feel something isn't right for our family, or for this baby, it's our duty to the children to respect that," Tabitha says.

"I remember that feeling, though. Of worrying we wouldn't be good enough, that something we said would make them shut our file and we wouldn't have Violet," John says.

Tabitha never even considered that fear. She and Perry had never doubted. What did they have to doubt? They had the money to give the children a comfortable life, they were old enough that they had perspective and experience but not too old to keep up with young children, they had a solid and happy marriage, and she was ready to devote herself to full-time parenting.

Except apparently Elizabeth, who seemingly never wavers in her confidence, and John, who is too boyishly unaware to question himself, had doubted.

"It's impossible to tell, isn't it? If someone looked at me, only knowing a tiny amount, how would they have guessed what sort of mother I would be?" Ginger asks thoughtfully.

"And no one asks people who just get pregnant if they'll be good parents. They just say 'Congratulations!'" Elizabeth says bitterly.

Tabitha imagined this vacation a thousand times but still failed to anticipate what being together like this would do, the way it would begin to strip away their armor, the way she would be able to see them more plainly. She had not known how much she did not know about these other people she calls her family; she had not known that they could infuriate her and touch her so deeply at the same time.

"Number six are both doctors. We'd never see them, either," Ginger says, flipping ahead.

"What about number seven? I like them," Elizabeth says.

Tabitha tries not to smile. Though she has intentionally not expressed her own opinion, they are her favorite. A couple together since college, married for six years – the moment it was legal, they said. A law professor and a florist. The professor was adopted from China as a girl, so she understands at least some of the issues present in adoption. They like to travel, but don't have to do so for work; they have friends but not family in the area, so there will be no confusion over their loyalties; and their schedules are flexible. The florist wrote the letter, which is funny and warm, and expressed interest in meeting the whole family, which Tabitha thought was lovely.

"Great, they're hired," John says, pretending to toss the packet to the side, but no one laughs. It is sobering to be on the other side of this, to think that this is a responsibility people have. They always say their family was formed through happy accident, but now Tabitha sees how intentional it has to be. She wonders why Sunny never mentioned this, how creating a family is a curious combination of deliberation and chance, the process, as Elizabeth points out, laced with unfairness and bias and seemingly random priorities.

"Shall we call them, talk to them a little more? And perhaps find a few other people to talk to as well?" Tabitha asks, relieved that they are settling on at least one couple.

There is silence for a moment, and Tabitha wonders if she has made an error.

"That's cruel, too, isn't it?" Ginger asks. "Leading them on like that?"

"Yeah, like getting their hopes up and then being like, 'jk, you can't have this baby'?" Elizabeth agrees.

Tabitha isn't sure what to say. She hadn't thought of it that way. "I suppose so, but isn't that— What is the alternative? We need to know these people as well as we can. We need to be able to tell Brianna that we have vetted them."

"Shouldn't she be the one to talk to them?" John asks.

"I don't think Brianna is in a state to do that. To talk to multiple families," Tabitha says.

She and Brianna have been texting, and the poor girl seems so labile. Excited one moment and despairing the next. Tabitha doesn't know what to do with her.

"It just seems so unfair," Elizabeth says.

"I understand," Tabitha says, "but what else are we supposed to do?" The others nod, bending their heads over their packets like it is college and they are studying together for someone else's final exam.

17

GINGER

"NOBODY'S ANSWERING THEIR phones," Sunny, the family's social worker, never says hello. She simply begins the conversation halfway through. Ginger has ceased to find this habit startling, but she still takes a moment to orient herself before replying.

"John and Perry are golfing, and everyone else went for a walk around the lake at Maroon Bells. Perhaps they don't have cell service," Ginger says. "Or Tabitha decided they should leave their phones in the car."

"Ha, that sounds like Tabby," Sunny says. She is the only one who calls Tabitha "Tabby," and whenever she does, Tabitha smiles in a politely pained way, but never says anything. They all live in a strange fear of Sunny, who gives the initial impression of being casually unprofessional, but can turn smart and sharp whenever she spots weakness, a shark smelling blood in the water. The parents' anxieties in her presence exist likely because their relationships with Sunny were formed in the cooperative yet adversarial process of home studies, of being evaluated for parental fitness. Ginger had never thought of herself as a person with secrets, but after each session in which Sunny rummaged around in her emotions and past, she felt exhausted and shaken. Then came the actual home evaluation, where Sunny led Ginger through her own apartment with a clipboard, ticking off all the hazards Ginger had never noticed. How had she been so foolish as to live without a fire extinguisher, an escape ladder, with blind cords just dangling within reach? Ginger considers herself a competent person, but that process exposed so many ways in which she fell short, and she still feels off-kilter in Sunny's presence, as though some other failing is always threatening to be exposed.

Sunny crunches into something on the other end of the line. She is even smaller than Tabitha, but is constantly eating lab-created artificial cheese snack foods: Takis, or Doritos, or Cheetos. There were orange thumbprints all over Phoebe's adoption paperwork.

At first, Ginger was startled by Sunny's casual approach to everything. It made it seem as though she didn't take her job seriously. After a time, however, Ginger recognized that Sunny's affect was mostly the result of professional fatigue, that though this was the first time she and Perry and Tabitha were all going through this process, to Sunny it was routine. And they were, Sunny constantly told them, an easy case, which made Ginger wonder what qualified as hard.

"How come you're not with them?" Sunny asks around the mouthful of whatever she is eating.

"I sprained my ankle," Ginger says. "I'm excused from all activities."

"Oh, right. Tabby did mention that. Bummer," Sunny says, though she sounds perfectly cheerful when she does.

Ginger is similarly undecided about whether her injury is a blessing or a curse. She greatly appreciates being excluded from most of the family expeditions, and at the same time finds herself at loose ends when they are gone and relieved when they return.

"Anyhoo, I actually wanted to talk to you in particular, so it's great I have you all to myself." Sunny laughs and crunches into her snack again.

"Me? Why is that?" Ginger tries to ask this politely, but feelings of cautious inadequacy rise again. There is no reason for her anxiety; the adoption is final, Phoebe is thriving, and the only reason Sunny is still part of their orbit has to do with Violet and now this other child, not because of Phoebe and the twins. But Sunny has not called Ginger directly since Phoebe's adoption was finalized.

"You're the only one I can count on to tell me the truth," Sunny says, and laughs again, as if she is kidding, though she likely is not. Truth is subjective, and in this family even more so. Tabitha is so optimistic she often sidesteps reality entirely, and Elizabeth vacillates between caginess and exhaustion. It falls to Ginger to be the voice of reason.

"What about?" Ginger asks.

"I'm just hoping to get the real scoop on what's going on. Brianna and Tabby both seem to think Elizabeth and John are going to adopt this kid, but Elizabeth said she told them no way. And I'm like, I can't help you if you aren't giving it to me straight, you know? One second Tabby is asking for parent profiles, and the next she's like, 'But not too many because Elizabeth is adopting.'"

"Right," Ginger says. "I can see how that is a problem."

"So give it to me straight, can you?"

"I can tell you all I know, which is that Elizabeth seems quite set against adopting again."

"Mm-hmm," Sunny says, either because she is chewing or because she is actively listening.

"And I believe Tabitha and Brianna are both hoping she will change her mind."

"Why is that?"

"Well, it would be easier, for one. Practically, but also emotionally. The level of disruption of simply having to find new parents, let alone incorporate them into the family. It's quite a lot. The children will have so much to manage already just with the baby."

As she speaks, Ginger wonders if she is as objective a source as Sunny believes her to be. She can feel herself tilting toward Tabitha's side as she talks. It is an eminently reasonable point of view, and terribly frustrating that Elizabeth has set herself so firmly against this. The irony of Ginger's injury is that being forced to the sidelines has given her even more time than usual to observe and consider everyone else's interactions. She tries to take people at face value, but she suspects that there is something more to Elizabeth and John's reluctance to adopt again than simply the loss of his job. Not that there is anything simple about that.

Perhaps they are getting a divorce? Ginger practically blanches at the thought. How have they never considered this eventuality? What would that do to the family? Every time she thinks this cannot get any more out of control, another worst-case scenario comes into play.

"Mm-hmm," Sunny says again. "Have you told the kids?"

Ginger pulls herself back to the conversation. "Not yet. We felt it would be more appropriate to tell them when we had more information."

"You worried about Phoebe?" Sunny asks, though it sounds more like a statement than a question.

"A little. She's already starting middle school, and the whole situation with Violet was quite upsetting for her. To have to go through another change in the family with a new baby when there is already so much else going on wouldn't be my preference, certainly." Pressing her fingers against her forehead, she forces herself to take a deep breath. She is becoming so emotional lately. It's this environment; it's all the pressures at once, making her feel not like herself.

"Yeah, Tabby told me about the whole moving thing, too."

"But we haven't decided about moving!" Ginger cries.

"Uh-huh," Sunny says, as if Ginger is an unreliable source on this topic.

For heaven's sake, does Ginger get to control nothing about her own life now?

"So does that mean you're not sending Phoebe to the charter school?"

The NSA, Ginger thinks, has nothing on Sunny. "I'm sorry, what does this have to do with the adoption?"

"Mmm, maybe nothing," Sunny says, sounding now like a detective in a cozy mystery who is simply nosing around the quiet port town that has been the inexplicable site of a dozen murders. "I'm just trying to get a sense of what's going on with you guys so I know what we're dealing with here. Normally it wouldn't matter, but you all are a special situation."

Ginger presses her lips together in a firm line. They have always been a special situation. She is tired of being a special situation, especially when it results in her boundaries being tested again and again.

"I'm not sure how it's relevant, but yes, Phoebe very much wants to attend The Global Academy next year, and I am working to make that feasible on our end."

"Why did you let her apply if you're not sure it's feasible?" Sunny asks, as if she is only idly wondering. She crunches a handful of snack food again, and Ginger finds the sound infuriating.

"I thought it would be a good exercise for her, managing the process of an application like this one. And TGA is an excellent school."

"So how come you're not sending her?"

"Well, she is going. We just need to make some arrangements first," Ginger finds herself saying. She has not committed to this aloud yet, but as she does, she realizes it is true. Phoebe will go. She just needs to figure out how to accomplish that without overturning their entire lives. "She'd be changing schools anyway," Sunny says, still in that infuriating musing tone.

"I'm aware," Ginger says, still prickly.

"And I can see how it could be an advantage to the kids

to all be closer together physically. Especially if you're so worried about how the shift in dynamic will affect Phoebe. It might be nice for her to have a good solid anchor of family around her."

Anchor, Ginger thinks. *What an apt metaphor. Something that weighs you down.*

"I said she was going to TGA, not that we were moving," Ginger says.

"Oh, sure," Sunny says, but Ginger has the feeling she isn't listening. "So where did you guys leave it with the potential-parent problem?" she asks, and then laughs to herself, as if pleased by her alliteration.

Ginger has to force herself to refocus, to stop the argument she is having with the other mothers in her head, with Tabitha about real estate, with Elizabeth about her nudging on Phoebe's school, as if it is her decision, as if she knows Ginger's child better than Ginger herself. She will do it. For heaven's sake, she will do it! She just needs time.

"The parents. Yes. We agreed to call some of the families that we thought might be good matches," Ginger says. They had agreed they would each call one family. The idea had been to relieve Tabitha of some of the work, or perhaps to interfere with Tabitha's steamrolling the process – she can hardly recall now. But the intent makes no impact on the fact that talking to a stranger sounds dreadful. The couple Ginger is scheduled to call do so much volunteer work she can't imagine how they would have time to have a child, let alone join this family with all its responsibilities.

"Okay, cool," Sunny says. "I'm keeping in touch with Brianna, so let me know what you come up with. Do you guys want me to be on the phone when you talk to the kids?"

"I hadn't thought about it, really. I think we can do it." This was, after all, not their first rodeo. "Should we have Brianna call in, though?"

"I'll ask. I don't think she'll be up to it, though. She's going through some things. So when are you going to talk to them?"

"I'm not sure. We were thinking maybe when we know who the prospective parents are?"

"Mm-hmm," Sunny says. That sound is beginning to drive Ginger mad. "You should do it soon. They'll be pissed if you keep something like this from them for too long."

Ginger is struck by two things about that sentence. The first is that Sunny is right. The children will be upset if they are left out of the loop for too long. The second is that this is yet another hill to climb, another source of tension and stress on this already quite tense and stressful trip. The previous year, when Brianna had told them she was pregnant, when she and Justin were still planning to parent Violet, Phoebe in particular had been quite upset. Why would Brianna parent this baby when she hadn't parented them? Justin's abrupt departure and Brianna's decision to look for an adoptive family had been reassuring to Phoebe, restoring stasis to her world, even as it threw the rest of them into chaos.

"Okay," Ginger says, more to end the conversation than to actually acquiesce. She isn't the one who makes decisions about when or how things are done in this family, which Sunny knows. So whenever the conversation with the children is going to happen, it will not be on her calendar. Though perhaps she should speak with Phoebe first. Alone. The twins are adaptable, and Violet is too young to understand the seismic changes coming their way. Phoebe should know first. Except if Phoebe knows, she is likely to want to tell the twins immediately, and that would infuriate Tabitha. Ginger presses her fingers to her forehead again.

"Cool. Thanks for the intel," Sunny says, though Ginger isn't sure what "intel" Sunny has gathered. She is all at sixes and sevens and can hardly remember what she said.

"Okay," Ginger says again, because it seems odd to say, *You're welcome.*

She thinks Sunny says, "Talk to you later," but it is hard to discern underneath the deafening crunch of more cheese-flavored snack foods. Then the phone beeps at her to let her know the call is over.

Ginger feels as if she has been played, but in what way precisely she has no idea. It occurs to her for the first time that perhaps in addition to ennui, Sunny's lackadaisical attitude may be an act, a performance designed to break down people's guards. In which case, brava, Ginger supposes, though she wishes she knew exactly what she was supposed to do now.

Ginger takes great satisfaction in her professional work, in taking a complex task and breaking it down into defined steps. She and Tabitha are alike in this way, she supposes, though Tabitha applies the concept of organization to life and people, while Ginger prefers to apply it only to the technical documentation she produces. Trying to think through their circumstances now with a more analytical mind only knots her up further. Phoebe's new school. Phoebe's moving into middle school. Moving to be closer to TGA. Brianna and the adoption. This couple she is going to call and all the people they have discussed, all of the personal details of their lives that now exist, unfairly, in Ginger's mind. Elizabeth and John's darkness. Tabitha's sharp fingers clutching at Phoebe's after-school time and Ginger's independence. There is no structure or sequence that can be applied to make sense of these things, to break them down into their independent parts and guide her through them.

This relationship is more like a marriage than a family, and a marriage of convenience at that. Each party entered into the arrangement not entirely of their own free will, with differing expectations and no contract on emotions. And like in a long marriage, they are wearing on each other, water on stone, the form they will take unknown.

18

ELIZABETH

WHEN ELIZABETH WAKES up, she can tell everyone else is already downstairs. She smells coffee and something sweet and breadlike, and her stomach growls. There is light coming around the edges of the curtains, which means it is later than Violet ever lets her sleep. Elizabeth has a vague recollection of punching John earlier in the morning when Violet woke up before passing out again, so he must have taken her. For once.

She is even more tired than usual, her body aching and her eyes heavy. The day before, while Perry and John spent the day golfing and Ginger lounged by the pool, Tabitha and Elizabeth had taken the children on a hike. Great views, but Tabitha and the twins had practically sprinted up the mountain, Phoebe and Elizabeth (with Violet in a backpack, and holy crap that kid must weigh fifty pounds) dragging behind. By the end, Elizabeth swore she was never moving again, and passed out, smelly and exhausted, before John and Perry even got home.

She rolls over to try to curl back into sleep, only to find John is still sleeping beside her. Sitting up bolt upright, she looks in Violet's crib, but she is gone, too, and she punches John again. "Where is the baby?" she asks.

"Tabitha," John mumbles, his face buried in his pillow.

"What?" she asks.

"Tabitha came when she woke up. So I gave Violet to her." He says all this without opening his eyes or moving his head, so he speaks half into the pillow.

"You couldn't get up with your own kid?" Elizabeth asks meanly. She had harbored the tiniest splinter of hope that she might get some rest this vacation, that she might feel better, happier, be a better mother, a better person. But no. Her creeping dread had been right. She feels meaner, sadder, more worried. Every time Tabitha slowed her sprint up the mountain the day before long enough for Elizabeth to keep up, she'd felt a momentary panic, fearing Tabitha was looking for a chance to insert some opinion, some passive-aggressive comment about the terrible lives of only children, or keeping their family special. The baby is hovering there like a threat, the sword that will break open her secrets.

Is it so terrible that she might want those secrets to come out? To have it all out in the open for once, for fuck's sake, so she doesn't have to do all this pretending, all this lying? Lying about why they aren't taking Violet to baby music class (it's too expensive, but Elizabeth told Tabitha it was because the schedule changed). Pretending to be happy, so happy, so fucking delighted to sing "The Wheels on the Bus" yet again and clean Violet up for the fiftieth time after she covers her face in beet puree, to do this endless repetitive slog of parenting that she had thought she would like so much.

God, at least if everyone knew, she could stop faking it.

John shifts up on his elbows and lifts his head so he can look at her with sleepy accusation. "Wait, you're mad I let Tabitha take care of Violet? Are you objecting to actually getting some sleep?"

He is right, and she doesn't have the energy to make up another reason to argue, so she collapses back into the bed.

The surge of adrenaline that caused her to start awake is no match for her guilt. Of course Tabitha is taking care of Violet, and probably doing a better job of it than Elizabeth ever could. By the time she makes it downstairs, Violet will no doubt be speaking fluent French and trying out for the Olympics in synchronized swimming.

She closes her eyes again. She won't be able to fall back to sleep – that skill disappeared as soon as Violet was born – but she drifts there for a moment, trying to summon up the energy to face the day.

She feels John shifting next to her, and then he says, "I want to talk to you about something, but you have to promise not to get mad."

Opening one eye, she looks over at him. "Why are you assuming I'm going to get mad?"

"I'm just saying hear me out."

"Fine, I'm listening," Elizabeth says, though she has to force her eyes open as she rolls over to face him. She's like one of those cartoon characters who is so sleepy they need to hold their eyes open with toothpicks.

"Perry offered me a job," John says.

"Wait, what? When?"

"Yesterday. When we were golfing."

Despite her best intentions, Elizabeth's first instinct is, indeed, to get mad. So that's why Tabitha dragged her on that hike. So Perry could bribe John with a job. She takes a breath in through her nose and lets her eyes close and then open again.

"See, I knew you were going to get mad," John says. He reaches up and rubs his face, the stubble on his cheeks making a pleasantly scratchy sound. He is blond, but the thickness of his beard always surprises her when she looks at it in the light. They haven't been in bed together like this, just the two of them, lazy in the morning, the air smelling of warm sheets and their dirty hair, in ages.

"I'm not mad. I didn't even say anything. I'm a little

surprised, but I'm not mad. Tell me more." She is mad, but she is not going to give him the satisfaction of admitting it.

"It would just be a temporary thing. They had some overlaps with clients, and they need someone to manage a few projects. He said about six months."

"Project management? Does he know you don't have any experience?" Elizabeth asks, and then backtracks. "Not that you can't do it. I'm just surprised."

"He does. We talked a lot about it yesterday. About what I did at my last job. He said he thinks enough of my skills would transfer, and that I could learn the rest. He thinks I'd be good at it."

Elizabeth looks at her husband, the hopeful expression on his face. She knows he idolizes Perry. Hell, she does, too. Perry is like Tabitha: everything he does is perfect, everything he does seems easy, but unlike with Tabitha, his perfection isn't obnoxious. It's just... perfect. John's father died when he was in college, so Perry is something like a father figure to him. Perry's compliments, his praise, mean something to John she will never entirely be able to understand.

"The other thing is, I've been thinking they were right to lay me off."

"What does that mean?" she asks, startled.

John looks a little sheepish. "I don't know. I don't think I was very good at sales. I'm not aggressive like they are, the really successful ones. I didn't like it when I had to follow up with someone a million times, or badger them into trying to make a sale. Like I figure that when I want something, I get it, and if you push me about it, I get annoyed. But Brian and the other guys said that isn't how sales works. It was starting to really drag me down."

With a shock of guilt, Elizabeth tries to look back over the last year. So much of it is a blur, but she remembers John often fell asleep on the couch, or didn't feel like talking when he came home from work. Sometimes, at the end of the day, he was short-fused, or after Violet went to bed he stared at the television, not watching whatever was on, really, just staring at it. She's been so focused on Violet – and her own misery, if she's being honest – that she didn't realize something was wrong, or anything more than the exhaustion they were both fighting. So often she has been angry with him for not doing as much as she does with Violet, but maybe what she had seen as laziness had been sadness.

"I never knew you didn't like your job," she says. It wasn't what he had wanted to do when they met, but who in this world ends up where they thought they would be? And John is so upbeat and good-natured, she'd always assumed that meant he was happy.

"That's the thing. I don't think I realized how much I didn't like it until they laid me off. I've been worried, but it's also been like ever since I got that call, I've had this huge sense of *relief*. I feel ten pounds lighter. In this job, I'll be working with people and helping things get done but not having to ask for a sale. That suits me better, you know?"

"Sure," Elizabeth says carefully. She does think, actually, he would be great at a role where he is thinking about how to make things happen. He's gifted in motivating people, good at helping people feel good. His baseball team in college had never been champions until he became captain. Same coach, same players, but John was so great at making them feel like a team, making their practices a place where everyone felt like they could achieve what they wanted to, that all of a sudden they couldn't stop winning. But like the person she used to be, funny and sharp and energetic, that John, the leader, the motivator, has disappeared, buried under too much disappointment and the granular daily struggles of parenting.

She should want this for him. She knows she should. But come on. Working for Perry? Why not just give up total control of their lives to Tabitha?

"You don't think I should do it," John says, seeing the way she is hesitating.

"No," Elizabeth says slowly. "It's not that. I mean, not

completely. I do think you'd be great. I want you to be happy. But I don't know. I don't like the idea of us being indebted to them. We're already so tangled up together."

"I'd rather be indebted to Perry than my uncle, to tell you the truth," John says. He pushes his hand through his hair, scratches his head. It is wild and a little scruffy, in need of a haircut, not that they have the money for that now. "With Perry, I trust that it will be just business, and with my uncle and my mom, things are likely to get sticky. Besides, this is only for six months, and then I can have something else to put on my résumé. He says I can even study for the project management certification while I'm working there, and that'll make it easier to get a job after."

Is this what they have been reduced to? Either his uncle or Perry? It's a catch-22. It feels too close, too hot. If Tabitha thought she could control Elizabeth before, wait until John is working for Perry. She doesn't want to sound like she's questioning him, and of course she doesn't want him to go back to something that makes him unhappy. But also, she doesn't want to be under Tabitha's thumb any more than they already are. It reminds her of her own family, of being told what to do and then being told how everything she did was wrong.

"Can't you look for something else? I mean, are you going to?" she asks.

"I can keep looking. But it would probably be in sales again. And it probably wouldn't be a very good job because I don't have a great track record now. The only reason Perry offered me something totally different is because he knows me. I have a good feeling about this." He rolls onto his back and looks up at the ceiling, his chin again. "Do you remember what it was like when we met Tabitha and Perry? When they first told us about Violet? How it felt like it was meant to be? Like this opportunity had been laid in front of us and it would have been crazy to turn it down? That's what this feels like. It feels like I would be crazy to turn it down."

"But Perry and Tabitha—" Elizabeth starts to say, but John does something she can't remember him ever doing before. He interrupts her. Sitting up, he pushes the sheets off his body and turns to her. They haven't looked at each other, really *looked* at each other, for so long. He looks old. Not old like Perry and Tabitha and Ginger old, but like a man, a grown-up, not the boy he was when they met in college and she thought they were so mature. They hadn't known anything at all then, and now they know too much.

"Elizabeth, listen. Perry and Tabitha are good people. I know your family wasn't great to you, but you cannot keep lugging that baggage into this one, assuming everyone here is out to get you. This is what family can do if you let it. It can help you. We can help each other. But we have got to trust each other. You've got to let go of whatever weirdness you're holding against Tabitha and whatever you're so mad about and let things get better."

When he stops talking, she doesn't know what to say. He doesn't understand. It's different for men. John doesn't understand the way mothers can be judged, the way she feels so small when Tabitha recommends doctors or educational toys and sign language classes, telling her how much the twins loved them, or buys Violet clothes like Elizabeth can't even dress her right.

"I don't know. I just don't know if I can handle her."

"Maybe that's the problem. Maybe Tabitha isn't something we should be trying to 'handle.'" He makes little air quotes with his fingers. "She's not a bomb we're trying to defuse. She's just a person who tries really hard to be nice."

"You always do that. You always make excuses for people. It's okay to say people are behaving badly when they are. She's a control freak. That's not niceness."

"Isn't it?" John asks.

Elizabeth says nothing.

"I don't think," he says slowly, "that Tabitha wakes up and goes, 'How can I control Elizabeth today?' I don't even think she wakes up and is like, 'Elizabeth is doing a terrible job and I must correct her.' She really is genuinely trying to help. It's just that's bumping up against all your feelings about not being good enough."

John's patience and thoughtfulness didn't just help take his baseball team to championships. It has sustained Elizabeth through some hard fucking times, when everything went wrong, when the nurses or doctors were impassive or confusing or downright incompetent, or the kids and (more often) the parents at work were driving her nuts. But sometimes it would be nice if he would get mad right along with her.

"It's like my sisters," he continues when she doesn't say anything. "They really don't know they're being hurtful when they say how easy it is for them to get pregnant, or whatever. But you can let people know when they're crossing boundaries without exploding at them. And you do that by remembering that people have good intentions."

Elizabeth tries to imagine this, tries to imagine John going to work at Perry's office, a hip industrial space in RiNo with views of the city and the mountains both, the office buzzing with creativity, voices bouncing off concrete floors. Tries to imagine the space it will take up having this family in their lives even more.

Then she tries to imagine the alternative: moving to Russell; quitting the job where she is set at long last to become team leader, to teach in Russell. John working for his uncle, that family's pressure on them instead. Something clutches at her heart, a feeling that something is being taken away, but not from her. From Violet. That her daughter will not sit in Phoebe's lap at Sunday dinner, Phoebe patiently letting Violet chew on her hair. That the weekly photos Tabitha takes of the kids, a way Elizabeth has learned to mark time, watching the tiny changes in all of them, would become more spaced out, months apart and then once a year, time accelerating out of control until Violet is Phoebe's age, her baby fat gone, leaving long, coltish legs and a shy hunch to her shoulders.

"How much does it pay? The job with Perry?" she asks, and when John tells her, she blinks. More than he would have made at the sales job, even if he earned out his full commission. Money they can use to pay down their debt, finally be able to breathe a little, let her stop hating herself for all her failures every time she watches a futile minimum payment whisk out of their anemic bank account, all interest, all past, no movement toward their future.

But the strings attached.

"What do you think?" John asks, and he looks at her hopefully.

FOR GOOD

It would make it so much easier if we didn't want a child. It's ridiculous to even think about bringing a child into the world – you're both setting them up for a dangerous future, a world where they literally will not be able to breathe, and making that future even more likely by adding another burden to the planet.

But I always wanted to be a father. I love babies when they are all sleepy and snuggly and coo and gurgle. But I also love toddlers and preschoolers and elementary-age kids when they're curious and determined to figure themselves out, and tweens and middle schoolers when they're both so needy and so independent, and teenagers when they think they know everything.

Allison and I met in college, volunteering for Habitat for Humanity over spring break. Community service is important to both of us. We serve meals and distribute supplies for folks experiencing homelessness downtown. She helps collect donations for Pine Ridge Reservation, and I've been a Big Brother for five years. We started a garden at our synagogue's school. With the little ones, we talk about planting seeds and how those tiny seeds become the plants that feed us all. They each get a tomato plant and a squash plant, and they are in charge of watering them and are so proud when they grow. With the bigger ones, we talk about different kinds of soil and how plants are hybridized and what GMO means. Often the older kids still want their own plants, so I give them a whole row. Everyone needs something to take care of.

We know the earth is too crowded, but we both come from big families, and always planned for a big family. But when Allison got sick, the only thing I cared about was keeping her safe. We could have delayed treatment so she could freeze her eggs, but the cancer was pretty advanced, and I said we could always adopt, but there was only one her.

It makes more sense for us anyway, doesn't it? We are so committed to making the world a better place, and isn't adopting a way to do that? There are so many children who need a loving home. If we adopt, we're not adding to the population. And we can raise them to be the type of people who care, who spend their time working to make our community better, who understand the value of taking care of each other.

19

TABITHA

TABITHA LOVES THE children's room in this house, despite its nearly deadly level of preciousness. It is designed to feel like being inside the crown of a tree, the corners rounded into a circle, tree limbs in basrelief spreading over the walls, six bunk beds nestled in between so when the children are sleeping they look like little woodland creatures curled up amid the leaves. The ceiling is domed, and hidden lights around the edges shine bright sunlight during the day but at night transform into a starry sky spread with constellations and a bright swath of the Milky Way. When she'd seen the house listed in the silent auction photos, it had been the picture of this room that had made her leap to outbid everyone else. The entire house is gorgeous, truly, wood and glass that make it look as if it has grown here instead of being built, but this room is something more than that.

Maybe she loves it so much because it manifests the precious magic of childhood she had only experienced in books and art but tries so hard to bring into Tate and Taylor's daily lives: adventure and wonder and whimsy. The children adore the room, started clamoring for something like it at home the moment they saw it. They are constantly swinging across the bunk beds and the ladders, hiding behind the tree limbs, and generally acting like they live in *Peter Pan*.

But when she walks in to shoo the children into bed that evening, she finds all three sitting on the floor with their bedding around them, playing cards. "What are you doing?" she asks, surprised.

"We're having a slumber party," Tate says.

"Oh?" Tabitha tries to sound casual, but the coincidence is odd. She hasn't talked to Tate about Serafina's party yet, has hardly had a moment to mention it to Perry, too busy taking care of Ginger and talking about the baby and finding prospective parents and keeping everyone fed. This vacation, which ought to have been so perfect, is feeling like a tremendous amount of work, like she is dragging the family around all by herself, the same way she had to practically drag Elizabeth up the smallest hills on their hike the day before. Perry had taken John out to offer him a job, and he reported John was excited, but that he had to talk to Elizabeth. Tabitha is attempting to remain sanguine.

"Tate's going to a slumber party, so we're practicing," Phoebe explains.

"Guys," Taylor moans. He is wearing sunglasses and holding his cards so close to his face he looks like a nearsighted poker champion. "Stop taking forever."

"Whose slumber party are you going to, Taters?" Tabitha asks in the same casual tone, though it is hard to get it out of her throat, which feels slightly constricted. Who told them? She knows Serafina has a phone, but she and Perry have not set up messaging on the twins' tablets, and Tate hasn't talked to any of her friends on the phone since they arrived.

"Serafina's," Tate says, too busy to look at her mother as she plays one card and draws another. "There, it's four now," she says to Taylor, who peers even more closely at his cards. Does he need glasses? Is that why he's wearing his sunglasses? She'll have to ask the pediatrician for a referral when they get back. "Didn't you see the invitation?" Tate turns to Tabitha. "It has unicorns."

"Oh, I saw it," Tabitha says. "It has unicorns and glitter." How had Tate seen it? She must have found it in the kitchen. That child can sense glitter and unicorns calling her from thirty paces. Dammit. Dammit, dammit, dammit.

"And it was purple with my name on it!" Tate adds cheerfully, and goes back to playing.

"So what are you practicing? For the slumber party?" Tabitha tries to sound casual. She needs to approach this with Tate directly, she knows, but first she has to come up with a plan to make sure Tate can make it through the night without an accident. She wonders if they can get on a cancellation list for the last doctor they'd gone to see before Tate went on strike regarding any further treatment.

"Mom, stop, you are making them take too long," Taylor whines, but Tabitha kneels down anyway. She sees now they have taken the duvets from their beds and folded them in half like sleeping bags, pillows at one end. She thinks of Kara with her comforter and ribbons and slumber party invitation, and there is a lurch in her chest. This will be fine. It will be fine. She saw an ad about some new pajamas for children with nighttime issues. Maybe they won't look too awful for Tate to wear.

"I'm sorry, sweetie," she says. "But it's time to get ready for bed anyway. Maybe you can all finish playing in the morning?"

Taylor throws down his cards in disgust to let her know what he thinks of this rotten idea. Normally Tabitha would ask him to pick them up, but her mind is spinning, trying to figure out how to manage Tate's expectations and the reality of her bodily issues, so she starts to tidy up after him without thinking. Taylor drags his pillow and duvet back over to the wall and climbs the ladder in the tree trunk to the highest bunk, where he nests himself inside the bedding and produces his muchloved, much-battered copy of *Charlotte's Web*, settling in to read it for what must be the twentieth time. Tabitha harbors strong suspicions Taylor is going to ask to move to a farm for their next birthday.

Phoebe looks at Tabitha with a certain tween disdain. "It's a slumber party, Aunt Tabitha. We're not going to sleep for *ho-urs*." She stretches this word out, long as saltwater taffy.

"Oh, right." Tabitha does know at least that about slumber parties. "Well. At this slumber party we're having right now, you're going to bed at bedtime."

"We're practicing!" Tate says again.

"Which is a fine idea," Tabitha says. "But right now it is time to go to bed."

"Can we still practice?" Phoebe asks.

"If practicing means sleeping on the floor, be my guest. If practicing means staying up until two o'clock in the morning and not brushing your teeth, then no."

"Okay, okay," Phoebe and Tate grumble, and then hop up and chase each other into the bathroom.

"Don't forget to empty your bladder!" Tabitha calls.

Tabitha climbs up and kisses Taylor good night and does the same when the girls return, minty and giggling. Turning the lights to the night stars setting, she picks up the rest of the cards and closes the door almost all the way so she can still hear them if they don't go to sleep.

She has stopped in her own room for a moment, catching herself biting her fingernails, a bad habit she hasn't indulged in since middle school, when her phone rings. It's Pamela, which forces her to stifle laughter she fears would be hysterical. Pamela Preston and her ridiculous glitter bomb of a slumber party invitation are the reason she is biting her nails right now.

Tabitha hesitates, finger hovering over the button to answer. She hasn't RSVP'd, but surely Pamela wouldn't call herself to find out about that, would she? She has a house manager to take care of the quotidian duties of reality.

Still, Tabitha answers slowly, staring at the phone as she

lifts it to her ear, taking so long Pamela is already saying, "Hello? Hello?" by the time she presses it to her ear.

"Pamela, what a lovely surprise!" Tabitha says. She isn't sure it is lovely, but she will fake it.

There is a click and crackle as Pamela starts talking at the same time as the connection fades out. "...aren't you on vacation?" Her voice snaps back into clarity.

"We are. We're in Aspen. It's so lovely up here during the summer," Tabitha says.

"It used to be. Now it's too hot for our taste, and too crowded," Pamela says. There is a tone of pity in her voice that makes Tabitha's nostrils flare in irritation.

"Maybe in less exclusive areas," Tabitha says airily, as though they haven't encountered a living soul the entire time they've been here and she couldn't possibly know what Pamela is talking about. "We're staying in a private home on Red Mountain."

Pamela ignores this. "Not that we're any better – we're actually in the Hamptons! Can you imagine? It's so two decades ago, though you'd never know it by all the people who still think it's the place to be."

"The Hamptons?" Tabitha looks at her watch. "But it must be almost midnight there!"

"It is, but who has time to get anything done during the day? I'm absolutely run off my feet! We were on the Cape at first and it was even more crowded, if you can believe that. I told Tom next summer we're going to a new island – Eroda. I saw some photos online and it looks gorgeous, and no one has ever heard of it. It will be so lovely to get some peace!"

Tabitha can't imagine Pamela Preston genuinely wanting to be somewhere isolated, unless it is the isolation purchased by renting a private yacht she can post selfies from. If no one is around to admire her, does she even exist?

She is startled by her own meanness. She only says, "I'm sure."

"Serafina is thrilled Tate is coming to her party. Those two

184

are peas in a pod, I swear. We should get them together for another playdate before school, though heaven knows when, I don't even know why they call it vacation, we're so busy. You're smart to only have two. With four, it's a nightmare! Thorpe is at Yale for another week, and then he's going to the program in Barcelona, so we have to get him packed before that, and Amandine is still at UCLA's summer film program, so I have to fly out and collect her next week." She says all these things in a rush, and Tabitha struggles to catch up. Since when are Tate and Serafina two peas in a pod? And "another" playdate? Tate has not been invited to a playdate with Serafina before.

"Listen, I'm calling because Kitty Calder is building that house on the beach in Rhode Island, you know, and it's absolutely cannibalizing her time."

Tabitha's heart lifts for a moment. Pamela is head of the committee that puts on Country Day's fundraising Gala every spring, and Kitty Calder is one of the members. Tabitha had asked about joining the committee in a brief conversation in the lobby of the auditorium before the Primary talent show. Membership on that committee would put her alongside all the mothers who matter; would help her make sure she – well, Tate, she means – is on solid social footing. Is Pamela possibly calling to ask her to take Kitty's place?

But what comes next is not an invitation to join the committee but a question. "Anyway, I have no idea why she wants to build a house there, out in the middle of nowhere, but she is heading up our digital efforts and I thought I remembered Perry owns a website company?"

"A digital design and marketing agency, yes. They do websites as part of branding," Tabitha says, her heart slipping back into place, a growing feeling of disappointed dread. She remembers this from when she worked in New York, how people would find out what she did and promptly ask for something: a tip on wedding planning, or a name-drop that could get them a discount or an appointment with the best caterer, an invitation to a private winter party at the Morgan.

"Right. So we were hoping you would be able to donate some hours for the Gala – in exchange for prominent placement in the program, of course. The website is in a shambles. I don't even know what Kitty has done with it, plus the online bidding and the program design, oh, goodness, they all need to be redone. So immediately I thought of you and Perry!"

"I— I would have to ask him," Tabitha says, her surprise making her fumble. Pamela was calling her to ask a favor from Perry? Or, not asking. Pamela didn't ask. Pamela assumed. Pamela wouldn't think twice about calling someone in the middle of the night to ask for something she needed. "Did you— were you looking for someone to step in for Kitty?"

"Oh, no. She's not leaving, just needs a little hand. I know you had that little party-planning business, but we're just full up. So if you could chat with Perry, or just give him Kitty's number, she can explain what needs to be done. Yes, that would be better – he can call her directly."

Tabitha is so floored she cannot even speak, but Pamela doesn't need her to. She's still talking, telling Tabitha all the amazing things her children are doing and how busy that keeps her.

Pamela is offering her so many things to be upset about she can't even decide where to begin. Her "little party-planning business"? She did the Javits Center! The Plaza! She consulted for Selldorf and Marino! And Perry doesn't own a "website company." For goodness' sake. She is going to have to press him to press some of the graphic designers and web developers to do some work for the Gala, which is ethically questionable at best, and especially problematic because the company is so busy these days they don't even have a moment to hire more people to help them alleviate the workload, which is the only reason Perry could offer John a job.

"Oh, and the house manager needs your RSVP so she can order Tate's nightgown," Pamela says, this new information cutting through the chatter and Tabitha's rising emotions.

"What nightgown?" Tabitha asks.

Pamela makes a noise of frustration, as though she has already explained this to Tabitha a dozen times even though she has not done so even once. "The party nightgowns. They have to match for the photos. Oh, they are darling. Wait until you see them."

Tabitha does not remember seeing nightgowns mentioned in the invitation. Which is a problem. Because all of her ideas on ways in which Tate could potentially attend this party hinge on her ability to control what Tate wears, and to have multiple versions of it, in case she has an accident. A required piece of clothing – for a party, for goodness' sake, purchased from heaven knows where – will derail this.

Dammit.

She sits there, staring at a blank page on her planner, even though she has at least two things to add to her to-do list: talking to Perry and emailing Pamela's house manager to order Tate's matching fucking nightgown.

She blinks at her own profanity. She is turning into Elizabeth.

Pamela doesn't want her on the Gala committee. She doesn't even remember Tabitha's asking about it! This is why they left her out of the Halloween parade sign-up, even though Asher's mom said she made a typo in the email address, which is ridiculous, because her email address is only her name and how hard is that? Tabitha knows it isn't true. They just didn't want her. Nothing she does is good enough; nothing is right. Now she is going to ruin Tate's chances, too, hasn't been able to fix Tate's issues because she didn't try hard enough, and now her failure as a mother is going to be revealed and Tate will be haunted by it for the rest of her life.

20

GINGER

IT'S NOT THAT Ginger hasn't thought about what Sunny said. She was going to call TGA. She really was. But before she can, they call her. It is the worst possible moment, really. Perry and Tabitha are both sitting at the table with her. Tabitha has been in a strange mood all day, snappish and sharp, and Ginger doesn't want her to overhear the conversation because she will only start pushing about moving again. But there is nowhere for her to go to talk privately without a great deal of fuss and assistance. She is doing better on the crutches now that her wrist is healing, but she still cannot move easily.

"I'm calling because we haven't heard from you about Phoebe's enrollment." They had met Dr. Jemison, the Dean of Students at TGA, at the open house. She looked as if she were five minutes out of college yet was unshakably confident and competent. Phoebe fell in love with her the instant they met. Ginger found her intimidating.

"Do you – could I call you back a little later?" Ginger asks. Her voice is both hopeful and pleading, almost squeaking at the end.

"Unfortunately, today is the deadline. There are other people waiting for Phoebe's spot, and it's not fair to them to delay, is it?" Dr. Jemison asks.

"No," she says, feeling chastened. *I was going to call*, she wants to say. Really, she was.

"So will Phoebe be joining us?" Dr. Jemison asks, with exaggerated patience. Ginger notes the way she has constructed this question, pointing out how tardy their decision is, how they have subjected other families to the pain of waiting, that they are talking about the school year that starts in August and that this is a ticking clock.

Ginger hesitates, looking over at Perry and Tabitha again. Perry is absorbed in his tablet, hunting and pecking on its virtual keyboard, and Tabitha is reading to Violet, stopping her from gnawing the edge of the board book for a moment when she turns the page. But Ginger knows Tabitha is always listening.

If only she could explain to Dr. Jemison how complicated things have gotten, that their already-delicate family is on even shakier ground, how even though Elizabeth and John are perfectly capable of adopting this baby, they are not and therefore there are going to be more people – two more people, plus the baby, which will make things even more complicated, and how will Phoebe make all these adjustments at once?

Unbidden, she hears Elizabeth's voice in her head: *Is it worth torpedoing something that might be really great for Phoebe because you're scared of change?*

Dr. Jemison will not be interested in her problems. Ginger can picture her sitting in her office, tapping a pen impatiently on the desk, waiting for Ginger to decline so she can forget Phoebe ever existed and move on to the next family, who will appreciate the opportunity that is being given to them, going to this school that was featured on NPR and produces spelling bee and science bowl and robotics champions, instead of Ginger, who apparently doesn't care at all.

"Yes," she says quietly.

"Excellent," Dr. Jemison says, though she doesn't sound particularly pleased. "I'll expect the forms in thirty minutes."

"I'll need to get a computer. We're on vacation, you see," Ginger starts to explain.

Dr. Jemison is also not interested in hearing about any potential technical difficulties. "Excellent. I'll look for them in the next half hour. We're so delighted Phoebe will be joining us. Goodbye."

Ginger hangs up and puts down the phone.

"Did you say you need a computer?" Tabitha asks, proving she had indeed been eavesdropping.

"Yes, please," Ginger says, defeated, as Tabitha is already rising to get out of her seat. For heaven's sake, if only she had paid attention when she had gotten off that idiotic horse. If only she had listened to her common sense and not gone horseback riding in the first place. She is trapped, absolutely trapped by this ridiculous injury, dependent on Tabitha, of all people, and it will only get worse when Phoebe is at TGA and they must rely on Tabitha every day.

But what is she supposed to do instead?

Ginger holds Violet while Tabitha goes to get the computer. She does not consider herself a baby person; doesn't dislike them, per se, simply prefers children when they are older, when she can have a conversation with them. But babies, including Violet, do not care about her preferences, and chews on Ginger's shirt cuff while babbling at her. Ginger stares at her. Another baby – so soon. More parents – so soon.

"Here you go," Tabitha says when she returns, exchanging the computer for Violet. The other kids are playing badminton with Elizabeth and John in the yard, and they can hear shouting, then highpitched laughter, mostly Tate's. "What are you working on?"

There is no point in dissembling; Tabitha heard the call. "It's Phoebe's school. They want her enrollment forms."

"For TGA?" Tabitha says, and she lights up, her foul mood disappearing in an instant.

"Yes," Ginger says reluctantly, and right on cue, Tabitha claps her hands together, so quickly it startles Violet, who jumps and cries and then spots a water glass on the table she tries to pull off. Tabitha foils this plot without even looking.

"Oh, this is wonderful. So you're going to move, right? Have you checked your email? My Realtor sent some ideas for places, and I sent some, too. You can look now, or when you're done with the forms. I'll call our piano teacher and the head of the soccer program – Phoebe will love them; it's mostly college students who coach and they're absolutely delightful." She is already reaching for her planner with her free hand, taking up her pen, and Dr. Jemison's deadline is *tick-tick-tick*ing in her mind.

"No, stop!" Ginger says, and this time it is her voice that startles Violet, and is apparently loud enough even to break through Perry's bubble because he looks up in time for Violet to start shrieking.

"What's wrong, Vi-vi?" he asks. "Is Aunt Tabitha being mean to you?" He takes Violet out of Tabitha's arms.

"She needs a bottle," Tabitha says.

"Then a bottle you shall have," Perry says, hoisting the baby up in the air and tilting her, which both makes her laugh and causes her to let a stream of drool out of her mouth that lands in Perry's hair. "Gross, kid," he says, and pulls her back down, taking her into the kitchen.

"Why are you so upset?" Tabitha asks, and she looks so hurt Ginger is amazed. How is it possible? How is it possible that Tabitha genuinely has no idea how she behaves?

"Because you won't stop! I give you an inch and you take a mile. I haven't said anything about moving, or what Phoebe will be doing after school, and you're already buying me a house and signing her up for soccer, neither of which I am likely to be able to afford. Can you just let me do one thing? Let me sign my child up for this school before they take her spot and not be thirty steps ahead of me, making every decision for my family?"

She finishes, not because she is done talking, but because she is literally out of breath, unused to speaking so loudly, so emotionally. It's only when the silence falls, heavy and hard, between them that she sees Tabitha's face and hears the echo of her own words, and her heart begins to beat faster.

The first time she met Tabitha and Perry had been at their house, only a few days after the children had come to live with them. Phoebe was still deep in grief and confusion, Ginger taking her to therapy appointment after therapy appointment, Sunny visiting almost daily. Phoebe hadn't cried much at first. Mostly she was silent and still and would not leave Ginger's side, leaning her head against Ginger's belly and slipping her index and middle fingers over the hem of her shirt. Sunny had only asked Ginger if she would take Phoebe temporarily, hadn't discussed anything long-term, and she still felt off-kilter, unused to the presence of someone else in her apartment, at sea over what to do other than to be present and wait.

But Tabitha had seemed unflappable, as she would every time Ginger saw her afterward. Her hair was perfectly smooth and fell back into place when she moved. The twins were dressed in matching outfits and playing with all-natural educational toys, looking for all the world as though they had never known another parent, another life, while Phoebe was utterly at sea, Ginger doing her best to rescue her.

Ginger is not a competitive soul, never has been, and was only vaguely aware the Mommy Wars even existed. Tabitha's perfection didn't inspire jealousy in her, only curiosity. *How does she do this?* was what she thought most often in Tabitha's company. Second most often: *Why does she bother?* And now a third question is coming to her: *Why can't she stop?*

"I am only trying to help," Tabitha says, her voice going quiet. She is a small person, thin and bird-boned, but she looks at that moment as though she has literally shrunk into her clothes, like she is disappearing.

"It doesn't feel like that. It feels like you are trying to

control me. Control everything," Ginger says. "I don't know if we're going to move. I don't know what Phoebe is going to do after school. She's not your kid. You don't get to make decisions for her."

"I thought we were a family," Tabitha says weakly.

"Our being semi-related does not give you license to run our lives."

"I'm just trying to help," Tabitha repeats.

Ginger leans forward, putting her face in her hands for a moment. Is she angry with Tabitha? She doesn't even know. Perhaps she is angry with Dr. Jemison, her no-nonsense sternness and Ginger's knee-jerk compliance, as though she isn't a grown adult who can take an hour to do something, or procrastinate until midnight if she wants to. Perhaps she is angry with Phoebe for applying in the first place. Or with Tabitha for suggesting this vacation.

Or perhaps she is angry with herself. For putting off these decisions. For her selfishness in not wanting Phoebe to go to TGA because *she* is the one who doesn't want to change, not Phoebe, and because it has taken her this long to admit it. For not being a mother like Tabitha who does give everything, who would move halfway across the country if Tate and Taylor required it, without even thinking, and Ginger can't even gin up the courage to move ten miles.

"I'm not a bad mother because I am careful about making decisions," Ginger says.

"No one said you were! You're a wonderful mother," Tabitha says, trying to smile so hard Ginger can't tell what she really means.

"Do you really think that, though? You already would have enrolled her in the school she wants to go to. You probably would have called the admissions committee the minute she got wait-listed and demand they admit her at once, and they would have been so scared of you they would have. You would build a house brick by brick next to the school so she'd be able to get there in time and do every after-school activity she wants. I am not you, Tabitha, and I don't want to be you. Leave me alone."

Tabitha opens her mouth but has nothing to say in return, and when Ginger looks at her, she almost wonders whether Tabitha might cry. But she doesn't find out because Tabitha only pushes her chair back from the table and walks away, and by the time Ginger sees her next, she has closed over whatever emotions had been brewing with a brittle, eager politeness.

21

ELIZABETH

THE INCREDIBLE THING about this vacation, Elizabeth thinks as the mothers drive to the spa for their moms' day out, is that it keeps going. No matter how many things go wrong, no matter how much is thrown at them, they soldier on through the itinerary. Fun must be had at all costs, no matter how unfun it is becoming.

She wants to talk to Tabitha about this job offer, about what it really means, not whatever line of bullshit John has bought into. But that morning both Ginger and Tabitha are seriously losing it. Tabitha is positively manic, chattering about how amazing the spa is going to be, hashtag girl time, hashtag we deserve it. Ginger is humming – humming! – to herself in the back seat. This vacation, all the hysteria about the baby and prospective parents, it's getting to them. They're going to come back from the mountains having completely lost what little was left of their minds.

When they arrive at the spa, a valet takes the car and they are ushered inside to the hush that comes with money. They are given robes so soft they are more like mattresses than clothing and flip-flops that are shiny silver and feel like there are tiny elves massaging the soles of Elizabeth's feet when she walks. They are given glasses with flower blossoms floating in them and escorted to chaise lounges in the Relaxation Room, a sun porch that looks out on a stretch of mountain where every tree is as green as if the spa arranged it that way, and at this point she wouldn't put it past them.

No payment is discussed, which is par for the course with activities Tabitha has arranged. She and Perry have a way of paying for things without asking. It took a long time for Elizabeth to notice this habit, as they have done so few family outings outside of Sunday dinner until now. Violet is still so young that taking her anywhere is a struggle. But now that they have been out in the world so frequently over the past week, the way Tabitha and Perry make issues of money disappear has become inescapable.

Money is so easy when you have a lot of it, and so incredibly painful when you have none. Elizabeth grew up in a family that had plenty, so she never worried about it until she had to, and by then it was too late. This is how the fertility industry tricks you. They prey upon your hope. Because next time, next cycle, next transfer, next drug, that will be the one. Sometimes it is. It feels like gambling, the rush of possibility, the holding of breath while the ball clatters around the roulette wheel, waiting for a place to land. Once you are in the game, how can you say no? What if the time you say no is the time it would have worked?

They went broke, as Hemingway said, gradually and then suddenly. When they did, the way she looked at the world changed. She is aware now, so aware, of what things cost, of who is paying, of who has what and who doesn't. She has somehow ended up handling the finances, and she doesn't think John worries about it nearly us much as she does, is as aware of it every second as she is.

Now, on this vacation, she sees the way Tabitha and Perry make questions about money invisible. They are magicians, and this is their sleight of hand. They buy tickets and rent equipment in advance so the question of who will pay for it or how the bill will be divided never comes up. They went out to lunch earlier in the trip and were halfway home before Elizabeth realized she never saw the bill, only that Perry went inside the restaurant and reemerged as Tabitha was gathering everyone up to get back in the car. Tabitha ordered all the groceries for this trip. She found the house, too, said they won it at the twins' school's fundraising Gala last year, and that was all dealt with as if it costs nothing, but Elizabeth has been to fundraisers, and she knows the prices things go for are often even more extravagant than their value.

The job offer, this is another way of making money disappear, of pulling the strings and making them dance. Surrounding them in softness so they never notice they are being suffocated. She can't let it happen. She has to say something.

"Tabitha," she whispers when the various attendants, carrying pillows and flower water and aromatherapy sticks, reminding her of the thousands of brooms carrying buckets of water in *Fantasia*, are gone. "Tabitha." She leans over toward Tabitha, who has leaned back and donned an eye pillow that smells so strongly of lavender Elizabeth has to sneeze. "This place is really expensive."

She hates to object to the treatments themselves. God knows she could use some help from professionals. Her hair is so dry she has to pull it back or she looks like she has been electrocuted. Her skin is dull, and the circles under her eyes are so dark it's like she's been punched by one of those fists on a spring; her lips are chapped because she keeps forgetting to drink water and it's so dry up here, and her feet are beyond description. To be somewhere so quiet, somewhere she literally cannot be summoned to deal with Violet or answer questions about where the wipes or the drops or the onesie with the little bunnies on it are, is so amazing she is half tempted to stow away and live here forever. But everything comes with a cost, even when it has no price.

"It's okay," Tabitha says. "I got a package because we're doing multiple services." She is speaking quietly, but an older woman across the room sits up and takes her eye pillow off to glare at them. Elizabeth would like to tell the woman to fuck off, but she feels that sentiment would not respect the spirit of the Relaxation Room.

"I can't afford it," Elizabeth whispers.

"Let's talk about it later, okay?" Tabitha says, and pats her hand in a way Elizabeth thinks is meant to be comforting but only feels patronizing. She fought her way out of her family, where she was never taken seriously because she was the youngest, right into John's family, where she is never taken seriously because she is the youngest, and then into this one, where it has happened again.

She cannot argue with Tabitha because at that moment, a heavily pregnant woman in pristine white scrubs, the top designed to wrap across her belly and tie on the side in a way that only makes its swelling more prominent, opens the door to the Relaxation Room, which has not, in point of fact, proved terribly relaxing, and says, with perfect cheer, as though her very appearance doesn't make Elizabeth want to hulk out and throw furniture, "Elizabeth?"

"No," Elizabeth says, but it is only a whisper, and even though she does not want to go, some combination of social conditioning and muscle memory kicks in and she is walking over to this woman, staring at her belly.

The woman introduces herself, "I'm Amber, and I'll be doing your facial."

Elizabeth might say something like *Hello* or *Thanks*, but she isn't sure. Because as they are walking to the treatment room, and while Amber moves around her in the dark, the compresses on Elizabeth's eyes only making her even more aware of the movement of the other woman's body, of the brush of her belly against Elizabeth's arms no matter how tightly she pulls them against her body, all Elizabeth can think is, *It should have been me it should have been me itshouldhavebeenme.*

By the time they sit down to lunch after their first round of treatments, she feels worse than when they arrived, tenser, tauter, achier, ridiculous, and suffering from terrible under-boob sweat in the overly thick robes. The lunchroom has a slightly less spectacular view, but Tabitha still stands by the window, looking out at the curve of the hills and the trees.

"I love Colorado skies, don't you? I've never seen anything like them anywhere else," she says. "I feel like I could take a million pictures of the sky here and never get it quite right."

"I read an article about this. Something about the way the human eye processes dark and light versus the way a camera does. A camera's image is mathematically accurate, but our eyes aren't," Ginger says. She is already sitting at the table, which is tile and metal and therefore cold, too, her foot propped up. She has been oddly talkative today, but also distracted, like she's high or something. Elizabeth wouldn't have guessed weed as Ginger's jam, but at this point, who knows anything anymore? Do they even know each other at all, or are they only strangers masquerading as family?

"Really? How interesting," Tabitha says, though it isn't.

The lady with the blossom water comes in with plates of salad, even though Elizabeth could demolish a bacon cheeseburger right about now. But salads are all the spa serves, and thank god hers has chicken on it because if it were some vegan fauxtein she would have torn this place apart, fake wood beam by fake wood beam.

Tabitha comes over, sitting at the head of the table, as she would, Elizabeth thinks meanly, though it was the only seat left after she and Ginger had taken theirs. Tabitha reaches out and grasps both of their hands and squeezes them and says, "I'm so glad we're all here together. I know you two have siblings, but I never did until now. I'm so glad I have you two."

Elizabeth stares at her. Her own head is still ringing with

that incantation, *It should have been me it should have been me itshouldhavebeenme,* her stomach still burning with anger at Amber, Amber and her perfect white scrubs and her perfect belly and her cool hands on Elizabeth's hot, paper-dry skin, and she knows that is unreasonable, too; this woman has done nothing to her, and she *has* a child, for crying out loud, and then she starts to hate Tabitha, too, hate her extra for being so perfect and so happy with her adopted children and attachment parenting, and so goddamned rich she can just get her husband to give John a job he isn't even qualified for, like it's a pity fuck, and she even hates Brianna, though she can hardly even admit that to herself, Brianna for whom it is so easy she just offers up a child like it's nothing at all.

"It all feels like it's going so fast! This whole trip will be over in a few days, and then we'll go back to our lives and who knows when we can do this again, especially with the new baby. I was just reading an article about sisters who go on vacations together. Wouldn't that be fun? When the children are old enough," she says, turning to Elizabeth. Tabitha's hand is still on the table, too close to Elizabeth's, and she grabs her fork and shoves a bunch of salad into her mouth to get out of reach. "We could go somewhere warm. Beachy. Turks and Caicos is beautiful – gorgeous white-sand beaches. Perry and I went there for our babymoon after our home study was approved, and really, the flight isn't even that long. Wouldn't that be perfect?"

"That sounds nice," Ginger says, still in that odd, tinny, not-Ginger-happy voice.

"Why do you do that?" Elizabeth asks, putting down her fork and glaring at Ginger. She can feel a piece of carrot lodged in her teeth, but she refuses to free it.

"Do what?" Ginger asks, turning to look at Elizabeth. Her reflexes are slow, like her voice and her movements are out of sync, a badly dubbed movie.

"Say things like 'Sounds nice' when it doesn't? You always do that, and then we end up doing things like this ridiculous spa trip, which is going to cost more than my car even when you should be in bed with a bunch of ice packs? Why don't you ever stand up to her? Why do you let her bully you?"

Ginger blinks owlishly at Elizabeth and then looks down at her salad. Elizabeth grabs her glass of water and gulps at it. There's no wine here, either, which is another strike against this ridiculous place. If Elizabeth were going to start a spa, she would have it serve bacon cheeseburgers and excellent wine and cheesecake, and everyone would leave fat and happy with really sparkly toenail polish. She thinks she might literally kill the blossom-water lady for a piece of cheesecake right then.

"I didn't…" Tabitha starts to say, an uncharacteristic stammer breaking her words apart.

"You always do this, Tabitha. You make these crazy plans in your head and you don't even talk to us before you start spinning out! I'm sorry you don't have sisters, but I do. I have a sister and she's fucking awful, and I have John's sisters on top of that, and they're fucking awful, too, but I still have to go visit them because they already complain every time we do something with this family instead of them, and I can't go running off to Turks and fucking Caicos for the hell of it just because you're rich and bored and lonely."

Her words fall, and everyone freezes. They are a tableau of unspent emotion for a moment – Elizabeth's breathing ragged from anger; Ginger still staring at her plate, her face gone red now; Tabitha frozen, one hand in the air, her fingers trembling.

There it is. She has said it. And she's not sorry. She's not. She cannot live like this anymore.

"I am only trying to make everyone happy," Tabitha says; her voice sounds strangled, like she is pushing to get the words out.

"You can't *make* people happy. Jesus. What the hell is wrong with you? You're not making anyone happy. You just make it worse. Perry has to give John a job so we can pay our rent next month and you want me to go to fucking Telluride for Christmas? Go to Turks and Caicos to keep you entertained?"

Elizabeth feels her voice going higher, getting hysterical, which is what she hates, what makes her feel out of control, makes her think of wrestling with her sister. She can't stay cool; she just loses it and looks like an idiot.

"I didn't mean to make you uncomfortable. I wanted to help! It's just a temporary thing, to help you. And then John will get a new job, and things will be better," Tabitha says. She is speaking calmly like she is trying to soothe a rearing horse, but that only makes Elizabeth madder because she cannot control her own fury.

"No, they won't be better. They will never be better. We are fucked. We are well and truly fucked. Do you have any idea how much IVF costs? We are broke. Worse than broke. It's not just John's job. It's five years of me failing to get pregnant or stay pregnant. We are going to be paying off my uselessness until the end of fucking time. So excuse me if I cannot be jetting off to Aspen every ten minutes, okay?"

Elizabeth stops talking with a gasp, both because she hasn't stopped speaking to breathe and because she cannot believe what she just said, cannot believe that she spilled this secret aloud.

But there is no other way to get Tabitha to stop! And as the silence settles over the time, she feels oddly free. Now they know everything.

"I'm just trying to help," Tabitha says, and it's sounds like she's about to cry, goddammit, like Elizabeth needs that right now. "Why doesn't anyone understand that I am just trying to help? I just want to make everything perfect for everyone. I just want everything to be okay!" She is not quite as high-pitched as Elizabeth, but Tabitha is falling apart in a way Elizabeth has never seen before. And what is *she* so upset about? Elizabeth is telling her they can barely afford to make rent and Tabitha's *feelings* are hurt?

"It's not going to be okay. It's not going to be okay!" Elizabeth says. She is losing control now, and Tabitha may cry, but Elizabeth will not; she will not do that here, not do that in front of them. "I hate this. I hate all of it. I hate being a mother, I hate being broke and having to worry about everything, I hate the way you just have to control everything; I hate this stupid family—" She breaks off because the thing she was going to say next is that she hates herself, and oh, god, she does, but if she says it, she really is going to cry, and instead she walks out of the room, disappointingly soundless in her silver shoes, and lets the door close on the wreckage.

.....

BOY MOM

.....

I was a tomboy. I had three brothers, which probably didn't help, but I was always more interested in "boy" things. I liked dolls, but I loved trucks. My dad worked in construction, and some of the first pictures we have of me are sitting in his lap in the cab of an excavator and I'm reaching for the controls and grinning.

My mom was a Mary Kay rep, and she was constantly trying to get me to "girl up," but that wasn't my thing. I wanted to be dirty and muddy and loud, and then, when we got to the age where girls started being mean to each other for no reason, I sincerely wanted no part of it. I joined the softball team and the field hockey team, and I focused on games and school and not on any of that ridiculous social stuff.

So of course our first child was a girl. I love her. I love her more than anything. She has dolls and trucks, and she likes to play with both of them. She hates the sensation of grass on her bare feet, but she also loves to play in the sandbox and has recently gotten into playing in mud puddles, which is thrilling for both of us. One of the things that's so amazing about being a parent is rediscovering things you'd forgotten were amazing, like watching pill bugs crawl across a sidewalk or how miraculous thunder is. But I can see that our daughter is more girly by nature, that she wants to wear sparkly shoes and draw instead of wrestle or climb. She's not a boy.

I still think of myself as a boy mom.

When they did the ultrasound, the tech asked if we were hoping for a boy or a girl, and we said, "Oh, we just want a healthy baby!" but I was trying hard to pretend that I was not actually hoping for a healthy boy. But when she said, "It's a girl!" it was really hard not to be disappointed.

That's horrible, I know. But it is probably one of those things a lot of us think and no one has the courage to say out loud because it is horrible, but it's also true.

I'm a boy mom. In my heart of hearts, I'm a boy mom.

And I want my husband to have the experience of being a boy dad. He is a traditional manly man, a mechanic who loves to camp and fish and hike, and we do all those things with our daughter, but it's different with a boy.

So here are our options. We can keep trying until we get a boy, which might not happen. I know, put some butter under your bed or have sex in a specific position or with some essential oil smeared on your belly or whatever, but I have done my internet research and those things are hooey. We can do IVF with genetic testing, but who has that much money?

Or we can adopt a boy.

I always thought I'd adopt anyway. There are children who need families, and we have a family that feels incomplete to us, so why not? Why not adopt a boy? He can play with dolls and trucks and jump in mud puddles and my husband can take him camping and we can play soccer together and we'll be a family and I'll finally be a boy mom who happens to have a daughter, too.

22

TABITHA

THERE WERE NO apologies, of course. After lunch, they finished their treatments and Tabitha took care of the bill and the tip as usual, and they drove home in silence and then buried themselves in the children. No apologies from Ginger. No apologies from Elizabeth.

Tabitha didn't sleep. She cannot stop thinking about the things Elizabeth said about her at the spa, wondering if they are true. Cannot stop thinking about Ginger – Ginger, of all people! – snapping at her and saying she doesn't want to be like Tabitha, doesn't want her help. Cannot stop thinking about Pamela wanting *Perry* to help with the Gala. Perry, who doesn't even care! Cannot stop thinking about how she tries so hard to be generous and they throw it back in her face.

Bully. Rich, bored, lonely.

Bully? She doesn't – she isn't a bully. She tries to do nice things. Rich, yes, though that is the result not only of the luck of birth and all the advantages that followed, but of hard work and focus and resilience.

Bored? She is busy every second of the day, most of it

caring for other people, not only her family but also the school community and all the organizations she volunteers for. She has no time to be bored.

But lonely.

She might be lonely.

She is lonely.

Tabitha has spent her entire life trying to surround herself with the family she never had, and somehow she is still alone. After all this time, after all she has, she is still lonely. That seems impossible. She has a wonderful husband and children who amaze her every day with their courage and curiosity and good humor. In addition to her own children, she has Phoebe and Violet and soon a nephew, and she is so, so lonely. She feels like she has been trying to outrun that lonely girl with a sleeping bag and no sleepover to go to, and she is in exactly the same place. Pamela Preston only calling her to ask for Perry's help with the Gala. Maybe even – oh, god, had Pamela only invited Tate to Serafina's party because of the Gala, too? Ginger yelling at her over just trying to help her find a place to live, and Elizabeth yelling at her because she'd suggested going to the beach, of all things.

If she weren't forcing this whole fake family on everyone else, none of them would ever spend time with her at all.

In the morning, her eyes dry and raw, Tabitha makes gluten-free pancakes, done worrying about the sugar, and bacon, because who cares about anything anymore. At breakfast, John talks to Perry instead of paying attention to Violet eating her yogurt, so she is absolutely covered, and the twins' faces are sticky with syrup as they attempt to gross each other out with mouthfuls of half-chewed pancake. Phoebe is reading as she works her way steadily through two helpings of eggs and bacon and pancakes, but Tabitha doesn't ask her to put her book away or tell the twins to close their mouths or instruct John to wipe off Violet's face. She simply cooks and ferries food back and forth. She has forgotten to put on her shoes and is tracking glitter back and forth on the floor, but she can't summon up the energy to care.

"Good morning," Elizabeth says, coming down late, her hair like a bird's nest. Tabitha is surprised to see this greeting is directed at her, as though nothing happened.

"Hi," she says curtly. There is still no apology. Is this how it will be? Elizabeth will pretend nothing happened?

And you know what the infuriating thing is? Tabitha stood up for Elizabeth! Tabitha pressured Perry to help them! Does Elizabeth even know that it was Tabitha's idea to offer her husband a job? This is what infuriates her most, that she is only trying to *help*. She knows what they need; if they would only just accept it!

Elizabeth sits down at the table and reaches for the coffeepot as Tabitha turns around with the pancakes and their eyes meet, sure as magnets locking together. Which means Elizabeth takes her eyes off what she is doing and knocks over the vase.

Those flowers. She should have known they were a sign everything was going to go wrong.

Elizabeth jumps up and Tabitha leaps forward, but Elizabeth is on the wrong side of the table and Tabitha has the plate in her hands and the vase teeters there for a breathless second before tilting over, sending a shower of flowers into the air as it performs a perfect swan dive and shatters on the smooth, rock-hard, glitter-strewn slate floor.

Everyone freezes.

Things move in slow motion. The vase, which looks sturdy but shatters quite impressively, splits into tiny pieces that bounce across the slate in beautiful arcs, catching the light as they go. She wants to stop and watch the satisfying beauty of this destruction.

"Stay back, everyone," she says, holding her arms out. "Perry, go get the dustpan and broom from the pantry. John, take Violet upstairs and get her cleaned off. Tate and Phoebe, scooch over on the bench. No, don't get down yet, you don't have any shoes on. Taylor, oh, you have shoes. Please go get the garbage can." She does not ask Elizabeth to do anything. Elizabeth has done enough. And Ginger can't do anything, not that she ever would.

"Shit," Elizabeth whispers, but not quietly enough. "Shit, shit, shit."

"Mama, she said a dollar word," Taylor announces, dragging the garbage can over to the table even though he is perfectly capable of lifting it.

"You said it five times! You owe five dollars!" Tate chimes in.

Tabitha is fairly sure Elizabeth said it four times, but she does not have the patience to argue. "Enough," she says. "Taylor, please go get my shoes that are by the front door."

He scampers off as Perry comes in with the broom and Tabitha picks up the flowers, taking them over to the sink to rescue them. When Taylor brings her shoes, she takes over for Perry, directing him to carry the children over the glass and send them upstairs to finish getting ready.

"No harm, no foul. It's only a vase," Perry says as he comes back from delivering Phoebe to the stairs and finishes sweeping. He claps Elizabeth on the back, and for once, Tabitha hates him for his boundless bonhomie.

"Can you please go make sure everyone is ready to leave for the bike ride in a timely manner?" Tabitha asks. Perry leaves, whistling, and she looks over at Ginger and Elizabeth, who are still frozen, their feet on the bar in the middle of the table legs as though they are playing a version of the Floor is Lava. Ginger has a shoe on her unbandaged foot, but not on the other, which really is still so swollen.

"I'm so sorry," Elizabeth says. "We'll pay for it, I promise."

At that, Tabitha wants to laugh. It is her fault, really, for choosing that particular vase, an enormous, modern heavy crystal column by Baxter & Motts with a smooth exterior and a beveled design inside. That's probably what made it break so beautifully – the delicate interior work that makes it thinner than it first appears. But she hadn't been able to resist using it; the glass had looked so lovely catching the light, and she'd thought for sure the children were old enough that they wouldn't knock it over. At least she'd been right about that, she thinks humorlessly.

In any case, Elizabeth will not be paying for it, because anything from Baxter & Motts easily costs twelve thousand dollars, and not only does Tabitha now know for a fact that Elizabeth and John do not have that much money, if she tells Elizabeth how much it cost, they will have a coronary event on their hands and therefore ensuing hospital bills.

She doubts the owners will care about, or even notice, its absence. There are two more equally stunning and equally expensive ones in the butler's pantry. But she will tell them and handle it if their insurance doesn't. "It's fine," Tabitha says. She spots some more glass on the floor near their feet and dives under the table for it, sweeping it into the pan, and then sits back on her heels, reaching forward, running her hand lightly over the floor, feeling for more shards.

Elizabeth is still talking when she looks over at her, but she hasn't heard a word. What is the point of listening?

"Tabitha?" Ginger says gently. Tabitha focuses and sees Elizabeth looking at her pleadingly, as though she has asked a question.

She tries, but she cannot find the energy to care.

"You know what?" She stands and walks over to the garbage can, emptying the dustpan into it one last time. She is sure they have missed some; like the glitter, they will be finding pieces forever. "I'll stay back while you all go. I've got some calls to make." Without packing the bag of snacks or taking care of anything else, she grabs her phone and her planner and goes into the office.

This is what she needs. Some peace and quiet. Obviously they are capable of managing without her, and this is what she needs. Cross a few things off the to-do list. Get back in control. Start fixing problems.

But once she is in the office, she does nothing. She hears footsteps, people moving around, calling to each other, and then the slamming of doors and the sound of the cars as they go down the driveway, fading to nothing as they turn onto the road to head down to the trailhead. It is quiet – maybe Ginger went with them. She's been complaining about being bored cooped up in the house, and what Tabitha wants to say is that Ginger ought to have been a little more careful and not sprained her ankle.

When everything is quiet, she opens her planner, makes a series of precise bullet points, and begins to order the haphazard notes she has been taking all along of things to do when they get home. She color codes and makes a sublist and leans back. There. She feels more like herself again.

Before the silence begins to seep in and push her back into thinking about her loneliness and her failure, she makes a call. The professor isn't home, but the florist – Shelley – is so happy to hear from her. So, so happy. No, they don't have family nearby, they had to move for her wife's job, but they've been here long enough they've developed close friends who are family. Yes, they understand Brianna will be involved. They prefer it that way.

Yes, they very much want to adopt a child from China as well, because the professor was adopted from China. Tabitha explains why the family doesn't normally look at couples who have other children, but agrees international adoption is different, but also they really want the children to feel like a family, but yes, she really does support their plans.

Yes, family is so complicated. Yes (and Tabitha congratulates herself for not even pausing), family certainly can be wonderful.

She likes the florist as much as she had on paper, but it all feels like it's happening far away from her, the conversation being conducted by a stand-in, by someone else entirely.

When they finish their call, she hangs up and looks out the window to the backyard, past the miniature indulgence of the putting green to the wooded hill. The florist is lovely. She has no doubt the professor is lovely, too. They'd be a wonderful addition to the family.

What is this family, anyway? Only a few days ago she was worrying about the flowers for the bedrooms – oh, the flowers – and now everything real has been revealed: what Elizabeth really thinks of her, what Ginger really thinks of her, how they will never be the way she wants them to be. She's held on to the hope that someday, when Violet was older, when Ginger and Phoebe moved closer, when they took this vacation together, things would be better; they would be a real family, just like any other family. But here they are, and they're even further from that idea than they were when they started. She should have left well enough alone.

Still, what other option do they have? She thinks of the way the children are when they are together, their sweet, fierce love for each other, the way the twins light up when Phoebe comes over to visit. They are a family now, whether they like it or not, which apparently no one does, but there is no other alternative but to keep being one, no matter how much it hurts.

23

GINGER

THE SECRET TO Ginger's surviving the spa day was that after her own disagreement with Tabitha she finally caved and took one of the stronger painkillers they gave her at the hospital. It was glorious. She had felt dizzy and disconnected, her brain and body floating loose as a balloon. She couldn't have summoned up a coherent sentence to help break up the tension between Tabitha and Elizabeth if she wanted to, and the best part about the pills was that she didn't even care.

Perhaps she has been wrong. Perhaps bringing someone else into the family will actually diffuse the tension, spread it around, give them more than a hand's width of space between them. Or perhaps it will only make it worse, more people to fight with. She feels hopeful for a moment, and then deflates. It won't matter. Ginger had just told Tabitha to back off herself before Elizabeth's explosion, and then Tabitha had been right back at it with the vacation and the sisters thing. Ginger hadn't used the words Elizabeth used, not exactly, but she wasn't wrong. Tabitha just pushed and pushed at Elizabeth until she practically fractured.

At least that conflict had yielded Ginger some peace and quiet. Upon their return from the spa, Tabitha and Elizabeth both disappeared. Ginger spent the better part of the afternoon dozing on and off, sleepy from the combination of stress and pills. But this morning had been no better, Elizabeth breaking that vase, which must have cost a pretty penny, and Tabitha thin-lipped and angry, going into the office and slamming the door.

Now everyone else is gone, and she is silent, not moving, not wanting to disturb Tabitha, not wanting to endure another fight. She can hear her talking on the phone in the office, and then silence.

She'll text the prospective family and set up a time to talk. That's what she'll do. But after she does, the phone rings almost immediately.

She stares at the screen in dread almost until it goes to voicemail and then grabs it, answering, "Hello?" in a wavery, querulous voice.

"Oh, it's Allison Cohen, I just saw your text – oh, and now that I read it, it just says you want to schedule a time to talk. I'm sorry. I was just so excited when I saw your message. My husband isn't home, but I can catch him up later. Can you talk now?"

Ginger hesitates and then says, "I can." She might as well get it over with. "Thank you for calling."

"I'm sorry," Allison says again. Her voice is bright and full of energy, and Ginger is immediately guarded.

"It's okay, really," Ginger says, and then there is awkward silence, and then they attempt to talk simultaneously. "I was going—" Ginger begins, as Allison asks, "How is your summer going?"

"It's fine," Ginger says, trying to remember what she is supposed to be selling. "We're up in Aspen. The whole family is."

"Oh, that sounds so wonderful," Allison says, and there is genuine longing in her voice, as if Ginger has something worthy of missing. "You're missing the most terrible heat wave here. I wither into a raisin whenever I'm in the sun for a few minutes."

"Oh, it's quite pleasant up here," Ginger says, still feeling awkward. When they divided up whom to call – had it been her idea? a case of temporary insanity? – they hadn't specified what they would say. Only that they wanted to learn more. A script would have been helpful. What do you even say to a stranger who might join your family forever?

"Are you – so who are you?" Allison asks. She laughs at herself, but it sounds warm and not nervous. "Which mom are you, I mean. Tabitha explained everything in her email, but I can't remember. I'm sorry."

Ginger squints at the ceiling. "No apology necessary. There are a lot of people to keep track of. I'm Phoebe's mom. She's the eldest."

"Right, of course! I'm so glad you called!"

"I know it's a little strange, I know, things being so unsure, but—"

"Oh, sure," Allison says, almost stepping on Ginger's last words in her eagerness. "It's okay, I understand. But how wonderful that you all take vacations together! And the family dinners – Tabitha mentioned those. Mark – my husband – and I love that idea. Family is so important, don't you think?"

Ginger contemplates whether to clarify to Allison that this is in fact the family's first vacation together, and with the way things are going, it may be their last, but decides that is better left unsaid. "Do you have close families?" she asks.

"Oh, very. Not huge, but we're all really close. I have two brothers and a sister, plus my parents are both remarried, but they all get along great and we spend all our holidays together, and Mark's father passed, but his mom is still alive, and he's got two sisters. Oh, and one of my brothers and his family lives in Washington, and my sister lives in Argentina, but everyone else is here, and we're all super close."

"That's great," Ginger says, but so many people does sound large and complicated, even without attempting to unravel their relationships. "We're a fairly expansive family ourselves, though. Already. Would you and Mark be okay with that?"

"Oh, my goodness, it's one of the things we love about you all. We really wanted lots of children. Things didn't work out that way. But we love our families, and if we could have even more family, we'd be thrilled! We're Jewish, did I mention that? We can host the high holidays here unless someone else celebrates?"

"Oh, well, no," Ginger says, and takes a deep breath. An entirely new set of holidays on the calendar means even more family time. And an opportunity for the children to learn something new. Tabitha will be thrilled.

"That's great! We love hosting and sharing traditions. And then if you all celebrate things like Christmas and Easter, we'll do those, too!" She has a light, tinkly laugh that makes Ginger nervous. "I have to tell you; something here feels really right. Mark and I have been waiting a long time. When I saw Tabitha's message, it felt like a dream come true. You all are so lucky to have found something so special."

"Sure," Ginger says. She rubs her hand up and down her face. Doesn't Allison realize what all those things she thinks are so "special" about this family mean? The Sunday dinners and the holidays and the school breaks and now the summer vacation, and Tabitha even talking about Christmas and vacations without the children, though that is certainly off the table since both she and Elizabeth have read Tabitha the riot act. This special family is full of pressure.

"Our families are amazing, but you can never have too many people in your corner, right? I don't know if Tabitha told you, but I had uterine cancer. It's why we can't have kids. Anyway, it was diagnosed right after we got married. I thought I was pregnant – isn't that funny? It wasn't funny at the time, but ironic or whatever. And our families rallied around us. My sister moved in with us so she could take care of the animals when Mark was with me, and both of my parents and his mom were all there when I had the hysterectomy, and they traded off staying with us when Mark had to work or when I had treatment. Everyone jokes about how terrible their mother-in-law is, but mine is the best. And both of my parents' spouses. Mark and I are perfectly responsible adults, but isn't it nice to have someone to share the load every once in a while? I mean, can you imagine having to manage that alone?" Allison finishes with another laugh.

Ginger has never considered family that way at all, has never thought of it as a shared load but only another burden. Though now she wonders if she has been missing that view of things, that this is how Tabitha has seen it all along, though she can't imagine how, given that Tabitha never lets anyone share the load. The fact that she agreed to let Elizabeth and Ginger each call one of the families felt like a major victory.

"I wonder, will you be too busy? With your own family? All your volunteer work? I saw you do quite a lot of community service."

"Too busy for what?" Allison sounds genuinely confused.

"For things. All the things we do. With this family."

She laughs that tinkling laugh again. "Oh, my goodness, what else is time for?" This sparks another train of thought for Allison, who begins running through a list of holidays and celebrations they can all have together, and trips her family has taken together and ones they want to take.

Allison is coming to the end of her giddy list, planning all these times for a family she may never be a part of, doesn't even know.

"That sounds great," Ginger says, not entirely sure what she has approved of.

"And the biological parents will be involved? When can we talk to them?" Allison asks eagerly.

"Our children's birth mother has asked us to take the lead. So we're just chatting with some families on her behalf, and then we'll share that information with her. I don't want us to seem capricious, just calling when we cannot make any guarantees—"

Allison cuts her off. "No, it makes sense. You can't decide a child's parents off a website! And I love that you're so close to her! We've been learning so much about how important open adoption is."

"It can be, yes," Ginger says. They are lucky, she knows, to have such a solid relationship with Brianna, but that doesn't mean it isn't complicated.

"Do you all have big families, too?" Allison sounds as if she wants the answer to be yes, and Ginger wonders exactly how big would be enough for this woman. Maybe she and Tabitha are meant to be.

"Not nearby," Ginger says, which is the easiest way to explain everything.

After Allison asks her a few more questions and the conversation fades into awkward silences, Ginger says goodbye and Allison promises to email Tabitha. When she hangs up, she puts the phone in her lap and looks at its silent screen.

Is this how they are supposed to be? Excited by the very idea of spending time together? Eager for more and more of them, excited for an endless sprawl of relatives? For disequilibrium and disquiet, for constant readjustments and shifts?

When it was only her and Tabitha and Perry, it was so much easier. Perry and Ginger let Tabitha do what she wanted. After all, she is so good at everything. What is the point of fighting it? She imagines their family plus Allison and Mark's family plus whatever strays Tabitha invites at Thanksgiving dinner. She closes her eyes against the imaginary noise of it, the temporary tables set up throughout the first floor of Tabitha and Perry's house, the gauntlet she would have to run to get a moment of fresh air.

But then she imagines Allison's family in the hospital waiting room, and then recalls her own hospital stay when she had a biopsy a few years ago. Until then, she never saw her loneliness as a problem, had preferred the silence and ease of it. She hadn't stayed the night, but she was in two recovery rooms, and in the second one, where they could have visitors, she watched other people coming in, kissing their loved ones' heads.

That had been before Phoebe, so she had not had anyone to tell. But if it had happened after and she had told the family, well, Tabitha would have moved heaven and earth for her, would have driven her to the hospital and come into the recovery room, ordering everyone around the way she had at the ER. She would have set up the guest room and demanded Ginger and Phoebe stay with them, shuttling Phoebe to and from school and hurrying home to make questionably healthpromoting foods like hemp smoothies and kelp soup. At the time Ginger would have said all those things sounded awful. Now she isn't so sure. Imagine going through those things alone, Allison had said. Well, Ginger had. And she'd come out fine, hadn't she?

Then again, she thinks, looking down at her leg. Now that the last pill has worn off, the pain has returned.

All she has to do is ask. All she has to do is say to Tabitha, *Something is wrong, I need help.* And Tabitha will leap to take care of her. Maybe Elizabeth, even.

Maybe the point is not that she can go through these things alone, but that she no longer has to.

24

ELIZABETH

IT IS AMAZING how much easier it is without Tabitha all day. Well, not entirely easier. The arrangements were chaotic, no one having packed snacks and wipes and bandages and all the other crap Tabitha regularly Mary Poppins–es out of her bag, and no one knowing where exactly they were supposed to meet the guide for the bike tour or what size bike the kids needed. But other than that, it was way easier. Elizabeth made John pull Violet in the bike trailer while she rode at the back of the pack, coasting down the hills with her feet off the pedals like a kid. Is this all it took to feel better? Having a nervous breakdown and spilling her guts, and breaking what had to be a three-hundred-dollar vase?

When they get home, Perry announces he is taking Tabitha out to dinner, so the rest of them play in the pool while Ginger sits on the deck, reading. John swishes Violet through the water as she shrieks in delight; Elizabeth plays Marco Polo with the twins and Phoebe, Taylor forgetting to keep his eyes shut and Tate shrieking he is cheating for looking, then doing the same thing when she is It. After, they wrap themselves in towels and sit on the deck as the sun falls behind the mountains and the chill of evening settles in and eat the ridiculously elegant sandwiches Tabitha left for them. Because that is also Tabitha. Sulking all day only to emerge and cook for the people she is apparently mad at.

"Would you rather…" Taylor says, thinking so hard he squeezes his brow down until he looks like a confused chimpanzee, "have lobster claws for hands or for feet?"

The twins and Phoebe have developed a new obsession with Would You Rather, a sweetly childish version in which poop and Dada-esque ideas like this lobster claw one predominate.

"That's a good one," John says. "They'd both make life pretty hard, right?"

Taylor rolls his eyes. "That's the point."

"I'd rather have lobster claws for feet," Elizabeth says.

Violet is sitting in John's lap, wrapped in so many towels to keep her warm in the creeping chill of the coming evening she looks like a chrysalis, one tiny hand emerging to reach for a glass of water on the table. Elizabeth moves it deftly out of her reach.

"Ewww, why?" The kids laugh.

"Because then I could have a sweet custom wheelchair to get around, but I'd still have my hands," Elizabeth explains.

"I'd rather have them on my hands," John says. "So I could pinch people." He reaches out and gently pinches Taylor, who giggles and squirms away.

"I wouldn't want either," Tate declares.

"You can't say that. That's not the game. You have to choose one," Phoebe says in exasperation.

"I don't want lobster claws at all," Tate says, looking so upset at the idea Elizabeth leans over and rubs her back briskly to comfort her.

"Which would you choose, Taylor?" Elizabeth asks, interrupting the fight before it has a chance to begin.

"I'd have them on my hands, and I'd be a fighter and hit

people with them, like pow pow," Taylor says, holding his arms out and swinging them wildly.

"Careful there, lobster boy," John says mildly when one of Taylor's arms swings too close to him.

"Okay, my turn," Elizabeth says.

"No, Aunt Ginger didn't say yet," Taylor says, with all a child's sense of injustice.

"I don't think she's playing," Elizabeth says. God fucking forbid they all have to wait for Ginger to make a decision about this. She takes a million years to decide whether she'll drink water or lemonade, lord only knows how long it will take to decide where she wants to locate her imaginary lobster claws. "Okay, here's mine. Would you rather eat a rotten tomato or a rotten fish?"

"Ewwww!" The kids are reunited in gleeful disgust. Elizabeth smiles at John, who winks at her, a pleasantly casual gesture that makes her feel lighter. He has been in a good mood all day, and she suspects it is due to the job offer, which makes her feel guilty for not supporting it wholeheartedly. It's just that Tabitha... and the vase... and the baby. Jesus.

"Point of order," John says, holding up a finger. "Are we going to get sick from eating them?"

"Excellent question. No, you won't get sick after," Elizabeth says, stopping her train of thought.

"Do I have to eat the head?" Tate wonders.

"No. Just the part of the fish you would eat regularly," Elizabeth says.

"Except rotten," Taylor clarifies.

"Right."

The kids debate this one for a while, finally settling on the fish because the tomato would be too squishy and feel gross. Ginger draws a grimace across her face, and Elizabeth matches it. She guesses the kids have never smelled a rotten fish.

"Okay, my turn," Tate says, bouncing excitedly in her seat.

"Would you rather have to change Violet's poopy diapers or have poop come out of your ears?"

"I would rather change Violet's poopy diapers," John says without hesitation.

"I'd rather have poop coming out of my ears," Elizabeth says.

"That's the dumbest choice!" Taylor objects, hopping up on his knees in his chair in excitement. "Violet's not going to have poopy diapers forever, but you'd have poop coming out of your ears until you *dieeeeeee*."

"Yeah. Violet's not going to be little forever," Phoebe agrees.

"It just feels like it," Elizabeth mutters.

Violet, who seems delighted they are saying her name, pounds on the table and grins gummily at her sisters and brother, who make faces back, distracted from the pressing question of poopy diapers.

John takes the older kids for a walk after dinner, while Elizabeth stays back to give Violet a bath and put her to bed. The baby squirms and whines, reaching for something in the empty darkness, and Elizabeth wants to scream. It was such a nice night. Phoebe and Tate and Taylor are so easy, and dealing with Violet is so endless. Every time she starts to figure out what her daughter needs or might want, Violet changes, pulling the football away just before she has a chance to kick it.

If she is completely honest, Elizabeth's desperate fear is that the magic she has with kids does not apply to her own, ones she cannot send home at the end of the day or otherwise return to their parents; that she is the kind of person who should have remained a beloved auntie; that the universe tried to tell her again and again and again that she wasn't meant to be a mother, and it was only her hubris and stubbornness that made her push and push and push until it happened.

Below that is the fear that Violet knows this, Violet knows not only that Elizabeth was not meant to be anyone's mother, but specifically not her mother, that Elizabeth is not Violet's *real* mother, she is not Brianna, that there is some essential connection missing there.

When she looks at Tabitha and the twins, or Ginger and Phoebe, she doesn't see the same disconnect. She even sees their mannerisms in the children – Tabitha's firmness and confidence, Ginger's gentle hesitancy. But Violet is nothing like her.

When Violet finally goes down, Elizabeth pads down to the kitchen. The lights are off, and when Ginger says, "I'm in here," Elizabeth nearly has a heart attack.

"Holy shit," she says, stepping backward and putting her hand over her heart before stepping forward and flipping on the lights. "You scared the crap out of me."

"That's why I said I was here. To try not to scare the crap out of you."

"What are you doing in here?" Elizabeth asks, and then, without waiting for an answer, announces, "I need chocolate. Do you want some?"

"Good luck with that. Tabitha exorcised everything with sugar from the kitchen before we even arrived," Ginger says. She doesn't sound mad, at least.

"You obviously don't know where to look," Elizabeth says, and disappears into the butler's pantry, coming back with a stack of gourmet chocolate bars. The foil on their wrappers glints in the dim light: buried treasure. She fans them out like cards in front of Ginger, who takes one and peels back the foil and takes a delicate bite from a corner. "Chocolate bars are kept in the liquor cabinet, obvi. You should take up drinking. It has all sorts of side benefits." Elizabeth slides onto the bench across the table from Ginger. "Oh, you want some water? I'll get some." She gets two glasses of water and delivers one to Ginger before sitting back down.

"How is your ankle?" she asks, seeing Ginger suppress a wince as she shifts, reaching for the glass of water.

"Not great," Ginger says. "Don't tell Tabitha. She's only

going to make me go back to the hospital. I'll be fine until we get home."

This is classic Ginger. Don't make a big deal out of anything, even if it is a big deal, which usually ends up making it more of a big deal. Ginger's leg could turn gangrenous and fall off and she'd still be like, *Oh, no, I don't need to go to the doctor, I'll just fashion a peg leg for myself out of this stick.*

"We can go to urgent care or something."

"No, it's fine," Ginger insists.

Gangrene it will be, apparently. Elizabeth snaps a square from her chocolate, but it comes off in a triangle, leaving a jagged edge. She eats it anyway.

"Are you feeling better today?" Ginger asks.

Elizabeth swallows the chocolate, thick on her tongue, feeling the relief of the sugar coursing through her. "What do you mean?"

Ginger sits back, raising her shoulders stiffly. She always sits like that, bolt upright, like she is standing at attention. It makes Elizabeth want to slouch even more. "At the spa yesterday. You were so upset."

Heat rushes to Elizabeth's face, but she doesn't want to apologize. Nothing she said was untrue. She regrets none of it. She feels amazing, because for once she was honest with Ginger and Tabitha about how she felt. God, this family would be so much better if everyone were just honest.

"I feel better now," Elizabeth says. Which is true. She understands the phrase about getting something off her chest now, the way she felt so light and free on the bike, like something had been lifted. Not being around either of them all day, and then being cushioned by the presence of the children tonight, has allowed her to feel free. But Ginger is looking at her levelly, and underneath her relief, Elizabeth feels a hot ball of lead in her belly.

"I thought you might. I imagine it feels difficult holding so much inside," Ginger says.

Elizabeth snorts. "Like you're the authority on being emotionally forthcoming."

"I never claimed I was. But I have not been carrying around something so heavy."

Elizabeth lifts her chin. She shouldn't have said what she had about the money. "It's just money. We'll be fine."

"I don't mean the money. I mean what you said about hating motherhood. At first I thought you were just overemotional, that Tabitha pushed you into saying that. But tonight, as I watched you playing with the children, it struck me that you are genuinely struggling."

The heat in her belly floods Elizabeth's face, and she is grateful for the darkness to hide it. "I'm fine."

"Are you," Ginger says, and it isn't a question. Elizabeth doesn't answer.

"You know, I don't always just knuckle under to Tabitha's demands," Ginger says. She folds the foil over the edge of her chocolate bar tidily and sets it down, and Elizabeth feels irritated watching her primness. As if in retaliation, she takes another large bite of chocolate and then has to reach for the glass of water before her tongue sticks to the roof of her mouth.

"Okay," Elizabeth says when she can speak again.

"I had words with her just the other day about the way she is pressuring us to move."

Ginger's words are clipped, her hands folded neatly on the table, and Elizabeth's stomach burns.

"Well, congratulations."

In response, Ginger blinks slowly, like a cat. "I am going to apologize to her," she says calmly.

"Why?" Elizabeth allows her voice to raise. "She was overstepping like she always does, right? What do you have to apologize for?"

"I have to apologize because while she was overstepping her boundaries, she was also trying to help. I know this about her. I shouldn't have let my emotions color the way I reacted."

Elizabeth stares at Ginger. Is she for real? "Aren't you self-actualized."

"I'm not completely blind to my flaws. And what you said the other day about my resisting change because of me and not because of Phoebe – that was helpful in allowing me to evaluate my own behavior."

This compliment softens her for a moment. At least Ginger is capable of change. But apologizing to Tabitha?

"Well, I'm not apologizing. You know how she is! She's pushing you into moving because it's what she wants! Do you disagree with anything I said about her at the spa?"

Before she answers, Ginger pauses. "No."

"Then what the hell?"

"Have you called the couple you are talking to yet?" Ginger asks.

"No," says Elizabeth sulkily. She has, in fact, been avoiding it, bracing for Tabitha to criticize her about procrastinating. She doesn't even know why – doesn't she want to find a family so they can rescue her from this endless prodding on changing her mind? But she is resisting, always too tired or too distracted or too angry and, today, too out of fucks to give.

"I called mine. The wife, Allison, shared how close they are to their families. She had uterine cancer – that's why they're looking to adopt – and as she spoke about their families stepping in to help while she was in treatment, it reminded me of how you all came to my aid when I injured my ankle. For all the times Tabitha has pushed and pushed and pushed, and there have been so many of those, even before you joined us, she has meant it with kindness. I am trying hard to remember that."

Elizabeth stares at Ginger. A few days ago, Ginger was resisting sending Phoebe to a school she would be an idiot to turn down, all because it would inconvenience her so-called lifestyle. Now she's Miss Magnanimous, lecturing Elizabeth on how wonderful Tabitha is.

"So that's it? Tabitha just wins? She gets to treat us however she wants and we say thank you?"

"Nobody's winning anything," Ginger says with a slow shake of her head. "If we keep thinking of it that way, we're all going to lose."

Elizabeth takes a large bite of chocolate, shoving the whole row of squares into her mouth.

"Taylor is right, you know," Ginger says, breaking the silence between them. "Violet isn't going to be little forever. It won't always be this way."

On the heels of her words, there is the sound of a car in the driveway, doors closing, and then the children shouting. Perry and Tabitha must have gotten back, and John and the kids, too.

"Madam, are you ready to be escorted upstairs?" Perry says as he slides open the door, and the sound of the kids' voices outside and then Tabitha's, directing them toward the house, falls in.

"Thank you, yes," Ginger says, pushing herself up from the table. Elizabeth finishes her glass of water, letting it loosen the ball of chocolate in her mouth until she can manage to swallow it.

"Shh, shh," Tabitha is saying when the kids spill in, their feet pounding on the floors, calling out to each other. "We don't want to wake the baby." To Elizabeth she says nothing.

The kids make a half-hearted effort to quiet down, going upstairs telling each other to be quiet in stage whispers, slipping off their shoes and tiptoeing like cartoon characters, noisily shushing each other, and generally making more noise than they might have if Tabitha hadn't told them to quiet down. Violet, blessedly, doesn't wake.

That's it, isn't it? That, right there, is what Ginger means. That even though Tabitha has no reason to be kind to Elizabeth right then, she still tries to keep the kids quiet so Violet won't wake up. If the situation were reversed, would Elizabeth have been so thoughtful? She doesn't trust herself to say yes. Tabitha may be rich, bored, and lonely, but she is also thoughtful, kind, and generous.

Tabitha is just, as she says herself, trying to help. Elizabeth isn't wrong, but she isn't exactly right, either.

NOT YET

"Why don't you just adopt?"

People say this to us all the time. They said it to us when we were first diagnosed; they said it when we started treatment, after our miscarriages, after we stopped trying.

"Just adopt!"

It's the just that really gets me. People who say this are making it obvious they know nothing about infertility or adoption. They think that when you find out you can't have biological children you just shrug and say, Oh, well! and head right down to the Healthy Baby Store and say, One, please! and everyone lives happily ever after.

Adoption isn't an exact alternative to having biological children. It's an entirely different process.

One of the things you have to think about with adopting is what sort of challenges you'd be willing to take on in a child you adopt, because the fact is – and the foster system is a whole other series of questions – that a lot of children who are eligible for adoption have special needs. Will you adopt a child who is missing a limb? What about one who was exposed to drugs or alcohol during the pregnancy? Will you adopt a child who will never be able to live independently? What about an older child? What about an older child who's suffered significant trauma? What about an older child who's suffered significant trauma and has behavioral issues? What if you adopt a child who looks like your perfect baby and then it turns out they have learning differences or health issues?

Then again, what does it matter? We have this illusion of control that stems from biology and genetics, this vision that our children are going to be a certain way and have a certain life. Sometimes it does work out that way, but sometimes it really, really doesn't. Children are born who they are, and sometimes that means you get one who's a carbon copy of you or your partner, and sometimes that's a good thing and sometimes it isn't. Children are born with medical issues all the time, even after a so-called perfect pregnancy. Children develop learning and behavioral challenges no matter how much love they get or don't, no matter how much money their parents have or don't.

It's just that at this point, we've already been through so much. Trying on our own. Trying with limited medical assistance. Trying with serious medical intervention. Fertility drugs and tests and procedures and scans and appointments and positive tests and negative tests and ectopic pregnancies and miscarriages and D&Cs.

We stopped trying. We couldn't do it anymore. We're just taking time to deal with the grief from everything we've been through already before we think about anything else. Thinking about the people we want to be. Yasmin got certified to teach yoga. I signed up for guitar lessons. We took a couple's cooking class. We're going on a river cruise in Europe in the fall. We go to therapy. We're healing.

It's not that we'll never adopt. We're just not ready. Not yet.

25

TABITHA

AFTER TEN YEARS together, Tabitha thinks the best part of being married is being *known*. No one has ever known her like Perry. Which is why when he noticed she was unhappy, he took her out to dinner. And why, instead of a restaurant with a wine list he would have preferred, he took her to the secret place they had discovered on one of their ski trips a few years ago, a grimy bar outside of town that serves her favorite secret indulgence: bacon cheeseburgers and French fries.

All of that to say that when she wakes up the next morning, it is far later than normal, her sleep thrown off by so much sodium and carbohydrates, not to mention the red meat. When she comes downstairs, everyone is already outside in the pool. The kitchen is a disaster, cereal and milk spilled all over the table like everyone was forced to abandon their meal due to an unexpected storm. Putting her hands on her hips – she isn't wearing her wedding ring because she is so bloated from that dinner, but mercy, it was delicious – she allows herself a self-pitying sigh and begins to clean up.

Perry comes in, holding his coffee cup in one hand. "Halt,"

he says. "I know it is impossible for you to endure a mess, but I am going to take care of this."

Tabitha looks down at the bowls in her hands. He is going to load the dishwasher wrong, and there is still glitter on the floor and the chairs, and probably still pieces of that vase – she has to call the owners today – which he is going to spread around even more, and Ginger takes sugar in her coffee, and he won't wipe that up, which will leave the counters sticky...

"And no complaining about my doing it wrong," he says, putting down his cup and taking the bowls from her, kissing her forehead. "Have a seat and I will serve you."

While Tabitha brushes off a chair, he puts the bowls in the sink and assembles breakfast for her, not cold cereal but gluten-free avocado toast with smoked salmon. "You must have gotten up quite early," she says.

He presents the pepper mill as though they are at a restaurant, and she nods. When he is finished, he bows slightly.

"I wanted you to be able to sleep in. Are you feeling better?" He sits down across from her, not bothering to wipe off his own chair, with a freshened cup of coffee for himself and a mug of green tea for her.

Tabitha takes a bite of the toast, which is quite good, really, and settles the churn in her stomach. "I feel like I ate a bacon cheeseburger."

"That is unsurprising because you did. But otherwise?"

Over dinner, her resolve weakened by processed foods, Perry extracted the full story from her. Until last night, they had not had time to discuss the slumber party issue fully, and she hadn't told him about Ginger's and Elizabeth's outbursts or Pamela's phone call at all. How odd that they came on a vacation only to feel further apart from each other. When she thinks of how close she hoped they would all become during these weeks together, she doesn't know whether to laugh or cry.

"The same, I guess." She does feel better having told Perry everything, if nothing else. When she mentioned Pamela's request, he said, "I told you she was a bitch," which had made her laugh – though that might have been the beer – but said that he would help the Gala committee if Tabitha wanted him to. She will have to think about that. She is still feeling sour.

"What do you want to do about Taters?" Perry asked.

"I don't know," Tabitha said. She pushed aside the avocado toast, half eaten. She'd felt better when they weren't talking about it. "There's no good solution."

"She could just... not go," Perry says, and then holds up his hands to ward off her immediate objection. "I know, I know. She wants to go. But we are the parents. We get to say no. I know you are concerned about her social life, which I respect, but we've got a few more years before we really have to worry about that."

"With all due respect, you don't know how girls operate. It's so different from boys. She has to find her place now," Tabitha says.

"With all due respect, my love." He leans forward and puts his hand over hers gently. "My beauty. My darling. The mother of my children, the love of my life. With all due respect to the wonder that is you, I think you are dragging a bit of history into this experience."

Tabitha pulled her hand away. "What does *that* mean?"

"It means you had a hard time of things when you were a girl, and you don't want Tate to suffer through the same thing. Which is admirable. But Tate is Tate. She is different than you were, and she has her own path."

"So we're just going to let her wet the bed until she's in college?" Tabitha retorts. His calm can be exasperating.

"You know I don't mean that. It is probably time to have her agree to go back to treatment, but that issue is separate from the issue of this party. It's separate from us, and whatever we're projecting from our pasts onto her experiences. Or Taylor's, for that matter."

Tabitha isn't listening anymore. "If only it weren't a slumber party," she says.

"Yet it is," Perry says. "Here's another suggestion. What if we make it Tate's decision?"

"I doubt she's ready for that," Tabitha says.

"You seem to think she's ready to torpedo her entire social life, so why not? We'll give her some options and let her choose."

Options. What options are there? She goes or she doesn't. If only it weren't a slumber party. If only she didn't have to spend the night.

Struck, Tabitha sits up straight.

Of course she doesn't have to spend the night. Just because it's a slumber party doesn't mean she has to stay. "I have the perfect solution," she says.

He sips his coffee and frowns. "This is terrible. I don't know how that machine works."

She gets up without thinking and starts to manage the coffee maker.

"I can do it," Perry says.

"No, I will," Tabitha says. She likes having her hands busy.

Perry gets up and dumps out his cup of coffee and then comes to lean by her. "Are you going to share your perfect solution for Tate?"

"Let me think about it a little more," Tabitha says, already miles away. She finishes her adjustments and slips his cup underneath the spout as the machine begins steaming.

Perry crosses his arms and leans over, looking into the cup as if awaiting some sort of magic. "Okay. Do you want to talk about anything else? About things with Brianna, or Elizabeth and Ginger?"

"No, thanks," Tabitha says. She is done solving their problems. Let them have enough rope to hang themselves. She'll focus on Tate.

After she finishes taking care of him, she is upstairs taking Tate's sheets off the bed, working through exactly how she will present her idea to her daughter, when Ginger comes thumping in on her crutches.

"Do you have a moment?" Ginger asks.

Tabitha pulls off the last sheet and drops them onto the ground, climbing down the ladder. Honestly, does she look like she has a moment?

"Yes?" she asks, but she picks up the sheets and holds them in front of her, making it apparent she does not.

Ginger shifts uncomfortably, and Tabitha can see her wince when her foot brushes against the ground. Honestly, Ginger could be bleeding to death and she would refuse any help. But Tabitha is not going to step in and rescue her. Not today. She raises an eyebrow impatiently.

"I talked to Sunny the other day."

"Oh?" Tabitha says. That is a surprise. She is generally the point person for Sunny, when it doesn't involve private information about another family. In fact, that very morning she had received a couple of emails from Sunny, with no mention of having spoken to Ginger.

Ginger looks around furtively, as though she is about to expose a state secret. "She thinks we should tell the children."

"Does she?" Tabitha asks. The sheets are damp, and she can feel the wet against her shirt. Now she is going to have to put on a new one, as if she doesn't have enough to do. "What is it that she wants us to tell them? Have you even called the family you are supposed to talk to?"

To her surprise, Ginger nods. "I did. Have you?"

"Of course I did. We simply haven't had a chance to discuss it. Ergo, we have nothing to tell the children. Do you mind if I go put this laundry in?" She moves forward impatiently, but Ginger stays still, wavering slightly on her crutches, and she has to stop again as Ginger is blocking the door. Tabitha notices Ginger's wrist is freshly wrapped, but poorly. Well. That's what you get when you do everything yourself.

"I think she's right. While we don't have the full information, they are old enough – especially Phoebe – that presenting it to them as a fait accompli wouldn't be fair."

Tabitha sighs impatiently because she knows where this

is heading. "You want me to arrange this family conference, I presume?"

"No, actually. We should, as the adults, have a brief conversation so we are aligned. I was thinking after lunch? We'll include John and Elizabeth even though Violet isn't necessarily part of the conversation. Then we can speak to the children at dinner."

"I see you have it all figured out then, so you don't need me," Tabitha says, with a tight smile, and moves again as if to leave, but Ginger is still blocking her way.

"You can't have it both ways, Tabitha," Ginger says. "You can't complain that you're the only one who does anything and then get upset when someone else tries to contribute."

Shifting the sheets to her hip – might as well ruin her pants, too, while she's at it – Tabitha stares at Ginger. They have worked well as a team for years, but now something has gone off-kilter. "Do you think that's why I'm upset?"

"I do," Ginger says.

"That's not why I'm upset. I'm delighted to have someone help manage this family. Delighted!" she says, raising her free hand in the air and then letting it clap against her thigh on the way down. "I am upset because both you and Elizabeth take for granted everything I do and then you assume the worst of me."

She can feel herself getting warmer, can feel her throat closing, and struggles to retain control.

"You're right," Ginger says simply. She shifts again, winces again, and Tabitha glances down at her foot. She must be wrapping it all wrong; it looks too swollen still. "You're right, and I am sorry. I owe you an apology for allowing you to do all the work. I owe you an apology for getting so angry with you when you were trying to help. I am sorry."

Tabitha doesn't quite know what to say to that. "Well," she says, her throat too tight. "Thank you."

"Elizabeth owes you an apology, too, and me, and I presume she'll be around with that in time. I was wrong. I was wrong to delay acting on Phoebe's decision to go to TGA, but I have resolved that now. I may be wrong to delay acting on moving, but that is my choice. And I need that choice to be respected. When I am ready for help, I will ask for help."

"Fine," Tabitha says. "May I go do the laundry now?"

Ginger hesitates, as if waiting for her to say something else, but Tabitha has nothing left to say. She is a Gordian knot of emotions, and she cannot bear to cut through it.

"Okay?" Ginger says, and Tabitha can see that is not the way she expected this conversation to end. She thuds clumsily to the side, and Tabitha brushes past her, sheets still in her arms, and rushes into the laundry room, where she closes the door behind her.

There was the apology she was waiting for, or at least one of them. Tabitha supposes she ought to apologize, too. Only she doesn't want to apologize. Or maybe she doesn't know how. She doesn't tend to argue with people, and as long as she and Ginger have known each other, they have never had anything to apologize for. Or if they have, she hasn't known about it.

All those years she was aching for a big, busy family, she never thought of the price that would come with it. Her own family had been quiet, disappointingly so, but peaceful, and Tabitha assumed this family would be the same, only louder. Only happier. But it reminds her more of design projects she oversaw in her business, of the way people have their own agendas, bring their own problems along with them when they should have left them behind.

What had Perry been saying about her past? Accusing her of bringing her own childhood to bear on Tate? Which is silly. What are we but the sum of our experiences? What is the use of living if we cannot apply our pasts to our presents, teach our children from what we have learned?

Then again, it is obvious that Ginger's past forces her to hold everyone at arm's length, to push away the most sensible option when it is staring her in the face. It is obvious that

Elizabeth, who is a wonderful mother and the Pied Piper of their clan, has absorbed such strange ideas from her past that she thinks she is beyond being treated to a pedicure.

If those things are true, well, then, it stands to reason Tabitha has brought something unwelcome to this family, too. If only she knew what it was.

26

GINGER

"WHY ARE WE having a meeting?" Tate asks, hopping up into her father's lap and curling up against him. Taylor is already sitting in Tabitha's lap, and Phoebe is beside Ginger, their fingers linked. Perhaps Elizabeth sees the way the children are all connected to their parents because she leans forward to pick Violet up from the blanket where she is crawling around. The baby squawks in protest, and Elizabeth leans back quickly.

"We have something to talk to you about," Perry says. Their conversation at lunch had been brief, interrupted by Taylor stubbing his toe and demanding a bandage, and then Phoebe claiming she was hungry, and Violet throwing an absolute tantrum when she wasn't allowed to handle the knives at the table. But they had decided they would approach the topic briskly and honestly, letting the children know that things were indeed still unknown.

Surprisingly, Elizabeth is the one who makes the announcement. "We wanted to tell you that Brianna is going to have a baby."

Tate, who is fiddling with Perry's shirt buttons, sits bolt upright, her mouth opening in a theatrical O of surprise. "A baby?" she asks, as though she has hardly heard of such a thing.

"A *baby*?" Phoebe asks with an equal amount of shock. She looks at Perry and then at Ginger, and Ginger wonders again if she should have told Phoebe by herself, just the two of them, to shield the blow a little more.

Violet had necessitated a series of conversations as the situation changed. Ginger recalls their telling the children about the baby, and then that Brianna and Justin weren't going to parent after all, but she can hardly recall what they told the children about Elizabeth and John. They must have told them all at once, she thinks, or close to it, because everything had happened so quickly – Justin's disappearance, Brianna's panic, Elizabeth hitting Tabitha's car and seemingly the next instant coming over for Sunday dinner to meet the children.

By then, Elizabeth and John had already met all the adults, including Sunny and Brianna, but they had still seemed quite nervous. Ginger recalls John's sleeves had been buttoned at the cuffs when they arrived, but the moment they came inside and he saw Perry with his sleeves rolled up, he promptly did the same, as though this small choice would ensure he belonged.

Elizabeth and John shouldn't have worried; the twins had taken to them immediately. Even Phoebe, often cautious initially, had warmed up to them quickly. She could see why: Elizabeth and John were used to being the favorite aunt and uncle and genuinely enjoyed children. That first night they had wrestled with Tate and Taylor on the floor and then given them piggyback rides. They had brought Shrinky Dinks, which none of the children had ever seen before, and Phoebe had shrieked with glee when she saw them crumpling up in the oven. Being with children is clearly Elizabeth's default state. Just look at how easy she was with Phoebe when they were talking about TGA.

"Wait, is this baby Violet? Didn't Mama Brianna already have a baby?" Taylor asks, suspicious.

"She did have a baby. She had Violet. But now she is having another baby."

Taylor collapses back against Tabitha dramatically. "How many babies are we going to have?"

Tabitha kisses his hair.

"That's something I can't answer. All I can tell you is Brianna is going to have one this year," Perry says. He always sounds so calm and confident.

"It takes nine months," Phoebe announces for Tate and Taylor's benefit.

"We know *that*," Tate says, with a dramatic eye roll for flourish.

"It does take nine months. But she has already started cooking this baby, you see," Perry says.

"Who is cooking the baby?" Taylor asks, panicked.

Tabitha has been quiet until now, perhaps still sharp and bitter from their conversation that morning. She pulls Taylor back against her. "Daddy's just being silly. He means the baby is already growing in Brianna's tummy. Like how Violet grew in her tummy, and you did, too," she says.

"Are you going to have a baby?" Tate turns to Elizabeth and asks accusingly.

Ginger sees Elizabeth hesitate for a moment. "No. I can't have babies," she says.

Ginger meets Tabitha's eyes for a moment, and they both look away just as quickly. They have never heard Elizabeth say this so frankly.

Had the children ever even asked why Elizabeth and John had adopted Violet? It's not the sort of thing that would have confused them. In their world, adoption is the default state. Ginger recalls Tabitha's explaining to Tate and Taylor when they were much younger, "Some people's mom and birth mom are the same person."

Taylor had looked horrified, and Tate had shaken her head in disappointment and said, "That is so boring."

It is all about one's perspective, Ginger supposes.

"No, this baby," Tate is asking impatiently. "Are you going to have this baby, Aunt Elizabeth?"

"She means are you going to adopt this baby," Tabitha translates.

"No, we are not," Elizabeth says bluntly. Ginger catches Tabitha's eye again, but she cannot read her expression.

"So Mama Brianna might be this baby's mom?" Phoebe asks. She turns back and looks at Ginger, concerned, and Ginger feels herself seize inside. She absolutely should have trusted her gut to have had this conversation with Phoebe alone.

Most of the time, Ginger feels being an adoptive mother is no different than if Phoebe were biologically hers. But the reverse is not true for Phoebe, old enough to have vivid memories of another life, wise enough to understand that her story contains pain as well as gifts.

Though she knows the other mothers think she is only being stubborn, and Elizabeth was right that a certain amount of Ginger's resistance comes from her own fear of change, her love for Phoebe is why she has been so concerned about TGA, about moving, despite the obvious benefits. She is not wrong to consider how much displacement Phoebe can handle at once, when this shift in their family will bring up wounds from the past that are smoothed over but never quite healed.

Ginger tries to find a gentle way to explain, to calm Phoebe's fears. "She will be this baby's birth mom as she is your birth mom. But she has asked us to help her find this baby's parents to take care of him, as she did with Violet," Ginger says.

This is the precise language of adoption, a way of trying to pick apart the spiderweb of emotions and connections of families that are composed in different ways, of guarding and honoring everyone's feelings. *First families* and *choosing to parent* and *making a plan for adoption* and *mothers* and *expectant mothers* and *birth mothers* and *open adoptions* and *failed adoptions* and a thousand other delicate names for the delicate tendrils that twine them together. At the adoption training she had rushed through when Phoebe had been placed with her at first, Ginger had felt like she was entering a new country, a new culture, with its own languages and customs, and she still finds herself tripping over unexpected edges.

"Him? It's a boy?" Taylor asks. "Finally! I'm sick of all these girls."

"We're sick of you," Tate says, slipping out of Perry's lap and putting her small fists up like she is ready to fight. Violet shrieks in delight at the promise of action.

"Okay, wait," Phoebe says, holding up her finger in a charming imitation of an adult. "Who is going to adopt the baby, then? You?" Now she points at Tabitha.

"Not us," Perry says.

"*Us?*" Phoebe turns to Ginger then. "*We're* adopting this baby?"

"Not us, either. We don't know this baby's parents yet. We're looking for them, and when we meet them, you will meet them, too."

"We're still going to be a family, though, right?" Phoebe asks nervously. Whether she means she and Ginger, or all of them, Ginger isn't sure, but the answer is the same.

"We'll always be a family," Ginger says. "Nothing will ever change that." She reaches over, slipping her hand over Phoebe's and giving it a squeeze.

Elizabeth steps in. "Families change. Like this family changed when Violet was born and we became her parents. People get married, people have babies, and those things make families change. But that doesn't mean they're not families."

"Right," Ginger says, agreeing, though she is startled by the complacent manner in which Elizabeth delivers this. Glancing at Tabitha, Ginger can see she looks equally uncertain.

Phoebe seems to be considering Elizabeth's statement on families seriously, and then she turns to Tabitha, Ginger especially tense as they wait for her next question. "Can we make s'mores again?" she asks, and the adults laugh with tight relief.

But after s'mores, after Ginger hoists herself upstairs and into bed, Phoebe knocks softly on the door and pads in, barefoot. "Marmee, I want to talk to you," she says. The light casts across the sharpening planes of her face, making her look incongruously older in her dinosaur pajamas.

"All right," Ginger says. "Hop on up." She puts down her book and her reading glasses and pats the bed beside her. The bed is absurdly high, as though the people who own this house think they live in Versailles and there will be courtiers to help them climb in and out.

Phoebe climbs up, but instead of settling in beside her, she sits down by Ginger's knees, crossing her legs and leaning forward earnestly. "I want to talk to you about the baby," she says.

"I presumed you might," Ginger says, trying to keep her tone light but respectful.

"The thing is," Phoebe says, "I don't want Mama Brianna to have another baby."

"Why is that?"

"Because there are too many babies already!"

She nods thoughtfully to show she is listening and asks, "What do you mean?"

Phoebe doesn't answer for a moment. Then she leans forward, spreading her hands out wide on the bedspread. "Marmee, I don't want to hurt your feelings, okay?"

"Okay."

"But Mama Brianna was supposed to be my mom. But she wasn't. And ever since then, she doesn't want to be anyone else's mom, either."

"Okay," Ginger says again. She is afraid of where this is going, but she nods again, encouraging Phoebe to continue.

"So was it me? What if it was my fault? I was the first baby, right? That was when she said she didn't want to be a mom, and Meemaw had to be my mom, and then you had to be my mom."

Ginger is not given to strong emotion, but the tortured look on her daughter's face pulls at her heart. When the children's grandmother died, Phoebe's confusion and sadness had been overwhelming, knotted together with the disruption of living in a new home with a new caregiver and without Tate and Taylor.

Because they were in crisis mode at that point, Ginger realizes how little attention they ever paid, despite the rounds of therapy, to the first loss Phoebe felt, the loss of Brianna and Justin as her everyday parents, a loss of something she never even had. It is not something she speaks of often, and even with Violet, it had not presented this strongly. Maybe it is Phoebe's age now, or the other changes she feels coming, or maybe she is only now able to make sense of it enough to ask. Phoebe's past has been complicated, and it feels like every new bump in the road unearths a new layer of questions, of anxieties, of emotions to cope with. Whatever the reason, Brianna's pregnancy and the questions surrounding it are hitting her hard, and Ginger wishes she had prepared better. If only parenthood came with scheduled alerts on coming changes and crises.

"None of this is about you. Mama Brianna loves you loves you loves you. All of you. And your Meemaw loved you, and I love you so much. Beyond measure. If there is one thing you should never, ever worry about it is about how many people love you. This is the best part of our family – you have so many people who love you. So very many."

Phoebe swallows hard, but doesn't say anything. Ginger leans forward, gritting her teeth against the sharpness of the pain in her leg, and strokes her daughter's arm gently.

"So why won't she be anybody's mom?" Phoebe asks. "If she loves us so much?"

"It's not about wanting, really." Ginger tries to think for a moment of how to explain this to Phoebe in a new way. "You know Charlotte's sister Rylka? She's fourteen, right?"

"I think so," Phoebe says.

"Mama Brianna was Rylka's age when she had you. She was fourteen. That's pretty young to try to be someone's mom."

This comparison has the intended effect – Phoebe's eyes widen. Phoebe has always been aware that Brianna was fourteen when she was born, but it is not until now, connecting that age with her best friend's older sister, and maybe with understanding how close that is to her own age, that she understands how young that was.

"So you see, she wasn't really ready to be anyone's full-time mom when you were born. Which is why you and she lived with Meemaw."

"But she wanted to be Violet's mom," Phoebe says. "Right? Until Aunt Elizabeth and Uncle John adopted her instead?"

Ginger squeezes Phoebe's hand again, buying herself time to think. There will come a time, maybe not too far from now, as bright and observant as Phoebe is, that she begins to peel apart the stories she has been told about Brianna and Justin, the ways in which their family's story has been whitewashed. They have never directly lied to the children, but Ginger has come to see how parceling out information in small amounts and offering the sunniest interpretation of facts is dishonest in its own way.

Though what can she do? She doesn't want Phoebe to resent or dislike Brianna and Justin. Whatever choices they have made, they are her family. Is it like this for all parents, Ginger wonders, or only adoptive ones, holding your breath as your children age and watching them come to understand the fullness of their own stories?

"She did want to try to parent Violet. She simply didn't

feel like she was ready to do it on her own. So when your – when Justin left, she decided she wanted Violet to have parents who were ready to take care of her."

Phoebe purses her lips. She is still leaning forward, frog-like, sitting like a child but dealing with questions that would frustrate the savviest of adults, caught somewhere between childhood and her future.

"So if she doesn't want to be a parent, then how come she keeps getting pregnant?" Phoebe asks.

Ginger opens her mouth and then closes it again. This is the complicated question only Elizabeth has spoken aloud and that none of them can answer. Who can speak to another woman's choices?

Yet she has to answer these questions somehow, even if it is only an answer that will hold Phoebe until she is ready for the next stage of the discussion, maybe about Brianna specifically, maybe about pregnancy and responsibilities and decisions in general. This constant excavation and discovery.

"Do you maybe want to talk to Mama Brianna about some of these questions you have?" Ginger asks. She is holding her breath slightly as she does. Sunny said Brianna was not up to talking right then, but she always says if the children have questions, they should ask.

"Maybe," Phoebe says, but she has already retreated back into her mind, and Ginger knows it will be a while before she is ready for that conversation. Ginger will have to reach out to Brianna in the meantime to prepare her, and make sure Phoebe has an appointment with her counselor when she gets home.

"I cannot speak for Mama Brianna. Only she knows why she makes the decisions she does. But I do know, and I really, really want you to understand this, Phoebe, my love," she says, reaching out and brushing her fingers under Phoebe's chin, lifting it gently until their eyes meet. "Your choosing me to be your Marmee is the best thing that has ever happened in my whole life. I didn't 'have to' be your mother. I *get* to be your mother, and it is an honor and a joy to think that I will get to be your mother every single day for the rest of our lives, because you are smart and silly and amazing and curious, and I love you very, very much."

Phoebe nods and lunges forward, hugging Ginger, who doesn't even notice the pain in her leg. She turns her head long enough to say, "I love you, too, Marmee," and then buries her face in Ginger's shoulder again, and Ginger holds her close, the way she did when Phoebe first came to her, safe harbor in the storm.

27

ELIZABETH

WHETHER IT IS the seriousness of the conversation they had with the children, or time, or the way things between the three mothers remain stiff and formal, the freedom Elizabeth felt after the spa has evaporated, leaving salty regret in its wake.

It makes her hot with shame to think she told Tabitha and Ginger the darkest secret she holds. There is nothing worse than a woman who hates motherhood. Except maybe an adoptive mother who hates motherhood, or an adoptive mother who put her family in an obscene amount of debt because she couldn't do the one goddamned thing women were put on this earth to do.

What would John think if he knew how she feels? What would he think about all the money they spent, all the years they lost, all the physical risk she put herself through, the humiliation of it all if he knew how miserable she is?

Maybe that is why she hasn't yet called the couple she is supposed to talk to. Yasmin and Peter. Because she has to lie to them, tell them that this is a wonderful family to join, that they will love being parents, and really what she wants to tell them is to *run*. But she has to call them. Angry as she is, Tabitha would call instead if Elizabeth asked her to, but isn't the problem that Tabitha is always doing everything?

She puts her head down on the nightstand for a minute and then forces herself to pick up the phone and dial.

"Hang on, let me get Yasmin," Peter says when she identifies herself. He has a deep, soothing voice, the kind you hear on classical radio, and when Yasmin answers, her voice is equally musical, bearing a soft accent Elizabeth cannot place.

"Okay, we're here," he says, and the contrast between his professional voice and his eager tone makes her smile, loosening the unnamable emotion in her belly.

"Hi, Elizabeth, we're so glad you called!" Yasmin says. They're on speaker now; she can hear the echo.

"I saw in your messages with Tabitha that you did fertility treatments at Fertility Innovations. We went there, too," Elizabeth says. It still stings, remembering that place, the atrium of the waiting room with warm light spilling in, the unsparing Colorado sunshine never matching her mood, the curious combination of hope and dread. She'd gone to college out east, where there were sometimes thunderstorms that lasted for hours, turning the day into night, and long, gray winters that allowed, even encouraged a good sulk and the coziness of a warm drink in the premature dark of the afternoon. Colorado's relentlessly blue skies had a way of refusing those comforts.

"Oh, you did? Who was your doctor? We had Dr. Ramirez until she left, and then Dr. Rogers. Who were you with?" Yasmin asks.

"That's so funny. We were with Dr. Ramirez, too. We stopped right before she left."

"Because you adopted your daughter?" Peter asks. There is a little scuffle on their end, and Yasmin whispers something.

"Yes. No. We were going to stop. We couldn't..." She thinks of saying they couldn't afford another round financially, which, while true, wasn't really at the heart of it. It was because they couldn't afford all the other costs. Her body, their hearts, their marriage, none of these could withstand the strain for another moment. "We were just done. Then we adopted Violet shortly after."

"We're done, too," Peter says, and she recognizes the weariness in his voice. "And we weren't even looking to adopt yet, frankly. A friend of ours saw your post – or your sister-in-law's post. I'm sorry, I don't know exactly how you're related."

Elizabeth laughs in acknowledgment. "Yeah, me either. It's complicated. I usually do say 'in-laws' when I'm talking to people who don't know our family, even though we're not in-laws. We're just… family. Anyway, it was Tabitha who posted it."

"My parents got divorced when I was little, and both my parents have been remarried multiple times, so I have lots of semi-relatives I don't have names for. I call them aunts and uncles and cousins anyway. It makes it easier," Peter says.

"Exactly. It doesn't matter, anyway. Family is family," she says, surprised by the confidence with which she says it.

"I only have a brother. My mother lives with him and his family in California," Yasmin says. "Can I ask…" Another scuffle, another whisper, this one from Peter. Elizabeth imagines them having a silent argument sitting on a sofa beside each other. Apparently Yasmin wins because she asks, "Can I ask how you knew it was time to adopt?"

Elizabeth pulls her lips into a perfect circle like she is blowing a smoke ring as she exhales. Her story is so long. Everyone's stories are so long, aren't they? A trail of victories and miseries that ultimately only matter to the people enduring them. "That is a good question. I don't think we were. We lucked into Violet. Adoption wasn't our plan at the time. We were planning, really, on living child-free." She thinks of those days, the cracked and empty shells they had become. Where would they be now if Violet hadn't come along?

"Anyway, when Violet came it just felt right." That isn't

entirely true, either, but she can't bear to get into it, not now. Violet had felt like a gift, yes, but Elizabeth also felt so blurry and out of control at the time she might have said yes to anything just to make the pain end. "When did you do your last cycle?" she asks, changing the subject slightly.

"A year ago," Yasmin says, and Elizabeth takes that in. They are living a life she and John might have had. If she'd left work five minutes later the day she met Tabitha, if she had been paying more attention to the traffic, if, a thousand ifs, none of this would have happened. They would be Yasmin and Peter.

But then she wouldn't have Violet. Something inside her lurches wild and raw at that thought.

"We've been in therapy for the past year. We were in therapy before, obviously, during treatment. We saw Laurel at FI – did you see her or the other counselor?"

There had been counselors at the clinic, Elizabeth remembers. But she had never wanted to go. It was easier to put her head down and keep plowing through. What was there to talk about anyway? They were sad. It sucked. What else was there to say?

"We didn't see anyone, actually," Elizabeth says, and she means it to sound careless, because it was, but Peter and Yasmin don't say anything for a moment, and their silence gives her space to wonder. Had everyone else been talking to someone?

She had intended to tell her family only after she was good and pregnant, and then after a while it was too late to tell them, and she was too raw to bear whatever criticisms they would have lobbed at her. John's family had known, and they had tried to be nice and supportive, but she just *couldn't* with them. All those Fertile Myrtle sisters-in-law and their stressful two months trying to conceive their fourth child – oh, the horror. Being with them was like living with that reality TV family with all the kids and the weird skirts. She had heard all the old wives' tales and stories of some friend of a friend who got pregnant when they stopped trying, just stop trying so hard, just eat more pineapple, just eat less sugar, just do yoga, just wear warm socks, just stop using lotions with parabens, just stop drinking caffeine, just *stop*.

None of it had worked anyway.

"Everyone is different," Peter says, that smooth voice making it sound okay.

Then Yasmin speaks, and her soft voice sounds sad. "I can't imagine going through it alone. You must be so strong."

"I don't know about that," Elizabeth says, and she tries to laugh, but something squeezes in her throat and she can't quite get it out.

Peter says, "In any case, it's only now we've even felt ready to consider our next steps. We have a lot of things to grieve. But when our friends sent us Tabitha's post, we thought we should at least consider the option."

"So, wait, you aren't looking to adopt?" Elizabeth asks, confused. She knows she should have looked at Tabitha's notes on them before she called, but she has no idea what she did with the packet.

"We were just starting to turn in that direction. It was probably the same for you, right? All that grief. All that loss. Did you have any pregnancies during treatment?"

"Four," Elizabeth says. Her voice cracks. She never tells this to anyone.

"Oh, my goodness," Yasmin says. "I am so sorry. So you understand. You know what it's like to grieve. Other people don't understand, do they? The grief of infertility is so specific. I'm amazed you went straight from your last transfer to adoption. It's been a really slow process for us. The grief."

Grief. Yasmin had said the word three times. Elizabeth repeats it silently, her mouth forming the word, a kiss that pulls back.

Mostly, when their cycles failed, she was angry. She punched things. She called the doctor incompetent and the nurses inept. She shut herself in her car and screamed so loudly and for so long she sprained her vocal cords and had to communicate at work by typing on her computer and having one of the students read her instructions aloud. She had been so, so furious.

She doesn't tell Peter and Yasmin that. "Grief. Sure," she says finally. "I know."

When she finally joins the rest of the family that afternoon, they go out for miniature golf, but the noise of the course and the nearby gokart track feels like too much, so she gets some soft ice cream and sits on an old wooden bench. Eventually, John comes by with Violet and asks if she wants to drive bumper cars with the kids. Normally she would be all over it, but she isn't in the mood. She tells him no, and he gives her Violet. She watches them driving, Perry's knees practically up by his ears in his car, the kids shrieking in pleasure. Ginger crutches over and sits down, and then Tabitha walks up the hill, fresh-faced from laughing so much, even though she was definitely the worst bumper car driver on the track.

Elizabeth puts Violet down and lets her surf along the edge of the bench. "Oh, she'll get splinters," Tabitha says, pulling her hands away.

"She's fine," Elizabeth says. "If she gets a splinter, she will survive."

Tabitha looks over at her quickly and lets Violet's hands go, which doesn't matter because she simply surfs herself over to Ginger's crutches and grabs on to them, giggling to herself like she has won the giant-stick lottery.

"I talked to Yasmin and Peter. The chiropractors who own that wellness business?" Elizabeth says. She's still looking at the bumper cars, watching John and Perry collide into each other, laughing like boys.

"Oh, what were they like?" Ginger asks. She had said they might be a little too woo-woo, but Elizabeth hadn't gotten that impression.

"Nice," Elizabeth says. What else is she supposed to say?

"You've been quiet today. Was it talking to them?"

Elizabeth stares at the bumper cars for another minute, trying to figure out how to explain. "It's funny, you know. I thought everything would be okay when I had a kid. And now I do, but my sisters-in-law get pregnant so easily, and when one of them is, I just want to…" She squeezes her hands ineffectually in the air, clawing at nothing. "It makes me so mad. When they complain about it, I want to scream. Like, do you know how lucky you are? Do you know I would have given anything to have swollen ankles or fatigue or stretch marks?"

She looks at Ginger and Tabitha, who are both looking back at her. They don't understand. Neither of them ever cared about being pregnant. They can't know. They can't understand.

"They're just so happy all the time. Everything is so perfect. Like their kids are these little miracles, and even when they're complaining, they're not really complaining. It's like, 'Hahaha, look at my kids who put grape jelly on the kitchen cabinets, hashtag mom life.' I just want to burn it all down."

Ginger turns away, looks out at the miniature golf course, the tiny windmill spinning so slowly it hardly moves. "Did you ever think," she says delicately, "that you should talk to someone?"

"I don't think talking to anyone is going to help me not be a terrible mother," Elizabeth says.

Tabitha speaks so quickly and forcefully that Elizabeth is taken aback. "You keep saying that, but it's not true. It's never been true. I watch you with Phoebe and the twins and you're a miracle. And you and Violet together – you are magic. Her colic was so hard on you, I know, and even at the best of times, being a new mother is an unbelievable adjustment. Perry and I were talking the other day, and he reminded me of how when we first got the twins, I had a crying breakdown like every five minutes."

Elizabeth raises an eyebrow. "You?" she asks.

Tabitha nods. "It was so exhausting, and I never knew what I was supposed to be doing, and the minute I figured it out, they would go through some developmental leap and I'd be lost again."

"It was the same with Phoebe," Ginger says. "She'd gotten so used to staying up late when their grandmother was sick, it took three months to adjust her bedtime back to normal, and then she started having nightmares. I don't think either of us got a full night's sleep the entire first year she was with me. Don't get me wrong, she was in no way a newborn, but it was a lot."

"Really?" Tabitha asks, looking at Ginger and laughing. "Did we ever talk about this? Or were we both such zombies at the time we didn't even register the other person was going through the same thing?"

"Probably the latter," Ginger says.

"It's just like— I prayed for this. Literally prayed for it," Elizabeth says.

"So do biological moms, and they get postpartum depression all the time. And adoptive postpartum is just as real as typical postpartum," Tabitha says.

Ginger nods. "Adoptive motherhood is motherhood. All terms and conditions apply."

Elizabeth looks back and forth between them, trying to decide if they are making this up so she will feel better. But it doesn't seem like it. If nothing else, Ginger and Tabitha have never lied to her.

"Tabitha," she says, "I'm sorry for what I said. At the spa. It wasn't fair to you. I've been so angry, but it's not your fault. I'm sorry."

The smile that cracks open Tabitha's face is one of happy relief, and Elizabeth feels it inside herself, too.

As if Peter and Yasmin are reading her mind from miles away, a message pops up on her phone. A name and a phone number.

In case you want to talk to someone, Yasmin says.

THE ARTIST'S LIFE

One of my first memories is of standing in the living room at my grandparents' house, frozen as I listened to a song on the radio. I don't remember what it was, or how old I was. I only remember that the music caught me and held me, and I could not move until it let go.

In school, I hummed to myself in class so often they sent me to see the nurse because they thought I had a problem. Whenever I went over to a friend's house for a playdate, if they had a piano, I would ignore them and go sit at it, pressing the keys and wondering at the sounds that came out, until my friends got sick of waiting for me and went off to play by themselves. I wasn't invited back to a lot of people's houses.

My parents weren't big on religion, but I begged my mom to let me go to church with our neighbors because at church they sang songs and there was always a piano in the Sunday school room I could play when the lesson was done. The moment we could join the school band, in fourth grade, my mother filled out the application for a loaner instrument – a trumpet, shiny and yellow in its dingy case. I didn't mind that my trumpet was used while the kids around me had ones that were new. I just wanted to play. In class, I wiggled my fingers on invisible valves while the teachers blabbered about things that didn't matter – science and math and reading.

My partner is a painter. We understand each other. A relationship is a series of promises, and one of the promises we have made to ourselves and then to each other is that our art will always come before money. We both teach a little – music and art – but we know that teaching too much not only robs your art of the time it needs to breathe, but it changes your relationship to it. You can only tell people how to change what they're doing so often before it starts to snake its way into your own work. I had to take a break from teaching and focus on performing last year when I couldn't get my own voice out of my head. It meant we had to move out of our apartment into a smaller place, but it made all the difference in how I was playing.

I see the salaries of ball players sometimes, and it's crazy that people who play a literal game make millions of dollars a year, while we do something that matters and are always scraping by. I don't want to be rich; I don't care about being rich. Neither of us grew up with much of anything, and I wouldn't know what to do with a lot of money if we had it. But it would be nice not to have to hold my breath when I swipe my debit card at the grocery store, or not worry whether we're going to make rent.

I would teach my kids that art is what matters. That they're not really living unless they are creating something. That whatever they want to do – make music, or paint, or dance, or act, or write, or whatever way they want to be creative – that's the thing that will keep them alive, the thing that will keep the world alive. When we're sad or angry, or even happy or in love, we don't turn to commercial real estate or personal injury attorneys. We turn to art.

That's how our kids are going to grow up. In a house that may not be big or fancy, but where we all know what matters. Where they'll be allowed to explore who they are, and where we'll always make music instead of watching TV, and we'll let them draw all over the walls because you can always repaint walls, but childhood doesn't last.

28

TABITHA

ONE OF TATE and Taylor's favorite treats is getting their nails done. They love the enormous massage chairs and the polish (the sparklier, the better), and are greatly offended when they have to take it off for school.

So when Tabitha says she and Tate are going to the nail salon but Taylor can't come, he is understandably disappointed. She explains that she needs to talk to Tate alone, and they will have a special outing just the two of them another day, but Taylor nonetheless elects to pitch a serious fit, a toddler-level tantrum. Normally she would deal with it, coax and cajole him into calm, but that day she looks at his Oscarwinning performance and she turns to Perry and says, "Good luck!" She and Tate take the big car, and she lets Tate listen to Radio Disney the whole way there. They have only a few days left on this trip and she has to let Pamela – *excuse me, the house manager* – know about Tate's RSVP. She is not above bribery.

"I've been thinking about Serafina's party," Tabitha says when their toes have been painted and they are waiting for them to dry, massage rollers buzzing against their backs. Tate is so small she vibrates along with the chair, and Tabitha has to fight to take her seriously as she watches her daughter's face shake.

"Me, too!" Tate says, as though it is an unexpectedly wonderful coincidence that they would both be thinking about this at the same moment. "Phoebe says when she goes to slumber parties they stay up all night and eat whatever they want."

Tabitha winces. When she saw the kids "practicing" the other night, she knew it was going to be trouble. But how can she stop Phoebe from wanting to usher her sister into this world of girlhood, and Tate for wanting to follow? If it had been her, she would have wanted to get there as quickly as possible, too.

"I'm concerned you're awfully young to be going to a slumber party, for one. It can be hard spending the night away from home."

"I spend the night at Phoebe and Aunt Ginger's all the time."

"It's a little different when it's family, but that is a fair point. Still, the thing is" – and she leans a little closer to Tate, even though the salon is empty other than the employees, who are gathered toward the back, relaxing and talking—"the other issue I'm concerned about is what you'll do about using the bathroom that night. I wonder what would happen if you had an accident."

There is a fine line Tabitha and Perry have always tried to walk between making it clear Tate's issues are not something she should be ashamed of and being honest about the fact that they need to be managed. Because this party invitation has made it evident that it can't be ignored any longer, especially when it comes to social situations.

Tabitha has gone over and over the possibilities in her mind, that Tate's accidents are a resistance to authority, some suppressed trauma over her grandmother's death, bodily disconnect – therapy has turned up none of these things, but perhaps Tate simply wasn't able to verbalize them at the time. Perry is right; they are going to have to talk Tate into going back into treatment. Maybe this will be the first step.

"I know," Tate says, visibly deflating. "I'm worrying about that, too."

"And what do you think?" Tabitha asks.

"I don't want to have an accident at Serafina's," Tate whispers, leaning forward to meet Tabitha so their foreheads are nearly touching.

Tate looks so worried Tabitha almost regrets bringing it up, wishes for a moment she had taken Perry's advice to simply decline and told Tate she was too young. It would have avoided Tate's feeling uncomfortable entirely, and she could have been mad at her mother's foolishness, which they both might as well get used to.

Instead she has been so certain it matters for Tate to go, but does it, really? The more she thinks about it, the more she wonders if Perry is right and Pamela Preston is actually a bitch, because what sort of sociopath invites a bunch of seven-year-olds to a sleepover? What sort of princess just assumes Perry and Tabitha will jump to her orders to help with the Gala without even bothering to invite her to be on the committee? What sort of idiot falls for a viral marketing campaign for an island that doesn't even exist (Eroda is fake – Tabitha looked it up) because she is so desperate to be first and best and special?

"So you don't want to go to the party?" Tabitha asks, unable to keep the hope from her voice. Maybe Tate will change her mind and then they won't have to worry about either part of it – dealing with Pamela or the accidents.

"Yeah, I do," Tate says, as if she were not aware grown-ups could be so dumb. "I just don't want to go if I'm going to have an accident." She whispers this last part.

"What do you think about wearing a pull-up? Just for that night?" Tabitha is still leery about whether this solution would actually work or not, as she has not seen the nightgowns in question, nor has she determined a way to ask about their design in a way that doesn't make her seem Amish.

As she suspected, the pull-up idea makes Tate no less anxious. "No way. What if they *see*? Or what if it makes *noise* while I'm walking around?"

"Good points," Tabitha says, as though they had not previously occurred to her. "So do you want to spend the night?"

"Not if I'm going to have an *accident*," Tate repeats in that same terrified whisper. She brings her knees up onto the chair, which is so large it makes her look even smaller, more vulnerable, and half leans over the arm, practically crawling into Tabitha's lap. The massage function is still making her face vibrate slightly.

"We don't know ahead of time if you will have an accident. Which is the problem." Tabitha puts her index finger against her lips and pretends to think again. "You know how I said I thought your grade was a little young for a slumber party?"

Tate rolls her eyes aggressively. "I am *not* too young."

"Oh, I know. I know you are quite grown up, but I am still your mommy, and it is hard for me to remember how mature you are. So one idea I have is to say that I am not ready to have you spend the night, but that you will go to the party and I can pick you up at, say, nine o'clock. How does that sound?"

Tate looks suspicious. "But everyone else will be spending the night and I'll miss all the fun."

"Not all the fun. I know Phoebe said people stay up all night, but she is older than you, and I suspect at this party everyone will fall asleep earlier than they do at slumber parties she goes to. You'll be there for cake and presents and games and really everything except the sleeping. We could even take you back over for breakfast in the morning."

"But everyone will know," Tate says.

"They'll know you're not there for the sleeping part. And there might be some things you will miss. But I can tell Serafina's mom that I believe you're too young for a sleepover, which is true, and then it's my fault and not anything to do with you. That I'm just mean."

"You're going to say you're mean?" Tate boggles at the idea.

"Not precisely. But your friends might think so. I'm okay with that because it means you don't have to feel uncomfortable." Tabitha has pictured herself saying this to Pamela, that Tate is too young for a slumber party, and in her mind, Pamela is taken down a peg or two by her pointing this out.

Tate collapses back in her chair, sticking her legs back out and staring at her toenails. Tabitha glances over at the television, which is silently playing a home-improvement show. The edges of the people talking are fuzzy. She is going to have to give in and get contacts. Or Lasik. She pulls out her planner and makes a note to call her optometrist as well as one for Taylor when they get back into town.

"I'm going to think about it," Tate announces as Tabitha closes her planner and returns it to her bag.

"That sounds like a good plan. You let me know if you want to talk about it more."

"Can we go to Paradise Bakery on the way home and have gelato? Just us?" Tate asks, scooting forward on her chair, ready to spring back into action.

Tabitha is about to say no, it isn't even lunchtime, and they've had so much sugar and dairy on this trip already they'll be eating nothing but lettuce for weeks to recover. She is still bloated from her indulgence with Perry the other night. But she looks at Tate, really looks at the shape of her, still a little girl but not for much longer. Being around Violet for such a long time has brought into sharp relief a lesson Tabitha apparently needs to learn over and over, that it goes fast, so fast, and if she doesn't stop thinking about what is happening next and focus on what is happening now, she'll miss it all.

"Okay," she says. "Just this once."

When they get home, Tate high on gelato and the power

of sparkly nails, Perry has coerced Taylor and Phoebe into playing horseshoes and croquet, in blissful ignorance of the fact none of them knows either game. No one cares; Taylor and Phoebe are having a grand time knocking the balls through the hoops in no particular order, and Tate runs up, grabbing a mallet and joining in without question. Perry is pitching the horseshoes with exaggerated panache, going into a deep curtsy, one leg thrust out behind him as he tosses them, the horseshoes falling comfortable feet away from the stakes.

"Hello," she says, giving him a kiss. "You're doing terribly."

"Beginner's mind," he says, tapping his temple as though this means something. "How did that go?"

"Okay," Tabitha says. "She said she'll think about it. Then she demanded gelato."

"Did you get her some?"

Tabitha nods seriously, and Perry feigns shock. "Scandal. I'm going to have to report you to the perfect mothers league."

"They've already heard about my violations, I'm sure. Where's Ginger?"

"Last I saw she was on the couch in the living room. Don't you want to stay and admire my form? I'm headed for the Olympics, if horseshoes are a sport," Perry calls after her as she walks away, but she only smiles back at him.

When she steps inside the living room, it is cool and dark, and Ginger is lying with her eyes closed and her foot elevated. "Are you okay?" Tabitha asks.

Ginger opens her eyes and squints for a moment until Tabitha moves so the sun isn't at her back. "Sure," she says. "How did it go with Tate?"

"Good, thank you," Tabitha says. She sits down on the edge of the couch, noticing that Ginger clenches slightly when she does. "Though I did want to say – talking to her made me realize you were right. I have been pushing you too hard about moving. About Phoebe's school."

Ginger looks taken aback. "Thank you," she says awkwardly, though Tabitha hasn't technically apologized.

"I am sorry," she says. "I really am. I know it doesn't matter because you've realized it's the right thing to do, but…" She hears herself begin to back out of her apology and forces herself to stop talking. "Anyway. I was just trying to help. I'm glad everything's working out."

There's a long silence between them, and Tabitha thinks maybe she needs to apologize more, or differently, but then Ginger says, "It's funny you bring it up, but I think I need a little help now."

"Sure, what do you need?" Tabitha asks, perking up.

"The thing is, and I haven't told you this because you would have wanted to go back to the hospital and I didn't want to, but my ankle isn't getting any better. I was going to wait a few more days until we got home, but I can't bear it anymore. I think we need to go to a doctor. Now."

Normally, Ginger's face is impassive, but as Tabitha looks at her now, she can see small lines of tension spreading across her forehead, the way her mouth is clamped shut.

"Can I see?" Tabitha asks, and when Ginger nods, she turns and kneels, unwrapping the bandage slowly. She hasn't seen it for over a week, since Ginger fell, but when Tabitha finishes pulling away the fabric from Ginger's ankle, if anything, it looks worse. The colors are mottled, and it is still round and swollen, the discoloration too fresh for an injury that should be half healed. "Oh," she says when she has pulled the bandage fully away, looking at the print of it on Ginger's tender skin. "You should have told me."

"I know," Ginger says with a grimace.

29

GINGER

"IT'S NOT A family vacation without a few trips to the emergency room," Perry says when they get home from the hospital. He's standing in the driveway, the children playing basketball behind him. Ginger didn't check the itinerary before she asked Tabitha to take her to the doctor, so she doesn't know what they are all supposed to be doing, but it doesn't seem to matter. Perhaps in the waning days of this surprisingly eventful trip, even Tabitha is too worn out to marshal them anymore.

"That is true, but I expected it to be the children," Ginger says.

"Oh, my gosh, what happened?" John asks, coming out of the house as Tabitha helps Ginger out of the car, Ginger's purple cast leading the way.

"Turns out it wasn't so much sprained as broken," Ginger says with game good humor, which may be partially due to the painkillers she accepted. She feels slightly drunk, the cheerful softened edge that makes the pain distant and the world a little rosier. Also maybe because it feels like she has been tensing all week, afraid of asking for help. But Tabitha had simply done what Ginger asked, and knowing her leg is going to heal now, Ginger feels a calm so great it is almost like joy. And maybe it is also a little bit because she is starting to let go, trying to see the coming changes as less of a tsunami and more part of the tides.

"Marmee, what happened?" Phoebe says, finally interrupting their game when she sees the cast.

"I'm okay, sweetie," she says. Phoebe runs over to Ginger, throwing an arm around her and clinging to her side. She is still holding the basketball with her free arm, much to Tate and Taylor's annoyance.

"Are we playing or what?" Tate calls out, hands on her hips like a tiny Tabitha.

"It's purple!" Phoebe says, looking at Ginger's cast.

"I chose it especially for you," Ginger says. They offered her a bevy of colors, far more than had been on offer the last time she had broken something, which had been in fourth grade, when all they had was dull white. She selected purple because it is Phoebe's favorite color. Had she realized how large the cast would be and therefore how lurid that much purple would look, she might have made a different decision, but what does it matter? She knew it would make Phoebe happy, and what is middle age for if not wearing purple casts?

"Are you going to be okay?" Phoebe asks, still clinging to her, and Ginger pauses from her labored walk to give her a real hug.

"I am. It's a small fracture, which is why they missed it the first time, and it's going to heal just fine."

"Okay," Phoebe says, and runs off.

"Always nice to have the loving concern of one's children," Perry says. "Where would you like to recline, m'lady?"

"We can sit by the porch," Tabitha says, pointing up at the chaise and chairs there.

They get Ginger settled, the echoing bounce of the basketball in the background, and Tabitha bustles around, surrounding Ginger with pillows as if she is transporting eggs, going back to the car and then in and out of the house while John joins the children under the basketball hoop and Perry sits down and looks at his phone.

A minute later Elizabeth comes down with Violet. "Wow. You just have to have all the attention, don't you, Ginge," she says dryly, eyeing the cast.

"It's true. I'm terribly dramatic," Ginger says. "Tabitha, will you sit down? You're making me dizzy," she says when Tabitha comes out of the house again, this time carrying a tray with a pitcher of herbal iced tea and glasses, each with a perfect tower of ice cubes inside as if she arranged them that way. Perhaps, Ginger thinks wryly, she did. Some things will never change.

"I just have to get the snacks," Tabitha says, setting down the tray.

"No one is hungry," Elizabeth says. "We all ate three minutes ago."

As if to prove her wrong, Violet grabs a handful of grass and starts to shove it in her mouth. Ginger leans over and gently pulls it away, and when she sits back, the disequilibrium gives her a pleasant rush.

"I'm hungry. I'll get them," Perry volunteers, and he stands up, heading for the kitchen without looking up from his phone, and walks straight into a glass door.

"That man is a titan of industry and he walks into a door," Elizabeth observes, watching him correct his course, still not looking up from his phone.

"It's infuriating, isn't it? Men go around walking into doors and they're still in charge of everything," Tabitha says.

"He can only do it because you're in the back, stage-managing everything at home," Ginger says. "You're the perfect mother and the perfect wife. You do everything and you never walk into doors."

"I walk into doors all the time!" Tabitha says, sounding shocked and defensive, and Ginger laughs out loud because it is such a funny thing to want to defend. "Metaphorically. I don't actually walk into doors."

"You'd never know it," Elizabeth says. "It's hard to be around you, Tee. You're like the ultimate Pinterest mom."

"I don't even know what that is," Ginger says.

"You know. One of those moms who makes all the perfect cakes or does all the perfect activities for their kids like they have on Pinterest. I tried to do this one thing with Violet where I made all this bubble bath foam with food coloring with a hand mixer, and she just ate some of it and then puked. That would never happen to you."

"I don't know how you got the impression that I am perfect. I am most definitely not," Tabitha says, and she sounds offended, which is odd, for someone who spends so much time making everything, including herself, perfect.

"It's intimidating to be around you," Elizabeth says.

"You're not intimidated by anything," Tabitha scoffs. "You probably came out of the womb punching."

"Elizabeth," Ginger says, closing her eyes and leaning back in the chaise, "is intimidated by *ev-er-y-thing*. Especially you."

"I don't think that's quite true," Elizabeth says, offended.

Ginger says nothing, her eyes still closed.

There is silence for a moment, and then Tabitha says, "The thing is, it doesn't do us any good to be comparing, does it? Because we aren't the same people, and we don't have the same children. Okay, so I do a lot of activities with the twins, but they need more activities than Phoebe. She's quite good at entertaining herself. Tate and Taylor do better with more stimulation. I'm guessing Violet is going to be like that, too," she says.

Ginger opens her eyes to see Violet handing Elizabeth the cups, one by one. Elizabeth takes each one, dropping it on the floor, where Violet picks it up and hands it to her mother again. It's mesmerizing to watch, like a Ferris wheel going up and around.

"It's like the kids I teach," Elizabeth says. "Their parents will be like, 'Susie's sister was never like this!' and I say, 'Susie is not her sister.' It's amazing how sometimes it's like they've never thought of that before."

"I've been wondering about something, Elizabeth, about the thing you said about hating being a mother," Tabitha says. She pauses to take a sip of the iced tea and then rattles the glass lightly, letting the cubes clink against the side. "The thing is, you're going to be a lot of different mothers over the course of Violet's life. It could be that you don't like being this mother, this infant mother, and no one would blame you for that, not a bit. It's really hard. They're energy vampires, and they take so much and give so little. But it won't always be this way. She'll be Tate and Taylor's age and Phoebe's age, and you'll be the mom she needs then, and you'll like some of those stages a whole lot more, and some of them probably less. None of this is written in stone. There's no finish line in parenting, no end to it. We just have to be in it with them the whole time."

It is strange to hear practical Tabitha speaking so thoughtfully, but Ginger cannot help but think she is right. There is an ebb and a flow to parenting, moments of tension and release. Yes, moments she has enjoyed more than others, though mostly it has been a mix. Right now, Phoebe's expanding world scares her, but it is also exciting, the two of them talking about a story they listened to on the news, going home to look up a country Phoebe has never heard of, Ginger learning, too. And then there are the flushes of tweenager, the obstinate streak and the dismissive posturing, which are less delightful. But like Tabitha, Ginger has been at this long enough to know it will pass.

"Do you remember the other night when we were playing Would You Rather and the kids said Violet wouldn't always be little? I keep thinking about that. God, is it terrible that I'm desperately looking forward to it?" Elizabeth says.

"No one expects you to miss the hard parts while you're in

them," Ginger says with a laugh. "When Phoebe was eight, I would have been glad to fire her into the sun for a brief stay. Now I miss it just a bit. But at the time? No, thank you."

"Just think, you've got middle school coming up, too!" Tabitha says.

"Don't remind me," Ginger says grimly. "I am not looking forward to having to help her navigate that."

"That's why you have meeeeee to help," Elizabeth sings, flashing a pageant-kid smile. She loops her arms around her knees and crosses her legs at the ankles. "The hardest part is watching them go through it because you know how much it hurts, but you also know how little it will matter in ten years. But don't say that to them. They don't like being told things will be better when they are old. I speak from painful experience."

"It's the same thing with parenting, then. What you're saying to the children. Or not saying. I know everything with Violet feels like it will be forever, but it's not forever. And when Violet is in middle school, she is going to be set, because you will totally get her, whereas Tate and Taylor will be on that rocket ship to the sun," Tabitha says. And then, "Hello," because Violet has crawled over to her and put her hands on Tabitha's knees where she is rocking back and forth and grinning up at her expectantly.

"The money, too. I know it feels insurmountable now, but it won't always," Ginger says.

"It's true," Tabitha adds. "It's only money."

"That's easy for you to say," Elizabeth says.

Tabitha picks up Violet and rocks her back and forth, dipping her down in exaggerated swoops, and Violet giggles, but then Tabitha stops to bounce her instead, looking at Elizabeth seriously. "When I first moved to New York, I was so broke. My parents supported me until I graduated college, but then I was on my own. I lived in this twobedroom apartment with six girls. We had curtains up in the living room to make an extra bedroom in there. I was working events and

I'd always bring Tupperware to take leftover catering home and that's what I'd eat. I still cannot tolerate mini quiches because I ate them for breakfast for a solid three years. One month I didn't have enough money for rent, so when the landlord called looking for it, I pretended to be one of the other girls. For three days, until I figured out how to get a cash advance on my credit card." She puts Violet down. Violet promptly reaches for Tabitha's glass of tea, and Tabitha helps her lift it to her mouth, the baby drinking greedily.

"Anyway," she says, "I thought I'd be broke forever. Thought I'd have to move back home. I can still remember how sick it made me feel when I'd go to an ATM and I didn't even have enough money to take out cash. But I got through it. You will, too."

Elizabeth looks down at her feet. Ginger wants to say something else, but there is nothing else to say. If Elizabeth wants to discuss it, she will, and Ginger will listen. She is, quite literally, she thinks, looking at her cast, which has picked up the damn glitter from that invitation and is now both purple and sparkly, not going anywhere.

30

ELIZABETH

WHEN SHE DIALS, a woman picks up on the first ring.

"Dr. Bailey," she says, her voice gentle and calm, as it should be, and Elizabeth freezes.

"Hello," she says awkwardly, after far too long a pause. "I'm sorry, I wasn't expecting a real person." She laughs nervously, which is great, because certainly now this woman thinks she is a complete idiot.

Dr. Bailey only laughs warmly in return. "It's okay. I always expect voice mail, too. But I had a patient cancel, so here I am. How can I help?"

How could she help? Oh, sister. Where to begin?

"I got your name from Yasmin Scott?" Elizabeth starts, uncomfortably tentative.

Dr. Bailey doesn't say anything. It occurs to Elizabeth that she doesn't even know if Yasmin talked to this lady or just sent her the name, and Dr. Bailey probably couldn't tell her anyway. She finds herself at a loss as to what to say next. "She said you could help. With some stuff. Fertility stuff. Infertility stuff."

She squeezes her eyes shut. She should have planned better. But seriously, what doctor answers her own phone?

"I do work a fair amount with people who are experiencing infertility. I used to be a clinic counselor at Fertility Innovations before I moved into private practice."

"Oh, yeah. I went there. My husband and I did. But we didn't do any counseling or anything."

"Is that what you'd like to talk about? Fertility issues?" Dr. Bailey prompts when Elizabeth doesn't say anything else.

"Yeah. I don't know. We're not going through treatment now. Not anymore. Except now we've adopted a baby. She's almost one. So I guess I shouldn't really need to talk to anyone anymore." She forces a little laugh, trying to sound less unhinged and only making herself sound more so. "But it was really hard. I had some miscarriages. And I don't..." To her horror, she feels herself starting to cry.

Dr. Bailey doesn't say anything for a moment, and Elizabeth wonders if – hopes – they have gotten disconnected. "It sounds like you've been through a lot."

This small recognition pushes Elizabeth over the edge of sadness and into tears. She pushes her fist against her mouth, trying to stifle the gasping sobs so the rest of the house won't hear. "I'm sorry," she gasps. "I shouldn't be like this. I have a kid, right? I'm so lucky."

She catches her breath for a moment, and in the silence, Dr. Bailey says, "Having a child doesn't cure infertility."

This is so shocking, so plainly true, it catches Elizabeth mid-sob, and she has to force herself to breathe once, twice, again. Of course it does, she thinks, and then, of course it doesn't. They have Violet, but they do not have those other babies they lost, and the ones that never were, that they only hoped for, eggs and embryos that faded before they ever became anything. They have Violet, but they still have the crushing debt of all the misery that came before her. She has Violet, but she also has the memories of that furious lack of control, of the hours and days she will never get back, punching wildly and pointlessly against an invisible enemy that laid her flat without ever appearing. She has Violet, but she still cannot have a baby.

"Oh," she says quietly, almost a whisper. "Oh."

"Would you like to come in and talk?" Dr. Bailey asks. It sounds like she is a new neighbor inviting Elizabeth over for tea. "It might help."

It is a struggle to say yes, not only because of the tears that are still choking her – she has never been good at crying, which is one of the many reasons she avoids doing it – but also because she knows it won't be like having tea with a new neighbor. She will go in and pay a hundred dollars they don't have in order to sit on a couch and cry, and it won't make her feel any better.

Or maybe it will.

"Are you free during the week, or do you need Saturday?" Dr. Bailey says.

"I'm a teacher. So I'm off right now," she says.

"How about Tuesday, then? Three o'clock?" Dr. Bailey suggests, and Elizabeth wonders if everyone this woman deals with is as slow and lost as she is.

No, she wants to say. *No.* Tuesday is both too close and impossibly far away. But she gives Dr. Bailey her information, and they set up the time and the doctor hangs up, but Elizabeth sits there with the phone still to her ear, not saying anything to anyone at all. How are they going to pay for this? She is going to have to cancel for that reason alone. Somehow this thought brings her no relief.

"Hey," John says, opening the door to their room. He's carrying Violet, and Elizabeth can smell the situation in her daughter's diaper even through her post-tears stuffy nose. When she turns around, John looks surprised, which she is sure is because she looks crazy, her hair probably standing up and her eyes and nose swollen and red.

"Oh, hey," he says again, looking down at Violet, who

is babbling at him and patting his shoulder, and then at her, trying to triage both situations at once.

"I'm okay," Elizabeth says. "I'll change her." She reaches out for Violet and takes her as John pulls the changing pad out and lays it across the bed. She remembers the first time they dressed Violet in the hospital, both of them leaning over her in the bassinet, trying to get her tiny body into the tiny onesie, terrified of breaking her. They had both been sweating and laughing, so happy and so scared. Now it is a ballet: he puts down the mat and she lays Violet on it, deftly removing the diaper and cleaning her with one hand while holding her in place with the other, John taking the dirty diaper and sealing it one of the scented bags they use for travel while Elizabeth puts on the new one.

Then she puts Violet down on the floor and they both wash their hands, and he stops her before she leaves the bathroom and asks, "What's going on?"

She can see herself in the mirror, and though she splashed some water on her face after she washed her hands, she looks no less swollen and red. "I made an appointment with a counselor," she says.

A few expressions pass over his face before he lands on something that looks like relief. "Really? I didn't know you were thinking about that."

She shrugs, looks over at Violet to make sure she isn't chewing on an extension cord, but she has only stood up and is circumnavigating the bed by holding onto the duvet cover. "I didn't know I was, either. But that couple I talked to, they said it had been helpful for them, and I thought it might be for me, too. Or for us."

"That might be good. I think it's great that you're going."

"You do?"

"Yeah." He stops and rubs his chin. "I thought we should go. During treatment, you know. Both of us."

"Why didn't you say anything?" she asks. It amazing how

you can be right next to someone and not know at all what they are thinking.

"Not to say I told you so, but I did bring it up, and you said no."

"I did?" Elizabeth feels a twist in her belly, a vague recollection of him saying this to her, holding her hands, looking into her eyes in the earnest way he has, half encouraging team captain, half sweet husband.

"You did. You said we were too busy."

She claps her hand over her eyes. "Ugh, you're right. We were so busy! God, it all took so much time. I was already at the fucking doctor every ten minutes. I felt like I was plagued by appointments. Endlessly. I couldn't manage another."

"Yeah, but I don't think that's why we didn't go," John says. "Hey, hey!" He ducks over and grabs a small jar of Elizabeth's night cream out of Violet's hand. "That's Mommy's."

Violet looks as if she is considering make a fuss about this but instead starts working her way back down the duvet to where she can gnaw on the bedpost.

"Why didn't we?"

"I'm not sure because you didn't say, but I'm guessing it was too hard. Emotionally. You don't like to cry or talk about your feelings," he says, coming back to her and rubbing her upper arms like he is trying to keep her warm.

"Not much," she agrees. When she was little and she cried, her father mocked her, screwing up his face and crying big fake tears, *wah-wah-wahing* right back at her. She has thought of that memory again and again over time, and once, she laughingly mentioned it to John, only to have him look at her, horrified. "That's awful," he said. "What a shitty way to treat a kid."

"He was just joking," Elizabeth said, dismissing it, but she had felt something tug inside her as she did, something that told her he was right.

"Babies cry. Kids cry. It's what they do. It's how they

communicate when they can't communicate. What kind of crappy parent makes fun of a kid for crying?"

She remembers looking at John's face when he pointed out her father's cruelty, the immovable shock and empathy as she worked through the realization, the humor in the story chased away by cold, hard reality. She had believed something that wasn't true: she had thought her father was being funny, and he was only being heartless.

It was then she had started to understand the lessons her family had taught her, to be spiny and prickly and defensive, to lash out wildly when she felt cornered, not to cry because someone would only mock you. How long ago had that been, and she still carried that message with her.

"You don't have to do this alone. And you don't have to pretend to be okay when you're not. Not with me, and not with anyone else in this family," he says, earnest and intense.

"I'm just so tired," she says, and she feels it as she says it, that bonedeep exhaustion that makes her want to crumple.

"I'm not saying I wasn't sad at all the losses and disappointments we went through. It was definitely harder for you, probably because you were carrying all the physical stuff, all the hormones, or maybe it just was because it was. And maybe now you're tired because you're still carrying it all around, and by yourself. You know, I talked to my family, and I get why you didn't feel comfortable talking to them about it, but you have talk to someone. It's too much to carry it yourself."

"Yeah, or maybe I'm tired because we have a baby," Elizabeth says, gesturing to Violet, who is focused on trying to pull a toy through the mesh side of her pack-and-play.

She was trying to lighten the mood, but John will not have it. "I know things have been hard with Violet. But I wonder if the way you've been feeling isn't really about Violet. Or not only about Violet. That we're both of us carrying around grief we haven't dealt with from before."

"Grief. That's what Yasmin kept saying when we talked."

"She would know."

They're silent again for a moment. Violet gets the toy free and squeals in delight, shaking it. "We did go so fast into adopting Violet."

"So fast. And I wouldn't change it. She is amazing. And you are an amazing mom."

"I'm so not," Elizabeth says, pulling away from him. She steps into the bedroom and finds her shoes where she kicked them off. She'd rather go barefoot outside, but it drives Tabitha bonkers for some unknown reason.

"You are. You so are. I don't tell you that enough. You are so good with Violet, so good at helping her figure things out for herself. So good at calming her down when she gets worked up. So good at reading the same book to her a thousand times. She loves you so much, honey. I wish I could see the two of you together."

"No," Elizabeth shakes her head. "I mean, the colic, and the formula, and the way she cries in the car—"

"Bethy, don't, don't. We're not doing anything wrong. Babies cry. And the colic, nobody knows, but it's not something you did. It's not something we did. You're a great mom. But something you're carrying around won't let you see that."

Elizabeth knows what it is, the core of it. People say it will happen when it is meant to happen. Whatever is meant to be will be. Except, what does it mean when it *doesn't* happen? Does it mean she wasn't meant for this? Wasn't meant to be a mother?

She has a million questions, but underneath it all lies that one. Maybe that is the grief talking. Maybe if they hadn't rushed into it, taken a year, talked to someone, things would be different, easier. Maybe she hasn't been angry at all. Maybe she has just been so, so sad.

"Do you remember what they said in our adoption training? About how adoption starts with a loss?"

"I do," Elizabeth says. She has turned that thought over in

her mind again and again. A loss for Violet – her first family not being the one she is raised in. A loss for Brianna – another child she is not parenting. For her and John, a loss of the family they thought they might build in exchange for the one they are building. She doesn't know how any of those losses will play out in the long term for any of them, but she cannot pretend they don't exist.

"So you've got every right to be grieving," John says. He rubs her shoulders, and she doesn't say anything. "What did you think of them? Yasmin and Peter, right?"

"I don't know. It was weird talking to them. They remind me of us. What happened. I feel like having them around would be this constant reminder, you know? Is that what we want?"

"I don't need reminders. I think about it every day. Don't you?"

"Yes," Elizabeth says, her voice so soft she hardly recognizes it. She thinks about it every day, even though she tries not to. When the thoughts come up, she pushes them down. It is like when her grandfather died. Her aunt was over, and she saw a picture of her grandfather on the mantel and she'd asked her mom, "Doesn't it make you sad to see him?"

Her mother had looked at the picture and tilted her head. "I'd be sad either way. It's not like I forget if I don't have a picture up. So I'd rather be sad and be able to look at him."

Elizabeth needs no reminders of what she has lost.

"I'm worried about how much it will cost to see this therapist," Elizabeth says. "Maybe I'll just go once or twice."

"No," John says, and he looks surprisingly stern, an expression she has never seen on him. "You'll go as much as you need to go. We'll figure it out."

"But the money – and your new job…"

"We'll figure something out. This is worth it."

There is a beat while they both sit quietly, and then John asks, "Do you think that maybe – so, the baby is due in December, right? Do you think that maybe after you have some conversations with the counselor, you might feel different? Because if we say no to this baby and then you change your mind…"

Elizabeth holds up her hand to stop him from talking. "I can't make that promise. Don't ask me to make that promise. It wouldn't be right. I don't want to say I'll think about it and then have the pressure of this baby coming. If it's not fair to Violet for me to feel like this, it would be even less fair to do it again."

"Okay," John says, but he sounds disappointed, and she can't fault him for it any more than she can fault herself. They are going to have to talk about whether they are going to expand their family further, and when, but she is not ready. He reaches out and rubs her back. "I want you to be happy. Violet needs you to be happy. Right now you are carrying around so much it's like you're at a breaking point all the time. Is that what you want for Violet?"

"No!" Elizabeth says, and it is a terrible thing to realize she doesn't want her daughter to be like her. At least not like that. It is yet another thing she didn't know about parenting, how much she would have to think not about what her child does but about what she does herself, and all the ways we pass on and inherit the things we never mean to.

•••••

DIFFERENT NOW

•••••

Things are different now. When I was adopted, closed adoptions were still pretty common, and a lot of people wanted them, preferred them, on both sides. So I have no idea who my bio parents are.

Look, I love my family. They are amazing and I have had a great life with them. But I can't stop thinking about the fact that somewhere out there I have this whole set of people connected to me who refuse to know me. I've done all the DNA sites, but none of them have shown up. Which, odds are, that's pretty strange, right? Not to get a single result?

My mom says she understands. Says she understands why I want to know, and they support me. It could be awkward talking about it, and sometimes I do feel bad, like I'm betraying them, but they say they don't feel betrayed. That it's okay to be curious. I ask why they agreed to a closed adoption and they said that's just how things were at the time. I don't know if it was easier for them, maybe, pretending I was biologically theirs. I can see how that would be awkward. They say it wasn't like that, but maybe a little bit deep down it was. Then again, they never made a secret of the fact that they adopted me. When I was little, I'd hop around in the park going, "I'm adopted! I'm adopted!" and it was always something they told me made our family special.

The problem is, it turns out my husband and I both have a genetic condition we don't want to pass on, so no bio kids for us. All this time I was thinking that when I had a family, I would have that genetic connection that's lacking. I would get to see which of my looks or my personality got carried over. Not in the cards, I guess.

It's a weird thing, being both the beginning and the end of your genetic line. My husband says it doesn't matter, but of course it doesn't matter to him. He has all his answers. People who aren't adopted don't understand.

We'd always planned to adopt. We just thought we'd have bio kids first. So that's been a shift. I didn't ever want a kid we adopted to feel like they were a second choice. It was just that we wanted to have bio kids while we were still young. So to make a long story longer, that was why adoption would come second. But we also knew adoption might take a while, so it's a good thing we'd started the application while we were trying to get pregnant.

I don't know how I feel anymore. I set up a special email account especially for the DNA and genealogy stuff, and I check it more often than I should. I also spend a lot of time looking at our family book on the agency website, and updating it whenever we do something fun. I try to picture my birth mom looking through my parents' book and being like, yes, these people are going to be this baby's parents. How do you even know? How do you even choose?

Things are different now, though. Because this adoption won't be closed. I told the agency we wouldn't even consider that.

It's for sure better for some kids if they don't have contact with their bio family, like if there's been abuse, but I want our kid to know their whole family. I want them to feel connected to their background, to never have to wonder about anything, like I wonder why my birth mom chose my parents, or who

I look like, or why my bio family didn't raise me. So our kid will have someone to ask all those questions to.

My kid will be lucky that way. And maybe they'll be able to have kids, bio kids, and then they'll get what I didn't have. Because things will be different then, too.

31

TABITHA

"I'M CALLING THIS family meeting to order," Elizabeth says. Tabitha has set out homemade tortilla chips, and Elizabeth grabs a handful before collapsing back into her chair.

"Who put you in charge?" Ginger asks.

"I'm not in charge, I'm just done waiting," Elizabeth says, popping a chip into her mouth and baring her teeth in a fierce mockery of a smile as she crunches into it.

"Your patience is yet another one of the reasons I married you," John says, reaching over and patting her on the leg. She gives him the same terrifying smile, tortilla shards stuck between her teeth. "That and your enviable dental hygiene."

"So we've talked to these three couples, right? And my lovely bride has passed along some additional candidates. Where do we stand?" Perry asks.

It is hard for Tabitha not to organize these things, but she is trying to stand back. Silly, of course, performative even, as all the information will be routed through her, but if this keeps the peace for a little while, she will do it.

"I've made my concerns about Allison and Mark clear – they're nice, but the size of their family is a drawback," Ginger says. "If we want things with us to stay like this, or close to it."

"What does that mean, stay like this?" Elizabeth asks.

"I don't know. Small. Closer. It feels like a lot of people to add in."

"People have families, though," Elizabeth says. "People come with people. You can't avoid that."

Tabitha nods, though she isn't sure who she agrees with. After the past two weeks, she can't imagine the family getting any bigger, having to manage anyone else. Then again, something in her still longs for that enormous extended family, tables spread out all over their house on holidays, people coming and going, too many to even fit so they have to go out into the yard to make a toast all together. But something feels tender and new about this family now, too, the way she and Ginger and Elizabeth have come together, and no matter who Brianna chooses to be this child's parents, things will have to change. She is both excited and fearful, holding their family in her palm like a new egg, wondering if it will crack, or if it will hatch.

"I also only talked to Shelley – the florist. She was absolutely as wonderful as we thought they would be. Except I do want to mention they have already started the adoption process to adopt a child from China. So I don't know what that means."

"Because we want the siblings just to be siblings?" Ginger confirms.

"Right," Tabitha says. "Though Shelley did point out that an international adoption would be different in that way, because that child wouldn't have the same connection to their birth family."

"Can same-sex couples adopt from China?" Ginger asks.

"I don't know. She said they had already started, so I presume they have some plan for that," Tabitha says. She is embarrassed that this question makes her a little hopeful. She really had enjoyed chatting with Shelley, and if she's being honest, the earnest progressive in her adores the idea of adding these women to their family, of expanding the way the children think of family, as if their definition isn't already wide enough.

"Yasmin and Peter were nice, too," Elizabeth says. "But…" She and John exchange a glance, and she goes silent.

"But what?" Tabitha prompts.

"They were in a similar situation to us. They actually went to the same fertility clinic. And when I talked to them, they said they weren't totally sure they were ready to adopt."

"Then what did they reply to the listing for?" Ginger asks.

"We weren't sure we were ready to adopt when we started, either," John points out.

"There's nothing wrong with that. We're not sure they're the right couple, either," Tabitha says, soothing. She does wish Ginger would take another pain pill. She's so unpleasant when her ankle starts bothering her. She's asked Tabitha to accompany her to look at some houses when they get back, and Tabitha is thinking they're only going to be able to do a couple each time they go out, or Ginger will get tired and cranky. Adults are so often like children. She knows everyone thinks she's crazy for bringing them snacks all the time, but there's really nothing worse than being around a bunch of hangry people. It's best to keep feeding them proactively.

"I just don't want to get down the path with them and have them change their minds," Ginger says. Tabitha glances quickly at her, wondering if this is a veiled reference to her hope that John and Elizabeth might change their mind. It is killing her not to ask about it again, but she is holding strong. At least so far. She does hope they will reconsider, and soon, because she can't imagine starting this process with another couple and then having to stop.

"I'd like to make a suggestion, if I could?" Tabitha asks tentatively. "I think we should have some special family dinners. The way we did with Elizabeth and John. Invite these couples over, and anyone else we may find." She lifts the new packet she has made – this one she has tabbed the edges so they can find the pages to discuss more easily. "Brianna can decide if she wants to come then, or we can have some of the couples back for another dinner."

"That's a lot of dinners," Ginger says immediately.

Tabitha sighs.

Ginger attempts to backpedal. "I just mean it's a lot of dinners to invite people to if they're not going to be part of our family. Isn't that what we've been discussing all along? Being kind to these hopeful adoptive families?"

That is not what Ginger meant, or at least not fully what she meant, but Tabitha appreciates the effort.

"So we will limit it to the ones we feel most strongly about, or perhaps share them with Brianna first and let her choose which one she would like to meet." Tabitha opens her planner, flipping to the next week. "Perry, you're supposed to go to that commercial shoot in LA, but you can send someone else, right? Because we could do weekend nights, and then, if we need more, we could do weekdays."

"Yeah, and Ginger and Phoebe can just stay at your house every night," Elizabeth says.

Tabitha opens her eyes wide. Why hadn't she thought of that? "That's a brilliant idea! Ginger, I'll drop the Realtor a line and see if she can do a couple of properties per day, and then you can come back to our house and rest before dinner. The twins have camp, but I'm sure they'll make space for Phoebe, so she'll be occupied during the day. I'll call them on Monday." She's jotting notes in her planner, the familiar fizzy excitement of having a project, a to-do list, bubbling inside her.

"Tee, I was joking," Elizabeth says. "I said she could spend the night, not move in."

Tabitha looks up, startled, and then around at the others. Ginger's face, as usual, is indecipherable. You would think after all this time that Tabitha would be able to read her, but no.

"No, you might be right about our staying over," Ginger says. "I'll think about it."

Tabitha isn't sure what that means, either. Often when Ginger says she'll think about something, it's because she doesn't want to say no, but she's smiling, so maybe this is different.

"Okay. Should we schedule the dinners then?" Tabitha asks tentatively. The anxiety she feels is familiar and disappointing. When she thinks about the plans she had for this vacation versus how it has gone, she could be heartbroken, but she is actually relieved. It has not been perfect, no, far from it. But they have had good times, and she sees them each carefully treading a new path. That as much as she is trying to draw back her tendency to forge ahead without asking, she can see Ginger trying not to withdraw, and Elizabeth working to view the others' efforts to help as kindness and not judgment.

"You can schedule them," Elizabeth says. "You're great at stuff like that."

This time Tabitha checks, but Elizabeth doesn't seem to be joking. A little puff of proud air releases in her chest. Relief not only because she did want to do it herself (she really is good at those things and enjoys doing it) but that Elizabeth isn't holding things against her for the sport of it.

"I'll text Brianna," Tabitha says, adding that to her list.

"Do we want to talk about these other parents?" Perry asks, rattling his paper.

"You did a way better job on the packet this time. Page numbers and everything," Elizabeth says, and this time Tabitha can tell she is teasing.

"Ha, ha, ha. Heaven forbid I make it easy for you to find who we're talking about."

"They look great," Ginger says approvingly. "Did you have any opinions on these folks you want to tell us about before we review?"

Tabitha opens her mouth and then closes it. "Why don't we all look at them together and then we'll talk?" she suggests, and they do.

She listens to the others talking, and though she does have opinions, they bring up things she hadn't thought about – this couple's history with a contested adoption, this one's arrest record (for protesting; does that count?), this one's indication that they are anti-vaccine. It is better, she sees, to allow them to talk it through. They will come out with the same opinions she did, she suspects, but it is better to come to them together, rather than for her to lead them there.

When had they become a family, anyway? Was it in the courtroom the day Phoebe's and the twins' adoptions were finalized? Or earlier than that, when they first met Ginger, or later, when they met Elizabeth and John? Or even earlier, when Lorna died, when Phoebe was born, when Brianna was born, or a million decisions and coincidences ago when everything was set in motion that brought them to this day, this moment, sitting here by the fire, the children sleeping upstairs, laughing and talking and arguing like a real family? Like any other family.

She thought she knew what made a family when she'd started dreaming of a different one as a child. She thought it came naturally with enough people. She thought it would be full of happiness, only happiness, everything easy and clean and comfortable. She'd been wrong. Maybe they haven't even begun to become one until now, until she is beginning to let go of the image of who she thought she wanted them to be, letting herself be seen and seeing everyone else for who they are and not who she wants them to be.

32

GINGER

"OH!" TABITHA SAYS when she comes into the children's room. "Thank you for getting them started!" Ginger has been sitting on one of the bottom bunk beds, directing the children's packing. Or trying to. She has rather less gravitas than Tabitha at her best, and given that she cannot chase them, her enforcement of the process of getting clothes into the actual suitcases has been less than successful.

"You're welcome," Ginger says. "Really, it's self-preservation. If I don't make Phoebe do it, it will not be done at all." Tomorrow they are renting a boat and will be on the water all day, and then they are going home early the next morning, so she was hoping to get a jump on the process, but if wishes were horses, etcetera.

"I was going to come in tonight and do the twins' after they were asleep."

"What, and miss out on all this fun?" Ginger asks, gesturing at them. Tate has gotten inside one of the bags and Phoebe and Taylor, giggling, are trying to zip her in.

"I've got to make Tate's bed," Tabitha says. "Can you scooch a little bit, please?"

Ginger obediently scooches, and Tabitha climbs up the ladder to the top bunks.

"Can we please make an effort to get some of the clothes into the bag?" Ginger asks, though she knows it is in vain. As usual, Phoebe will wait until the last minute to throw her things in, even though she has been warned a dozen times. Tate kicks open the zipper from inside and falls out of the bag, rolling over and landing by Ginger's feet. Ginger looks down at her. "At least if you're ever kidnapped in a suitcase, your mother will know you can escape."

"That is quite comforting," Tabitha says, finishing with the blanket and climbing back down. "Taylor, don't sit on your sister's head," she calls. She starts gathering some of the twins' clothes. "I should probably do a load of laundry before we go, but I hate the way clothes smell when they are shut up in a suitcase and I always end up rewashing them anyway at home. Hey, are you going to be okay?" she asks abruptly, stopping. "We haven't talked about how you're going to manage at home."

Ginger starts to speak and then stops. They've arranged that John and Perry will drive her car and she will ride with Elizabeth and Violet while Phoebe goes with Tabitha and the twins, but they have not planned beyond that, how she will get back to their apartment and then how whoever drives her there will get home, who will help them carry their things up the stairs because their apartment is on the third floor and there are no elevators, who will help her shower.

"I don't know," she says.

"I don't know if you've thought about it any further, but the offer stands for you to stay with us." She holds up her hand as if to stop Ginger's objection before it begins, even though Ginger was not actually going to object. "I know it's not your first choice, but I promise we'll give you lots of space and privacy. You can have the guest bedroom with the bathroom, and Phoebe can sleep in Tate's room, which I'm sure she'd prefer anyway, and we'll set you up and won't bother you at all. I can take you to the doctor or wherever else you need to go. Or you can get a rideshare. I'll set up the app on your phone." She stops herself, either because she's getting breathless or because she realizes what she's been doing, rushing ahead without asking, making decisions for Ginger.

Two weeks ago, Ginger thinks, she would have felt like she was caught in a wind tunnel. Now she pauses and considers. It will be a lot to go straight from two weeks with Tabitha into… well, two weeks with Tabitha. Maybe too much. Then again, back in Denver she will have work, and Tabitha will be busy doing whatever Tabitha does, and it will not feel so close, so claustrophobic. She doesn't have to let it swallow her whole. She gets to choose how she reacts.

"You know, that's actually a good idea," Ginger says. "It will get us through some of the family dinners and looking at some properties, as well as my figuring out how to navigate with the cast."

"Really?" Tabitha asks, and she sounds like one of the twins when she says it, so amazed her voice nearly squeaks at the end, eyes like cartoon saucers.

"Really," Ginger says. She is not sure, but she thinks Tabitha might look a little teary.

Neither of them has been paying attention to the children, but she notices Tate by Tabitha's elbow then, her eyes gone the same wide and round. "Wait a minute," Tate says, with the slightest touch of a New York City accent in her voice – *waiddaminit*. "Are you guys coming for a sleepover when we get home?"

"For a little while, yes," Ginger says.

"Until Aunt Ginger's leg gets better," Tabitha says.

"PHOEBE!" Tate shouts, turning and running back to Taylor and Phoebe, who are building a tower of playing cards. "YOU ARE GOING TO LIVE AT MY HOUSE."

"WHAT," Phoebe shouts.

"Shh, you're going to wake the baby," Tabitha scolds.

"Baby's awake," Elizabeth says, bringing Violet in. She's holding Violet's hands, letting her stagger along, toes dragging on the ground. "We're about to head to bed."

"BABY!" Taylor shouts, and all three mothers shush him at the same time. Violet looks startled by the noise for a moment and then lights up as her brother and sisters descend on her. Elizabeth lowers her to the ground and Violet crawls to meet them, diving headfirst along the way into the pile of dirty laundry Ginger had been attempting to have them pack.

The children start wrestling each other among the clothes, tickling Violet and laughing as she squirms around in delight. "That's nice," Elizabeth says. "I hope no one had any plans for those clothes. What's going on? I heard Tate saying someone's living in her house."

"Phoebe and I are," Ginger says, and laughs as Elizabeth slowly raises an eyebrow. "For a while, until my leg is better. The stairs at our place would be insurmountable. And Tabitha will keep cooking for us."

"Good point. Maybe I will move in, too," Elizabeth says. "But not John and Violet. They can stay home and eat Hot Pockets like the savages they are."

"Nope. Only one guest room, all booked up," Ginger says.

"Actually, there's another one in the basement," Tabitha says.

"Suck it," Elizabeth says to Ginger, pointing finger guns at her. "God, I would love to get a night away. Just so I could sleep."

"Why don't you let us take Violet tonight? We can move the packand-play into our room," Tabitha suggests.

Elizabeth looks surprised, then regretful. "No. You've taken her a bunch of times in the morning. It's fine."

"No, really. I don't know why I didn't think of it before. Get at least one good night's sleep before we go back. Honestly, it would be a treat. I love waking up to a sleeping baby."

Elizabeth looks cautious, but Tabitha is smiling easily.

This is what Ginger tried to explain to Elizabeth, and that she will need to remind herself of again and again. That whatever the motivations – rich, bored, lonely – Tabitha really does mean well, is never happier than when she is helping someone else.

"Take her up on it," Ginger says.

Elizabeth looks over at Violet. "You don't think that makes me a bad mom?" she asks.

"Because you're getting some sleep so that you will be better rested and, in fact, be a better parent?" Ginger asks. "No, I do not think that at all."

"Okay," Elizabeth says, after pausing one more time. "That would be really nice." She smiles the first real, wide, genuine smile, without reservation, that Ginger has seen on her in a long time.

"Perfect," Tabitha says, clapping her hands together like a delighted child. "It's been so nice having Violet around. Can you believe we're going to have a new baby, too?"

"I really can't," Elizabeth says. "I feel like Violet was a newborn about two seconds ago."

"I can't believe we're going to have more parents," Ginger says. The thought still gives her pause, makes her anxious, but she is trying not to struggle so hard against it.

So much will change for her and Phoebe, too. A new house, a new school. A new era. Ginger isn't the sort of person to wish away her life, or her daughter's, but she sees it unspooling now more quickly than it had before, picking up speed as it goes. Phoebe will be in middle school and then high school, and then perhaps college, given her interest in world events, and then she will be gone. What will the family look like then? Violet and this baby still under ten. Will she still go to family dinners when Phoebe has moved out on her own? Will Phoebe still come if she lives in the area?

She takes a breath. She has to stop herself from spinning out like Tabitha, making a list of a thousand things to worry about before she has finished with one. Phoebe's new school, which will begin before they move. The baby's parents. A new mother, or mothers, or perhaps only new fathers; there is a lovely couple, two men, in this new group they all really like and are going to invite for dinner after Elizabeth talks to them on the phone.

"It's a good thing we didn't book a Christmas vacation," Elizabeth says. "Who knows how many people we'll have to plan for?"

"Don't worry about it," Tabitha says, patting Ginger's knee, though she hasn't said anything. "It's going to be okay. However it happens, it's going to be okay."

"We're going to have a busy few months," Ginger says.

"That's why the good Lord gave us Tabitha," Elizabeth says.

Tabitha looks at her sideways, her hand still on Ginger's knee above her cast, the warm pressure of it surprisingly calming. For someone who had purposely avoided physical touch for so long, Ginger finds she has become surprisingly used to it. Not only from Phoebe, but also from the twins, who are quite physically demonstrative, and from Violet, and the other parents.

"What do you mean?" she asks.

"Your crack organizing skills are going to get us through the next few months. Thank heavens for that because if I had to manage it, I would lose my mind and the baby would be born without any parents," Elizabeth says.

"I'm not going to do it all myself," Tabitha says, and whether this is an objection or an apology, Ginger can't quite tell. Perhaps both.

"No one expects that. For instance, Ginger will be in charge of packing her own apartment, and I will be on hand to offer snarky commentary whenever necessary," Elizabeth says. Ginger laughs, partly because she is not wrong, and partly because she knows Tabitha would pack up their apartment, and do a better job of it than she would, in a heartbeat. She only needs to ask.

"How are we even going to know if we pick the right people?" Ginger asks.

"I think we'll just know," Tabitha says.

"That's magical thinking," Elizabeth says. "It's not fate."

"You don't think you were fated to be Violet's mom?" Tabitha asks. She sounds curiously disappointed, looking over at Violet, who is letting a truly impressive stream of drool fall into the laundry. It's a good thing Tabitha didn't wash them after all, Ginger thinks.

"I don't think anyone's fated to be anything," Elizabeth says.

"Oh, I do. I believe it was fate that I met you that day," Tabitha says. "What else could it have been?"

"Bad luck?" Elizabeth says, but it is a joke that doesn't land.

Does Ginger believe she was fated to be Phoebe's mother? It was certainly a strange turn of events, that she, who never had much interest in children, had felt compelled to volunteer for the church's literacy program instead of one of the others. Or that the church set up its program at that particular school. Or that she joined that church at all, when there was one much closer. Or that she got a scholarship to a college in Colorado, which had brought her here in the first place. How much can you ascribe to fate? She considers herself as an eminently practical person, but for some reason it makes her sad to think that Violet's mother could have been someone else, or Phoebe's, or Tate and Taylor's.

"It doesn't matter," Ginger says. "Because we'll never know, will we? We'll never know if we were wrong or right, or if it was coincidence or fate. We're going to like the people we like, and then Brianna will decide. And then we will learn to love whomever she chooses."

"Even if they're a gigantic pain in the ass?" Elizabeth asks.

Tabitha nods. "Of course. After all, that's what we had to do with you."

Ginger and Elizabeth swivel their heads slowly toward

Tabitha, who, to their knowledge, has never made a joke in her life, let alone at someone else's expense.

When their shock fades, they both start to laugh and laugh and laugh, and after a moment, even Tabitha cracks a slow, self-satisfied grin.

"Hey, what's so funny?" Tate asks, the children looking up from their pile of laundry, but all the mothers can do is laugh even harder, leaning against each other as if they can't even sit on their own.

33

ELIZABETH

WHEN ELIZABETH WAKES up, she is disoriented. The curtains are drawn, but she can see a strip of light outside, too bright for early morning. Panicked, she bolts upright, looking for Violet, who never sleeps this late. The pack-and-play is gone, and it takes her a frantic moment to remember Tabitha took Violet last night, dragging the playpen and suitcase – because of course the kid has her own fricking suitcase – into her bedroom. Should she have felt bad that after she put Violet down and closed the door, she didn't feel any guilt or disappointment at all? Only a delicious sense of relief? Nigh giddiness?

John's side of the bed is empty, too, and when she rolls over to look at the time, she has to blink repeatedly at the screen to be sure she has read it properly. It's ten o'clock? She hasn't slept past, what, five thirty, since Violet was born. She's never been able to sleep when she knows Violet is awake, all her anxieties kicking into gear. But maybe knowing Violet was with Tabitha took all her worries away. Tabitha may drive her crazy on the regular, but even Elizabeth has to admit she trusts her with her child's life.

The surprising thought she has, as she pulls herself out of bed, is that she misses Violet. Wants to see her.

Normally she dreads the march of the day, the flood of demands and tasks from the moment Violet wakes up, but in what must be a strange case of sudden-onset maternal Stockholm syndrome, she suddenly misses it. The part she minds, she realizes, is that Violet always cries when she awakes. It is hard to start the day with a scream. But that may pass, too. Or maybe they can do something to alleviate it. Tabitha probably knows someone who can help, a baby nurse or a sleep consultant. She'll have to ask her later.

When she goes downstairs, John is sitting in the kitchen, reading the news on his phone. "Hello," he says. "How do you feel?"

"Amazing," Elizabeth says. "Amazing." She does feel amazing. The night of sleep has not cured her problems, but it has given her hope, reminded her that, as the kids pointed out the other night, Violet won't be little forever. She won't always need a diaper change or wake up crying. And it has shown her that she has options. What if they took Violet over to Tabitha and Perry's on a Friday night and she spent the night there, and Elizabeth and John went out, or just slept in? Violet's colic is gone – finally, praise all the various gods – and despite the fact that she still wakes up appallingly early, at least she sleeps through the night. It's no longer a burden to ask someone else to take care of her occasionally. That is, as Tabitha would say, what family is for.

"Where did everyone else go?" she asks.

"They left for the reservoir already, but Tabitha said we should take our time. They can bring the boat to meet us when we're ready."

"Is it okay if I eat something first?"

"No rush," John says. "I'll get you some coffee and the plate Tabitha left for you." He stands up. "Hey," he says, reaching out for her and giving her a kiss. "We're going to be okay."

"I know," she says, and holds him close. "I know." Maybe it is the sleep, or having a plan to meet these potential families, or talking to Dr. Bailey, but she really does believe it.

When they get to the reservoir, the family picks them up on the boat Perry has rented. He is wearing a captain's hat, and Elizabeth laughs at him, but John asks to try it on and if he can drive, and then Elizabeth laughs at him, too. She hopes whoever joins their family has a good sense of humor and a high tolerance for her goofy husband.

"Mama!" Violet claps when she climbs on board.

"Hello, lovebug," Elizabeth says, reaching out for her daughter, who is sitting firmly in Ginger's lap, wearing a life jacket. "Has she been okay?"

"She's been loving it," Ginger says, handing Violet over. "It's the motion of the water. She'd probably fall asleep if the others didn't keep bothering her."

"Hear that?" Elizabeth says to John. "We're moving to a houseboat."

"Okay," John says agreeably.

"That was easy," Elizabeth says cheerfully. She turns to Tabitha. "Thanks for packing Violet's suitcase." When she had gone up to get her things and change into her swimsuit, she found Violet's suitcase perfectly packed, her clothes organized into tiny soldiers on one side of the suitcase, all the other supplies laid neatly on the other, so orderly it looked like an advertisement. And though she will admit to rolling her eyes at Tabitha's precise management of a baby's suitcase, of all things, what she really felt was gratitude that someone else had done it for her.

"Happy to do it," Tabitha says. "Taylor Grayson Basnight, stop that right now," she says to Taylor, who has a sandwich in one hand and is dancing around his twin sister, pretending to push her into the water.

"Sorry," Taylor says, not sounding sorry at all.

"Can we stop to eat?" Tabitha asks John, who disappointedly eases back on the gas. As the boat slows to a drift, Perry drops the anchor.

"We can eat while we're going," Tate objects.

"I would prefer not to have my lunch all over my front, thank you," Tabitha says, handing out plates and napkins, because this is what Tabitha would do for a picnic on a boat.

As the children noisily clamor for their lunches, John slips over beside Elizabeth and puts his arm around her. "I love you," he says. "It's nice to see you happy."

Violet reaches out for his sandwich and he gives her some, which she immediately peels apart, dropping the less palatable bits, which Elizabeth barely manages to catch on her own plate, in order to get to the bread.

"It's nice to be happy," Elizabeth says. "I really can't tell you how much better I feel after a good night's sleep." It is amazing to her how her entire view of the world feels different this morning. She is still tired, imagines she will be tired for years more, but while she has felt hopeless every day for months, today she feels like there is something worth being there for.

"I'm so sorry I didn't understand how worn out you've been. We'll have to make sure you can get more nights like this."

"If we can. I'm sorry I didn't realize how unhappy you were at your job."

"We'll figure it out," he says. She is still a little nervous about this job with Perry, what will happen if it goes wrong, but for now they will just have to move forward. John looks happy, and it is startling to her how foreign an expression that has become for both of them.

"Let's promise to talk more," she says.

"Deal," he says, and gives her a gentle, slow kiss.

"GROSS!" Taylor says, seeing them. John slips his arms

around Elizabeth and pulls her closer and then dips her back, kissing her with a fake ferocity that nonetheless gives her a surprising little frisson of pleasure, a reminder that he is more than the person she hands the baby to when she needs a minute to go pee. She holds on to Violet as she leans back on the seat, laughing.

"So gross!" Tate says. "Can we swim, Mom?" she asks Tabitha.

"You've only eaten one grape," Tabitha says. "Aren't you going to eat anything else?" She is wearing a black swimsuit and white capri pants, and she looks as elegant handing out sandwiches on this boat as she does when she's dressed up for Christmas.

"I'll eat after we swim," Tate says, and without waiting for any further permission, she climbs over to the back of the boat, Taylor hot on her heels, shoving her in as she bends to dive. Her life jacket makes her bob to the surface quickly, gasping in surprise. "It's freezing!"

Phoebe comes up behind Taylor and pushes him in, and when he pops up, he doesn't complain about the cold, only looks sadly at his sandwich, which had been in his hand when he entered the water and is now a soggy disaster. She jumps in after him and then swims back to the boat to announce, quite seriously, "It really is freezing."

"I can't believe we're going home tomorrow. This has been an enjoyable trip," Ginger says to no one in particular.

"Except for the fighting, and Brianna's unexpected pregnancy, and your ankle, and my breaking that vase," Elizabeth says. Violet is squirming, so she hands her to John so she can eat her sandwich, surprisingly starving even though she just had breakfast. She realizes with some dread that she is going to have to go back to being in charge of feeding herself after two weeks of having someone handle the cooking. How depressing.

"Other than those things, yes," Ginger agrees.

"At least none of the kids had to go to the ER, though," John points out helpfully.

"Chin up, the day is young," Elizabeth says. "I find the odds of accidents increase the more tired they get."

"That is indeed something to look forward to," Perry says. He's sitting in the captain's seat, legs stretched out, hands clasped behind his head, looking for all the world like a master of the universe. She thinks about what Tabitha said, about how hard things had been for her in New York when she was younger, and wonders if in twenty years she and John will be more like Perry and Tabitha are now, if they will be confident and calm, if they will have the money and the grace and the experience to handle anything. She feels a sudden rush of gratitude for their steadiness, and for Ginger, for the advice and calm she offers. This is the flip side of being the youngest she never experienced in her own family, of someone not only laying out the path ahead, but turning back to guide her and encourage her instead of mocking her for not being further along.

Soon she will have the chance to do this herself, since none of the new families will have been parents yet. She will be the teacher instead of the taught, something she does all the time with kids but has never done with other adults. There's another nice couple she quite likes that she is going to call later. They are a few years younger than her and John, and she imagines being able to help them through those first few bleary months, telling them the things she learned along the way that she wishes she had known before. It's almost a waste not to have another child now that they know so much more. Maybe… but no. She chases the thought away.

"I've had a good time, too," Elizabeth says. "Thank you, Tabitha, for doing this."

By this she means many things – the boat rental, the lunch and all the cooking, taking Violet last night so she could sleep, the endless activities she arranged. But she also means the family. For being at the right place at the right time. For helping her find the thing she had most wanted, and reminding her she was capable of doing it. Tabitha and Ginger and Perry and John and the twins and Phoebe. And Violet. Whether it was fate that made them family or the dumb luck of the universe, they are here now, and they are going to go forward together.

EPILOGUE

"VIOLET, NO," ELIZABETH says for the fiftieth time, pulling her daughter away from the oven. She has been a holy terror since she started walking. The other day it was eerily quiet, and when Elizabeth went to find Violet, she had camped herself in front of the pantry, happily eating a sleeve of saltines, crumbs all over the floor, and Elizabeth was so surprised she couldn't stop laughing, which made Violet grin, pleased with herself.

"Put her in with the kids," Tabitha says, stepping around them as she carries a cutting board over to the stove and smoothly slides chopped green onions into a pan. "There's a baby gate in there now."

"There is? God, you are a miracle," Elizabeth says, walking Violet over – because she now cries whenever she is carried instead of walking – to the playroom and lifting her over the gate. "Nobody step on Violet," she warns the kids, not entirely optimistic that anyone will listen.

"When are they coming?" Ginger asks when Elizabeth returns. She's out of the purple cast, but her foot is still elevated and in a walking cast. When they got back from vacation, she and Phoebe stayed with Perry and Tabitha for two surprisingly low-stress weeks, and then went back to their apartment to start packing, having found a house only a mile from the school, albeit in the opposite direction from Tabitha and Perry's. It was good to maintain some boundaries.

"Any minute," Tabitha says, glancing at her watch and then out at the backyard. "Elizabeth, will you go get the boys? Tell Perry if he wants to let that dessert wine breathe, he should open it now."

Elizabeth obeys, heading outside while Tabitha finishes the last steps of dinner, pushing the pan back to the warming area and then turning back to the appetizers, sitting on the island in front of Ginger, who is flipping through a magazine, her bad foot balanced on one of the other stools, where Tabitha hopes it won't leave a mark.

"It's all going so fast," Ginger says. "We still have a few months before the baby comes, but that's already so filled with school and birthdays and everything, and we're still not done unpacking the new house."

"It has been a little bit of a whirlwind. Even more than with Elizabeth and John, don't you think?"

Ginger looks up from the magazine to squint at the ceiling, trying to remember. "It really has been. It's funny, though, because we knew so much earlier with this baby. I guess it feels faster because we had more than one couple to meet. It was boom, boom, boom."

"Do you still think about them?" Elizabeth asks, returning to the kitchen. She hops up on a stool beside Ginger's foot and reaches over for a piece of cheese. Tabitha moves another piece to cover the gap it has left, restoring the plate to symmetry.

"Who? The other couples Brianna didn't choose? Absolutely," Ginger says.

"Definitely. It's so weird that we got this really close view into their lives and now they're just… gone," Elizabeth says. "This is really tasty," she says to Tabitha.

"It's yak cheese. From that ranch we drove by on vacation," Tabitha says.

"Never tell anyone else that," Elizabeth says. She makes a face and puts the rest of the cheese on a napkin.

"We can't not think about them. We just have to trust that they'll find their families. We can't rescue them," Tabitha says.

"No," Elizabeth says, but she knows they all feel more than a pinch of sadness at the families that could have been theirs. Loss again. So much sadness and so much happiness tied together.

Tabitha steps back from the island, drying her hands with a towel. "Okay, dinner is ready whenever they get here."

Once Brianna chose the intended parents, they'd been invited to Sunday dinners, and gamely started coming every week. Brianna joins them, too, occasionally, and those are Tabitha's favorite times, the whole family together, twelve with lucky thirteen on the way. The children are happiest then, especially Phoebe, who is struggling with the arrival of this new child, but feels steadied when Brianna is around.

Tonight it will just be the new parents-to-be, and that will be fine, too, getting to know each other before the baby comes and everything is upended. Elizabeth has tried to warn them, but there's no warning anyone about the way family changes you.

"They're here, they're here," Tate shouts from the playroom. She practically hurdles over the baby gate, running for the front door before the bell even has a chance to ring. John and Perry come in, and Perry starts fussing with drinks while John eats the rest of Elizabeth's yak cheese, and Tabitha goes to undo the child lock on the front door so Tate can open it and let the new parents in, each of them thinking, in a warm way, that they are happy not to be in any other family but this one.

AUTHOR'S NOTE

"Were your son's birth parents really young?"
"Isn't it weird that he knows his real parents?"
"How much did it cost?"
"He looks just like you!"

I hear questions and comments like this regularly since my husband and I adopted our son four years ago. Though they aren't always polite, they don't bother us; before we adopted, we didn't know much about it either, and though we respect our son's privacy and that of his biological family, we're otherwise happy to share our experiences.

As we have gone through the process of adopting and developing our open adoptive family, we are regularly surprised by how our reality differs from many people's ideas about adoption.

Just as every family is different, every adoptive family is different, and adoption has changed dramatically over the years. The more I talked to people and saw how little we understand the complexities of adoption and adoptive families, the more I wanted to write a story to encourage conversation and raise questions around those topics.

Though they are not always possible, arrangements like our son's open adoption, where we have a close relationship with our son's birth parents and their families, have become more common as we learn how beneficial that can be to everyone involved, especially the adoptee.

DNA testing services allowing previously closed or secret adoptions to become open, a decreasing number of unplanned pregnancies due to availability and acceptability of birth control (not to mention a pandemic that kept us six feet apart!), shifts in foreign relations and changes in regulations around international adoptions, a relaxing of societal pressure on single parenting – these are just some of the factors that affect the constantly shifting nature of adoption, for better and for worse.

There are a thousand topics related to adoption I could not even begin to fit into this novel. Most notable is the absence of the biological family's and children's sides of the story, but I also had to sidestep central issues of race and class, foster care, mental health, international relations, access to reproductive health care and information... I could go on for pages. My decision to focus on the issues in the particular adoptive family depicted here does not diminish the importance of those other pieces.

My greatest hope with this book is not that I have written a complete exploration of adoption – that would be impossible – but that I have helped open space for us to think about the way we create families, the trust we put in each other, the experience of parenting, and what adoption means and can look like, even as all of that continues to develop and change.

ANSWERS:

- *Nope! Just not ready to parent.*

- *We think our son is so lucky to know his biological parents and their families. It's not any more confusing to him to have parents and biological parents than it is for a child to have parents and grandparents. Our relationships with him are different, and we play different roles in his life.*

- *Our son was adopted through a process called "designated adoption," which cost about $14,000. Adoption from foster care is quite a bit less expensive; private infant adoption or international adoption costs quite a bit more. The cost of the adoption process is a pressing issue we need to work on to make it accessible to more families.*

- *He's the spitting image of his biological father, especially in sunglasses!*